PENGUIN BOOKS

Judy Nunn's career has been long, illustrious and multifaceted. After combining her internationally successful acting career with scriptwriting for television and radio, Judy decided in the '90s to turn her hand to prose.

Her first three novels, *The Glitter Game*, *Centre Stage* and *Araluen*, set respectively in the worlds of television, theatre and film, became instant bestsellers, and the rest is history, quite literally, in fact. She has since developed a love of writing Australian historically based fiction and her fame as a novelist has spread rapidly throughout Europe, where she has been published in English, German, French, Dutch, Czech and Spanish.

Her subsequent bestsellers, *Kal*, *Beneath the Southern Cross*, *Territory*, *Pacific*, *Heritage*, *Floodtide*, *Maralinga*, *Tiger Men*, *Elianne*, *Spirits of the Ghan*, *Sanctuary* and *Khaki Town*, have confirmed Judy's position as one of Australia's leading fiction writers. She has now sold over one million books in Australia alone.

In 2015 Judy was made a Member of the Order of Australia for her 'significant service to the performing arts as a scriptwriter and actor of stage and screen, and to literature as an author'.

Visit Judy at judynunn.com.au or on
 facebook.com/JudyNunnAuthor

T0363455

Books by Judy Nunn

The Glitter Game
Centre Stage
Araluen
Kal
Beneath the Southern Cross
Territory
Pacific
Heritage
Floodtide
Maralinga
Tiger Men
Elianne
Spirits of the Ghan
Sanctuary
Khaki Town

Children's fiction
Eye in the Storm
Eye in the City

Short stories (available in ebook)
The House on Hill Street
The Wardrobe
Just South of Rome
The Otto Bin Empire: Clive's Story
Oskar the Pole
Adam's Mum and Dad

Araluen

JUDY NUNN

PENGUIN BOOKS

PENGUIN BOOKS

UK | USA | Canada | Ireland | Australia
India | New Zealand | South Africa | China

Penguin Books is part of the Penguin Random House group of companies
whose addresses can be found at global.penguinrandomhouse.com.

First published by Random House Australia, 1994
Published by Arrow, 1999, 2007, 2011
This edition published by Penguin Books, 2020

Cover photograph © Photolibrary/Corbis
Cover design by Blue Cork
Typeset by Midland Typesetters, Australia

Printed and bound in Australia by Griffin Press, an accredited
ISO AS/NZS 14001 Environmental Management Systems printer

 A catalogue record for this
book is available from the
National Library of Australia

ISBN 978 1 76104 122 8

penguin.com.au

The author would like to thank
Dr Grahame Hookway in Perth,
Robyn Gurney and Sue Greaves in
Sydney and Carmen Duncan in
New York for invaluable assistance
in the researching of this book.

For my husband Bruce Venables

For one sweet grape who will the vine destroy?

WILLIAM SHAKESPEARE
The Rape of Lucrece

Come ye back to Araluen
Ancient warrior distant traveller
Tread ye softly wake me gently
Whisper to me all your woes.
Let the place of waterlilies
Soothe your pain and ease your sorrow
Sleep forever on my hillside
Where the timeless vine doth grow.

ANON

BOOK ONE

The

Old Days

(1849 - 1873)

CHAPTER ONE

George and Richard

IT WAS A HOT, harsh day, mid-January in the Southern Hemisphere. George and Richard stood at the portside bow of the barque *Henrietta* and watched the rugged coastline slipping by. Neither spoke. After three months at sea even Richard had run out of words. Bored and restless, no longer homesick, no longer seasick, they simply ached to set foot once more on solid ground.

But as the vessel rounded the southern headland, their torpor lifted and they gazed ahead, awestruck.

'My God!' Richard breathed. 'They told us it was beautiful. But look at it, George. Just look at it!'

And the *Henrietta* sailed into the womb of Sydney Harbour.

George and Richard Ross were remittance men. They'd been banished to the Colonies by an irate father who was sick to death of buying them out of trouble – gambling and women, mainly.

3

Howard Ross had paid for their passage to Australia, given them each the healthy sum of five hundred pounds to get started and told them not to return to England for five years.

'Both of you will receive one hundred pounds remittance every quarter,' he announced. 'If you've not straightened yourselves out within five years, then I wash my hands of you. You forfeit any further monies and you're on your own.'

Howard was a tough man and he meant it, despite the tearful protestations of his wife, Emily, who was particularly worried about Richard, the youngest of her brood of seven.

'He's not yet twenty, Howard, and he has a weak chest.'

'Rubbish – it's all those cigars. He's a malingerer.' Before his wife could protest further, he added, 'If he's consumptive, the dry climate'll do him good.' And that was the end of the argument.

Howard didn't like Richard much, he never had, but he was sorry to see George go. He had a soft spot for George. But he couldn't show favouritism, he told himself. Both boys appeared to have inherited the weak strain that ran in the Ross family and the only way to strengthen them was to boot them out of the nest. The remaining boys had proved that they were more than capable of running the highly successful family business and the two girls had been satisfactorily married off. The House of Ross had a reputation to uphold, a reputation not only for the manufacture of the highest quality steel cutlery, but for the exemplary behaviour of its members – members of one of the finest families in the county, or so Howard firmly believed.

George was devastated by his father's decision. Although he was only twenty-one, he had a strong sense of family and had presumed that, after sowing a few wild oats, he would take his correct place in the dynasty. He would work alongside his older brothers. He would marry and he would produce sons as a true Ross should.

No amount of argument could dissuade his father and George certainly refused to beg. Not that begging would have changed the situation. Even if it could have, George would beg to no man. Despite his father's opinion, young George was not a person of weak character. His penchant for women and gambling had been directly attributable to youth and to the influence of his younger brother. Indeed, it was his younger brother who was George's one true weakness. He had inherited his mother's need to nurture Richard. Richard was fully aware of this and used it unashamedly.

'For goodness' sake, George, old man,' he chaffed, 'stop being so melodramatic. It's only for five years. We'll have a wonderful time – it will be an adventure.' The idea of travelling halfway round the world was exciting to Richard and he was not the least bit daunted by the prospect of what might be in store for him at the other end. After all, George was with him. George would look after him. George always did.

So it was, then, that on a crisp autumn day in mid-September, 1849, George and Richard Ross set sail for the Colony of New South Wales aboard the *Henrietta*.

It was a sweltering Sydney summer. Even the nights afforded no relief from the oppressive heat. 'It's not always like this,' George and Richard were informed. 'This is a heatwave – things will get better.' But such reassurances couldn't change Richard's mind. His desire for adventure quickly waned in Sydney. It wasn't just the heat. After the first flush of excitement at the sight of its magnificent harbour, he had decided that Sydney was a grubby town. He missed the green hills of Cheshire.

'This is a hateful place,' he complained. 'Look at it! Space all around us and yet people build these horrid little terraced houses in imitation of the squalid parts of London! You'd think they'd know better.'

'Rubbish,' was George's retort. 'There are some magnificent houses in Sydney.'

But, as usual, Richard wasn't listening. 'There's nothing here but dust and heat and flies and scrawny trees with no colour,' he continued. 'Can't we go somewhere green?'

'No, we can't,' George answered dismissively. 'The whole of the country's like this – you'd better start getting used to it.'

'No, it isn't,' Richard insisted. 'Do you remember that German chap on the boat? The one who was joining his brother in Adelaide? He said there were valleys outside the town that reminded him of the Rhine. Why don't we go there? Please, George, let's go there.' When George looked as if he might be starting to weaken, Richard coughed pathetically and added, 'Besides, this dust is shockingly painful to my lungs.'

George laughed out loud. 'And you are shockingly painful in your transparency, Dickie.'

Richard just grinned back. It was wonderful having a big brother like George.

Three months after their arrival in Australia, George and Richard Ross bought fifty acres of prime, green land in a valley not far from the township of Adelaide.

Richard was not strong enough to involve himself in physical labour so he stayed in town while the homestead was being built. Between sating his desires at night and trotting out in the dray several times a week to see how George and the men were going with the building, he was thoroughly enjoying himself.

Adelaide was a far more pleasing town to Richard than Sydney. It was less grubby and cramped, and he found the freestanding stone cottages charming. Although Sydney Harbour had been impressive, he preferred the tranquil beauty of the Torrens River, and the surrounding green hills reminded him of Cheshire.

But it wasn't just the bucolic aspect of the town which appealed to him. Beneath its tranquil facade, Adelaide had plenty to offer the hedonist in Richard. He quickly acquainted himself with its more select brothels and gambling dens and soon became a popular member of the flamboyant Adelaide society which flourished after sundown.

George was aware that Richard was behaving true to form, but after one token lecture he gave up trying to amend his brother's behaviour. He didn't have time to reform Richard. There was too much to be done. He kept a tight hold of the purse strings, however, handing over a moderate weekly allowance and turning a blind eye. If Richard wished to lose his money in a poker game, then that was his choice.

George was also fully aware that Richard was using his weak physical condition to escape any form of physical labour, but he didn't care. It didn't bother him one bit, because George was filled with a joy he'd never known was possible. He loved this land. He revelled in the physical exertion and the feeling of well-being it gave to his body, which was turning harder and browner by the day. And he loved the freedom from his domineering father and the stultifying family business. Who the hell needed cutlery anyway? he decided with abandon. Eat with your hands. Do everything with your hands – fell your trees, build your houses, till your soil. And, as the sweat poured from his brow, he'd clutch fists full of earth to his chest and laugh for sheer happiness.

'Araluen. That's what we're going to call the place,' he announced one day.

'Araluen?' Richard queried. 'What on earth does "Araluen" mean?'

' "Place of water lilies",' George explained. 'It's an Aboriginal term. I learnt it from one of the locals.'

'I haven't seen any water lilies.'

'That's because you never look. Take a trip to

the creek down at the eastern end of the valley. There's a waterhole there covered in them.'

'Very well. Araluen it is, then.'

George didn't pay too much attention to Richard's many helpful suggestions regarding the building. They were usually made to impress whichever young woman had accompanied him that day to view the site and the emerging homestead.

'But don't you think the door should go there, George?' Richard would question his brother with a nudge and a wink that said 'make me look good', and George would grin and reply, 'Good idea, Dickie, damn good idea'. Despite everything Richard's charm was irresistible, and he invariably managed to make George laugh. He's incorrigible, George thought with a wealth of fondness.

Once the homestead was completed, Richard was bored. He sat on the spacious verandah watching George and the men building the barn and wished he was back in town. It was much more diverting there.

'You'd be less bored if you did something,' George finally snapped back. He was becoming a little fed up with Richard's whinging.

'What exactly did you have in mind?' Richard asked petulantly. 'Digging up mulga roots? Building woodsheds?' The cough that followed was deep and rasping and, although George knew it was a bid for sympathy, he was concerned. The

Australian climate had had little effect on Richard's lungs.

'Father was right,' he said sharply. 'Give up the cigars.'

'You get more like him every day,' Richard answered. 'You're turning into a tyrant, George.' But he smiled as he sipped his port and puffed his Havana and, as usual, it was impossible for George to take offence.

'I know what you can do, Dickie,' George said one night as they sat on the verandah in the gathering dusk watching Thomas cart wood up from the shed.

'Oh yes,' Richard answered warily. 'And what is that?'

Thomas went through the side door into the kitchen where they could hear him talking with Emma. Thomas and Emma were a middle-aged ticket-of-leave couple George had hired several months earlier and they were proving invaluable. Most of the Colony's domestic labour was employed from the ranks of convicts granted a ticket-of-leave, the conditions of which allowed them to serve their sentence under parole conditions but forbade them ever to return to England.

'Study. That's what you can do,' George continued. Richard stared blankly at him and sipped his wine in silence. George rose, walked to the verandah rail and spread his arms expansively. 'Look at that. Isn't it magnificent? And it's ours, Dickie. All ours.'

The view was certainly impressive. The long straight drive up the hill to the homestead, the massive stone barn to the right and, to the left, the stables above which were the servants' quarters. But Richard knew that George was referring to the land. The acres and acres of land which had been painstakingly cleared. Richard didn't think it looked magnificent at all. He thought it looked embarrassingly denuded and he vastly preferred the green trees and grasses that had been there before. But of course one had to clear the land and plant one's crops to survive, so he nodded dutifully.

'Yes, George, it's magnificent. You've done a fine job. So what exactly do I study?' he asked, feigning interest and hoping Emma would soon announce dinner. He was starving.

'Crops,' George answered. 'Wheat, I presume – that's what most of the locals seem to favour. The land will be ready for planting soon and we need to know the correct time, the correct depth, the correct – '

'Good God, how am I supposed to go about that?'

'The locals, Dickie. Charm the locals and learn their methods.'

'Oh.' Richard was suddenly interested. Here was a valid excuse to get away from the homestead and into town. 'Very well. I shall start my inquiries tomorrow.'

George smiled. Richard's response was eminently readable. 'And don't confine your inquiries to the township, will you, Dickie? You must visit the properties and talk to the farmers.'

11

'Yes, George, of course.'

But strangely enough, it was in the township that Richard found the answer.

'Vines! We'll plant vines!' Richard exclaimed three weeks later upon his return from the doctor. His cough had worsened and a worried George had insisted he seek medical advice.

'What are you talking about, Dickie? I thought you'd been to see the doctor.'

'I have, I have, and he says we should plant vines. He's given me some cuttings. They're in the dray. Come and have a look.'

'But what about your chest? What about the blood you coughed up the other day? What did he say about ... ? George followed his brother out to the verandah.

'Oh bother the chest – just look at this!' Richard reached into the back of the dray and held aloft a handful of vine cuttings. 'Here is our future, George.' He joined his brother on the verandah and thrust one of the cuttings into his hand. 'Here!'

George had never seen him so excited. He stared blankly at the cutting then back to his brother. 'What sort of vines? What are you talking about?'

'Grapes, man, grapes! When Dr Penfold came out here he brought grape cuttings with him from some of the finest wine areas of France and he's succeeding! Already! After only seven years!'

'Wine?' George said incredulously as realisation dawned. 'You mean make our own wine?'

'Yes, George, yes!'

'But we're not wine-makers. Wine-making is a science.'

'We're not farmers either. And the science is called oenology.'

'But we know nothing about it.'

'Then we'll teach ourselves. We'll start with these.' Richard held up the cuttings. 'Dr Penfold will help – he knows everything about viticulture – and in ten years we'll be among the top vignerons in the country. You see,' he boasted, 'already I know the language of wine.'

George was shaking his head but Richard continued regardless. 'If we must become men of the land, why not grow something we can enjoy, for God's sake? I insist you come with me to look at Dr Penfold's property tomorrow – he's offered us an open invitation to The Grange.'

Again George tried to interrupt but Richard took no notice. 'He'll be at his practice in town but his wife Mary will accommodate us. Now go and nag Emma about tea, there's a good chap, while I unharness old Ned here, who's dying for a drink too.'

'And tell Emma plenty of cake and scones,' Richard called as he led the horse and dray off to the stables. 'I'm starving!'

As usual, Richard had his way and, although George maintained his doubts about the wisdom of cultivating grapevines, he agreed to donate ten acres of the property towards the establishment of a vineyard.

'But if, in five years, it proves to be a non-viable proposition ... '

'Ten, George – you have to give me ten. It will take at least ten years to establish.'

'Very well. Ten,' George agreed. 'But if, after ten years ... '

Richard burst out laughing. 'Listen to you, George, just listen! You sound like father at his pompous best.' And George found himself laughing in agreement.

They were a hard ten years and there were many times when George wanted to give up but, surprisingly enough, it was Richard who insisted they persevere.

'It takes time,' he said when George repeatedly suggested they convert their vinegrowing acres to grazing land for the sheep he'd acquired. 'It'll be worth it, believe me.'

George continued to be sceptical all through the early experimental years when failure constantly seemed to outweigh success but finally Richard's refusal to give in started to pay off and George was forced to admit his brother had been right.

But Richard's triumph was costly. Years of endless hard work took their toll, years of pruning, harvesting, and irrigating. And when he wasn't working among the vines, he was walking among them. Through the searing heat of summer and the biting mid-winter frosts, Richard walked endlessly between the rows and rows of his precious vines like a shepherd guarding his flock. Shortly after his thirtieth birthday, he became seriously ill.

When Dr Penfold visited the property he warned George that Richard simply could not continue at such a pace.

'Try to tell him that,' George replied. 'We have workers, of course, but he tends the vines as though they were his children and will allow no one else to oversee the operation, not even myself.'

Dr Penfold and his wife were among the most successful vignerons in the country and it was this fact rather than the good doctor's excellent medical reputation which finally persuaded Richard to employ an overseer. Dr Penfold was, in Richard's opinion, the only person qualified to announce that the vines were now firmly established and the only person qualified to recommend an expert worthy of the task of tending them.

Such an expert did not come cheap, of course. Neither did the extra labour George insisted hiring in order to impress upon Richard that there was no necessity for him to set foot outside the house. 'At least not until the start of summer – the spring frost is not good for your chest.'

'We can't afford it, George,' Richard protested feebly. 'We're only just starting to make good as it is.'

It was true. They had recently finished paying off their acquired debts, and funds were in short supply, the support from their father having long since been withdrawn.

Howard's remittances had arrived quarterly, as promised, for the first five years, always accompanied by a letter from Emily, but with never a word from Howard himself. At the end of the fifth year, a brief note informed them that there would be no further monies forthcoming and that George and Richard were to return to England within six months.

They had corresponded intermittently with their mother, but, apart from acknowledging receipt of their remittances, neither George nor Richard had seen any reason to communicate with Howard. Upon receiving his father's instructions, however, George wrote informing him that they would not be returning in six months, that they had no need of further monies and that they were happily settled in their adopted country. He concluded with a formal thanks for the assistance they'd received and a promise that he intended to honour and serve well the name of Ross in the new Colony. Richard added a postscript promising to send a bottle of his best vintage as soon as it should come available.

They didn't hear from Howard after that and even the letters from Emily dwindled over the years, as if she'd given up hope of ever seeing her youngest sons again. Or perhaps Richard's surmise was correct and Howard disapproved of her contact with them.

Whatever the reason, George and Richard managed to survive without their quarterly income. And, in accepting the fact that they were each other's sole family and that it was unlikely they would ever again see their home country, an even closer bond was forged between them.

It was with great difficulty, therefore, that George once again communicated with his father. Only Richard's illness and the fear for his brother's life could have forced him to take such a measure.

Ten years and two months after Howard had watched the *Henrietta* set sail for the Colonies, he opened George's letter informing him of Richard's illness and requesting funds.

'The boy must think I'm an imbecile,' he stormed. 'What does he take me for?' Despite Emily's pleas, he flatly refused to send any money. 'It's a ploy,' he said. 'Richard's a scoundrel. Always was. And he's pursuaded George to join forces and milk what they can from their estate. I must say I'd have expected a little more of George. Well, they'll be back when they realise how uncomfortable it is to starve.' And Howard would hear no more on the subject.

That summer was hard and seemed to go on forever. George quickly realised that he'd lulled himself into a false sense of security when he'd pursuaded Richard to remain indoors and away from the spring frosts. Summer started early, suddenly and with a vengeance. And, as the hot winds seared through the vineyards, threatening to devastate the entire crop, George could see that any attempt to dissuade Richard from working was useless. All he could do was work alongside his brother, erecting whatever wind protection they could and tending the vines regularly to ensure their supplementary water supply.

That was the summer that did it. George was

sure of it. Richard lasted another five years, but it was the summer of 1860 that was his undoing. George watched, powerless, as his brother wasted away, refusing to give in to his illness until the very end.

Richard died in 1865, six weeks before his thirty-sixth birthday, and he died content. His success as a vigneron was unquestionable – even Dr Penfold himself said so – and Richard toasted his own end with a glass of his finest Syrah.

'Did you send that bottle off to father?' he asked.

'Yes, it went with Martin Longford on the *Tag-lioni*. He said he'd deliver it personally.'

'But that was nearly six months ago. And there's been no word?'

'Come along now, Dickie, you know it can take all of nine months for word to get back to us.'

'Rubbish,' Richard smiled. 'Father's disowned us and you know it.' He coughed and, as usual, the cough took over.

It pained George to watch his brother's frail body fighting for air but finally the spasm was over and Richard lay back against the pillows, exhausted. He's near the end now, George thought as he reached for a tumbler of water. Dr Penfold had said as much. Not to Richard himself, but Richard knew, George was sure of that.

Waving the water aside, Richard gestured for the glass of wine he'd insisted George pour for him earlier. He sipped at it, examined it lovingly and, when he could finally trust himself to talk without precipitating another attack, he said with a proud nod, 'Sixty-two – one of our good years. In ten years' time it'll be a prize drop. Get yourself a glass, George, I want to make a toast.'

When George rejoined him with a fresh glass Richard was looking content and comfortable. Almost serene, George thought. Yes, he certainly knows.

'Father always said we'd inherited the weak strain of the Ross family,' Richard commented as he watched George pour the wine. 'Me, at least. I suspect he held hopes for you somewhere along the line.' He held his glass aloft. 'Well, old chap, if we are the weak Rosses, God protect the world from the strong ones. To you, George.' He clinked their glasses together. 'You're a fine brother.'

'To us both.' It was all George could trust himself to say. Any more and the tremor in his voice might betray him.

'Mind you,' Richard continued, oblivious to his brother's emotion, 'you're also a very stupid fellow.'

The insult was genuine and effectively curbed the threatening sting of a tear. 'Stupid? How?'

'Your letter to father all those years ago – which quite frankly I found a trifle pompous – when you promised to honour the family name in the new Colony.'

'What of it?' George demanded defensively. 'I meant every word.'

'Confound it, man, how are you going to honour the family name when there is no family?' George looked at him blankly and Richard fought back the desire to laugh, it would only bring about another coughing fit. He smiled broadly instead and, emaciated though the face was, the smile was

19

as engaging as ever. 'Stupid, you see? Take a wife, man, take a wife. You're thirty-eight years old and you're not going to last forever. One of us has to start breeding and, at the moment, I'd say you're the safer bet.'

The laugh finally erupted. A coughing fit followed and it was several minutes before Richard could continue. By now he was so weakened and his chest ached so much that all he wanted to do was sleep. But he smiled at George nonetheless.

'You're so like father, with your determination to found a Ross dynasty.' George was about to defend himself again but Richard continued. 'There's nothing wrong with that. You'll do a good job and, unlike father, you'll look after your own.' He shrugged. 'Personally, I couldn't give a damn about the family but I'd like you to promise me one thing.' George nodded and bent closer, Richard's voice was now very weak. 'Look after my vines.'

'Yes, of course,' George nodded.

'Good.' Richard closed his eyes. 'I'll see you in the morning. Wake me around dawn.' And within seconds he was fast asleep.

George didn't wake him at dawn. The following morning Richard had lapsed into unconsciousness and he died at nine o'clock that night.

George grieved for his brother and felt a loneliness he'd never experienced before. After the grief came the anger. He was convinced that Richard had died needlessly. If they'd been able to purchase modern labour-saving devices, if they'd been able to employ extra workers, if Richard had been hospitalised ... In other words, if Howard had forwarded the funds George had requested, his youngest son would be alive today.

The anger continued to gnaw away at George. He didn't inform the family of Richard's death – not even when, two years later, he received word from one of his sisters that his mother was dying. Although he was initially saddened by the news, he hardened his heart to it – Emily was an accomplice in Richard's death, after all, as were his brothers and sisters. They had each denied their own.

It was then that George made his decision. As far as he was concerned, the Ross family started here and now. *His* Ross family. Born of the Colonies. And he took Richard's advice and searched for a wife worthy of the name.

He found her in Sarah, the only daughter of strict Methodists, Henry and Elizabeth Cusack. Sarah's parents were greatly relieved to see their daughter wed; she was twenty-five, after all, no great beauty, and her dowry was mediocre.

'Sarah was sort of unexpected, you might say,' Henry explained to George, a trifle embarrassed. 'We'd put our money into getting the lads started by the time she came along.'

'The lads' were Sarah's five older brothers and the reason George wanted to marry Sarah. She was strong, good breeding stock and males ran in the family.

'No matter.' George said, waving aside the

dowry. 'I have more than enough for our needs.'

In the past few years George had done well. He had converted over half of Araluen to vines and was currently in the throes of purchasing a small neighbouring vineyard. All thanks to Richard, George thought. If only he'd lived to see it.

For propriety's sake, Elizabeth wanted to delay the marriage by several months. 'After all, you and Sarah only met three weeks ago, Mr Ross.'

But George was brutally honest. 'I am forty years old and childless, Mrs Cusack. I need sons.'

The truth did not endear George to Mrs Cusack but, as her husband pointed out in private, she really had no option. Her pride was salved a little, however, when George readily agreed that any off-spring were to be brought up strictly in accordance with the Methodist teachings.

George and Sarah were married on the first day of spring, 1868. Nine months and one week after the wedding, their first child was born, a strong healthy girl whom they called Catherine. For Sarah's sake, George hid his disappointment as best he could. But a year later, when Sarah gave birth to a son, there was no disguising George's elation. He handed out cigars with abandon and openly talked of Charles being the first in a new breed of Ross. One who was born to look after his own. No one knew what George was talking about but put it down to overexcitement at the birth of his first son.

Mary's birth two years later was a complicated one. Doctors fought to save both mother and baby and they succeeded. But they told Sarah that she would never have another child.

It was surprising how quickly George came to terms with the fact that he was to be denied the family of sons he'd had his heart set on. So the dynasty would take a little longer to establish itself – what matter? he asked himself. It was quality not quantity that counted.

The truth was that George had grown to love Sarah and the thought of losing her terrified him. They were a family now and the future would look after itself. Charles would have sons, the girls would marry strong men. The dynasty was founded.

So secure was George in this knowledge that, when the letter arrived from his father's personal secretary, he had no second thoughts as to how he should reply.

' . . . in these the last few months of his life,' the secretary's letter read, 'your father wishes to make his peace with you both.' The letter went on to say that, if George and Richard were to make haste to their father's bedside, Howard was prepared to reinstate them in his will. Evidently, he wished his entire family to be present at his deathbed and that included his two youngest sons.

George's reply was brutal and damning. 'Inform my father that his youngest son is dead,' he wrote. 'His youngest son has been dead for eight years and his second youngest son hereby severs all ties with his father.

'There is new Ross stock, bred from the Colonies, which, from this day, owes no allegiance to, and will accept none from, Howard Ross or any of his direct family.'

There was certainly no going back now, George

23

thought, and he felt elated as he put his seal to the envelope. There probably never had been, he supposed. But this – he looked down at the letter on the desk before him – this was irrevocable. This was uncompromising. This was the beginning.

BOOK TWO

The

Early Years

(1915 - 1946)

CHAPTER TWO

Young Franklin

FRANKLIN HAD VIVID MEMORIES of his grandfather despite the fact that he'd been barely ten years of age when old George died in the summer of 1915. The image was blurred – an old, old man with leathery skin, massive sideburns and a striking grey beard – but the impact Grandfather George had upon him remained with Franklin throughout his life.

Even on his deathbed Grandfather George was impressive. He ordered the entire family to his bedside and laid down the law for the final time. They'd heard it all before – George had laid down the law time and again over the years – but the fact that they were all together, his children, their spouses and his five grandchildren, made it quite an event. And the fact that he openly announced his intention to die within the week made it positively awe-inspiring. Certainly to Franklin, the youngest member of the family.

There was another awesome event occasioned by George's imminent death – the return of the infamous Aunt Catherine.

Franklin stared at her, mesmerised. To think that she lived in Paris! That she was an artist! That she had rebelled against Grandfather George! Rebelling against Grandfather George was the most astonishing fact of all. And here she was answering back to him, even on his deathbed.

'I'm sorry I kept you waiting, Father,' she was saying, 'but ships can only travel so fast, you know.'

'And you've still not married,' George complained. 'Good God, woman, you must be nigh on forty years of age by now.'

'I'm forty-six.' Catherine held her handsome head high. She even looked like an artist, Franklin thought, with her wild grey-black hair. 'And yes,' she continued as she saw George about to interrupt, 'I'm well aware I'm past child-bearing age but you have your grandchildren from Charles and Mary and four of them males at that, so I don't see what you have to complain about.'

It was said with good humour but it was shocking nonetheless. Franklin stared at his grandfather and waited for the explosion. But there wasn't one. Something quite different happened instead. Something quite astonishing. George actually smiled.

'Twelve years since I've seen you, girl, and you haven't changed a bit, have you?' His voice had lost its edge.

'No, Father, and I don't intend to, but I have always been thankful for your support. You know that.'

There was something in the old man's face that Franklin had never seen before and it suddenly occurred to the boy that Aunt Catherine was very special to Grandfather. He had certainly never looked at Father like that, Franklin thought. Or Aunt Mary, for that matter.

The adults in the room had also registered the old man's fondness but it was no surprise to them – certainly not to Charles and Mary. Catherine had always been their father's favourite. She'd nearly broken his heart when she'd announced she was going to Paris to study art. George's refusal to allow her to go had meant nothing – she'd merely threatened to run away and work her passage aboard the next ship bound for Europe.

True to his doctrine of 'always look after your own', George had funded her studies and her trips home to see the family but he'd missed her sorely between times. Her rebellious, carefree spirit reminded him so much of Richard that at times his heart ached and deep down, he knew that she was the son he wished he'd had. It made him feel guilty that he couldn't love Charles the same way. His son was a good man, he knew that: solid, reliable, trustworthy – his word was his bond. Not unlike George himself, really. But that was where the similarity ended. Charles had no romance in him, no true love of the land or the vines. The man didn't even drink, for God's sake. The only time wine passed his lips was when they tasted the new vintage.

It was the one thing George hadn't reckoned on when he'd allowed Sarah full rein with the children. A promise was a promise, after all, and he'd given his word to her parents that all offspring

29

were to be brought up in strict accordance with Methodist teachings. For ten years George hadn't afforded it another thought as Sarah took the children off to church regularly each Sunday morning and read to them from the bible for half an hour each evening. It was only when Charles was ten and steadfastly refused the first taste of wine offered him that George remembered with horror that Methodists didn't drink alcohol. Sarah had told him as much years ago and of course she never touched a drop herself, but George hadn't thought for a moment that such a doctrine should apply to his own children.

'For God's sake, woman, the boy's going to inherit a vineyard!' he exploded. 'How in hell can he *not drink*?'

But Methodist they were and, at ten years of age, Charles was the staunchest of them all. It was Catherine who had thrown her religious instruction to the winds and become a free spirit and, yet again, George wished that she'd been his son.

His youngest daughter, Mary, was another matter altogether. Mary was quiet, calm, acquiescent. Mary was also enigmatic, and George felt that he'd never really known her and probably never would.

George looked at his family gathered around his deathbed. They weren't such a bad lot, he supposed. A good enough start for a dynasty. Then why did he feel vaguely dissatisfied? Because something was lacking, that was why. There was no spirit or challenge. No adventure. Maybe he'd made life too easy for them – maybe they hadn't had to fight hard enough. Surely they couldn't all have inherited the weak Ross strain, he reasoned, but as yet he'd seen no indication of the fighting spirit. With the exception of Catherine, that is – and of what value was the fighting spirit in a woman who insisted upon remaining childless? Moreover, because she'd refused to return to the family home for the past twelve years, he hadn't even been able to enjoy the pleasure of her company.

Not long to go now, George told himself, as he ploughed on with his address to the family. He'd already given his lecture on 'looking after one's own' and 'the family comes first'.

'Control of The Ross Estate must pass to the first-born male of each generation,' he continued. 'So when your father dies . . . pay attention, boy!' He'd turned to Kenneth, Franklin's older brother, and caught him gazing out the window.

'So when your father dies, you will be the one to inherit Araluen and you will be responsible for the welfare of the family . . . Are you listening to me, boy?'

'Yes, Grandfather. I'm sorry, Grandfather,' Kenneth said guiltily, aware of the admonishing looks from both his mother and father. But he was bored. On such a beautiful sunny Saturday afternoon he should have been out riding with his cousin. They'd planned on racing the horses to the far north paddock and swimming in the dam.

The old man was aware of the unrest amongst the young ones. 'Very well,' he said finally, as he allowed his head to sink back on the pillows, 'that is all I have to say. You may go.'

The younger members of the family left the room with indecent speed. All except Franklin – he remained transfixed, staring at the old man in the bed. Then the adults filed out slowly until only Catherine and Franklin were left.

'Shall I come back and read to you after your nap, Father?'

'Yes.' The old man closed his eyes. 'Thank you, Catherine, I'd like that.' He felt tired. There was no real pain apart from the general ache of old age but he longed to leave this world. There was nothing left for him. There'd been nothing left for a long time now. The exercise of hanging on to a life he didn't want until Catherine came home had been an interesting one. Quite a test of strength. A number of times he'd wanted to slip away in the night. As he'd felt himself drift off to sleep he'd had to consciously remind himself that he must wake up in the morning. It was like setting an alarm clock, he thought. And now there was no need to set the clock any more. How peaceful.

'Come along, Franklin.'

George opened his eyes. Catherine was at the door, her hand held out to Franklin who had remained staring at his grandfather.

Over the years, George had taken few pains with his grandchildren – they were still not at an age to be of interest to him – but something in the boy's face now arrested his attention. It was natural for a child to be fascinated by old age and death: fascinated or repulsed or just plain bored by something so foreign – it was to be expected.

But as the boy stared unwaveringly at him, there was something else in the face that intrigued George. It was a challenge.

'It's all right, Catherine. Leave him with me for a moment.' Catherine closed the door quietly behind her. 'What is it, boy?'

Franklin took a deep breath. 'Can you really do it?'

'Do what?'

'You said you were going to die within the week. Can you really do it?'

Yes, George thought, it was a challenge, all right. The boy was personally challenging him. He smiled. 'I think people can do whatever they set their minds to,' he said, 'if they're strong and they have the will.'

Franklin nodded. That made sense. 'When will you do it?'

'Not tonight. Maybe the night after.' George paused. No, that wasn't fair, he thought, he needed to be more decisive than that. 'Yes,' he said, 'the night after. Sunday seems a good idea, don't you think?'

Again Franklin nodded. He believed Grandfather George implicitly. 'I won't tell anyone,' he promised.

'Good,' George agreed and he closed his eyes once more. 'Instruct your Aunt Catherine to wake me in an hour.' Such trust must not go disappointed, he thought, and as he drifted off, he felt a great sense of joy. The boy had what the others lacked. The boy had spirit.

The next day, when Franklin brought in his lunchtime soup, they smiled at the secret they shared and, later that same night, at around eleven o'clock, George died peacefully in his sleep. Franklin was deeply impressed. Grandfather George had been a man of honour – he'd remained true to his word until the very end.

Franklin noticed a lot of changes after the death of Grandfather George. Uncle Harry, Mary's husband, went off to the war and Aunt Catherine stayed on in the family home – only for three months, she said, while her belongings were shipped out from France. Then she was going to Sydney to open an art gallery.

Catherine became a firm favourite with Franklin. She was 'different' and he deeply admired her. His brother Kenneth also liked her, as did Mary's brood who lived only a few miles away. But, popular as she was with the younger members of the family, the adults kept their distance. Catherine was too Bohemian for them. They took their lead from Charles who actively disliked his older sister. He maintained that she had deserted the family and he didn't approve at all of her single lifestyle.

'A very selfish woman,' he said one day at the luncheon table. 'And decidedly peculiar.'

'Well, of course she's "peculiar",' Franklin boasted later to Kenneth. 'She's an artist.'

Two months after the death of Grandfather George, Charles announced stiffly to the family that a friend of Aunt Catherine's would shortly be arriving from Paris and staying for a week before accompanying Catherine to Sydney. It was quite obvious he disapproved of the visit.

How exciting, Franklin thought. Catherine had told them she was going to Sydney to open an art gallery, but she'd said nothing of a friend from Paris.

'Is your friend French?' Franklin asked as he watched the bold charcoal strokes take form on the page before his very eyes. Like magic, they became a vineyard. Rows and rows of vines stretching into the distance. Franklin never tired of watching Catherine sketch.

It was nearly dusk and they were seated beside the old stone cellar, Catherine on her little camp stool and Franklin on the ground beside her.

Catherine looked out over the vineyard. These were the oldest vines, planted by her uncle Richard. They had always been her father's favourites. 'Yes, French – like the vines.' She looked up at the sky, then back at her sketch and smudged the clouds with her thumb. The cloud and light formations over the vines were thrilling. 'Very French, and very nice, and you'll get on famously, I know it.'

Catherine leaned back against the cool stones of the cellar walls. Second only to the homestead the cellar was the oldest building on the property and she remembered hearing her father's proud boast when she was a very young girl, 'Of course, it was just a barn in the beginning. Huge, it was. Nearly broke our backs building it.' Then he shook his head in disbelief. 'Whoever would have thought it would one day be the birthplace of some of the finest wines in the country.'

Catherine had stared spellbound as her father held a half-filled glass of rich purple wine to the light.

'Because they are, Catherine. Among the very finest. And one day they'll be among the finest in the world.' Catherine always loved the way her father spoke to her as an adult. 'Here. Try it.' And he handed her the glass.

It was the first time Catherine had tasted wine and, despite the strict rulings of the Church, she didn't question her action for a moment. To the contrary, she felt deeply privileged to be sharing such an experience with her father. And of course George loved her for it. There was such pride in his voice as he said, 'I knew I could rely on you, Catherine.' She hadn't known that, only two days before, her father had been bitterly disappointed when Charles had refused to take even one sip.

She'd been eleven then. Around the same age as Franklin is now, she thought. And that moment in the cellar had formed the basis of the lifetime bond she had shared with her father.

'Why have you stopped drawing, Aunt Catherine?'

Startled out of her reverie by young Franklin, she looked up at the sky. 'We're losing our light. Let's do something else instead, shall we?' Catherine packed away her sketching things. 'Come along.' And Franklin clasped the hand she extended to him and followed her into the cellar.

Franklin had been inside the cellar only twice before. And then briefly and in the company of his father, the children being forbidden to enter unless accompanied by an adult.

It was a fascinating place. Dark but not gloomy; cool but not dank; musty but not stale. It excited him and, as he drank in the smell and the look and the feel of it all, he barely noticed Catherine pouring a glass of wine from one of the sample bottles on the heavy wooden counter.

Suddenly the half-filled glass was before him. 'Try it,' she said. And he stared at the rich purple wine. 'Go over there and hold it up to the light. It's a beautiful colour.' He crossed to the doorway and held up the glass.

'If you roll the wine around gently you can see where it sticks to the glass,' Catherine said. 'That's a very good sign.' She watched as the boy examined the wine from every angle. It was a solemn exercise and he was utterly engrossed – just as she herself had been at his age. She watched as he gently sipped from the glass. A bond was being forged between the two of them, just like the bond that had been created between her and her father all those years ago.

'Do you like it, Franklin?' she asked.

Franklin paused for thought. 'It tastes like wet flour sacks,' he said finally.

Catherine laughed. 'Have you ever tasted wet flour sacks?'

'No. But it tastes the way wet flour sacks smell like they'd taste.'

It was a very serious assessment so Catherine didn't laugh again. 'Is it a taste you like?'

'Yes,' he nodded. 'Yes, I think so.'

Franklin wasn't sure whether he liked the taste

or not. But 'taste' wasn't really the right word anyway, he thought. It wasn't a big enough word. He was enjoying the whole experience – the smell, the texture, the colour of the wine. And he was enjoying being in the cellar and the closeness with his Aunt. How could he put all that into words? He took another sip instead. 'Yes, I like it,' he said.

How unlike his father he is, Catherine thought fondly. 'Come along, we'd better go inside. It'll be dark soon.'

Two days later, the shocking news arrived. Uncle Harry, Captain Harold Johnston, Sixth Division, South Australian Light Horse, had been killed in action. He was one of many, many Australians who had fallen in battle at a place called Gallipoli.

Mary contained her grief and it was frightening to see. She closed herself off from them all. She was fine, she said. People died in a war; it was to be expected – she wasn't the only widow. She must accept her lot.

Her behaviour wasn't natural. They all felt disturbed by it. The whole family. But no one could break through the barrier. She insisted on seeing to the funeral arrangements herself, she didn't shed a tear during the service and, the day after Harry was buried, she started packing away his clothes and personal belongings for Charles to deliver to the Salvation Army headquarters in town.

* * *

Surprisingly enough Catherine was the one who finally made the breakthrough.

Late one afternoon, Mary turned up in the trap, a large trunk on the seat beside her. 'Charles says you're going into town to collect your friend tomorrow.'

'That's right,' Catherine nodded.

'I've packed the last of Harry's belongings and I wondered whether you might drop them at the Salvation Army for me. It would save Charles an unnecessary trip later in the week.'

'Of course. Come on, hop down and have a cup of tea while the boys unload the trunk.' Catherine signalled to one of the farm hands who was sweeping out the stables.

'No, thank you.' Mary kept a firm hold on the reins.

'For heaven's sake, Mary. We can't unload it ourselves. Well, I certainly don't intend to. What's more, your horse looks as if he could do with a drink.'

After a moment's hesitation, Mary agreed. 'Very well,' she said, but she ignored the helping hand Catherine extended.

'You can't go on like this, you know that, don't you?' Catherine spoke brusquely and she didn't look at her sister as she busied herself stoking the fire in the wood-stove. 'You've closed yourself off for a fortnight now and everyone's too unnerved to talk to you.'

Mary sat staring into the open grate,

mesmerised by the sparks produced by Catherine's vigorous stirring.

'Well, I'm not letting you out of this kitchen until you talk to me.' Catherine slammed the grid closed and Mary was startled. 'Did you hear me?' She knew she was being brutal but maybe bullying Mary was the only way to get a response.

'Talk to me!' she demanded. 'Cry, for God's sake! Get angry! Why did he have to die? Tell me how much you loved him!' As Catherine pressed on relentlessly, she saw Mary's cheeks start to flush. 'Please, Mary. Talk to me!'

Mary didn't move. She gazed steadfastly out the window but there was the glistening of tears in her eyes and Catherine knew she was fighting the urge to cry.

'Oh, Mary. Dear little Mary.' She gathered her sister in her arms. 'Let go, my darling, let go.'

Mary resisted only for a moment, then the floodgates opened. She sobbed until her eyes were swollen, her nose ran and her chest ached and Catherine held her all the while.

When the outburst was over, Catherine cleaned her face with a fresh tea towel and Mary blew her nose as she was told like an obliging child.

Then, as Catherine rose to fill the teapot from the now boiling kettle, Mary leaned back, exhausted, and started speaking, more to herself than to her sister.

'Father never knew that Harry didn't want his children to bear the name of Ross. He didn't know that it was I who insisted upon it and that Harry agreed simply to please me.' Catherine looked at her, surprised.

40

'Yes,' she continued, 'just for me, Harry did that – and it cost his pride, I can tell you. He received a medal in the Boer War, you know, and he was proud of his record and rank and name. Captain Harold Johnston of the Australian Light Horse Contingent. And just for me he allowed his children to become Ross-Johnstons. It was no mean thing, Catherine.

'But then, Harry would do anything I asked him,' Mary continued. 'Anything except stay home from the war. From that filthy, shocking war.'

Her eyes filled with tears and she started to cry, softly this time. 'My Harry, my beautiful Harry, I begged him not to go, I begged him to stay home with me. But he said, "My country needs me, this is what I'm trained for."' She rocked back and forth in her chair. 'I begged him. I begged him and I begged him and it was the only time he ever denied me.'

Catherine put the pot on the table before them and sat quietly waiting for the tea to draw. She didn't dare say a word. Gradually, the sobs once more subsided and Mary, her energy expended, started to talk quietly.

'Father never really liked me, you know. I think perhaps he blamed me for Mother's ill health, my birth being such a difficult one.' She shrugged. 'Whatever the reasons, he considered me weak and uninteresting, I'm aware of that. You were the one he admired, Catherine, you were the strong one and he loved you for it.' Mary smiled, without animosity. 'It doesn't matter now. Anyway, Mother's love was enough for me.'

41

'Yes.' Catherine finally spoke. 'I was always jealous of Mother's love for you.'

'Were you?' Mary looked genuinely taken aback. 'So we were jealous of each other, then – how strange for us not to know it. When Mother died,' she continued as she watched Catherine pour the tea, 'I was perceived as the frail younger sister, of little value to anyone, and I didn't seem to have the voice to prove otherwise. I had neither your defiant courage nor Mother's quiet determination. But I did have a will of my own, Catherine. Truly I did. And that's what Harry recognised. I was my true self with Harry – he was the one person in the whole world who really knew me.'

She stared guiltily down at the cup of tea Catherine placed in front of her. 'God forbid I should say this, but I feel that even my own children don't know me.' She stirred the tea, watching it swirl in the cup. 'You escaped the destiny of the Ross women,' she said. 'We're breeders, you see – that's our sole purpose.' She finally looked up at Catherine and there was no rancour in her smile. 'Unless one subjugates one's will entirely to the men, this is a harsh family for women.'

'This is a harsh *world* for women!' Catherine felt an overwhelming mixture of emotions. She felt guilty that she'd never known her sister. She felt guilty that she, like the others, had assumed that Mary was weak and uninteresting. And all the while Mary had been crying out for recognition. Catherine was excited by the prospect of enlightening her.

'But it won't always be a harsh world for us,

Mary!' She knocked her teacup over in her enthusiasm. 'Things are changing. Already women have been granted the vote in Australia, it is why I came home. I tell you, my dear, this country is leading the world in women's rights.'

Catherine grabbed the tea towel and dabbed at the mess. 'Good heavens, within the last ten years three Nobel Prizes have been awarded to women. Well, two went to Marie Curie. And one of them she had to share with her husband,' she admitted. 'But I'm sure that was only a matter of protocol.'

Catherine's zeal was so amusing that Mary surprised herself by laughing out loud. 'What about the other one?'

'Other what?' Catherine also was taken aback by Mary's laughter.

'The other Nobel Prize. Who won it?'

'Oh. Baroness Bertha von Suttner, who died only last year. Her novel *Lay Down Your Arms* created a furore in the nineties. She was a great crusader – and she felt the same way you do, Mary. She actually called war "an obscenity" – isn't that brilliant? She was awarded the Peace Prize about six or seven years ago. So you see we can do anything! Anything!'

Catherine's ineffectual dabbing had not stemmed the flow of tea which now found its way to the edge of the table.

'Here, let me,' Mary said. She reached over to take the tea towel but Catherine snatched it back.

'No, don't dismiss me like that,' she continued vehemently. 'It's the duty of all of us to do things, you included. They don't have to be momentous.

43

Just exercise your mind and your rights.' She put down the tea towel and took hold of Mary's hand. 'Read and study and ... '

'I read a great deal,' Mary interrupted.

'Then express your opinions on what you read. Let people know you, Mary. And when I open my art gallery in Sydney you must come over and see my first exhibition. You must – '

'Yes. I'd like that.'

Catherine stared back at her. 'You would?'

'Yes, I'd like that very much.'

'Oh my dear, please do come, please! You'll be proud of me, I promise. My gallery is going to specialise in the work of the Impressionists. Do you know of them?'

'I've read of the *French* Impressionists, yes,' Mary nodded. 'But ... '

'Well, there is an Impressionist movement afoot in Australia. I've been in communication with them. A group of young artists, several of them women, are founding a modern school of art in Sydney and I intend to champion their cause. Oh, thank you.'

Mary had put a fresh cup of tea into her hands and Catherine, who hadn't even noticed her pouring it, automatically took two sips before continuing anew. 'Cezanne, one of the greatest of the French Impressionists, has had a vast influence upon the Australian Moderns ... and I knew him, Mary! I actually knew him!'

As Catherine gabbled on, Mary watched her affectionately, aware that she was closer to her sister than she had ever been before. And, for the first time in two weeks, she relaxed. The painful

44

sense of loss and the ache for Harry were still there, of course – the void would never be filled – but the raw, screaming nerves had gone. She would be able to cry now, even in front of the children, if she wished.

'A wonderful man,' Catherine was saying. 'A gentle giant. Surprisingly humble, and such a liberal thinker. Now, there's a point, Mary – Cezanne never thought of women as inferior. Mind you, he never thought of his work as superior either.'

Catherine laughed. And when she laughed, Mary laughed with her, even though she hadn't heard what her sister said. They talked for a further hour – well, Catherine did – before Mary finally left, resisting the invitation to stay the night.

'Goodnight, Catherine,' she said as they embraced. 'I shall most certainly come to the opening of your gallery.' And Catherine knew that she meant it.

Two days later, when Catherine returned from town with her friend, she was surprised to see Mary waiting in the drive, her three children lined up either side of her.

'Mary! What are you doing here?' she said as she handed the reins to the stablehand.

'We came to meet Gabrielle, of course.' Mary walked over to the trap and offered her hand in assistance to the pretty, fair-haired woman seated on the passenger side. 'These are my children,' she said after she'd accepted Gabrielle's enthusiastic hug and a kiss on each cheek.

That must have shocked her, Catherine thought. Mary was certainly not accustomed to the European form of greeting – and it was a particularly effusive one, at that. Gaby, having been warned to expect otherwise, was delighted by the welcome.

Franklin and Kenneth charged down the steps from the verandah and were also introduced. Which left only Charles and his wife, Sybil. Catherine looked up at the house and saw them standing in the doorway. Charles' eyes met hers and he initiated the move, Sybil taking the lead from her husband, as always. They walked slowly together towards the edge of the verandah; when Charles stopped, Sybil stopped. They didn't venture down the steps but waited for the others to come up to them.

Yes, this is what I expected, Catherine thought and flashed an apologetic look in Gaby's direction.

Gaby didn't see it, however. She didn't have time. In an uncharacteristically familiar gesture, Mary had taken her arm and was ushering her up the steps towards the house.

'Come along, Gabrielle. Sybil has the kettle on and I brought over a batch of my scones which are delicious if I do say so myself.' They were on the verandah now. 'This is my brother Charles and his wife Sybil.' Mary allowed only a moment for the nods of acknowledgement before sweeping Gaby inside the house. 'Now do come inside and relax. It's such a jarring ride from town, isn't it?'

Sybil and Charles were left on the front step, jaws agape, and Catherine bounded up to them laughing. She was still laughing as she went inside.

46

Dear Mary, what a tower of strength. Who ever would have thought?

Gaby was a personable woman and the children warmed to her immediately. She was blonde, petite and pretty. She spoke with an attractively pronounced French accent, and she had a bubbly, youthful personality which belied her thirty-nine years. Franklin found her fascinating.

Aunt Catherine told him that Gaby was a talented sculptor, that her father was a prominent art dealer and that she knew all the most exciting people in Paris. It added to the allure and, to Franklin, Gaby represented everything that was romantic about the world outside. That vast world which lay beyond the Ross property, beyond Adelaide, beyond Australia itself. That world of adventure and opportunity which Franklin would one day conquer.

It was Sunday, a week after Gaby had arrived and the day before the two women were to depart for Sydney, when Franklin did a wicked thing. 'I'll meet you at the church, Mother; Aunt Mary is going to pick me up.'

It was a lie and Franklin knew he would be heavily punished when it was discovered, but he was quite prepared to pay the consequences. Because he never lied, his parents didn't question him for a second.

Franklin stood in his Sunday best watching the rest of the family drive off in his father's brand-new automobile and, when they were out of sight, he went to his room and changed into his dungarees.

Neither Catherine nor Gaby attended church, much to his father's disapproval. Half an hour earlier, they had taken their sketch books and gone walking.

As Franklin wandered around the deserted grounds – the servants and labourers were also at church or visiting relatives – he wondered which was the most likely walk the women would have decided upon. The old vineyard probably.

But they weren't there. And they weren't at the poplar grove near the eastern dam, another favourite sketching haunt of Catherine's.

Franklin was frustrated. Thirty minutes had gone by and, if he was going to have to suffer the inevitable beating for his blatant disobedience, he wanted it to be worthwhile. It was his last opportunity to have Aunt Catherine and Gaby all to himself and he wanted to sit at their feet for hours, listening to their stories and watching their sketches appear magically on the page.

They must have gone further afield than usual, he thought. The quickest way to find them would be to saddle up Old Black Joe.

Franklin opened the stable door. He didn't see them at first. In fact he heard them before he saw them. A harsh, rasping sound. For a moment he thought one of the horses might have colic. He walked through the stables in search of the sound.

They were in one of the empty stalls right at the far end, lying together in the fresh straw, their bodies entwined, and they were kissing, roughly, insistently.

Franklin had never seen two people kiss in such a way. Only once had he seen his parents kiss and it had been gentle and discreet. It had also been very brief – when his father had noticed him watching he had immediately broken away. And here were these two women, feverishly feeding upon each other's mouths.

Gaby's bodice was undone and her breasts were exposed. Franklin stared in horror as Catherine's mouth travelled down the long, slender neck. Her lips engulfed a quivering nipple and Gaby, eyes closed, mouth open in ecstasy, cried out, dragging at Catherine's skirts, exposing her legs and her undergarments and the rhythm of her grinding pelvis.

As he watched them grunting together in the straw like animals, Franklin felt repulsed, but he couldn't turn away.

Pulling herself up onto one elbow, Gaby lifted her own skirts and started to tear at her underclothes.

Catherine's hand was between her legs and Gaby was parting her thighs, moaning loudly.

Then Catherine's voice, thick and guttural. 'Oh mon amour, mon amour *tu est belle* ... ' Her hand moving quicker. Gaby, arching her back, her eyes opening wide ...

'Oh God, the *boy*!' Gaby hissed. 'Kate, the boy!' Quickly, Gaby covered her breasts and pulled her skirts down, but Catherine made no attempt to repair her disarray. Slowly she raised her head and looked at Franklin. Her skirts were bunched around her thighs, her thick, grey-black hair had broken loose from its pins and fell around her shoulders, pieces of straw sticking out of the tangled mess.

She stared at Franklin for what seemed an age and he stared back at her, powerless to move. Gaby looked from one to the other, waiting for Catherine to say something.

Eventually, Catherine sat up and straightened her skirts. 'You'll tell your father, I suppose,' she said. More a statement than a question. Franklin continued to stare back at her.

Oh God, Catherine thought, how had she let this happen? Apart from holding hands on their walks together – and then in a way that could only be construed as friendship – she and Gaby had risked no physical contact. They hadn't visited each other's rooms in the dead of the night, they hadn't shared embraces when they were sure nobody was looking – it hadn't been worth the risk. And now, with only a day to go, convinced that the entire property was deserted, they'd abandoned themselves. If only they'd lasted one more day! Just one more day!

Catherine cursed herself. And now, of course, the boy would tell his father. And Charles would withhold the allowance granted her under George's will ...

But there was a regret far more important than the loss of her family inheritance. It was in the boy's eyes as he met hers. Utter disillusionment. She'd been his idol, she knew that. And Gaby had fascinated him.

Oh well, one day he would come to understand

sex, Catherine told herself. Then maybe ... But she knew it was futile. The boy would never understand the love she and Gaby shared. He was repulsed, sickened by the sight of the two of them.

She tried to shake off his accusing stare. 'I said, I suppose you'll tell your father,' she repeated.

'No.' Finally Franklin found his voice. 'No, I shan't tell him.' Catherine looked at him disbelievingly. 'You have my word,' Franklin said, and he turned and walked out of the stables.

That night Franklin received the beating he'd anticipated for lying to his parents but his mind was so preoccupied that he barely felt it. 'The boy', he kept hearing as the bamboo rod seared the back of his legs. 'Kate! The boy!' Gaby had hissed.

Was that all he'd been to them – 'the boy'? And all the time he'd accompanied them on their walks, had they been wishing he wasn't there so they could do their filthy things to each other? He hated them. But he would keep his word. Like Grandfather George, he would always keep his word.

The next day Catherine and Gabrielle left Araluen, bound for Sydney. It would be over fifteen years before Franklin saw them again.

CHAPTER THREE

Franklin

SURRY HILLS, SYDNEY'S seedy backyard, was still a colourful area in 1930, despite the City Council's determination to strip it of its original charm. But then its original charm had always been an arguable point. There were a few old-timers who recalled peaceful rolling hills, grand estates and sheep grazing in nearby Hyde Park. Others romanticised the turn of the century when the 'larrikin pushes' – the hooligan street gangs – pelted each other with 'Irish confetti', a mixture of gravel and broken bricks. And for some, Surry Hills was at its most alluring in the 1920s when the hardened criminals took over and business boomed for the sly grog and cocaine traders.

So, when the Council started systematically demolishing whole blocks of Surry Hills under the guise of 'cleaning up the rat-infested inner city streets', the die-hard residents pragmatically decided that it was just another phase the suburb was going through. Many of them refused to be pushed out of their homes to make way for the businesses, warehouses and factories that would command higher rates for the Council and higher rentals for the landowners. Surry Hills was a residential area, they said. Surry Hills was their home. And if it meant more people had to be crowded into fewer of the tiny terrace houses and cottages, then so be it. Everyone agreed, after all, that no matter how the face of the suburb changed over the years, it was the people who made Surry Hills. And in the face of adversity, the bond forged between the people of Surry Hills always became stronger. Always had and always would, they said.

To twenty-five year old Franklin Ross, it was an exciting place. But then the whole of Sydney was an exciting place – if Franklin had any regret at all about leaving the comfort of rural South Australia, it was the fact that he hadn't done it earlier.

He sorely missed Araluen and the vineyards, but that couldn't be helped. One day he would buy a vineyard of his own, he promised himself. One day. In the meantime, he had to make his fortune.

The break with the family hadn't been all that difficult – but then of course he'd presented his arguments with clarity and precision.

'Kenneth is the next in line, Father. He will be here to look after the family. And if we don't start broadening our horizons, the wines of The Ross Estate will always be considered colonial.'

Charles wondered what was wrong with 'colonial' – it suited him perfectly – but he didn't say so. He'd never really understood his youngest son. Franklin had many of the qualities Charles most admired: he was a serious, responsible young man, not in any way frivolous. But there was a ruthlessness in him, an ambition, that was quite foreign to Charles.

'Your grandfather was proud of being colonial, Franklin. He worked hard to establish our roots here and I'm sure – '

That was when Franklin knew that he'd won and he couldn't disguise the triumph in his voice as he interrupted. 'Grandfather also worked hard to break into the Sydney retail market. He hoped it would be the first step to an international reputation. And it's not happening, Father! The distributor's doing nothing! Grandfather George would be the first person to send me to Sydney. I know he would!'

That clinched it. Charles stopped arguing. He gave Franklin a sizeable sum of money to get started and agreed to send him a comfortable monthly allowance for a period of ' . . . shall we say three years?' he suggested.

'It may take longer, Father,' Franklin replied diplomatically. 'I intend to work very hard at establishing our interstate market.' He didn't think it was necessary to tell his father his true intentions. He felt his father didn't quite have the vision to understand.

Franklin's true intentions were to conquer as much of the civilised world as he could lay claim to in his lifetime.

He had told his father no lies; he would most certainly deal with their Sydney distributor, and the wines of The Ross Estate would one day rank among the finest in the world – Franklin would make sure of that. But his vision was far broader.

Franklin had sensed very early in his life that his

father was not a leader. His father was the protector of a small rural community and he was training his first-born son to follow in his footsteps. Surely that couldn't have been what Grandfather George had intended for The Ross Estate, Franklin reasoned. Not Grandfather George!

Franklin meant to follow his grandfather's patriachal doctrines to the letter. He believed in them implicitly. He would marry sensibly, sire as many sons as possible and allow the eldest one to take over the reins. But the reins to what? That was where the difference lay. Franklin Ross's first-born would not simply inherit 'a family' – he would inherit an empire.

What's more, he would be trained to do so. He would be trained to be strong. A leader. And Sydney was where it all started.

Sam Pritchard, the distributor, was a tough little cockney who didn't like being ordered about by a smooth-talking member of the landed gentry who'd probably never seen a hard day's work in his life. 'I'm aware The Ross Estate wines are good, son, of course I am. I know my business.'

'Do you?' Franklin stared down at the man, willing him to look up from his order books. 'Do you really know your business?'

It worked. Sam looked up. And he met such a steely glint in the young man's eyes that he decided not to push his luck.

'Look, Mr Ross,' he explained patiently, 'I can't spare a salesman to personally deal with your range – be reasonable now, you couldn't expect me to, could you? But I'm quite prepared to give you a full list of all our outlets and you can have a bash at them yourself. I can't be fairer than that now, can I?'

'Thank you. I would appreciate it.'

Sam was annoyed as he watched Franklin Ross walk out of the offices. Why had he allowed himself to be intimidated? On first appearances there was nothing unusual about the young man. He was well dressed, well spoken, pleasant looking – a gentleman, certainly. But there were plenty of those around. A minute or so in his company, however, and one realised that there was something dangerous about Franklin Ross. Something unrelenting. You wouldn't want to cross him, Sam thought.

Franklin stepped out into the hustle and bustle of Goulburn Street and looked up at the bright blue sky. The glorious summer's day seemed to heighten the grime and diversity of Surry Hills. Squalid little terrace houses were jammed in between factories, shops and warehouses. Around one corner was a hive of industry, around another, the unemployed. Dozens of them, spilling out of pubs, lounging around in tiny doorways of tiny houses. Children and dogs played on the dusty curbside. Unemployment. Overpopulation. The Great Depression. But it wasn't depressing to Franklin. This was a big city – weakened and wounded, certainly, but not dead. It was the perfect place to make things happen.

Surry Hills was where he would live, he decided.

He would find accommodation this very afternoon and book out of his city hotel immediately.

It had always been Franklin's intention to find cheap lodgings. He had already invested most of the money his father had given him and he meant to bank all of his considerable monthly allowance and exist upon whatever part-time job he could get while he serviced the wine outlets and investigated business prospects.

'Perfect,' Franklin said, as he looked around the sparsely furnished room. It was clean, it was tidy and it overlooked busy Riley Street – that was what Franklin liked best about it. He glanced out of the window before turning back to the nuggety, dark-haired man leaning in the doorway. 'Perfect,' he repeated. 'I'll take it, Mr Mankowski.'

Solomon Mankowski grinned and offered his hand to Franklin. 'Solly,' he said. 'My friends call me Solly. And you have not yet seen the bathroom. Follow me.'

Solly led him back down the single flight of stairs to a workshop on the ground floor and out through a door at the rear. A small weatherboard shack had recently been attached to the house – in it were an enamel bathtub and a washstand with basin. There wasn't room for anything else.

'You see?' Solly turned on the bath tap to prove that it worked and stood back proudly. 'Good, yes? A whole many houses in Surry Hills do not have bathrooms.'

The lavatory wasn't quite as impressive. It was housed in a rickety wooden box right down the end of the narrow backyard. 'No matter,' Solly said reassuringly. 'The owner, he say he will give me a new one next year.'

Franklin had presumed from his proprietorial air that Mankowski himself was the owner but it appeared that Solly rented the house, conducted his successful boot-making business on the ground floor, lived in the basement and sub-let the two rooms on the first floor.

'Millie Tingwell, she has the other room upstairs. Do not concern yourself,' Solly added hastily, 'she is very quiet.' Then his face became a mask of tragedy. 'Poor woman, two years ago she lose her husband. A factory accident, very sad.' He led the way back to the shop at the front of the terrace house. 'I do what I can to help her, of course. For no extra rent I let her use my kitchen.' He stopped at the door which led from the work-room to the shop.

The smell of leather was overpowering but not unpleasant, Franklin decided. Just as the chaos of the workroom itself was not unpleasant. The half-finished boots, the heavy industrial sewing machine on the scarred wooden table, the strips of leather and twine hanging from hooks everywhere – it all spelt industry.

'For a little extra rent you maybe want to use my kitchen too?' Solly asked.

'No, thank you.' Franklin shook his head and followed the man into the shop.

They sat opposite each other across the counter, surrounded by displays of boots, shoes, belts and assorted leather goods and for a full ten minutes they haggled. Franklin was aware that Solly had assessed the quality and the price of his suit, his waistcoat, his shirt, his hat and, above all, his boots and had come to the conclusion that here was an easy bet.

Having already enquired as to the average price of rooms in Surry Hills, Franklin was also aware that Solly was asking over four times the accepted amount.

Eventually they agreed upon a sum to their mutual satisfaction. Franklin could have pushed it down a little further but he decided to let Solly have the extra couple of shillings. Mankowski was a shrewd fellow, he knew the area and its people well and he could prove useful.

'You drive a hard bargain, Mr Ross.' Solly grinned amiably; he enjoyed a good haggle.

Franklin paid him three months rent in advance – unheard of in Surry Hills – and said he would move in the following morning. 'I shall no doubt be doing some business locally and would appreciate your advice from time to time,' he said.

Solly pocketed the money and nodded eagerly. 'Anything, Mr Ross. Anything you want, you ask Solly Mankowski. And I tell you what – for no extra rent you use my kitchen. Come. I show you.'

'No, thank you.' Franklin rose and crossed to the door. 'That won't be necessary, I prefer to dine out.' Useful as Mankowski may prove to be, he didn't want to encourage over-familiarity.

As he opened the door Franklin collided forcefully with a woman on her way in. 'I'm so sorry,' he said and put out a hand to steady her.

'I'm perfectly all right, thank you,' the woman replied and smiled reassuringly.

'Millie, this is Mr Franklin Ross – he's going to be your neighbour.'

'Oh.' Millie Tingwell looked taken aback. She had presumed the posh gentleman leaving the shop was someone from the outer suburbs purchasing a pair of Solly's boots. Solly had a number of wealthy customers. 'Well, fancy that.' Millie smiled again, her dimples flashing alluringly. 'How do you do, Mr Ross.'

'Mrs Tingwell.' Franklin raised his hat and tried not to stare too hard. The woman was astonishingly attractive.

Millie was in her early thirties and she wasn't beautiful. Her features weren't fine enough to be beautiful. Her mouth was a little too generous and her jaw was a little too wide. What's more, she was a redhead, and her curls were a little too lavish to be in good taste. They were natural – everything about Millie was natural – but, like her hair, everything about Millie was unruly. It was a constant source of frustration to her. She was conscious of style, very much wanted to be 'chic', and tried desperately to maintain some control over her appearance. But no amount of pins successfully anchored her hair, her generous body refused to be disguised by her modest choice of dress and her dimples flashed disobediently even when she was at her most serious.

'Welcome to Solly's,' she said. 'I'm sure you'll be comfortable here.' Then she excused herself and went up to her room. She had just finished a ten-

60

hour shift at Gadsden's Fabric Bag and Sack Factory and she was exhausted.

Solly had noticed Mr Ross's reaction. It was the same reaction he noticed in every red-blooded male who came in contact with Millie. Indeed, it was the same reaction Solly himself had experienced when she'd first moved in five years ago.

So attractive had Solly found her that, after Millie's husband died, leaving her in financial trouble, he had even suggested there might be an alternative method of rental payment he would be happy to discuss. As a landlord he had never before contemplated such an arrangement – Solly never mixed business with pleasure.

But Millie appeared unaware of his proposition, agreeing that she would be only too happy to do his washing, ironing and mending in exchange for the rent.

'That wasn't exactly what I had in mind,' Solly said.

There was a definite plea in Millie's voice as she added, 'Perhaps even a little cooking now and then?' Solly shook his head and started to feel embarrassed, not wanting to spell it out. Finally, Millie straightened her back, looked him directly in the eye and said, 'I shall be moving out next week, Mr Mankowski'.

Solly felt terrible. So terrible that he did a totally uncharacteristic thing, surprising not only Millie but himself into the bargain. He let her forgo the following month's rent altogether until she found herself a factory job. They never again mentioned his proposition and a genuine fondness grew between them.

61

Now, despite his soft spot for her, Solly prayed that her presence would not disrupt the household. He prayed that she would not overly distract or upset Mr Ross. In the fifteen years Solomon Mankowski had been sub-letting around Surry Hills, he had never once had a tenant as classy as Mr Ross. It was an excellent sign. Money bred money, class bred class and Mr Ross had both. And he had something else as well. He had determination. Solly recognised a winner when he saw one – and one must cultivate winners, particularly in a Depression. But one had to be subtle, one mustn't be intrusive – Mr Ross was a private man who didn't welcome intruders. No, Solly decided, he would wait until he was needed. Over the next few days while Franklin settled in, Solly kept well out of his way.

Much as he would rather have avoided it, Franklin knew he had to contact his Aunt Catherine. She was a prominent figure in Sydney, with a successful art gallery and many worthwhile contacts. If anyone could help him secure a well-paying job, she could.

'Franklin! My dear!' He was engulfed in a fervent embrace. A strand of her hair found its way into his mouth and he could feel her ample breasts against his chest. The strong, musky scent she was wearing, mingled with the smell of oils and varnish and tobacco, was suffocating. Finally she released him. 'Let me look at you,' she said.

Franklin attempted a smile as she held him at arm's length. There was no point in alienating her – she was too useful. But he found her repulsive. She's gross, he thought, gross and vulgar.

Catherine was certainly large. She'd always been a big woman. Big-boned and handsome. But at sixty-one she'd lost her looks. Her thick, grey-black hair was still abundant but now it was white with a yellowish tinge, like straw. She was no longer statuesque but shapeless, and the face had become fleshy and dissipated. But if Franklin had cared to look closer he would have noticed that the smile was as generous as ever and the eyes as clever and humorous as they'd always been.

But Franklin didn't care to look closer and Catherine sensed it immediately. She too had not forgotten that day in the stables but she'd hoped by now Franklin may have developed some tolerance. Obviously he hadn't. Well, she'd just have to work on him and see if she could break through. She hoped he hadn't turned into a boring prig like his father.

'Come on through to the studio. Gaby's working and she's dying to see you.'

Catherine led the way. It was an elegant house, built in 1860, and Catherine had retained its original splendour. Strange that she could be so slovenly herself and yet live so graciously, Franklin thought.

As though she'd read his mind, Catherine said, 'Gaby looks after the house. I live mostly in here.' And she flung open the doors to the studio.

Anything but elegant, it was a huge modern open-plan room built onto the side of the old home. Its massive windows looked out through a leafy green garden to the streets of Kings Cross. There was a long work bench against one wall, with an assortment of brushes and jars and tubes and tins scattered all over it. The floor was made of bare boards and leaning against the walls were dozens of paintings and sculptures in various stages of completion. The sun streamed in over everything and the effect was one of highly lit chaos. Franklin had to admit that it was rather exciting – in a Bohemian way.

'Franklin!' Gaby looked up from her work. She was in one corner of the room by the windows, a plaster cast on a pedestal before her and, although she was messy from her elbows down and had a smudge of plaster on her face, she managed to look neat, presentable and very attractive – the antithesis of Catherine.

'I am so sorry I couldn't come to the door, but look at her.' She gestured to the bust on the pedestal. 'If I let her dry, I am lost.'

Franklin joined Gaby and she kissed him on both cheeks, holding her wet hands aloft. He didn't find the physical contact with her at all offensive. In fact, if he eradicated the repulsive image of her in the straw with Catherine, he found her immensely attractive. She would be well into her fifties by now, Franklin thought, and yet she looked so young.

'She's beautiful,' Franklin said, nodding at the bust. 'Who is she?'

'A prostitute,' Catherine said before Gaby could reply. Gaby flashed her a look of rebuke but Catherine ignored it. The boy needed a dose of the truth. 'A notorious prostitute, famous in the

64

underworld, very beautiful and quite a nice girl too.'

She's doing it deliberately to shock me, Franklin thought, annoyed.

'It will be a bronze,' Gaby said, getting back to her work. 'This is the early stage.' Much as she loved Catherine, Gaby wished she wouldn't go out of her way to antagonise people the way she did. And not Franklin, she felt like begging. Not your Franklin. You've been so looking forward to seeing him, don't ruin it for yourself.

And Catherine thought irritably, 'Dear, stylish, oh-so-nice Gaby. She'll go out of her way to be all the proper things the boy expects people to be. Someone has to teach him a lesson. And I suppose I'll have to be the ogre who does it.'

Franklin lunched with the two women and, throughout the meal, Gaby continued to charm him and Catherine continued to grate on him.

'What timing, Franklin!' Catherine laughed, when he told them of his plans. 'We are in the grip of a Depression, there is a massive labour movement afoot in the city and you decide to make your capitalistic bid for fame and fortune!'

'And I shall succeed, Aunt Catherine.'

Catherine didn't need Gaby's warning glance – even she couldn't fail to notice the steely glint in her nephew's eyes.

'I'm sure you will, my dear.' An attempt at mollification. 'And let's drop the "Aunt", shall we? Call me Catherine.'

'Very well,' Franklin answered stiffly. He didn't like being laughed at.

After lunch, they drank their coffee in the

garden outside the studio, Catherine smoking little black cigars, much to Franklin's disapproval. Through the leafy green trees he could see the bustling streets of Kings Cross and he listened with interest as Gaby told him a little of the suburb.

'It is Sydney's Montmartre,' she said. 'Very Bohemian.' Her accent was as charming as Franklin remembered from his childhood. 'I feel at home here,' she continued, 'despite the fact there is a dangerous underworld influence.'

'Rubbish,' Catherine interrupted. 'That only makes it all the more colourful. What about that bust you're doing of Nellie Cameron? One of the best things you've done in years – you find her quite inspirational, you said so yourself.'

Catherine lit up a fresh cigar. 'There are a lot of powerful women in Sydney, Franklin. Particularly in the art world.' She puffed at the cigar and coffee slopped from the cup in her other hand.

'And the underworld,' she added. 'The underworld has very powerful female leaders. There is a current war between Tilly Devine and Kate Leigh as to who is the true queen, even though they operate in different fields. Tilly controls the prostitution racket and Kate deals in sly grog and cocaine.'

Franklin missed the sharp glance from Gaby and the bravado in the tilt of Catherine's head as she returned the look. 'Now let's discuss this job you're after,' she said, changing the subject.

Half an hour later, Franklin had to admit that Catherine's offers of help were very generous.

Gross, vulgar, offensive she might be, but she was prepared to offer him invaluable assistance and he was extremely grateful. She knew of the right position for him – it would be lucrative and he was bound to secure it so long as they went about it the right way.

'Gustave Lumet is his name,' Catherine said. 'And you must meet him socially – impress him with your style and breeding and the fact that you don't really want the job at all but you might accept it as a favour to him.'

Gustave Lumet, it appeared, was the chef-owner of the very chic restaurant next door to Catherine's art gallery.

'He passes himself off as French aristocracy, born in Paris,' Catherine explained, 'but we all know he's half-Belgian and that he started out as an assistant pastry cook in Lyons.'

Gustave's restaurant was a very popular meeting place for the Bohemian set of Kings Cross, as was Catherine's art gallery, and the two of them worked closely together to their mutual advantage.

Over the past twelve months Gustave had been dissatisfied with the succession of managers he'd hired and he constantly complained to Catherine and Gaby. 'No style,' he'd say, 'they have no style. I do not mind if they know little of managing a restaurant – my staff is good, my maitre d' superb. All I ask is that they meet, greet and welcome my diners with style!'

' "Style" is Gustave's favourite word,' Catherine explained to Franklin. 'Gaby, for instance,' she said, waving her cigar in Gabrielle's direction, 'he's convinced that Gaby's the only woman in

Sydney with true style. The silly man's nearly twenty years younger than she is but he's madly in love with her. Sees her as a fellow aristocrat, probably. The French are such snobs.'

Franklin looked at Gaby to see if she was offended but she was smiling indulgently at Catherine and seemed genuinely amused. Franklin could quite understand how Gustave could be madly in love with her and he agreed with the man implicitly – she had great style.

Catherine's plan was perfectly simple. There was to be a minor showing at the gallery the following week. 'A trial half-dozen pieces by a new artist,' she said. 'But everyone will be there to check out the latest competition. I shall introduce you to Gustave and I suggest you offer him a sample range of The Ross Estate wines. It means you'll be meeting him on equal ground and that should do the trick.'

Several minutes later, as Franklin was preparing to take his leave, the side gate leading to the street swung open and a burly, casually dressed man carrying a gladstone bag sauntered through the garden and up to Catherine. He didn't remove his cloth cap – Franklin thought him terribly rude. He wondered whether he should reprimand the fellow.

'Delivery from Kate,' the man muttered and Catherine waved him towards the studio door.

'Wait for me inside, please,' she said. 'I'll be with you shortly.'

Franklin was aware of a sudden tension and he made his farewells as brief as possible. 'No, please,' he insisted as Gaby shepherded him towards the studio. 'It's just as easy for me to go through the side gate. You have your business to attend to and I want to explore the streets of Kings Cross for a while.'

Gaby pointed him in the direction of the art gallery which was only two blocks away. 'Roslyn Street,' she said. 'You can't miss it.'

'But don't go into the Cafe Gustave,' Catherine warned. 'He mustn't meet you until next week.'

Franklin thanked them again and left. Gaby watched him go, then frowned and was about to say something but, before she could, Catherine kissed her quickly and forcefully upon the lips.

'You've done it again, you temptress,' she said with a cheeky smile. 'The boy's mad about you.' Then she disappeared into the studio.

Gaby remained staring after her. The cocaine was more than just fun now, she thought, it was an essential part of Catherine's life. But there was nothing one could do about it. Catherine was incorrigible. She refused to grow up and still thought of herself as the young rebel Gaby had first met in Paris forty years ago. She would never change and, apart from a futile hope that the cocaine would not damage her health, Gaby didn't want her to.

When Franklin returned to Surry Hills he was surprised to see a gathering of people on the pavement outside the terrace house two doors down from Solly's. Solly himself was there, as were Millie and several other faces Franklin recognised as neighbours.

'What's going on?' he asked, joining Solly and tipping his hat in acknowledgement to the flash of Millie's dimples.

There was a motley collection of furniture on the pavement and a large, balding man in the centre of the crowd was holding aloft a cracked porcelain washbasin.

'Old Arch is way behind with his rent,' Solly explained, 'so the bailiff's auctioning off their stuff.'

Franklin looked at 'old Arch' and his wife. They were seated on their front doorstep watching the proceedings with a profound lack of interest. It was difficult to tell whether Arch was really 'old' or not and the same applied to his wife. They both carried the careworn, lacklustre stamp of poverty and over the years they had come to look alike. Franklin felt sorry for them.

Nobody bid for the washbasin. Nobody bid for the chamber-pot. Nobody bid for the rickety old bed with its broken springs. So, when the bailiff pointed at a small chest of drawers and still no bids were made, Franklin felt such a sense of pity that he was compelled to raise his hand.

'Don't, Mr Ross,' Solly muttered and Franklin quickly lowered it.

'Why?' he asked. 'They need the money for their rent. Why is no one helping?'

'They are.' It was Millie who answered. 'They're helping by not bidding.' Franklin looked confused. 'Arch's belongings wouldn't fetch a quarter of the rent they owe. Whatever money they made would go straight in the bailiff's pocket and they'd be evicted anyway.'

'Oh. What will happen then?'

'They'll pilfer whatever they can of the smaller stuff and they'll be gone by the morning. The bailiff doesn't know it but this . . . ' she gestured at the mock auction ' . . . this buys them time.'

'Surry Hills people – we stick together,' Solly explained, and there was no mistaking the pride in his voice. 'Sometimes if it is a widow being sold up, everyone put in money. Buy all her stuff. Then give it back to her the next day.'

The entire gathering of locals stayed for the duration of the 'auction' to ensure no stranger put in a bid. Everyone was quiet, and there was no heckling or jeering at the bailiff, which made the unfortunate man's job even more frustrating. When he finally called an end to the farce there was a polite round of applause and people drifted away.

The bailiff started stacking the belongings and Franklin walked over to him. 'How much rent is owed?' he asked quietly.

'Six pounds, five shillings, Guv',' the bailiff said.

'Here.' Franklin pressed a ten pound note into the man's hand. 'And give them back their furniture.' As he turned to go he noticed Solly and Millie several yards away, staring at him. They had both witnessed the transaction. They were impressed. But they didn't acknowledge it – it wasn't the done thing.

'You come to my place for a vodka, Mr Ross, yes?' Solly asked. He deliberately ignored Millie even though it was quite obvious she would love to be included in the invitation. Now was the time, Solly decided, to start convincing Mr Ross of the

71

true value of Solomon Mankowski. If the evening evolved into a business discussion, Millie might prove a little too distracting. 'Good Polish vodka,' he added.

'Thank you, Solly, I accept.'

'Greedy, you see? The landlords, they are too greedy.' It was an hour later. An hour, and three-quarters of a bottle of vodka later. Solly had explained to a fascinated Franklin the background of Surry Hills and the rigours that beset its inhabitants. The property owners had moved out long ago. And, from their comfortable existences in the wealthier outer suburbs, they were ruthless landlords. The fact that their tenants were forced to live in decaying houses with rats and shocking drainage and sewer problems appeared to be of little concern to them.

'My landlord, he is of course different,' Solly admitted. 'Just as I was different. I too was a good landlord.'

Franklin had been about to excuse himself. Interested as he was, the vodka was starting to have an effect upon him and he didn't like to drink too much. But the fact that Solly had been a man of property was too interesting to go unquestioned.

'You were a landlord?'

'Yes,' Solly answered. 'A good one.' He was pleased with himself. He'd sensed that Mr Ross was about to leave and he'd timed it perfectly. 'Two houses I owned. One here in this very street. Number sixty-four.' He picked up the vodka bottle. 'The other, in Darlinghurst, near the police station. I sell them both fifteen years ago.' He filled their glasses again and Franklin didn't protest. 'I was a good businessman, Mr Ross. Still I am a good businessman. But ... ' He left it hanging in the air and Franklin, aware of the man's theatricality, refused to ask 'but what?'.

'But ... I gamble,' Solly finally admitted. He downed his drink in one gulp. 'Not always. Only when I drink too much vodka.' He picked up the bottle as if to emphasise the point and poured himself another. Then he proceeded to tell Franklin his story.

Solomon Mankowski came from the wide, sandy plains and heathlands of central Poland. He was the youngest of nine children and an unwelcome mistake – there was nearly ten years' difference in age between him and the next youngest. It was a lonely childhood; his brothers and sisters didn't want to know him and to his poverty-stricken parents he was merely an added burden. So at fourteen he left the small poultry farm near Poznan and found his way to Krakow. He apprenticed himself to a leather merchant and worked hard. By twenty he was an accomplished craftsman, had done well at his trade and was ready to conquer the world.

'Such a big world, so much to see.' Solly held his arms out expansively. 'You drink your vodka, Mr Ross, do you good.' Franklin did. He was starting to enjoy it. 'So, I decide to go to America.' He filled up their glasses. 'But I come here instead.'

'Why?'

'I meet an Australian woman. She is married, travelling with her husband. But not happy,' he

73

hastened to add as if to vindicate himself. 'Her husband, he is wealthy, but he does not love her, so ... ' He swigged back the vodka and poured the remaining half-inch from the bottle into his empty glass.

'When she leave Poland,' he continued, 'I follow her to Australia, but when I get here ... ' he shrugged philosophically, ' ... it seems she is happy after all.' Solly grinned and rose to get another bottle of vodka. 'I was nineteen and foolish. She was a middle-aged woman and I was her holiday.' He took a fresh bottle from the cupboard and nodded at Franklin. 'Come along, drink.'

Franklin automatically did as he was told. There was something very authoritative about Solly. Far from making the man drunk, the alcohol seemed to be giving him a strength and a charm that hadn't been there before. Or maybe it had been and Franklin hadn't noticed. Whatever it was, Franklin thought as he held out his glass, there was something eminently likeable about Solly Mankowski.

Solly could feel the young man relax. Good, he thought. This is what Mr Ross needs. A night of vodka and talk and camaraderie. Soon we will be friends. He needs friends. He is too stern for one so young.

'Yes,' Solly heaved a sigh and leaned back in his chair. 'A boy I was. Just a boy. Not much younger than you, Mr Ross.'

Franklin sensed a question. He didn't mind. 'I'm twenty-five,' he answered.

'And I shall be forty in one month.' Solly's grin

74

was triumphantly boyish. 'I do not look forty, hey?'

Franklin laughed and shook his head. It seemed the right thing to do.

The grin vanished as quickly as it had appeared and Solly leaned forward in his chair. 'I have saved, Mr Ross. Since my ruin I have worked hard. When you start your business, you think of Solly, hey? I would make good partner.'

Franklin downed his drink, held his glass out for another and only vaguely questioned why teaming up with Solly seemed like quite a good idea.

They drank the second bottle of vodka and talked until three o'clock in the morning. Franklin told Solly of his love for the vines.

'They're timeless, Solly. They're young and they're old. They're the past and the future. When you stand among them, you could be anywhere. In any place. In any civilisation.' Franklin had never talked like this in his life before. He was enjoying it.

'Rows and rows of them,' he said, seeing them in his mind, 'stretching across the hills and the valleys – and what do they symbolise, Solly? Tell me, what do they symbolise?' Solly shook his head and waited for the answer. He didn't want to break the mood; it was good to see Mr Ross so freed of his inhibitions. 'Harmony,' Franklin announced. 'Harmony, friendship, conviviality . . . and I'll tell you why.'

There was no stopping Franklin now. He desperately wanted Solly to understand, he needed to explain. 'They're not cultivated for survival, you see? They're not wheat grown for bread or cattle raised for beef. The vines are grown to make wine. Wine for men to share at their table – they're the bond between us all.' He downed his vodka. 'There can be no war among men who share a love of the vines,' he concluded.

Solly waited a full thirty seconds before he replied. He wanted to be sure Mr Ross had finished. Then he nodded gravely. 'You must travel, Mr Ross,' he said. And, in Franklin's eyes, a fresh dimension was added to the man's strength and charm – Solly was wise. 'You're right,' he said, 'You're right.'

Then Solly talked about Poland. It had been twenty years since he'd left, but he thought of her daily. His Poland. His beautiful Poland.

Solly didn't actually think of Poland daily but, when he was drunk, he could swear he did. And it was true he did love his motherland. He had blocked out the harsh reality of his childhood and remembered only the good parts. He communicated regularly with several of his brothers and sisters and always planned one day to go back.

'I worry, Mr Ross. I worry. This Austrian with his National Socialist Party, this Hitler – oh sure, he is doing good things for Germany, but he is greedy. Just like the landlords, you know? He will want more, only a matter of time. And Poland will be first. Always she is. Always, Poland is the sandwich.' Solly drained the last of the bottle and then noticed that Franklin had passed out.

'It was a good night, Mr Ross,' Solly said the next morning. He was fully aware that Franklin's reserve was back in place. No matter, the break-through had been made. There would be other times. 'You remember what I say.' He nodded conspiratorially. 'When you are ready to do business, we talk, hey? You ask around Surry Hills. The people, they tell you I am a good businessman.'

Franklin did ask around Surry Hills. He wasn't sure why. Just a passing interest, he told himself – Mankowski was a colourful character. His inquiries revealed that Solly had not only been a man of property, he had been a good friend to many. A bit of a rogue at times but a kind-hearted man and one who kept his word. A terrible gambler with vodka in him, Franklin was warned. But then Solly had admitted that himself, hadn't he?

Franklin was quite impressed. Yes, he thought, Solly Mankowski could well prove useful.

Several days later, as Franklin left for the art gallery and his designated meeting with Gustave Lumet, he bumped into Millie Tingwell on the landing. It was ten o'clock in the morning and an odd time to find her home. Her shift hours at the sack factory were from five in the morning till three in the afternoon.

Franklin raised his hat in greeting. 'Mrs Tingwell. You're home early.'

'Hello, Mr Ross,' Millie replied. She'd been laid off that morning. Always the way with casual labour, she thought wearily – they never gave you any notice. Seeing Mr Ross cheered her up. Such a fine man, helping old Arch the way he had. She admired him tremendously. 'Yes,' she said. 'I

77

handed in my notice at Gadsden's – the hours were simply too long.' No point in being depressing company, she thought. 'Perhaps you'd like to celebrate with me over a cup of tea in Solly's kitchen.'

'I'd like that,' Franklin said, and most certainly would have, 'but I have an engagement this morning.'

'Oh well, never mind.' Millie opened the door to her little back room. It was much smaller than Franklin's front room and overlooked rows of narrow backyards, disintegrating picket fences and sagging clotheslines always heavy with the weight of the daily wash. Millie found comfort in the uniformity of it all. She would like to be married again. She would like to stay at home, keep house, wash and cook. She hated factory work. 'Another time, perhaps,' and she smiled once more as she started to close her door.

Although it was unintended, the twinkle in Millie's eyes and the dancing dimples appeared to hold such promise that Franklin was loath to relinquish the opportunity. 'Perhaps you'd care to dine with me?' he said. It came out with such a rush that it took him by surprise.

Millie was equally surprised. 'When?' she asked.

'Tomorrow evening?'

'Oh.' Dine with Mr Ross? This couldn't be happening. For dignity's sake she appeared to give it a moment's thought – as though she were regularly extended invitations to dine from gentlemen of the calibre of Franklin Ross – and then she nodded. 'Very well,' she said.

78

When the door was safely closed behind her Millie kicked off her shoes and tried not to squeal too loudly. Dinner with Mr Ross! Fancy that!

As Franklin hailed a cab, he wondered why on earth he'd done it. What would they talk about over dinner? He had nothing in common with the woman. Nothing at all.

But the subject of Millie bore no analysis. Franklin sat back in the cab sure of only one thing. He desperately wanted Millie Tingwell. He looked out the window and thought of Bronwyn. Bronwyn was the only woman Franklin had ever slept with.

Franklin Ross was still a virgin at twenty when Bronwyn came to work as mess cook for the farmhands.

Bronwyn was a big woman – not fat, but buxom. And capable. Strong. She must have been thirty, Franklin supposed, and definitely experienced.

'One of the young masters,' she said when she first met him. The voice, with its soft Welsh lilt, came as a surprise. 'I'm pleased to meet you, sir.' The token curtsy which followed teased and mocked him and suddenly he found her highly desirable.

Over the ensuing weeks, Franklin observed that she never behaved the same way with Kenneth, nor any of the farmhands, for that matter. Surely she couldn't have set her sights on him.

But Bronwyn had.

It was a Sunday, in the stables. The same stables where Franklin had witnessed the shocking coupling of Catherine and Gaby.

He was saddling his horse to ride to church. He never travelled in the trap with Kenneth and his parents. His father had disapproved at first; the family should arrive together, he said. But when Franklin turned eighteen, Charles was forced to concede that as long as the boy attended the Sunday service, his means of transport should be his own choice.

One Sunday, Bronwyn was waiting in the stables for him.

'The young master,' she said. 'You look grand.' She was sitting amongst the fresh straw at the end of the stables, leaning back against the wooden planking of the far wall.

He stood there, framed in the light of the doorway, the bridle in his hand. He knew what was going to happen. He wasn't sure how to go about it, but he knew he'd been aching for it for weeks. The bridle dropped from his hand as Bronwyn came towards him.

'We wouldn't want to spoil our Sunday best now, would we?' she murmured as she slipped his jacket from his shoulders. 'And the trousers, such a nice fabric.' He scarcely dared breathe as she knelt before him and undid the buttons, sliding the trousers down. So slowly down. Everything had become slow motion to Franklin and, as she rose to her feet, he still didn't move.

She took his hand. 'Come, young master, let us lie down in the comfy hay.'

She'd undone the buttons of her blouse and he

longed to touch the swell of her breasts as he blindly followed her to the straw, but he was powerless.

Then, with the strength of a farmhand, she pulled him down upon her and Franklin was no longer mesmerised. He ripped at her blouse, at her skirts, he thrust his hand between her legs and, in an equal frenzy, laughing all the while, she ripped at him.

His mouth was full of her breasts, her lips, her neck. His hand was discovering territory he'd never known existed. She was soft and moist and she kept laughing as he felt her. Then she was wet and open and inviting and, before he knew it, he was plunging himself into her.

It was over in seconds but Bronwyn didn't seem to mind. 'Next time will be better, I promise you.' Franklin left the stables in utter bewilderment. Better? How could anything be better?

Their affair continued twice a week for the following four years. They would steal into Bronwyn's room in the servants' quarters above the stables in the dead of night. Their couplings were always furtive as they choked back their grunts and animal noises for fear someone might hear them in the still darkness.

It was the furtive aspect itself which excited Franklin. He found the blackness and the strangled grunts and the anonymity immensely erotic as they bucked about on her tiny bed in the corner of her tiny room.

Their sexual encounters were always aggressive and the more energetically he pounded away at her, the more forcefully Bronwyn thrust herself back at him until, having both made full use of each other's bodies, they exploded in an orgy of fulfilment.

Then she'd get up, turn on the light and douche herself in the basin of cold water she'd set under the bed in anticipation of their rendezvous. 'You wash it all out, you see,' she'd explain to him in her soft Welsh lilt. 'That way you don't have a baby.'

Franklin looked away when she douched. He found it disgusting and wished she would go to the servants' bathroom downstairs. He would concentrate on dressing himself as quickly as possible by way of distraction.

Bronwyn didn't seem to mind the haste with which he left. 'I'll see you next Wednesday, yes?' she'd whisper as she opened the door. 'Save it up for me, mind.' And she'd smile and he'd leave and he'd tell himself he wasn't coming back. But of course he always did.

Then, very abruptly, Bronwyn fell in love with the new foreman employed on Mary's neighbouring property. She married him and, six months later, was once again giving Franklin the eye. But, by this time, Bronwyn had become thoroughly abhorrent to Franklin and he found it very easy to resist her advances.

That had been the limit of Franklin's sexual experience and the year of celibacy which followed was no hardship to him. He decided that sex was a little disgusting and, pleasurable as it was for one brief moment, it was considerably overrated. What's more, it was distracting – one could be far more productive by concentrating all of one's energies on work, achievement and success.

And now here was Millie, reminding him of the beast within. Franklin found it rather unsettling.

Catherine's friends were just as pretentious as Franklin had anticipated. At least that's what he told himself. Having no knowledge of art, he actually found some of them a trifle daunting but he refused to admit that, even to himself.

'But a wheat field isn't that colour,' he said to Catherine and a group holding court before a particularly gaudy landscape. 'I've lived in the country all my life,' he insisted, 'and wheat fields simply are not that colour.'

'Oh yes they are. To many people they are.' Catherine smiled. She wasn't being patronising and she wasn't being aggressive either, which was a welcome change. 'Yours is not the only vision, my dear.' And then she introduced the artist. 'This is Margaret,' she said.

Franklin refused to be daunted. 'But I see what I see and a wheat field is not bright orange.' He looked argumentatively about at the group. Who the hell did they think they were, anyway? 'I realise that impressionism must mean it's some person's impression of what a wheat field looks like to them,' he said, glaring an accusation at Margaret, whose expression was particularly patronising, 'but I don't have to recognise that and I don't have to like it.'

'Of course you don't.' Catherine refused to be offended. 'But quite possibly you see what you *expect* to see: brown earth, green trees, yellow daisies. Perhaps you need to liberate your senses a little more. Allow yourself to see more freely.'

'And how exactly do you suggest I liberate my senses?' he asked.

There was a touch of scorn in his voice but Catherine refused to acknowledge it – he was only being defensive. 'You need to free your eye from the focal point,' she said. 'Come on, I'll show you.' And she led the way out to the small back garden, Franklin reluctantly following.

'Look up at the sky,' she instructed. Franklin did. Might as well keep the peace, he thought. 'Close your eyes,' she said, 'and try and think of nothing.'

Catherine watched him as he stood with his head back and his eyes closed. He was so young and so serious. She wanted to hold him to her and tell him that there was joy in the world, and magic. She wanted to teach him to let go, to say yes to it all.

But then the first few sniffs of cocaine always made Catherine feel like that. Vital, attractive, inspired, as if she were young again and it were her mission in life to share the magic of the universe. She knew she abused the drug. She knew that later in the day she became loud and aggressive. But what of it? Many of her friends indulged too. They understood, Gaby understood.

'Now open your eyes,' she said, 'and without focusing on anything, be aware of the colours in your peripheral vision.'

Franklin concentrated on doing exactly as she instructed. He was starting to find the exercise rather interesting and, as he stared ahead at the empty sky, he became aware of an insistent yellow glare to his right and a flash of red somewhere down near Catherine's feet to his left.

Catherine could see the young boy holding the glass up to the light. She could see him study the wine reverently and she could hear his solemn pronouncement, 'It tastes like wet flour sacks.'

'The red flowers,' Franklin said and he pointed at the patch of geraniums in the corner. 'Those ones. They stood out the most. And so did the balcony of the restaurant.' He pointed next door to the wrought iron which Gustave had painted an outrageous yellow.

'Excellent,' Catherine applauded him. 'Now apply that lesson during certain times of the day when the light plays tricks or in places where the colours are deeper and you'll find that the wheat fields really are orange and that the earth is red and the mountains purple, and all sorts of astonishing things. It's very exciting.'

She didn't want to push it any further than that. She felt she'd made a remarkable breakthrough. She wanted so much to win back Franklin's love and respect. 'Let's go inside. I'm deserting my guests.'

As they passed by the gaudy painting of the wheat field Catherine said, 'Have another look at it. And concentrate on the sky this time; you might like it.' Then she smiled wickedly and muttered, 'Even if you don't, it's going to be worth a lot of money one day.'

Franklin looked at her, surprised. 'I'm not mad on it myself, actually,' she said, casting a critical glance at the wheat field, 'but I sure as hell know what the critics like and Margaret's it.' She took him by the arm. 'Come and meet Gustave,' she said.

Franklin was relieved to discover that Gustave Lumet held no mystery for him whatsoever. Here was no connoisseur of art, no man with a magic vision of the world. Here was an out-and-out snob, a self-made businessman with pretensions of grandeur. Franklin had met his type often before in the wine trade, where they abounded. And he knew exactly the way to play him. Within an hour of their meeting Gustave was taking him on a guided tour of the restaurant next door and suggesting Franklin sell him a selection of Ross Estate wines. Of course he knew of The Ross Estate, he insisted; there would be no need for samples, he wanted to lay in stock immediately.

'Very well, I'll deliver them myself,' Franklin offered graciously. 'We'll have a small private tasting of the newly released vintages, shall we?' It would be interesting to test the man's palate as well as his business sense.

The idea of a private tasting with the vigneron himself was very appealing to Gustave, who prided himself on recognising a genuine patrician when he met one, and Franklin Ross was definitely that. If he had thought for one moment that he could secure Franklin's services, he would have gone down on bended knee.

Gustave insisted on breaking open a bottle of Dom Perignon to celebrate their agreement and they sat talking about wine, food and restaurants and thoroughly enjoying one another's company.

When Franklin called in next door to thank

Catherine nearly two hours later, the exhibition was well and truly over. Many of the guests had gone and those remaining were very loud and gregarious. A lot of champagne had been consumed, more was being passed around and a party was obviously well under way.

Catherine was nowhere to be seen so he tapped quietly on the little sitting room door marked 'Private' at the rear of the studio. It was ajar and, as there was no reply, he pushed it open gently and peeped in.

She was slumped in an armchair, her chin resting on her ample bosom. Her right hand was also resting on her bosom, her fingers loosely curled around a tiny silver spoon. The top two buttons of her blouse were undone and Franklin could see that the spoon was attached to a slim chain around her neck.

Catherine's eyes were closed but he could tell that she wasn't asleep. She was breathing deeply and rhythmically but each exhalation was like a groan. Painful. There was white dust encrusted around her nostrils and her lips and, from one corner of her mouth, a slow dribble of saliva was starting to wind its way down among the several layers of her chin.

The door to the bathroom opened and Gaby appeared, carrying a glass of water. She saw Franklin immediately but she barely acknowledged him. 'Come along, my darling,' she said, kneeling beside Catherine. 'Drink some water.' She removed the silver spoon from Catherine's hand and replaced it with the glass, firmly pressing Catherine's fingers around the base. 'Come along now.'

'Yes, yes, yes.' Catherine's eyes sprang open and she pulled the glass away. 'I can do it, I can do it.' As she gulped greedily at the water, spilling it down her chin, Gaby slipped the silver spoon on its chain back inside the blouse and did up the top two buttons.

'Franklin has come to say goodbye,' she said. And she rose to her feet and crossed to him. 'Be kind,' she whispered, 'it is the cocaine.'

For the first time Franklin noticed the small, open-lidded silver box full of white powder on the coffee table beside the armchair.

'Goodbye, Aunt Catherine,' he said tersely, forgetting to drop the 'Aunt'. 'Thank you for inviting me.'

Catherine focused on him for a second or so, registered who he was, and mustered up a dignity from somewhere out of the past. She inhaled deeply. 'Goodbye, my dear, thank you so much for coming,' she said. And Franklin disappeared into the afternoon, grateful to be gone.

CHAPTER FOUR

Franklin and Millie

DINNER WITH MILLIE was initially awkward. The restaurant was expensive, the diners were obviously wealthy, and Millie felt self-conscious in her checked skirt and jacket and her best blouse with its mismatched button.

She'd lost the button a year ago and had searched everywhere for a matching one, but to no avail. She'd chosen the closest match and put it up the top, presuming that the odd one wouldn't show as much there as it would in the middle of the row. Now, at dinner, she kept a hand at her throat to avoid people noticing and talked a little too much and a little too quickly. If only Mr Ross would put her at her ease, she thought. He seemed so withdrawn. It was probably the blouse. He was ashamed to be seen with her. He was probably dying to get out of the place. Millie felt uncharacteristically nervous.

Franklin concentrated on the menu to distract himself from the fact that Millie was looking particularly alluring tonight. He had very set ideas on women. There were the Bronwyns of this world and there were the women like his mother. Millie broke the rules. Millie was somewhere in between and he didn't know how to handle her. The sexuality of the woman was undeniable and yet she looked so demure in her neat little suit, her hand modestly at her throat, her voice soft and pleasing. When she'd suggested he order for her and hadn't even looked at the menu, Franklin had liked that.

He ordered the food and the wine, annoyed that they didn't stock Ross Estate (he'd be back tomorrow to sort that out) and finally he had no choice but to direct his attentions to her.

'You look very pretty tonight,' he said.

Millie suddenly recognised his awkwardness as desire and her tension vanished. He hadn't been embarrassed by her at all, she realised. He'd been embarrassed by his lust for her. She felt a huge relief.

All her life Millie had been attractive to men. She didn't know why, but she'd ceased to question it long ago. She liked men; vastly preferred them to women. They were simple, uncomplicated and, despite their need to dominate, vulnerable. She was content to let men hold the upper hand if it made them happy and she'd never quite been able to understand what the suffragettes' cause was all about. In her own simple, ingenuous way, Millie was a dangerous woman.

She took her hand away from her throat – it didn't matter at all about the button now – and smiled happily at him. 'Thank you,' she said in reply to his compliment. Franklin smiled back at her. It was impossible not to.

The food was exquisite. Well, it certainly was

to Millie. Franklin was too distracted by his sexual desire to taste much of whatever it was he was putting into his mouth.

Facing each other on the first-floor landing outside the doors to their rooms, Franklin didn't quite know what to say. Seduction wasn't his strong point. Millie saved him the trouble.

'It's a pity I can't offer you a cup of tea,' she said. 'Would you like to sneak into Solly's kitchen?'

'Why don't we have a drink in my room?' Franklin countered gratefully. 'I have cognac and port.'

'That would be lovely.'

While Franklin poured their drinks into the glasses he'd purchased that very afternoon, Millie looked out of the window. 'What a nice view,' she said, although she actually preferred the view from her own room. Looking out over backyards was more homey, somehow, than looking out over a main street. 'And it's a nice big room; lots of space.' There was too much space, Millie thought. It was very spare. He could do with more furniture and more pretty things about, a bit of colour ...

'Thank you,' she said, accepting the cut-crystal port glass. 'Oh, isn't that lovely!' She held up the glass, examining the sparkle of the light on the crystal and the velvet colour within. 'It's too pretty to drink.'

'We can always fill it up again,' Franklin said, as he toasted her with his brandy balloon.

What an attractive man he is, Millie thought, sneaking a look at him over the rim of her glass as he inhaled the brandy fumes. With his thick hair starting to curl at the collar and his fine cheek-bones and patrician nose – and those eyes, above all those compelling blue eyes! She looked away in case he should glance up and catch her staring at him. When he didn't, she stole another look. The way he carried himself, the way he wore his clothes. He was a good deal younger than she was, Millie was sure of that, but there was no callow youth about him. His air of authority and command was palpable. All night she'd noticed the effect he'd had on others – not only the waiters in the restaurant, but those dining as well. Once she'd established the fact that they weren't staring critically at her, she'd been aware that the other diners were wondering who the aristocratic young man was. He was class, Franklin Ross, all class.

Far above her station, of course, but she could fantasise, couldn't she? He obviously found her desirable and if she allowed him to sleep with her ... well, anything was possible, wasn't it? 'Allowed' him to sleep with her? Why pretend? She wanted to sleep with him. She wanted the touch of his hands on her flesh, she wanted the weight of his body on hers, she wanted to feel him inside her.

Millie genuinely missed a man in her life. Not only did she want to cook and housekeep and sew for a man, she needed a man in her bed. It was a terrible thing to admit, but the truth was that Millie liked sex. She knew she wasn't supposed to, but she did.

So when Franklin wasn't quite sure where to start, it was Millie who took the initiative.

'Thank you for a lovely evening,' she said after he'd poured her a second glass of port and seated himself next to her on the uncomfortable hardback sofa, a little too close, obviously unsure of what to do next. Millie put down the glass and turned to him. 'I enjoyed myself very much.'

Franklin could contain himself no longer. Suddenly his mouth was on hers, his hand seeking her breast, his body pressing against her at an uncomfortable angle.

Millie was taken aback. She hadn't expected this. She'd registered that Mr Ross was shy, but this was gauche, this was ungallant, this was ... She pulled away from him, unsure whether to slap his face or ... Then she saw the desperation in his eyes. The desperation of a boy embarking on his first sexual adventure. Mr Ross was inexperienced – that was it! Perhaps he was even a virgin.

As Franklin once again lunged towards her, Millie deftly avoided his embrace, rose from the sofa and walked to the door. 'I think I should be going now, Mr Ross,' she said formally.

Franklin was mortified. He walked over to her. 'I'm sorry, Millie, I'm extremely sorry. That was unforgivable of me, I – ' He stopped.

Millie had reached up and taken his face in both of her hands. 'Thank you again,' she murmured. 'It's been a beautiful evening.' She stood on her tiptoes and he allowed her to gently lower his head until their lips were touching. Then her arms were about his neck, her mouth was slowly parting as her body melded itself to his.

Franklin lifted her in his embrace and carried her to the bed. Again he forced himself upon her, brutally, demandingly.

Millie pushed him away with all her strength, averting her face from him. 'No, please,' she said, 'please. That's not the way.'

'I'm sorry.' Although he was apologising again, Franklin wasn't quite sure why. She was obviously going to allow him to have sexual intercourse with her. So why did she keep stopping him? He watched as she rose and turned off the overhead light.

'Gently,' she said. 'Gently. Turn on the bedside lamp.'

He did. She stood before him in the rosy glow and slowly showed him how to undress her. When everything but her shift was removed, she stopped him.

'Now you,' she whispered. Together they undressed him. Each time he tried to rush the process she made him linger, tantalising herself as well as him. Finally, when he stood before her, naked, she lowered her shift.

Franklin had never been naked in the presence of a woman, nor had he seen a woman fully naked. In their wild couplings above the stables, Bronwyn had always kept her shift on and he had never bothered to remove his upper garments.

Millie's full, lush body with its milky white skin was a source of wonder to him, and, as he gently ran his fingers over a breast and watched the nipple harden, he thrilled to the pleasure he could sense in the woman. He let his hand stray over her stomach, the small of her back, her hip, until finally, with the tips of his fingers, he touched the copper-gold thatch between her legs.

'Yes,' Millie murmured, her head back, her eyes closed, 'yes.' And her fingers returned his caresses, travelling down his body, over his chest, his buttocks, his groin.

Then they were on the bed again, Franklin quivering with the desire to plunge himself into her, the ecstasy almost more than he could bear. But he was aware that he mustn't. He must hold back. He must take his lead from her. Her pleasure was exquisite to him and he mustn't break the spell.

She lay on her side facing him and, as she kissed him deeply, he felt her legs part. He was rock-hard and, when she placed her hand upon him, he shuddered in anticipation. But she didn't guide him into her, she clamped her thighs tight around him then moved herself backwards and forwards along the shaft of his penis. He could feel her, moist and ready, and her thrusts quickened as the friction stimulated her desire. Finally, when they both felt they could resist no longer, she opened her legs and took him into her.

They'd so prolonged the agony of their pleasure that the final act didn't last long. 'Oh yes! Oh yes!' Millie cried. 'Now, now, now!' And, as Franklin responded to her urgency, his own excitement reached fever pitch. He clasped her tightly to him, buried himself deep inside her and let go with a strangled cry.

For several seconds he lay next to her, fighting

to regain his breath, overwhelmed by the experience. And then confusion set in. It was over. He found their nakedness confronting. And, as Millie snuggled up against him like a contented kitten, he leaned over and turned off the bedside lamp.

She was aware of his confusion and waited for him to say something. When he didn't, she propped on one elbow, kissed him gently on the lips and said, 'I must go back to my room.'

He made as if to protest – he supposed he should – but she interrupted.

'It's too small a bed to sleep two.' And she was up and dressing deftly in the dark, leaving him fumbling for his trousers.

'Shall I see you tomorrow?' he asked.

Millie wasn't sure whether he meant it or not but she smiled reassuringly. 'If you wish.'

Franklin certainly did wish and the following evening found him tapping on her door.

'I wondered whether you might care to dine,' he asked, aware that he was actually asking much more and wondering how he could avoid it sounding the way it did. He couldn't, but Millie's engaging grin banished any need for embarrassment.

'I'd be delighted, Mr Ross.'

He smiled back. 'Do you think, under the circumstances, we could make it Franklin?'

Millie dined, and slept, with Franklin three times over the next ten days and, on the fourth time, exactly a fortnight since their first evening together, Franklin mentioned that he had a surprise for her.

'There you are. What do you think?'

He'd opened the door to his room to reveal the

brand-new double bed which sat in pride of place beneath the bay windows. 'Now you can stay the whole night,' he said. And Millie thrilled to the words.

'Yes,' she answered. 'The whole night. Oh, Franklin.'

They kissed deeply and later, in her passion, she cried out, 'My darling, my darling', again and again.

Franklin learned a lot that year. He learned how to become a good restaurateur from Lumet, who was only too eager to appoint him manager of Le Cafe Gustave; and he learned how to become a good lover from Millie, who was only too eager to teach him the joys of sex.

Franklin grew very fond of Millie and took great pleasure in his new-found sexuality, but he couldn't rid himself of a deep-seated guilt. It didn't seem quite right, somehow, to be so abandoned. His plan had always been to marry a respectable woman who would bear him sons. But there would be time for that, he supposed. And Millie seemed to quite happily accept the relationship as it was; she made no demands upon him, and appeared to have no false expectations.

Indeed, when Franklin had discovered that she'd lost her job it had taken all of his powers of persuasion to convince her that he should pay her rent. 'Very well,' she agreed finally. 'But only until I find another position.' As Solly accepted the money he said, 'You're a kind man, Mr Ross', fully aware of the situation. Of course Solly had been fully aware of the situation even before the double bed had arrived. The lust shared by Millie and Mr Ross was positively palpable.

Gradually Franklin's room took on a new look. As Millie grew bolder, she insisted he allow her to buy a new counterpane, a pretty lace tablecloth, fresh flowers daily. Franklin liked it. When a job opportunity came Millie's way he told her not to take it. The hours were too long, he said, and she hated factory work. Eventually she agreed to accept his support, insisting upon doing his washing and mending by way of exchange and all the time wishing that they had a real home so that she could cook and keep house. But the idea never seemed to occur to Franklin and of course Millie never dared suggest it, so they continued to live in their separate rooms.

Eighteen months after they'd been working together, Gustave Lumet suggested a deal which Franklin was only too quick to accept.

A partnership in an upmarket new restaurant was the offer. Gustave had already chosen the site, a prime piece of real estate overlooking Sydney Harbour. The house was of the grand colonial style, built in the eighties, surrounded by wide verandahs, with large rooms, high, decoratively moulded ceilings and open fireplaces. A grand central staircase led to a second floor, the rooms of which opened out on to balconies bordered by ornate iron lacework.

'Elegant,' Gustave explained. 'People pay for

elegance. We cater for the rich, *mon ami*.'

It would be a costly exercise – not only did they plan to buy the property, but the conversion from house to restaurant would be expensive and it would most certainly take time to accumulate clientele.

Gustave dismissed the severe economic climate with a derisive snort. 'There is always money, *mon ami* – in times like these it just takes a little longer to find it.'

Once they'd acquired the property, the plan was for Franklin to front it. No one was to know Gustave was involved. 'A different image,' he said. 'You understand? I am known to cater to the Bohemian. We need a true aristocrat, a man who will be known to cater to the patrician.' He smiled indulgently. 'And to those who pretend to the patrician.'

It had taken Franklin quite a while to recognise the fact that Gustave wasn't really a snob at all. He was a very astute assessor of people and their requirements and he played his role of the flamboyant French poseur purely because it was the image which most suited his purpose.

Franklin's accumulated funds would not stretch to a half-share in the deal and his only option appeared to be an appeal to his father. He loathed the idea of fielding all the questions Charles would ask and putting up with all the lectures on the responsible handling of family finances. And, after putting himself through the ordeal, who could say what the outcome would be anyway? He would end up being either refused or deeply in debt and answerable at every turn to his father. The prospect of that was odious.

He said as much to Millie one night – she had become his regular sounding board.

'But you don't need your family at all,' she answered. When he stared at her uncomprehendingly, she spelled it out for him. 'Solly. Solly, my dear. He has finances. He is quite a wealthy man and you know he has always wanted to go into business with you. In fact, he's been biding his time for just such an opportunity.' When Franklin was about to interrupt she concluded, 'What's more, he's a very good friend and an honourable man.'

Solly was, of course, thrilled with the idea and they found that, between the two of them, their funds were more than adequate for a half-share in the venture.

Franklin thought it only fair he tell Gustave that he was bringing in a partner. He wondered how the Frenchman would react to a Polish bootmaker from Surry Hills being a part of his elegant project aimed at the patrician market.

Gustave merely laughed. 'You think the money I put in is all my own? I too have silent partners, my friend.'

Of course. Franklin remembered Catherine telling him that Le Cafe Gustave had been quite a front for the sly grog trade in the earlier days of prohibition and Gustave had formed a cosy alliance with Kate Leigh. Well, no questions would be asked – if Kate and her mob were Gustave's silent partners, it was all right by Franklin – just so long as there was nothing illegal expected.

Gustave was quick to read Franklin's reaction. 'A property investment only,' he said. 'My partners remain silent, I promise.'

Solly didn't remain silent. In fact Solly was so excited by the whole prospect that he was more voluble than ever. And many of his ideas were excellent. They should furnish the five bedrooms on the first floor luxuriously, he said, and rent them out to top-class clientele. And when Franklin had set up his wine cellar, they should convert the smaller adjoining room to a showroom.

'People come to dine, they taste the wines,' Solly said. 'That way you teach them about your Ross Estate.'

Regular wine tastings – what an excellent idea, Franklin thought.

It was hard work but it was exciting, and to Millie it was positively thrilling. Far from being left out, she was very much a part of the whole project. Again, Solly's idea.

'I tell you, Boss, you give Millie a job.' For the past six months Solly had taken to calling Franklin 'Boss'. Despite their being partners, he couldn't quite come at 'Franklin' – it didn't seem right somehow. 'You give Millie a job and she will do the work of three people, you just see. You will have housekeeper and maid as well.' It was a deliberate ploy. Solly had been aware of Millie's utter devastation when they had decided that Franklin should occupy one of the rooms at the house. This way she could remain a part of his life. 'You could even move her in with you,' he said boldly.

Franklin stared back at him. 'You mean live together?'

What was so bad about that? Solly wondered. The woman would lay down her life for Franklin.

They spent most of their nights in the same room and in the daytime Franklin was out working. Why not let her keep house for him? Why not even marry her, for God's sake!

But, because he could sense Franklin's disapproval, Solly made light of his suggestion. 'Just an idea. Sure. Why not?'

Franklin could have told Solly why not, but he didn't. He changed the subject instead.

There were specific reasons why Franklin Ross would never marry Millie Tingwell. He believed he loved her. He probably loved her as much as it was in his capacity to love a woman. But there was a much stronger driving force to be considered. He was twenty-seven years of age; he must start a family before he turned thirty. And with the right woman. The right *young* woman. A woman of breeding, no older than twenty-five, with plenty of child-bearing years ahead of her. Millie was working class and in two months time she would be thirty-five years old.

It was a pity, Franklin thought. Millie could have made him happy. There was nothing he would like more than to have her cook and keep house for him the way he knew she wanted to. He was fully aware of how deeply she loved him.

He never discussed the situation with her, careful not to encourage false hopes in any way. And he was most particular about the precautions they took to prevent conception. Each night after they made love, he would insist that Millie douche herself immediately. When she wanted to curl up beside him, he ordered her out of bed. 'Straight away, Millie,' he'd say. 'It doesn't work if you don't do it straight away.' And Millie would dutifully traipse downstairs and out the back to the bathroom. She did it to keep the peace more than anything. She wasn't actually sure if douching worked and she wasn't even sure if she could conceive anyway. She'd certainly wanted to during her eight-year marriage but it had never happened.

For the first year Millie hadn't questioned the need to avoid conception – of course it made sense. She quite understood that Franklin would one day seek a young wife of his own class and in the meantime she was only too grateful for his support and friendship. But as she grew to love him and as she sensed his love in return, she couldn't help but feel hurt. She knew she had no right to, Franklin had never promised her anything. But each time she squatted in the bath and flushed herself out, she felt humiliated and rejected.

They called the restaurant The Colony House and it took them nearly two years to get it up on its feet but eventually it proved every bit as successful as Gustave had predicted. The Colony House gained an international reputation and catered to the elite from all corners of the globe.

'Didn't I tell you, *mon ami?*' Gustave boasted as they set up a private poker game for a guest in one of the upstairs suites, 'there are always people with money. You just need to give them a little time to sniff you out.'

Gustave was often at The Colony House, not because it was necessary but because he loved the place. The Bohemian set of Kings Cross bored him now; he preferred to mingle with the international crowd. He always posed as a guest, though, never letting it be known he was Franklin's partner.

Gustave particularly liked the evenings when they hosted a night of blackjack or poker. Those were the nights when the really big spenders swarmed about The Colony House like bees around a honey pot. Not that Gustave himself was much of a gambler. He put in bids just high enough to keep him in the game and lost only the amount he was prepared to lose, but he adored people who spent money. Lots of it. With style.

The gambling nights, always organised at the request of a well-known or well-referred guest, were as borderline illegal as Franklin was prepared to go. The Colony House did not operate as a gambling casino, it merely hosted the evenings of its guests' choice. And if the guests chose to gamble with their own money, Franklin reasoned, who was he to stand in their way?

Solly was a problem on gambling nights – or rather, when gambling nights coincided with vodka nights, Solly was a problem. And it was difficult to escape him. With a bottle of fine Polish vodka inside him, Solly could sniff out a poker game a mile away. Three times he'd lost every penny he owned.

'With the American in town it will be a big game tonight – what are you going to do about Solly?' Gustave asked as he finished setting up the bar in the corner of the suite. Gustave didn't care much for Solly. The man was colourful, certainly, but he had very little style.

Franklin shrugged. 'Solly won't be any trouble. He can't be, he has nothing left to gamble.' He opened the french windows and stepped outside onto the balcony. He didn't think it necessary to tell Gustave that just last week Solly had gambled away his bootshop. Franklin had been appalled.

'I know, I know, Boss.' Solly had been deeply penitent. 'It's the vodka. I tell you, no more, never again.'

It was Millie who'd persuaded Franklin to loan Solly the money to buy back his business.

At first Franklin had refused. 'Why should I?' he'd demanded. 'Solly's a fool. Good God, next time he'll probably put up his share in The Colony House – that's all he's got left to gamble.'

Millie had quickly seized upon the fact. 'Then take that as your security,' she said. 'Make Solly sign over his share of The Colony House to you until he repays your loan.'

Eventually Franklin did as she suggested – it was sound reasoning after all – and Millie was the one left a little confused. She didn't know why she had fought Solly's case so vociferously. Something had warned her that if Solly was ruined, she would be too. Perhaps it was a case of Surry Hills people sticking together. Perhaps it was just that. But things were changing, Millie could feel it – they were moving too fast, and she didn't want them to. She wanted the comfortable faces and places from the past around her and she often wished

Franklin was still living in the front room above the bootshop in Riley Street.

Not that Millie didn't love The Colony House. She did. She not only loved its beauty but, during that first year, she loved the hard work as they struggled together to make a success of the restaurant.

Solly had been quite right when he told Franklin she would do the work of three. Millie was maid, housekeeper, and kitchenhand. Each morning she would walk from Surry Hills to Point Piper. Her first job was to service the suites. As she opened the french windows to air each room, she loved to step out onto the balcony and look at the sparkling blue harbour waters and the occasional big ship steaming its way towards the far distant heads and the open sea. She loved sitting in the parlour making out the lists of housekeeping supplies needed and she loved polishing the beautiful crystal wine glasses in the restaurant and setting the tables the way Franklin had taught her.

Millie didn't hostess or wait at table. Franklin never asked her to and she was rather grateful for that. But a year or so after the restaurant was established, when the gambling evenings started to prove popular, he suggested she host them with him.

'They don't want regular waiters and maitre d's,' he said. 'They want to feel they're among friends.'

Millie was very flattered and she came to love the evenings, for several reasons. She was working closely with Franklin, for a start – with the burgeoning success of the business, she had been seeing less of him – and it kept her away from the restaurant. Millie was a little in awe of many of the people who now dined at The Colony House. She was self-conscious and aware she was out of her class. The gambling nights were different. The atmosphere was far more relaxed and, as the company was predominantly male, Millie was more often than not a major attraction. She enjoyed the mildly flirtatious attitudes of the men – they meant no harm, and it was good for her ego.

But what Millie loved most of all about the gambling nights was the fact that they started late and invariably went through until the early hours of the following morning, which meant that she spent the remainder of the time in Franklin's bed.

They allowed themselves to sleep in and 'dawdle into the day' as Millie put it. As they drank their morning tea together gazing at the harbour, Millie would fantasise that they were married. This is how it would be, she would think.

'The American has stamina.' Gustave lit up one of his foul-smelling imported cigarettes. ('They taste much better than they smell,' was his jovial excuse when people turned away in disgust.) 'His ship does not arrive until late afternoon and he wants a poker game his first night in town.' Gustave nodded approvingly. 'I shall look forward to meeting him.'

No one had met the American but he came with excellent references and credentials. Not only did he own property all over the globe, including film studios in Hollywood and a cattle station in Queensland, he had been referred to The Colony House by no less than three well-respected guests, each of whom had suggested that a poker game, involving major players only, be set up for Big Sam.

Samuel Crockett was indeed a big man. In every sense of the word. Big in body, voice and temperament. 'How do, Mr Ross,' he said, taking Franklin's hand into his massive paw and shaking it effusively. 'Samuel David Crockett, and I'm happy to make your acquaintance.'

Sam's grandfather had always claimed that Davy Crockett was his first cousin, so Sam's father had been called David, Sam's middle name was David and Sam himself, always prepared to go one step further, had recently christened his first-born son Davy. The fact that no relationship to the legendary hero had ever been traced was immaterial to the entire family. 'Hell, nobody kept records back then!' They were Crocketts from Tennessee and Davy, they maintained, was their ancestor.

'I've heard a lot of fine things about your magnificent establishment,' Sam continued. They were standing on the front verandah, and he looked about at the lavish grounds and the wide stretch of grass sloping down to the harbour. 'And I see that it's all true.'

'You must be weary, Mr Crockett. My driver tells me your ship docked less than an hour ago.'

'Weary? Hell, no. Nothing like a sea voyage to

get you up and going.' Sam gestured at the harbour. 'What a remarkable sight.' He shook his head admiringly and Franklin realised he was referring to the Sydney Harbour Bridge.

'Yes. Two years old now. Magnificent, isn't it?'

'It surely is.' Sam walked to the edge of the verandah and gazed across the water. The bridge was indeed impressive in the early gathering dusk. 'It surely is,' he repeated.

'Your first visit to Sydney, Mr Crockett?' Franklin asked, joining him.

Sam nodded. 'I got me a cattle station in Queensland four years back. Near Quilpie.' He laughed. 'I thought Sydney'd be kind of like Brisbane.' Franklin wondered whether the man intended to patronise or whether he was actually a bit stupid.

'I thought all Australian cities'd be like Brisbane.' Sam continued to stare at the bridge and, when he turned to Franklin, it was with a huge grin of genuine admiration. 'I sure didn't think you'd have a place like this down here. It's some town, I tell you.'

Franklin realised that Sam was not being intentionally patronising, nor was he stupid. With the exception of his cattle station in outback Queensland, he was genuinely ignorant of anything pertaining to Australia, and he was the first person to admit it.

Sam Crockett was exceedingly arrogant and Franklin didn't much like him but he recognised an honesty in the man which demanded respect.

Sam's staying power also demanded respect. Dismissing the idea of a rest before dining, he insisted Franklin join him for champagne on his

109

balcony so that they could watch the sunset over the harbour. 'Bring some friends,' he said. 'Introduce me to some company.'

Sam had already boasted of his newborn son, Davy, and his wife of one year, Lucy-Mae, so Franklin wasn't sure if he meant 'female company'. In any event, not associating himself with such requests, Franklin discreetly referred the enquiry to the maitre d', who did. But it appeared Sam simply required convivial drinking companions. So Franklin asked Gustave and Solly to join them.

Solly was the first to arrive. Despite the fact that he still worked hard in his boot-making shop and, although he had recently come close to ruin, Solly looked prosperous. He enjoyed his elevated position as Franklin's partner and for some time now he'd consciously set about improving his image. Always easy company, he was quick to delight the American.

'You know, when they build the bridge, Mr Crockett,' he said as Sam once more admired the construction from the balcony, 'they start from both sides of the harbour and when the two halves meet in the middle they are less than one inch apart.'

'No, you're kidding me.' Sam was fascinated.

'It is true. An engineering masterpiece.'

The sun was setting over the harbour and the old-fashioned gas lanterns, which Franklin had insisted on installing at great expense, had just been lit. There were thirty of them. They lined the main circular driveway and the grass harbour frontage, their reflections shimmering in the darkening waters. Beyond them, across the bay, reared the massive Harbour Bridge and the combination of old and new was breathtaking. The three men sat admiring the view for several minutes before Solly broke the silence.

The champagne was mingling rather unpleasantly with the half-bottle of fine Polish vodka he'd consumed a little earlier, but it was certainly not apparent. Apart from his compulsion to gamble beyond his means, Solly's behaviour never appeared drink-affected.

'Of course you have wonderful bridges in America too,' he said expansively. 'San Francisco, I have always wanted to see San Francisco.' He encouraged Sam to talk about his homeland in general, his Hollywood film studio, his Queensland cattle station, and, by the time Gustave arrived, the air was thick with camaraderie.

Solly had his reasons for charming Sam. He'd heard of the impending poker game and he fully intended to participate. He had not yet paid back his creditor and Franklin's money was burning a hole in his pocket.

Solly loathed being in debt and he'd become obsessed with the notion of doubling the money on a poker table, buying back his business and repaying Franklin in one fell swoop. When he'd accomplished that, he swore to himself, he would never gamble again.

Sam insisted that his new friends join him for dinner and he was effusive about The Ross Estate wines.

'Amongst the finest I've tasted,' he enthused. They were the words Franklin always loved to hear from an overseas visitor. Through The Colony House, The Ross Estate wines were earning an international reputation. Not only did guests take wines back with them to their homelands, but in the past year Franklin had received orders for six consignments from various small buyers in Britain.

Tonight, however, Sam's opinion meant little to Franklin. The man was swilling the wine as if it was water, just as he had the champagne earlier, and he was becoming noticeably drunk.

Over coffee and cognac Franklin made a tentative suggestion. 'I'd be quite happy to postpone our game tonight, Mr Crockett, if you're weary.'

'No. Good God, man, no! And it's Sam. All my friends call me Sam.'

'It would be no trouble at all to inform the other players, I assure you,' Franklin persisted. 'We could just as easily arrange it for tomorrow evening if you wish.'

'I do not wish, Mr Ross.' The big face lost its joviality and the brown eyes burned into Franklin's. Sam had sensed the inference and he was angry. Very angry. Was this young upstart of an Australian daring to insinuate that Samuel David Crockett couldn't hold his liquor? Although Sam was only five years Franklin's senior, he felt superior in every way. 'I most definitely do not wish,' he repeated scathingly, defying Franklin to pursue the matter.

'Very well.' Franklin gestured to the waiter for more coffee and sighed inwardly. He could sense trouble ahead. Drunkenness and gambling were not a good mix and he tried to avoid it whenever possible.

'And the two of you are going to join me for the game, are you not?' Sam's large toothy grin was once more back in place and his voice reverberated with bonhomie as he turned to Gustave and Solly.

'Thank you for the invitation, but I am afraid the stakes will be a little high for me,' Gustave smiled apologetically.

'I accept with pleasure,' Solly said and he pretended not to notice Franklin's reaction.

For the next fifteen minutes, while they finished their coffee, Solly resolutely refused to meet Franklin's eyes, but finally there was no avoiding the confrontation.

'Well, gentlemen, if you'll excuse me.' Franklin rose from the table and looked at his watch. 'The other players will be here in an hour and there are things to be done. Solly, I need your help.' Solly put down his coffee cup and rose reluctantly. 'We shall meet in your suite at eleven, Mr Crockett, if that's suitable.'

'Excellent, excellent.' Sam nodded affably and helped himself to another cognac.

When they were safely out of earshot Franklin turned to Solly. His voice was like ice. 'Would you care to explain yourself?' Solly tried to look bewildered but Franklin continued. 'How the hell do you intend to gamble if you have no money and you're in debt to me?'

'Ah. Yes.' Solly nodded, pretending a sudden realisation. 'I am sorry, Boss, I should have paid back your money last week.' Franklin continued to stare at him. 'I have big win in a game last Friday,' Solly explained. 'Yes, yes ... ' He held up his hand as if to ward off interruption even though it was evident Franklin was not about to say anything. 'I should not have been playing I know, but, well . . . ' A shrug and an apologetic smile. ' . . . the vodka.'

Franklin continued to stare back at him. Solly's charm had been wearing decidedly thin for quite some time now.

'I have your money,' Solly insisted. 'Honest I do. It was a big win.' Somewhere in Solly's brain he was justifying the lie. He did have the money, didn't he? It was waiting for him. On the poker table. All he had to do was double what was in his pocket. He'd done it before.

'I've never known you to be a liar, Solly.' Franklin felt deeply disappointed. The money was not the issue to him. If Solly's gambling addiction had reached such proportions that he could renounce his honour, then Franklin had lost a friend. 'It doesn't become you,' he said and walked away.

The other players arrived punctually and Franklin and Millie escorted them to the suite. Each of the three men had been hand-picked by Franklin. Robert Mitchell was 'old family'. His parents owned half of Sydney and he was a womaniser, a rake and a very astute card player. Paddy Conway was a one-time sea captain who had retired early in life. No one knew where his money came from but it was rumoured he used to run guns. He was a bold gambler who won big and lost big. Viscount Peter Lynell was one of the richest men in the Commonwealth. He lived in London but regularly visited Australia to oversee his vast mining interests. He always stayed at The Colony House and genuinely enjoyed the fine wines. He and Franklin got on particularly well.

'Mrs Tingwell, this is Mr Crockett.' As Franklin started on the introductions, he realised that the American was even more inebriated. He wasn't staggering and his speech wasn't slurred but there was a general air of aggression and Franklin sensed that the man had done away with niceties. Crockett obviously considered himself to be among inferiors and seemed to hold them all in contempt.

'Mrs Tingwell.' Sam lifted Millie's hand and brushed his lips over the back of it. The gesture was somehow obscene. Franklin bristled – surely the man would not behave like that amongst his own set. Did he think Millie was a whore?

'Sam Crockett, this is Robert Mitchell ... ' Curbing his annoyance, Franklin introduced the other players. Sam shook Robert Mitchell's hand vigorously but still allowed himself to be distracted by Millie. ' ... Paddy Conway and Viscount Peter Lynell,' Franklin concluded, hoping that the men were not as aware as he was of Crockett's blatant rudeness.

'Sam. Call me Sam.' The American finally gave his attention to the others and pumped their hands effusively. 'Let's not stand on ceremony. Drinks!' he roared. 'Where are the drinks?' He took Millie by the arm and shepherded her towards the bar with a familiarity bordering on lewd. 'What about you, little lady, what are you having?'

Millie gave him the prettiest smile and gently

disengaged her arm. 'I rather think that's my job, Mr Crockett.' The dimples danced. 'What may I get you?'

Although Millie lacked confidence in sophisticated mixed company, she was perfectly in control among men. Particularly when she knew they were attracted to her – which was invariably the case. It had always been a talent of hers. Even before Franklin had tutored her in the social graces, she'd been able to manipulate men with ease, never offending, never annoying.

Now, as the American nodded amiably and ordered a bourbon, Franklin felt very proud of her. She was a great asset.

'Gentlemen,' he said, taking over, 'if you'd care to place your orders with Mrs Tingwell or myself we'll look after you throughout the evening. Cigars and cigarettes are on the table; feel free to take off your jackets.'

Half an hour later, as the game was about to get under way, Solly arrived. He knew the other players and was gracious in his apologies although no one seemed to mind, certainly not the American who was still busy ogling Millie.

Solly placed a request for a large vodka with Millie and sat himself down at the table, carefully avoiding eye contact with Franklin. Their earlier confrontation had been very upsetting. Solly had known that Franklin was right, that he was not behaving like a man of honour. After Franklin had walked off, he'd had to go home to boost his morale.

Half a bottle of vodka later, the self-loathing had disappeared. What did the Boss know? The

Boss was not a gambling man. Only a fool would ignore the signs, Solly told himself.

Solly was going to win tonight, he knew it. All the signs told him so: the law of averages told him . . . he'd lost three times in a row; the numbers told him – it was a nine day, things always went well for him on a nine day; and he had right on his side – he was playing for somebody else. He was playing for the Boss. And it was common knowledge that when you played for something other than greed the odds were in your favour.

Solly took the glass of vodka from Millie. He felt good. Positive. A winner. Tomorrow, when he handed back the money he'd borrowed, together with a healthy amount of interest, Franklin would know that he'd been right. Solly would then beg forgiveness, swear off gambling and once more be a man of honour. But tonight was his night. Solly leant forward and cut for the deal. He turned up a three.

An hour later, Robert Mitchell retired from the game. 'Well, gentlemen, I think I'll make an early night of it,' he said, rising from the table. 'If you'll excuse me.' The American was playing like a fool, he thought, forcing the stakes up too high too early. Robert preferred a more skilled, cautious approach to the game. Besides, if he popped into the downstairs lounge now, one or two of the beautiful women he'd seen dining might still be there. Admittedly, their husbands would also be there, lingering over their cigars and brandies, but that never bothered Robert.

Peter Lynell also rose and excused himself. 'Maybe another hand a little later,' he said, although he had no intention of returning to the game. He too was not enjoying the American. Not that he minded the style of play – he rather enjoyed a bold game himself. But the American, who was obviously an experienced player, was throwing his money around in such a vulgar fashion that Peter found it extremely insulting. It was as if the man couldn't be bothered with the game at all. Furthermore, he was drunk and loud and Peter loathed drunkenness. 'Excuse me,' he said and stepped out on to the balcony.

Solly didn't mind the American's drunkenness, vulgarity, or style of play. Solly didn't mind anything. Solly was winning. He'd been right, he thought, knocking back another vodka and nodding for Millie to fill the glass. This was his night.

'As a young man I was going to go to America,' he said while Paddy shuffled the cards. 'But I come here instead. From Poland. She is a difficult country to live in, Poland. But she is beautiful. So beautiful.'

Sam stared balefully at him. Who the hell cared about Poland? And how come the yid was winning every hand? The bonhomie he'd felt towards Solly earlier had long since soured. Sam now found him irritating. But then Sam was finding the whole evening irritating. He wasn't enjoying the game and he wanted it to be over. It wasn't because he was a poor sport. He normally weathered his losses well. But he was too distracted to enjoy the night. He was too distracted by the woman.

Sam could see her lush body through the fabric of her modest, well-cut dress. Who did she think she was fooling, dressing like one of the gentry? She was a working woman, Sam could see that. And who the hell did Franklin Ross think he was, introducing her like she was a woman of class? She was no lady. Sam could sense Millie's sexuality and it was driving him mad. The more he drank, the more he became consumed by his lust.

As Millie put the glass of vodka down beside Solly, Sam held his own glass up to her, deliberately brushing her breast with the back of his hand. 'Another bourbon,' he said and he held her look before allowing his eyes to travel down her body.

No one had noticed. Paddy was busy dealing the cards, Solly was leaning back in his chair, waxing loquacious and Franklin had just stepped out onto the balcony to join Peter Lynell and escape the cigar smoke.

Millie felt her cheeks flush. It wasn't the American's desire that was insulting, it was his assessment of her. She knew he saw her as working class. She knew, furthermore, that he saw her as the type of woman who was accessible to men. The type of woman who would moan in bed as she gave herself to a lover. The final humiliation for Millie was her knowledge that the man's assessment was right. She walked back to the bar, deeply disheartened. How could she ever have thought there was a place for her in Franklin's life, among his class, when she could be so easily read?

'Now more than ever Poland will be a difficult

place to live,' Solly continued, enjoying his own conversation. 'This Adolf Hitler, he is greedy, and now that he is Chancellor of Germany there will be a war, I know it. A big war that will involve everyone. Including Australia.' He picked up his cards. 'Australia will ally with Britain just like in the First World War and it will be a bloody one, I tell you. I put my money on it that I am right, you just see.'

'Try putting your money on the table,' Sam growled. 'It's your bet.'

Paddy smiled at Solly. 'If there is a war there'll be a lot of people making a lot of money, you can bet on that,' he said amiably. There was no need for the American to be so rude to Solly, he thought.

Solly grinned back. If anyone knew about making money out of a war it was certainly Paddy Conway.

'Not just guns, mind,' Paddy corrected. 'People get rich a lot of ways in a war.' And he turned his attention to the cards.

That was when the idea hit Solly and he stared back at the Irishman. Of course! That was it! That was how he was going to repay Franklin. That was how he was going to once more become a man of honour in Franklin's eyes. He was going to make Franklin rich! Everything was suddenly clear to Solly.

'Are you in or out, for Christ's sake?' the American barked.

'Sorry. In,' Solly said and he opened the bidding.

* * *

120

An hour later, Solly's money was gone, but he was happy. He'd won what he'd set out to win and he had the piece of paper in his pocket to prove it.

Franklin had been downstairs fetching more bourbon and vodka and hadn't witnessed the final bidding. Peter Lynell had retired for the night, Paddy Conway had been well and truly cleaned out and the play had been left to Solly and Sam. Solly had called the American's bluff. A big risk. All or nothing. But he'd won. He couldn't wait to tell Franklin.

'Thank you, Mr Crockett,' he said as he put on his jacket. The American's belligerence was so extreme now that even Solly couldn't ignore it so he'd dropped the first name and the camaraderie. 'I have enjoyed this evening.'

'Yes, I'll bet you have,' Sam said, hauling himself to his feet. 'Get me a drink.' He clicked his fingers at Millie.

'Mr Ross is fetching another bottle of bourbon,' she answered stiffly. 'He shouldn't be long.'

Sam looked at her. 'Mr Ross.' She called him Mr Ross. He wondered whether they were lovers. Of course they were. They didn't let it show in public, but of course they were. Franklin Ross knew the woman's body. He'd caressed her breasts. She'd opened her thighs for him. She'd panted like a bitch on heat for him.

'He's taking too long,' Sam said, crossing to her. 'Let's go downstairs and find our own bottle.' He put his arm around her and, before she could pull away, his hand was on her breast.

'Let her go.' Franklin was standing at the door.

Sam took his hand from Millie's breast but kept

121

his arm draped around her and looked malevolently at Franklin. Millie tried to edge to one side but Crockett gripped her shoulder.

Franklin handed the two bottles he was carrying to Paddy. 'I said, let her go,' he repeated.

'I thought I might take the little lady down to the lounge for a drink.' Sam's smile was insolent. 'Away from this cigar smoke. It's so close in here.'

Millie stared at the floor. Why did she feel guilty? Why did she feel responsible for this hideous confrontation?

Franklin saw her reaction and he felt a rush of anger. He walked over to Sam. 'I'll say it one last time. *Let her go.*'

'Oh come on now, Mr Ross, I'm a guest in your establishment.' The smile was now goading. 'A drink with the little lady, that's not too much to ask, surely?'

Franklin pushed Sam's arm roughly from Millie's shoulder, took her by the hand, and led her away.

The American's smile faded and his face turned ugly. 'What's all the fuss about, Ross? Who do you think you're kidding anyway? She's a working woman.'

It all happened in a split second. Two paces back to the big man, then Franklin's arm shot out and Sam was on the floor, dizzy, clutching the side of his face. He stared up in disbelief.

'You're drunk, Crockett,' Franklin said tightly. 'We'll forget this happened.'

If Sam was drunk, he certainly didn't feel it. Not any more. He felt enraged. Angered beyond belief. His eyes were stone cold sober as he pulled himself

122

to his feet and confronted Franklin. 'I demand satisfaction.'

'You'll have none. I refuse to fight.' Franklin turned away.

'A duel.' Sam picked up his jacket which was hanging over the back of his chair. He reached inside it and pulled out a Colt .38 revolver from its leather holster sewn inside. 'I demand a duel.'

Millie, Franklin, Solly, Paddy, all stared at the American in disbelief. Was the man mad?

'A duel,' he repeated. 'You owe it to me.'

Paddy Conway was the first one to try and reason. 'Don't be a fool, man,' he said. 'Put the gun away.'

'You struck me to the ground and I demand satisfaction,' Sam repeated, not taking his eyes off Franklin.

'Paddy's right,' Franklin said. 'Don't be a fool. This is 1934. No one fights duels any more.'

'You refuse?'

'Yes.'

'So you're a coward then.'

'No,' Franklin replied evenly. 'I don't have a gun.'

Sam took one step forward and, with the back of his hand, struck Franklin hard across his right cheek. 'I say you're a coward,' he repeated.

A shocking second passed. A second when Franklin didn't move but his eyes turned to steel. 'Now I come to think of it,' he said, and the voice was deadly, dangerous, 'I know where I can find a gun.' He turned to Paddy Conway and held out his hand.

Paddy reached inside the jacket he'd kept on all

123

evening and took the Webley .455 from its shoulder holster. He handed it to Franklin.

There was a gasp from Millie but, apart from that, silence as Franklin broke the breach and checked the cylinder. Then he turned to Paddy and Solly. 'Are you prepared to act as seconds?' he asked. The two men agreed and Franklin turned again to Sam. 'Acceptable to you, Mr Crockett?' Sam nodded. 'Then make your choice.' Sam chose Paddy Conway.

'I think we'll find the light is best on the lawn,' Franklin said and he led the way. No one spoke as they followed him out of the suite, down the central staircase and into the main hall.

Through the arch to the left, a number of guests were still gathered in the lounge. There were several houseguests playing cards in one corner and a group of late diners were dawdling over final cognacs and being entertained by Robert Mitchell. They all turned and stared at the two men and the guns they carried as Franklin paused and motioned for Robert to join him. 'Stay with Robert, Millie,' he muttered. And, before he could protest, he and the others had walked away.

The guests followed at a respectable distance and they were joined by The Colony House staff members who were still working. Everyone spilled out onto the front verandah to watch as the men crossed the main driveway and walked towards the harbourside lawn.

A couple of staff members disappeared upstairs and, several seconds later, french windows opened and people appeared on balconies.

Finally the hushed whispers died down and an

eerie silence settled upon the proceedings. The men took up their positions on the grassy slope in the hazy light of the gaslamps, their reflections flickering in the harbour waters behind them.

Paddy Conway was elected duel marshal. 'I'm not positive as to the correct etiquette, gentlemen. Back to back, fifteen paces. Does that sound all right?' he asked.

'It'll do.' Sam gave a curt nod. 'Call the paces out loud. At fifteen we turn and fire in our own time,' he instructed.

Solly took Franklin's jacket and stood to one side. He muttered a quick 'Good luck, Boss', but Franklin didn't acknowledge it.

'Are you ready sir?' the American demanded.

'I'm ready.'

They stood back to back and Paddy started counting slowly and loudly. 'One . . . Two . . . Three . . . '

From the front verandah and the balconies, a crowd of people watched, breathless. Although it was a warm, balmy night Millie started to shiver. How had it come to this? What had she done? She knew she was somehow responsible, but what had she done? It had all happened so quickly. 'Five . . . Six . . . Seven . . . ' What if Franklin were killed? Oh God! She started to shake uncontrollably. Robert Mitchell put his arm around her shoulders and supported her.

'Nine . . . Ten . . . Eleven . . . ' Paddy Conway's voice rang out clear in the night air. Solly watched Franklin, each step precise and measured, his back, as always, ramrod straight. Solly couldn't see his face but he could see the tilt of the head and he knew the jaw would be set and the eyes cold and clear. Sure, the Boss was a strong man, not easily frightened, but what did he know of duels?

'Thirteen ... Fourteen ... Fifteen.' The two men stopped. They turned. Paddy Conway's voice hung in the air, then the crack of a pistol shot rang out in the night and a spurt of flame leapt from the American's gun.

Franklin, his right arm extended, revolver pointing at the American, felt the bullet enter his body. It was rather like being hit with a hammer, he thought vaguely. Although there was no immediate pain and although he was still standing, he felt the warmth of his blood as it rolled down the skin of his arm from the hole in his left shoulder. But he continued to stare along the barrel of his revolver. There was no rush now. Plenty of time. One shot each, that was the agreement. He squared his gun sights.

Solly had been right, Franklin knew nothing of duels. But Franklin knew a great deal about guns and targets. He'd been taught at a very early age. And as a child, whether he'd been sighting on the potatoes his father had placed on the top of the fence posts or whether he'd been sighting on the marauding birds over the vines, Franklin had always liked to take his time.

Now the sights of his revolver were perfectly set on the bridge of the American's nose. The bullet would hit right between the eyes. The back of Sam's head would be blown away and he'd drop like a stone.

Franklin waited for the American to falter,

waited for him to show some sign of fear, perhaps even to beg. But he didn't. He stood motionless, waiting, a massive figure in the lamplight. Franklin had to admire him for that.

As Samuel Crockett looked at the unwavering barrel thirty paces away he realised that Franklin Ross knew his business. Franklin Ross was going to kill him. Sam cursed himself. He'd been too eager, had fired too quickly. Unlike him. It was the liquor of course. What a fool he'd been. And why wasn't the Australian firing back, damn him? Because he wants to make me sweat, that's why, Sam thought.

Beads of perspiration sprang out on his upper lip and his brow. Well, I'm sweating, you bastard. Shoot!

A tiny vein started to twitch in Sam's left temple. He wants to break me, he thought. He wants me to beg. Be damned, Ross! I'll die before I grovel to any man.

Samuel Crockett stood his ground.

At the very last second, just before the gunshot rang out and the flame flashed, Sam saw Franklin alter his aim. Then he felt a tearing pain in his left shoulder and he dropped to his knees.

Slowly Franklin walked over to him. Sam rose to his feet to face him, his left arm hanging uselessly by his side.

'A shoulder for a shoulder, Mr Ross?' he said.

But Franklin didn't answer. His wound was starting to ache and he was annoyed that he'd allowed himself to be landed in such a situation. The whole thing was a wasted exercise.

'Would you care to accompany me to my doctor's rooms?' he asked and he handed his gun to Paddy Conway.

The following afternoon Sam and Franklin sat down in the front lounge for coffee and a business meeting, their shoulders bound and their arms in slings. The meeting had been arranged at Sam's suggestion.

'Mr Mankowski tells me we're partners,' he'd said when he'd tapped on Franklin's door an hour ago. 'Let's meet for coffee and discuss the situation.'

Franklin had been utterly mystified but the man seemed amiable enough, besides which he'd actually apologised for his behaviour towards Millie. In a very oblique way, admittedly: 'May have overstepped the mark a little' was what he said. But Franklin took it as an apology. 'The front lounge in one hour?' he suggested.

'So,' said Franklin, lifting the steaming coffee to his lips, 'in what way are we partners?'

'I believe you own fifty per cent of my Queensland beef cattle.' Sam also took a sip of his coffee. 'Good and strong,' he said approvingly. 'I like it that way.' Then he put his cup down and continued. 'And that means Mandinulla, my ranch – well, you call them stations down here, don't you?' he corrected – 'and my one hundred square miles of grazing land as well as my prime stock.'

He shook his head in disbelief. 'That was some win, I tell you.'

He drained his cup and exhaled loudly as it burned the back of his throat. 'Mind you,' he said, pouring himself another coffee, 'I was gambling like a fool last night.'

Franklin continued to stare at the man, bemused, thinking that perhaps the duelling wound had addled his senses. 'I don't know what you're talking about,' he said. 'I wasn't betting.'

'No, but your friend Mankowski was. And when I met him this morning to discuss our debt, he said he was winning for you.' Franklin looked at the American, dumbfounded. 'You mean you didn't know?' Sam asked and when Franklin shook his head, he shrugged. 'Well, I guess you better sort it out with Mankowski, but he was very insistent and I've contacted my lawyers to start drawing up the necessary papers.'

Sam dropped his air of indifference and leaned forward in his chair. 'I must say, Ross, if I have to share my property with anyone, I'm honoured that it is a man of your character and courage.'

It was a big thing for the American to say and Franklin realised that, whether he liked it or not, he had probably won a friend for life. 'Thank you, Sam,' he said.

'What the hell do you mean, you were winning for me?' Franklin demanded.

'Just what I say, Boss, and the proof – here it is.' Solly took a piece of paper from his pocket and, with a flourish, handed it to Franklin. Sure enough, it was a letter of agreement from Samuel Crockett signing over a half-share of his Queensland holdings.

Solly couldn't wipe the grin from his face. He

had never before seen Franklin Ross at a loss for words. 'I do good, eh?'

After a moment's dumbfounded silence, Franklin looked up from the letter. 'You're a madman, Solly,' he said. Solly nodded in happy agreement. 'What the hell am I going to do with a cattle station in Queensland?'

'Get rich, Boss. Very, very, very rich. There will be a war in Europe, I tell you ... '

'Yes, time and time again you tell me.'

'And Australia, she will ally with Britain like the last time. And the army, the army, it will need supplies.' There was no stopping Solly now. 'Paddy Conway, he say it, "People, they can become rich in a war".' Then he added hastily, 'Not bad rich, Boss – good rich. Sell beef to the army, sell leather goods to the army.' Solly's eyes were shining enthusiastically. 'I design good boots and belts, we buy a factory and we make thousands and thousands ... ' He stopped briefly. Franklin's expression was still enigmatic. 'Of course, we always give good price for the army,' he added. 'We help the allies.'

Finally Franklin had to give in. 'You're a madman but you're right,' he agreed.

They talked for an hour or so and, as usual, many of Solly's ideas were excellent. They both agreed that Franklin should start making some firm contacts in the British military. And soon. For two reasons. Inside information on the state of the European situation was needed, and, with well-established contacts, Franklin would automatically be one-up on his competitors when it came to bidding for an army contract.

It was time for Franklin's appointment with his doctor. The dressing on his shoulder had to be changed daily. But, as he was about to leave, Solly had one last request.

'Hey, Boss, I look for factory to buy. You trust me?' Franklin nodded.

A week later, Viscount Peter Lynell returned to England with a request to prepare his considerable contacts in the British military for Franklin's arrival in six months. He was more than happy to oblige.

Franklin accompanied him to the passenger terminal and shared a brandy with him in his stateroom on A deck. 'Don't forget to bring some prize vintages with you,' Peter added after they'd made their farewells. 'We'll educate the top brass in Australian wines. That'll get them on side.'

It was late afternoon when Franklin arrived back at The Colony House and he was tired. He'd been tired for over a week. Although the shoulder was healing well, it ached constantly, which was debilitating. Also debilitating was the camaraderie it bred between him and Sam – or rather, the camaraderie Sam chose to believe it bred. Sam told everyone about the duel, referred to Franklin as a legend, calling him 'partner' to his face and boasting of their undying friendship. The man was utterly exhausting and Franklin couldn't wait for him to go back to America.

'Come on up for a drink, partner!' Sam called. He was sitting on his balcony with a set of cronies, preparing to watch the sunset as he did each evening.

Franklin waved back with his good arm. 'Sorry, too busy,' he said and ducked inside. It wasn't as though Sam were starved for company, after all.

Safely in his suite, Franklin had no sooner sunk into an armchair than there was a tap on the door. It was Millie. She was pale, but her eyes were glowing and she looked excited.

'I need to talk to you, Franklin,' she said a little breathlessly.

'Of course, my dear.' He rose, kissed her on the cheek and crossed to the cabinet. 'May I get you a drink?'

'No, please,' she said. 'Sit down, you look weary.'

Franklin took her by the hand, led her to the sofa and they sat together. He waited. There was a hesitancy about her. 'What is it, Millie?' he asked.

She hadn't prepared a speech. She'd decided she would just come out with it. She had no idea what his reaction would be but there was such tenderness in his eyes now, surely it would be the one she'd been praying for. Indeed, he'd been very loving towards her for the past week. Ever since the duel.

'I'm going to have a baby,' she said. There. She'd done it.

His reaction was unlike any of the possibilities she'd contemplated. It was nothing. He simply stared ahead, as if he hadn't heard her.

'Franklin?' she said, finally. 'Did you hear me, I said I'm –'

'I heard you,' Franklin replied, still not looking at her. And he crossed to the cabinet and poured himself a brandy. 'How far gone?'

Millie felt a tightening in her chest. *Far gone* – what did he mean, talking like that? 'The doctor said I'm between six to eight weeks.'

'Still time to get rid of it, then.' He took a deep swig of brandy.

The tightening in Millie's chest shifted to her stomach and she felt suddenly nauseous. 'You can't mean that.'

'What are the alternatives? Marry you, is that what you want? Or acknowledge the child out of wedlock – which is it to be?' He drained the brandy, then turned and looked at her for the first time. 'I will never marry you. And I will never give my name to a bastard.'

There was no anger in Franklin's eyes. Millie would have preferred it if there had been. Instead, they were cold and dead. 'You haven't played by the rules, Millie,' he said.

The sick feeling in her stomach slowly disappeared as Millie realised what the outcome was to be. 'I won't get rid of it.' It came out a whisper but her decision was just as irrevocable as his.

'Very well.' Franklin put down his glass. 'I shall make arrangements for a monthly allowance to be transferred to a bank of your choice. Under the proviso, of course, that you are never to contact me nor ever to divulge the identity of the father of your child. Should you do so, all funds will be – '

'I don't want your money, Franklin.' Millie suddenly felt very strong. 'And I promise you, you shan't see me again.'

'Very well.' Franklin opened the door for her. 'That is your decision.'

'But you can't do this, Boss ... ' Solly was shocked almost speechless.

'I'm not telling you in order to elicit your opinion, Solly.' The eyes were still cold and dead. 'She won't accept my money but when she becomes desperate she will no doubt accept yours – for the child's sake. I am going to open a separate account from which you may draw funds and I expect you to see to her needs.'

'That I would have done anyway,' Solly answered.

Before he could continue, Franklin interrupted. 'She will need to move out of that poky little room at some stage. You will see to that too and, when you do, I have no desire to be informed of her whereabouts.'

'You're a hard man, Boss,' Solly said as Franklin turned to go. 'You want to watch one day that it does not catch up with you.' But the words hung in the air, unheard.

Franklin had closed his mind to Millie. She belonged to the past and he must concentrate on the future.

CHAPTER FIVE

Franklin and Penelope

VISCOUNT PETER LYNELL stepped out onto the balcony of his club and breathed deeply. The dozen or so friends with whom he'd just dined were all smoking cigars and he was grateful to escape the stale air of the club lounge.

London was well into spring but the evenings retained a winter nip and the breeze which now swept up from the Thames was chilly. Lights glowed along the Victoria embankment and intriguing pinpoints flickered on the black waters as the night traffic made its mysterious way up and down the river.

Peter could hear the men carousing in the lounge behind him. He even heard one of them mention the name Franklin Ross. Yes, he thought, pleased with himself, the wheels were well and truly set in motion. Everyone was looking forward to meeting the Australian.

It was the story of the duel that did it, of course. It impressed men and women alike, but particularly the top brass, and it was the military, after all, that Franklin was out to impress. Peter con-

135

gratulated himself. He'd done well. He was looking forward to Franklin's arrival next week. It would be amusing to show a novice around London.

He looked at his watch. Eleven o'clock. Time to pick up Miss Greenway from the theatre. It was the final performance of *Quality Street* and she wanted him to accompany her to the closing night party. He didn't particularly fancy a gathering of theatricals but he certainly fancied the company of Miss Greenway.

Penelope Jane Greenway had forgotten the time when she used to be Penny Green from Brighton-Le-Sands, Sydney, and she'd made sure that everyone else had forgotten too. Not that she had anything to be ashamed of. Brighton-Le-Sands was a good, middle-class suburb, her parents were good, middle-class people and her upbringing was as proper as that of every other good, middle-class girl of the twenties. But Penny knew she could do better. So, in 1933 at the age of twenty-one, she set sail for Europe aboard the SS *Invercargill* and, despite the fact that she shared an eight-berth cabin on F deck, she was Penelope Jane Greenway when she arrived. Penelope Jane Greenway, actress.

The six weeks at sea were eventful and Penelope learned a lot. Most importantly, she learned the power of her beauty. She'd been aware of it before, of course. She'd been aware throughout her childhood that she could use her beauty to bewitch her parents and their friends. During her school days, and at Ladies Business College, she'd been aware that her contemporaries wanted to be like her. And of course she'd been aware that her many young suitors were very much in love with her. But it was aboard the SS *Invercargill* that Penny realised she could use her beauty to manipulate men. It was there she discovered male lust and the fact that she could evade it, control it and turn it to her advantage.

It started with the besotted purser who smuggled her regularly into first class where she partied and flirted with the wealthy. That was when she decided to become Penelope Jane Greenway. And 'actress' sounded glamorous. It was what she wanted to become, after all, and she'd played Cecily in the Brighton-Le-Sands Amateur Theatrical Society's production of *The Importance of Being Earnest* so she knew what she was talking about.

The purser was easy enough to keep under control. She opened her mouth for his kiss, even though she detested the feel of his tongue. And she let his fingers stray briefly to her breast. But the moment he pressed his groin against hers and she felt his awful hardness, she excused herself and headed for the eight-berth cabin.

Deluded by the belief that he would one day bed her in his comfortable cabin on B deck, the purser continued to be accommodating and the following evening saw Penny once again mingling in first class.

His hopes were futile. Penny intended to keep her final gift for the man who bought the full article. Penelope Jane Greenway was a professional virgin.

London proved as easy to conquer as the SS *Invercargill*. She kept her part-time secretarial job a secret while she attended the elitist social functions to which she was invited by virtue of her beauty and the influential contacts she'd made in first class and, over the next six months, her field of contacts broadened to include actors of note and influential entrepreneurs. Finally, Penelope Jane Greenway got her break. She was cast as Poppy Dickey in *Rookery Nook* and the critics were kind.

'Miss Penelope Jane Greenway is a beguiling Poppy. Tall, slim and dressed in camiknickers, she displays a generous amount of well-proportioned leg while singing 'Yes Sir, She's My Baby'. However, with her short-cropped auburn hair, porcelain skin and perfect features, she rises above the possible tasteless nature of the role.'

A number of minor roles followed 'Poppy Dickey' and, although the critics rarely commented upon her talent, or lack thereof, they were unanimous in their appreciation of her beauty and charm.

Amongst the wealthy patrons of the theatre who fell under her spell was one Viscount Peter Lynell and, although Penelope wasn't particularly attracted to him, she allowed him to fete her with roses, after-show suppers and, when she wasn't performing, opening nights at the ballet and opera.

He was a little old for her, she felt – he must have been in his early forties at least and she was only twenty-two – but he was immensely wealthy and she actually rather liked him. Besides, he wasn't as demanding as the purser or some of the other admirers she'd encouraged. His goodnight kiss occasionally became a little persistent and his hand occasionally brushed her breast as if by mistake, but it was nothing Penny couldn't control. She was starting to feel rather tempted. Peter certainly appeared to be the wisest choice.

And then he introduced her to his friend from Sydney.

'Penelope, this is Franklin Ross. Franklin, Penelope Greenway.'

Penelope hadn't been particularly interested in meeting Peter's friend. Apparently the man had fought a duel over a woman and had been shot in the shoulder and everyone seemed to find that fascinating. Not Penelope. She thought it was a rather stupid thing to have done. Besides, Peter's friend was Australian. From Sydney, what's more, and Sydney held little interest for Penelope Greenway. As it turned out though, Franklin Ross was an extremely attractive man.

'How do you do, Miss Greenway.'

They shook hands. Penelope met the steel-blue eyes and knew immediately that the man was attracted to her. She was used to that. 'Mr Ross,' she said nonchalantly, and made to release his hand. But he held on to her for that fraction of a second too long and his eyes didn't waver and Penelope felt a little disconcerted. If he found her overwhelming, then surely he should be the one to feel uncomfortable?

'I believe you're from Sydney,' she said. Damn, she hadn't meant to bring Sydney into the conversation but he was staring at her and she had to say something. Now he'd probably ask her where

139

she came from and she'd have to admit to Brighton-Le-Sands and the respectable childhood she'd escaped.

'Yes,' was all Franklin said.

Penelope started to feel something akin to panic. No one had ever had this effect on her before and she wasn't sure if she liked it.

'Franklin's originally from South Australia.' Mercifully, Peter Lynell continued the conversation. 'His vineyards produce some of the finest wines in the country.'

'Peter tells me you're an actress, Miss Greenway.' The eyes hadn't left hers.

Before she could answer, Peter was called away to welcome some newly arrived guests. 'Excuse me,' he said, 'back in a moment. Look after Franklin for me, Penelope.' They were at a cocktail party in Peter's Chelsea townhouse.

Franklin suggested they step outside onto the small balcony which overlooked Elm Park Square. There was little Penelope could do but oblige.

'When may I look forward to seeing you in the theatre?' he asked.

Penelope focused on a park bench in the middle of the square, terribly aware that his sleeve was nearly touching her arm as he leant against the railing. 'I've just completed a season in Mr Barrie's play *Quality Street*,' she answered. 'He came to the opening night – a lovely man.' Then, before Franklin could ask her which role she'd played (it was a very minor one) she continued, 'How long are you planning to be in London, Mr Ross?'

'I leave one month from today,' he answered.

'I'm afraid I shan't be performing during that time. I'm between engagements.'

Penelope hoped he wouldn't ask her what her next engagement was, she didn't have one. But it appeared he wasn't interested anyway. For the first time, he took his eyes off her, looked up at the night sky and breathed deeply.

'The air is so different here, isn't it?'

It was sheer willpower that dragged Franklin's eyes away from Penelope Greenway. He could have sat and drunk his fill of her all night. The patrician bones, the chiselled nose, the perfect mouth which held such promise. She was graceful and feminine, and yet there was something unyielding in the set of her brow. She was a strong woman, he recognised that. And she was well-bred. Young. In fact she was ideal. And she was as attracted to him as he was to her, he could sense that.

Franklin decided to test Peter Lynell's intentions and the following night, when they were dining at Peter's club, he brought up the subject of Penelope Greenway.

'I admire your taste, dear chap,' Peter agreed. 'She's fascinating. But totally unobtainable, I'm afraid. At times I wonder whether it's worth the chase.'

'So what are your intentions then?' Franklin asked.

'My intentions? Good God, man, to get her into my bed, of course.' Franklin Ross never ceased to amaze Peter. How could a man with such style and breeding be so naive about women? He was an Australian, of course, but nevertheless . . .

Although Peter had helpfully spread the story all around London of Franklin's duel, he secretly thought the man was a fool for having taken such a risk. And for a factory girl no less! A highborn lady perhaps, but ... And now the chap was making serious inquiries as to one's intentions toward a young actress.

'She's an actress, for goodness' sake, Franklin,' he said with a touch of exasperation. 'And not a particularly good one at that. And I have the distinct feeling that she wants me to marry her before she'll acquiesce, which makes her a gold-digger into the bargain.' He signalled for the waiter to clear the table. 'We play a ridiculous game,' he continued. 'I allow her to call the tune because of course one can't force the issue. But one does get a little tired of her delusions of grandeur.'

Distasteful as Franklin found Peter's comments on Penelope, he was thrilled at the prospect that she was under no obligation. Peter's scorn for her in no way affected Franklin's view of the girl. After all, Peter came from such a blue-blooded line that little short of royalty impressed him. Franklin was convinced the man wouldn't know good, true stock if he fell over it. Typical of the English, Franklin thought, their upper classes are far too inbred – it's not healthy.

Franklin admired Penelope even more for not succumbing to the Viscount's charms. Peter Lynell was a man of extreme wealth and a dashing aristocrat into the bargain. Many a girl might have been tempted. But not Penelope. Franklin was convinced she was a virgin and, the more he thought about her, the more convinced he was that she should become his wife. He set out to court her.

No matter how often Penelope told herself she wasn't remotely interested in Franklin Ross from Sydney, Australia, it didn't work. She'd never met anyone like him before and she was immensely attracted to him.

His lack of guile was confusing. She realised that she could have told him the truth and it wouldn't have made any difference – she wasn't used to that. She *didn't* tell him the truth, of course – Penny Green had lived a life of fantasy for so long that she'd lost sight of what the truth was. She painted her pictures as vividly as she always had and Franklin quite happily believed that Penelope Jane Greenway was an extremely successful actress in the theatre and that it was only a matter of time before she would embark upon a career in films and become a star.

Franklin didn't question any of Penelope's tales about her past or her present because he had no need to. He wasn't particularly interested in what she had to say – it was the way she said it. She was beautiful, young, strong and well bred. He didn't care whether she was middle class or upper class; the stock was there, she would be a good breeder. Even her deep commitment to her career failed to concern him. She was a born mother, he could tell it. Once she had given birth, her priorities would change. Most women's did and Penelope would be no different. And the strength and dedication she now poured into her career she would later pour into her family. She would be his total support and she would rule his dynasty alongside him with a strength to equal his own.

In their own self-obsessed ways, Franklin and Penelope were falling in love, the only way that each of them knew how.

It was a Sunday and Penelope had wanted to see the ocean, so Franklin had hired a chauffeured limousine to take them to Worthing for the day.

For the past fortnight he'd been hiring transport rather than availing himself of Peter Lynell's standing offer: 'One of my vehicles and a driver is at your disposal any time, dear chap, feel free.' It was a generous gesture, but Franklin was highly critical of Peter's cavalier attitude towards Penelope.

'Good God, man, you're mad,' he'd said when Franklin had tentatively mentioned his desire to court her. Then he'd shrugged and added, 'Good luck'. Franklin had found his tone rather insulting.

Worthing was a pretty coastal town with stone cottages in the back streets, grand holiday houses along the ocean front and an impressive stretch of promenade and pebbled beach.

Franklin gave the driver a handsome tip, told him to amuse himself for two hours and instructed him to have a chilled bottle of champagne awaiting them on their return. Then he and Penny lunched at a little tea house overlooking the sea and Penny found herself actually admitting that Worthing reminded her of Brighton-Le-Sands.

'I only ever think of Australia when I'm by the

144

sea,' she said, 'and then I remember the beautiful blue bay and the little boats and I think of my childhood.'

It was the most truthful admission Penny had made to anyone, including herself, in years.

They walked all the way along the promenade, passing other couples, old and young. Passing families and tourists and locals. Worthing promenade on a Sunday was a popular spot. And then the houses thinned out and there were no more people and Franklin kissed her.

He'd kissed her before. Several times, when he was saying goodnight. But his tongue never explored her mouth and his hand never sought her breast, even though she would have allowed it. Franklin always exercised control and Penny was grateful for that. This time was different though. This time she wanted him to demand a little more.

And Franklin certainly wanted more. Much more. He ached for her. But he kept his distance so that she wouldn't feel his erection, his hands avoided the swell of her breasts and, as he felt her mouth start to respond hungrily to his kiss, he broke the embrace.

'Will you marry me, Penelope?' he asked.

Penny looked back at him, somewhat shaken. She wasn't shaken by the actual proposal; she'd been more or less expecting that. She was shaken by her response to the kiss. It was the first time she'd wanted a kiss to continue. It was the first time a kiss hadn't been simply the return of a favour, or a promise of things to come in order to maintain the status quo. And it was the first time she hadn't been the one to stop the embrace. She was confused and off-balance and not at all sure that she liked someone else calling the tune.

'Oh,' she murmured, pretending to be taken aback by the proposal and buying time. She looked out at a ship on the far distant horizon. 'I don't know what to say, Franklin.' When she felt she had regained her composure, she turned. 'Shall we go back to the car?' she suggested gently.

Neither of them spoke during the long walk back along the promenade. The driver was waiting for them and Franklin instructed him to open the bottle of champagne.

'Well?' he asked finally, returning the bottle to its bucket and handing Penelope a glass. 'Will you marry me?' He leaned back and watched her as the car started slowly wending its way through the streets of Worthing.

Having now fully regained her composure Penelope was in no quandary as to her answer. 'You would want me to return to Australia, wouldn't you, Franklin?'

'Naturally. That's where my home is. My work. My properties.'

'Then it's impossible, I'm afraid.' She smiled sadly. 'My career, you see. I couldn't give up my career.'

The reply didn't altogether surprise Franklin and he was not discouraged by it. 'I'm willing to wait,' he said.

But Penelope shook her head. 'There will never be a career for me in Australia,' she answered. 'It's not a matter of time.'

Inwardly, Franklin disagreed with her. She was very young and he was sure that the desire to have her own home, to be a mother, would eventually win out. Besides, he'd felt that moment of hunger in her as her mouth sought his and he knew, if he kept his distance, it would only be a matter of time before she would want him as much as he wanted her. All he had to do was speed up the process – he didn't want to wait too long. It suddenly occurred to him.

'If I could advance your career,' he asked, 'would you marry me?'

Penelope looked at him closely. Was he serious? Yes, he was. She took her time answering. 'You know how extremely fond I am of you, Franklin,' she said, 'and you know how important my career is to me. If it were at all possible to combine the two ... ' She smiled charmingly and Franklin thought she had never looked more beautiful. ' ... it's greedy of me, isn't it ... but, if I could do that, then yes, I would marry you.'

'So be it.' Franklin toasted her and downed his champagne in one draught.

As soon as Franklin got back to London, he sent a telegraphic cable to the United States. Then he cancelled his passage to Australia and waited for Samuel Crockett's reply.

The following afternoon he was on Penelope's front doorstep. 'How soon can you leave for America?' he asked.

'America?'

'Well, you want to be in movies, don't you?' And he handed her Sam's return wire. *Expect you both as house guests as soon as possible* STOP *Of course there will be a movie role for your fiancee* STOP *Eagerly await details of your arrival* STOP *Samuel David Crockett, Minotaur Movies, Hollywood.*

Wide-eyed, Penelope looked from the telegraphic cable to Franklin.

'May I presume we are now officially engaged?' he asked.

Ten days later, they sailed for America on the *Queen Mary*. Franklin had booked separate cabins but Penelope was wearing an extremely expensive diamond ring on the third finger of her left hand.

'I expect to be the first person on the invitation list,' Peter Lynell said as they were about to board, and he shook Franklin's hand warmly. 'Just as soon as you set the date.' Peter had changed his attitude towards Penelope and whatever rift had crept into his friendship with Franklin was now well and truly healed.

'I'm deeply grateful to you, Peter. For everything.' Franklin meant it. His business in London had gone exceedingly well and he considered Peter Lynell directly responsible for his success. Through Peter he had acquired valuable contacts in the Home Office and had already secured an army contract for the supply of a range of leathergoods.

Samuel Crockett lived in Bel-Air and his house was exactly as Franklin had envisaged. It was huge and opulent – ostentatious perhaps, but not in bad taste. In fact the furnishings and decorations were of the highest quality. It was a mansion, and testimony to Samuel Crockett's wealth, complete with kidney-shaped swimming pool, outdoor tennis courts, billiards room, and private movie theatre.

Sam himself was as big and as loud and as effusive as ever – and just as arrogant. But not with Franklin. Franklin Ross was the one man who had earned Sam's respect, the one man to whom he owed his life – and big Sam Crockett wasn't ashamed to admit it.

Together with his wife, Lucy-Mae, Sam was a generous host and the two of them made Franklin and Penelope feel immediately welcome.

'I've heard all about you, Mr Ross. Now you don't mind if I call you Franklin, do you?' Lucy-Mae dragged his face down to hers, kissing him on both cheeks and, before Franklin could answer, she took Penelope's hands in her own and stood back in open admiration. 'Why, Penelope, you're pretty as a picture, I swear. Welcome to you both.' More kisses on Penelope's cheeks, then came introductions to Davy Junior.

Sam hoisted the child up with one hand, holding him aloft like a sack of potatoes, and the two-year-old squealed with delight. He was a solid, beefy infant who held every promise of growing into a replica of his father.

Lucy-Mae wasn't beefy. Despite the fact that she was nearly seven months pregnant, she was tiny and birdlike, pretty in a slightly beaky way, with eyes that darted about, not missing a thing. But Lucy-Mae wasn't fragile. She wore gold bracelets that jangled when she moved and she was extremely confident and assured of her place in the scheme of things. She was Sam Crockett's wife, mother to his son and heir, and just about to give birth to his second child. Furthermore, she ran his home and household staff with the precision of a sergeant major and entertained his guests with true Southern hospitality and style. It never occurred to Lucy-Mae that her existence was in any way subservient and she would have been appalled if anyone had suggested it.

Penelope obviously passed muster with Sam, and for a brief moment Franklin couldn't help but compare the respect he afforded her with his insulting treatment of Millie. But it was only a fleeting thought – Millie Tingwell was rarely on Franklin's mind. He had no regrets about his actions and no desire to discover the sex of the child she must have given birth to since his departure from Australia. The rare thoughts he had of her were purely carnal and a result of his state of celibacy.

Although Sam was indeed aware that Penelope was a good middle-class girl, the respect he afforded her was actually part and parcel of the respect he afforded Franklin. Over the ensuing weeks, however, he recognised Penelope's strength and decided that if the girl could rid herself of her silly career fixation, she would make a fine wife for Franklin.

Several days after their arrival, Sam took them on a guided tour of the elite areas, pointing out the homes of the Hollywood stars. Most of them were mansions nearly as grand as Sam's and Franklin realised that to live like this was de rigeur in the upper echelons of Tinsel Town. He also realised that he vastly preferred the elegance of The Colony House.

'HOLLYWOODLAND – you see that?' Sam had instructed the driver to take them to Mount Lee and now he pointed to the massive letters which successfully destroyed the beauty of the virgin hillside. 'Just about sums up this town,' he said. 'They all come here like it's some special fairyland that's going to make their dreams come true.'

He again indicated the sign. 'That there's become quite a favourite suicide spot ever since a kid who couldn't make it threw herself off the "D" a few years back. A whole heap of them have done it since. They just can't get it through their skulls that movies aren't magic, movies are money.'

'Which "D"?' Penny asked.

'Pardon?' Sam looked at her blankly.

'Which "D" did she jump off?'

'The one at the end, I do believe.'

Sam was true to his word and, less than a fortnight after they arrived, Penelope Jane Greenway was tested at the Minotaur studios.

The test was a formality only, the studio executives having been instructed that Penelope was to be cast regardless of the outcome. They gave their customary sigh of resignation at the waste of time and prepared to shove her somewhere in the background of Minotaur's latest low-budget B-grade.

But the test was surprisingly successful. It revealed that Penelope Jane Greenway's beauty and charm did not escape the camera lens and, as with the several stage productions in which she'd performed, an absence of talent did not necessarily put her out of the running.

'She could well play the third blonde in the Thelma Todd movie,' the director said to the producer. 'She's the same build as Thelma – stick a blonde wig on her and she'd be perfect.'

True Blonde was a vehicle Minotaur had purchased hoping to attract Jean Harlow. They hadn't, but, after lengthy negotiations, they'd managed to entice Thelma Todd away from the Hal Roach farce she'd been about to accept, and they were due to go into production in three months' time. As *True Blonde* was a comedy about mistaken identity, the next step was to find three blondes who could easily be mistaken for Thelma. They'd found two and Penelope appeared to be an ideal number three.

'It's a nice cameo role, number three,' the producer said with a touch of uncertainty. 'We wouldn't want her to fuck it up. Let's shove her in the party scene of *Harlequin Horror* and see how she goes.'

Two weeks later, Penelope was engaged to play a 'guest' in the final scene of a low-budget horror film which the studio was just completing. Along with twenty other people in harlequin costumes she was required to witness a particularly horrific murder.

The movie was being shot in a grubby old tin shed in the backlot behind the modern studios. The tin shed, fondly referred to as 'The Sweatbox', had been the original studio in which a string of successful silent films had been made in the twenties. When the talkies arrived and many studios

152

found themselves on the brink of extinction, it was Sam Crockett who stepped in and saved Minotaur and the old tin shed. He bought the company for a song and, although he didn't know much about movies, he appointed people who did. Minotaur blossomed, a whole new studio complex was built and it was only the old tin shed itself which was threatened with extinction. However, a band of die-hards who had survived the transition from silent movies to sound appealed to Sam's senti-mentality and now the old studio remained as a symbol of a bygone era. But Sam demanded that it earn its keep, so he set up a sound stage there. All year round, Minotaur's cheapies were churned out of the old tin shed.

During summer, every single cast and crew member who worked in The Sweatbox dropped at least half a stone, and a new term was born into a profession which thrived on in-house slang. When actors were out of work they were 'resting' and when they were filming a low-budget movie for Minotaur they were 'dieting'. To the many actors and crew who spent their entire lives 'dieting', the term became one of endearment. Why sneer? There was quite a lucrative living to be made out of 'dieting'.

The party scene of *Harlequin Horror* was a garden setting and the day's shoot included a number of fetching shots of Penelope. Penelope peering from behind an imitation Trevi Fountain. Penelope leaning up against a palm tree. There was even a close-up of Penelope looking attrac-tively horrified as a severed jugular gushed forth copious quantities of blood.

The close-up was the true test. The director, aware that the censorship laws wouldn't allow him to have the screen awash with blood, needed to cut away from the slit throat to the reactions of the onlookers.

'You must reflect the horror of what you see,' he instructed Penelope when it was her turn and, while the make-up artist prepared her face for the close-up, he described in ghastly graphic detail what would happen when a person's jugular vein was severed.

To inspire her to greater heights, he repeated the description during the shooting of the close-up, but Penelope found it difficult to equate his grisly details with the semidecapitated wax dummy lying on the fake grass beside the fake fountain under the fake palm tree.

'You're horrified,' the director said. 'As you watch, the blood spurts from his open neck like water from a burst main . . . ' The dummy stared up at her with an idiotic grin on its face. 'You're repulsed,' the director continued. 'The blood is spouting with such force it's like the jets of the fountain behind him . . . ' Penelope could see the stagehand, sweat pouring from his brow, fiend-ishly working the water pump which fed the Trevi fountain. 'His body is twitching in death. His blood splatters the grass and the nearby palm tree like spray from a sprinkler . . . ' The director very much believed in the inspirational power of the metaphor.

Penelope was doing her best. She looked at the palm tree and tried to imagine it splattered with blood. But the palm tree was a cut-out, propped up with a sandbag. She'd made the mistake of leaning against it in an earlier shot.

'No, don't *lean*,' the director had shouted.

'But you told me to.'

'No, honey, *pretend*. Don't lean. Just *pretend* to lean.'

Everything was pretend and Penny found it a little confusing. In the theatre she'd been accustomed to weeks of rehearsals where actors discussed sub-text and motivation and inter-relationships. In Hollywood it appeared such depth wasn't necessary.

Confusing it may have been, but it was also hugely exciting and Penny decided if it was pretend they wanted, then pretend they'd get. She looked down at the dummy and started pretending for all she was worth.

Ten minutes later, the director tried a different tack. 'Tell you what, sweetheart, we'll give it another go and this time around let's do nothing, OK?'

'Nothing?'

'That's right. Don't move a muscle. Just stare at the body.'

'But what about the blood?'

'Forget about the blood, don't think about the blood, don't think about anything. Just stare at the body.'

So Penelope stared. And she continued to stare while the camera moved in closer and closer and closer.

'Love it. Stunning. Love it.' The producer and the

155

director were sitting in the darkened theatrette watching Penelope's face on the screen as the camera moved in closer and closer on the porcelain skin, the clear brow, the wide, hazel-green eyes and the perfect mouth, lips unwittingly parted.

'Freeze that, Joe,' the director called to the projectionist. 'We can use a still of that close-up for the publicity campaign. "What did the girl see? – buy a ticket to *Harlequin Horror* and find out".'

The producer nodded in agreement. 'Good idea. I'll get publicity on to it.'

'You can read into that face whatever you want to read into it,' the director continued enthusiastically. 'The secret is to stop the girl trying to act.'

The producer nodded again. 'Give her the third blonde.'

'I got the job! Oh, Franklin, I got the job!'

Franklin had been secretly hoping that she wouldn't, but the sheer joy in Penelope's face made him glad that she had.

'And it's a big-budget movie. Well, middle, really,' she corrected herself; one had to be truthful. 'It means I'm not dieting any more, I'm out of The Sweatbox.' Penelope was always quick to pick up on the current jargon.

'But you don't need to diet.'

'Some people work in The Sweatbox for years – their whole lives even – and I'm out in just one movie.'

'Congratulations, my darling.' Franklin gave up

trying to work out what she was talking about. That evening they did the rounds of the nightspots Sam recommended. Aperitifs at the Seven Seas, dinner at the Brown Derby then on to the Trocadero, and ending up at the Cotton Club. Everywhere they went Penelope recognised faces she'd seen on the screen. It was the kind of evening she adored and Franklin loathed, but he was prepared to humour her.

The following day they discussed their plans. Although *True Blonde* didn't go into production for two months, Penelope was on call for costume and wig fittings, publicity stills and numerous other studio requirements. Franklin needed to return to Sydney.

'When you finish filming,' he said, 'you're to join me in Australia. It'll be an autumn wedding, my darling, and then – '

'But Franklin ... my career. I told you ... '

'I know, I know, don't worry, I've planned it all perfectly. We'll come back together – well before the premiere and in time for your promotional tour.' Franklin smiled as he put an arm around her. 'See? I've learned all the correct terminology. I checked things through with Sam and they intend to finish shooting the movie by February, then there's several months of postproduction before you're required for promotions. Time for us to marry in Sydney and honeymoon on the way back. Just think! An autumn wedding and then a sea voyage, the two of us, in the finest stateroom, aboard the finest passenger vessel ever to travel the Seven Seas. What do you say?'

There was very little Penelope *could* say. She

didn't relish the thought of returning to Australia but there was no longer any question in her mind that she did want to marry Franklin. She gave in with good grace.

'That sounds perfect, my darling,' she said. They kissed deeply and, as usual, Penelope wanted the kiss to go further. Ever since that day in Worthing she'd been waiting for Franklin to demand a little more but he never did.

Franklin had not only 'checked things through' with Sam, he had asked Sam's advice about Penelope's apparent obsession with her career. They'd discussed the whole situation in depth.

'How do I get her over this movie craze, Sam? I know she loves me, I can feel it, but I'm going to have one hell of a battle getting her back to Australia.'

Sam had the perfect answer to the immediate problem. During the production break Franklin was to take Penelope to Sydney and marry her. And as to the future, well Sam's solution seemed to be equally simple.

'Get her pregnant as soon possible,' he said. 'That'll do it.'

A while back, Franklin would have agreed but now he wasn't so sure. The studio had held a party to introduce the cast of *True Blonde* to each other and he had watched Penelope as she posed for publicity shots with Thelma Todd and the other two actresses. She looked radiant – far and away the most beautiful of the four women, despite the blonde wig she was wearing for the shots, which Franklin found loathsome. There was no possible way she could follow a career path if she was to marry him and bear his children but he didn't want to break her heart.

Sam knew that Franklin was in a dilemma, although personally he couldn't see that there was a problem. 'You've given the little lady a taste of a career. Fine. Now get her pregnant and she'll soon forget about making movies, I swear.'

When Franklin still appeared unsure, Sam racked his brains further. 'Course there is one other possiblity. It would give you control of the situation and make her feel like she had a career.'

'What's that?'

'Buy into a film studio in Sydney.' Franklin stared at him, bewildered. 'You don't need to know anything about the business,' Sam continued. 'You just hire the people who do.'

Then he warmed to his theme – he was talking money now and Sam enjoyed talking money. 'There's a movie boom about to happen, partner. Thirty-five has been a good year. The post-Depression struggle is over and by my reckoning mid-thirty-six'll see the exhibitors' gross receipts hit the highest peak in years. And it's a world-wide trend, I tell you, bound to flow through to Australia.

'A lot of people have lost a lot of money making movies,' Sam admitted, 'and I'm certainly not advising you to sink a fortune into the business. But your New South Wales government has just proclaimed a Quota Act to encourage Australian entrepreneurs – that's a good sign for your local industry. And I could certainly open doors for you with Twentieth Century Fox. They control distribution in Australia,' he explained, 'so you'd be off to a damn fine start.'

'You seem to have made quite a study of the situation, Sam.' It was a question more than anything.

'Yep, sure have. That's what I was doing down there last year. There's been some good movies come out of Sydney recently and a number of us are keeping our eye on you Australians. We reckon you might be heading to establish an international film industry. And that's fine of course, good luck to you all. Just so long as you make your movies with a local flavour.' He grinned patronisingly. 'It wouldn't do to try and compete with Hollywood now.'

Franklin nodded. The whole idea was certainly an option in the solving of the Penelope dilemma, although he rather hoped such drastic action would not be necessary.

'Thank you, Sam, I'll bear it all in mind.'

Lucy-Mae wouldn't hear of Franklin renting an apartment for Penelope or setting her up in an hotel while he was away. 'Why, I couldn't dream of such a thing,' she insisted, her bracelets jangling alarmingly. 'Penelope's our house guest and I, for one, would be deeply insulted if she didn't accept our hospitality in the spirit in which it is offered.'

She darted a birdlike frown at Sam who took up his cue immediately. 'Lucy-Mae is quite right, Franklin – don't you even suggest such a thing.' The home-front was Lucy-Mae's realm and the one area where Sam always did as he was told.

* * *

Penelope wept quietly as she and Franklin made their farewells. He was touched and gratified and, as he gently kissed Penelope, he felt a deep and sincere love for her. 'It's barely five months, my darling, and then you'll be aboard a ship home and we'll be married in March.'

Penelope didn't like the sound of 'home'. Sydney was not 'home' to her, but Franklin had promised they would return to America immediately after the wedding and he never broke his promises. She continued her gentle weep, aware that he was enjoying it. To her, it was a mere indulgence and she could easily have stopped. But it was true she would miss him and, with his strong, protective arms around her, she allowed herself to feel vulnerable.

'You won't be with me for Christmas,' she sobbed.

'Not this time. But we'll have every Christmas together for the rest of our lives, my darling.' And he stroked her hair comfortingly.

Franklin didn't really enjoy the forty-day sea voyage to Sydney. It wasn't just that he missed Penelope; he was anxious to get back to work. He'd maintained cable contact with Solly at The Colony House and, via the Quilpie post office, with Kevin Everard, the station manager at Mandinulla, and everything appeared to be going smoothly. Between Solly and Gustave, The Colony House was in good hands, and as far as Mandinulla was concerned, Franklin and Sam had both agreed that Kevin Everard (known as Never-Never

161

because he refused to go near a city) was far better left on his own. Nonetheless Franklin missed the activity. He missed being at the hub of things, and he very much wanted to pave the way with the Australian military. Peter Lynell's contacts had not only confirmed the probability of war but the fact that the British military was well and truly in preparation for it.

While Franklin impatiently paced the promenade deck of the SS *Pacific Star* watching his fellow passengers enjoy the tranquillity of the endless ocean, Penelope threw herself joyfully into the Hollywood scene.

She was flattered when Thelma Todd paid her far more attention than she did the actresses cast as Blondes One and Two. Indeed, Thelma even invited her out nightclubbing on several occasions when she was 'doing the town' with a gang of her cronies.

Penelope was aware that several of the cronies were 'gangster types' but they were suave, snappy dressers who threw money around like confetti, all of which made them glamorous. And Penelope was at a stage in her life where she was very impressed by glamour.

Little did she realise that Thelma Todd was, in turn, rather impressed by Penelope Jane Greenway and her background. The studio publicity department had concocted an imposing biography, leaning heavily on Penelope's theatrical experience in London's West End.

The biography wasn't exactly a lie but it intimated that she'd starred in every production in which she'd appeared and there were also pictures (copies of which were supplied to the department by Penelope) of her with Noel Coward, Gertie Lawrence and Jessie Matthews. She neglected to tell anyone they were taken at a party thrown by Peter Lynell. There was even a photograph of Donald Wolfit kissing her hand – again, she didn't tell anyone it was the one and only time she'd met him. It was the opening night of *Quality Street* when she'd gone with the gang to the Garrick Club. The overall inference was that Penelope had starred on the legitimate stage with the British theatrical elite.

Thelma was further impressed by Penelope Jane Greenway herself. The regality of her. The tall, slim body, the patrician face and, above all, the mid-Atlantic accent. Thelma enjoyed introducing such a class act to her friends – it was good for her image.

Sam gave Penelope a gentle warning about Thelma's friends. 'I wouldn't want you to be alone with some of those characters, my dear. They're a pretty racy set and I feel responsible for you with Franklin away.'

But Penelope laughed it off. 'Bless you, Sam, I can look after myself.' She gave him a grateful peck on the cheek. 'We're always out in a crowd and they always behave like gentlemen, each and every one of them, I assure you.'

A fortnight before Christmas, Minotaur threw an open-house party at the Beverly Hills mansion of one of its executives. Sam never offered his home for such events – he didn't enjoy actors en masse

163

and he liked to be able to make a quick escape. Besides, there was always a number of the studio hierarchy queueing up for the privilege of hosting a party – their wives liked to boast that Tyrone Power or Gary Cooper or Joan Crawford had been to their homes.

Thelma took it upon herself to invite several of her friends, including 'Lucky' Jim Lonetti. Lonetti was a favourite of Penelope's. Whenever she'd gone out with Thelma's crowd he'd been most attentive and she knew he was deeply attracted to her. He was handsome in a brooding Sicilian way and she enjoyed flirting with him – it was harmless, after all, and he always treated her with great respect.

'Jim. Hello. What a nice surprise.' She refused to call him Lucky. 'It sounds like something out of a gangster movie,' she'd said when they first met.

'Penelope.' He kissed her hand. She always liked that.

It was a good party and Penelope was enjoying herself. Grateful for the opportunity to meet the hierarchy, she had worked hard to create a good impression. She'd spent time with Sam, Lucy-Mae and several members of the board. And she'd chatted to Thelma Todd, the producer, the director and, finally, to Blondes One and Two.

Having observed protocol, and in the correct order, Penelope allowed herself a dance with Jim and then let him escort her to the banquet room where they served each other delicacies from the gigantic buffet table. She laughed as she opened her mouth to accept the wedge of toast with Beluga caviar.

After she'd eaten, she excused herself and adjourned to one of the many powder rooms to freshen her make-up. Since her arrival in Hollywood, Penelope had been appalled to witness women applying their lipstick in public, and had vowed she would never do such a thing.

Although it was early, people were starting to get drunk and cigarette and cigar smoke was permeating the rooms. For Penelope, who didn't drink (apart from the odd glass of champagne) or smoke, it was time to get some fresh air. Besides, she wanted to explore the gardens. They were even more impressive than Sam and Lucy-Mae's.

The air was biting but invigorating and she clasped her wrap tightly about her as she set off on her exploration. Although it was dark, the paths were easy to follow – throughout the huge landscaped gardens, various trees, rockeries, and statues were floodlit.

It was a night-time fairyland and Penelope was enchanted. There was a little wooden bridge over a floodlit pond stocked with huge, golden carp. She stood there for a full ten minutes before the cold drove her on.

And then she came to a pergola. She could hear noises. Feverish, wet noises. A man's guttural breathing. A woman's moans, desperately demanding fulfilment. And there they were right in front of her, bucking and plunging and writhing and, in the reflected glow from the garden, Penelope could plainly see the man's buttocks as they pounded frenziedly between the woman's out-stretched thighs.

Penelope was shocked at the audacity of the couple. How could they be so brazen? Anyone could see them. She was also horrified. Horrified at the loveless desperation she was witnessing. It was ugly. Wasn't lovemaking supposed to be a caring exchange? But she was also fascinated.

Quietly, she stepped back into the shadows. She wanted to leave, but she couldn't. She even averted her eyes. But she couldn't escape the noises. And now the woman was gasping, as though she was in pain. Faster and louder and faster and louder, and then time suddenly stood still ... there was no sound from her at all. Penelope could hear the thrusts and grunts of the man as he struggled towards his own climax, but what was happening for the woman? Was this what it was like? Then the woman gave an ecstatic moan, followed by waves of strange quivering sounds from the back of her throat.

She backed further into the dark. Confused, she turned to go, panic setting in. She had to get away from the place before the couple saw that she'd been watching. How humiliating. She hurried back towards the party.

She was nearly at the house – she could see the lights of the main driveway ahead, and the sea of parked cars – when a voice from out of the dark stopped her. 'Penelope.' She whirled about, star-tled. 'I've been looking for you.' Lucky Jim Lonetti stepped out of the shadows.

'Oh, Jim,' she gasped. 'You frightened me.'

He came up to her and took her by the arm,

presumably to escort her back to the party. 'Now why on earth would you be frightened of me, Penelope?'

She smiled and started to walk towards the driveway and the lights and the cars, but his hand was suddenly like steel. 'You were watching them, weren't you?' She stared back at him. 'I saw you watching them. You liked it, didn't you? Would you like it to be you?'

Penelope felt more humiliated than frightened. Humiliated and angry. 'I don't know what you mean. And I'd like you to take me back to the house . . . right now.'

'Would you? You'd like me to take you now? Right now? Well I guess I'd better do as I'm told, hadn't I?'

A set of car headlights was switched on in the main drive. They shone down the garden path, for a moment dazzling them. Lucky dragged her roughly into the shadows and Penelope realised that now was the time to be frightened.

'Jim, please.' She tried to reason. 'You're behaving ridiculously; you've had too much to drink. Now come back to the party.'

'Come on, baby. Admit it. You want it.' He'd forced her up against a tree and one hand was holding her by the throat while the other ripped at her blouse. She felt the buttons tear away, then his hand on her breast and, all the while, his groin was thrusting at her.

'Stop it! For God's sake, stop it!' She tried desperately to push him away. 'Please, Jim! Please!'

'Shut up, bitch!' There was an explosion in her head as he smashed her hard across the face. She stopped resisting and stared at him, in a state of shock. 'That's better,' he said quietly. 'Now why don't you call me Lucky like everybody else, eh?' He still had her by the throat and his free hand was now pulling up her skirt.

'Cock-teasing sluts aren't allowed to call me Jim.' His voice was terrifyingly soft and his face was no more than an inch from hers. 'Only my mother calls me Jim.' She whimpered as she felt her panties tear. 'Thought you could get away with it, didn't you? Giving me the eye and flashing your goods and never paying out. He was undoing the buckle of his belt. 'Cunts like you deserve everything they get.'

'Leave it right there, buddy.'

Sam was standing on the path only several yards away. In his hand was the gleaming Colt .38 revolver.

Lonetti's hand instinctively slid towards the breast of his jacket and the shoulder holster he always wore.

'I wouldn't even think about it if I were you.' Sam extended his arm and the barrel of the gun pointed unwavering at the bridge of Lonetti's nose. 'In fact, I suggest that you hightail it out of here just as quick as you can,' he said. 'And I also suggest that you tell Thelma we don't want your sort anywhere around Minotaur again. Not at the studios, or mixing with the employees – is that understood?'

Lonetti didn't answer but he stared at Penelope as he did up his belt buckle. 'You'll keep,' he muttered and then he left, Sam watching him every inch of the way. It was only when the man was well out of sight that Sam turned to Penelope. 'I

168

guess I don't need to say I told you so.'

The relief was too much for Penelope. She burst into tears and was gathered into Sam's huge embrace. 'Come along now, little lady. You've learnt your lesson. There's no real harm done.' And he escorted her to the waiting car with its headlights still on and an anxious Lucy-Mae waiting in the passenger seat. 'Just as well we decided to leave when we did, eh?'

Penelope calmed down during the drive home and begged Sam and Lucy-Mae not to tell Franklin of the night's events. 'He'd only worry,' she said. 'And I promise I won't associate with Thelma's friends any more.' She wasn't sure why she didn't want Franklin to know. There were so many things she needed to sort out in her own head, she didn't want the confusion of having to explain things to him.

She had most certainly learned a vital lesson, though. Not only was flirting dangerous, it was unnecessary. After all, she was going to marry Franklin – she didn't need any more favours from men.

But the sounds of the woman's ecstasy still rang in her mind – and though she hated to admit it, Lucky Jim Lonetti had been right in a way. She wanted it. She wanted to know what it was like to experience what the woman in the garden had felt. She remembered the kiss on the beachside at Worthing and the way she'd felt whenever Franklin had kissed her since. She wanted more. She wanted the touch of his hands on her, she wanted ... Suddenly, Penelope longed for Franklin.

When the *Pacific Star* docked in Sydney, Solly was there to meet Franklin. Hanging off his arm was a dark-haired, buxom woman in her late twenties.

'You think you are the only one to fall in love, Boss?' he grinned. 'This is Zofia – isn't she beautiful? Maybe we make a double wedding, eh?'

'Hello, Zofia. You're a brave woman to take on Solly.' Franklin kissed her hand lightly and she laughed and clutched Solly all the more tightly.

'She don't speak such good English yet but she is learning.'

Solly didn't stop talking all the way to The Colony House. It appeared Zofia came from a little town near his own childhood home in Poland. He was deeply in love with her. She worked hard with him side by side in his shop, which had never seen such a profit. She had stopped him gambling and he intended to marry her just as soon as possible.

The week after Franklin's return, two cables arrived from America. There was nothing sinister about the first: *Healthy baby girl, Louisa Mae* STOP *Seven pounds two ounces* STOP *Born Saturday one am.* – but the second, delivered two days later, was chilling: *Thelma Todd murdered* STOP *Movie cancelled* STOP *Penelope distraught* STOP *Suggest immediate return* STOP

Franklin instantly set about hiring an aviator and aircraft. After several inquiries he found Frederick Howell, a young pilot who had been involved with Kingsford-Smith and Ulm in the forming of their short-lived Australian National Airways Company. Howell was obsessed with Ulm's plan to set up a regular airmail service across the Pacific, despire the fact that Ulm himself had died investigating the possibilities only one year previously.

Young Frederick Howell had made several trips across the Pacific since the death of Ulm and he seized Franklin's offer with great alacrity. Five thousand pounds! To make a flight he would have been prepared to make for nothing! To be paid to investigate his own business opportunities! Frederick suggested they take off in three days' time.

The morning before their departure, The Colony House receptionist rang through to Franklin's suite to announce a visitor.

'Have her shown up immediately,' Franklin said. 'And have some coffee and refreshments prepared.'

Several minutes later there was a tap on the door. 'Miss Juillard, Mr Franklin,' the house butler announced.

'Gaby,' he said, as he embraced her warmly. 'Come in.'

She smiled her attractive smile and allowed him to take her parasol. 'Thank you, Franklin. It is so hot, is it not?' She seated herself in the chair Franklin indicated and took a small ivory fan from her purse. 'All these years and never have I become accustomed to Sydney summers.'

She was still an attractive woman, still slim and

171

elegant, but was starting to look her age, Franklin thought. And she looked tired. Very tired.

'How have you been, Gaby?'

'I have been well.' She decided to come straight to the point. 'Not so your Aunt Catherine, I'm afraid. She has cancer, Franklin. She is dying.'

'I'm sorry to hear that,' he said.

'Yes.' Gaby gave a weary sigh. She'd cried enough; there was no more energy left to be spent on tears. 'I know that she would dearly love to see you.' Than she hastily added. 'If you don't wish to come you will not disappoint her. I have said nothing.'

Franklin stared down at the bed, trying to equate the emaciated form in it with the aggressive, arrogant, dominating presence he remembered as his aunt. The skin hung from the once large frame in folds; so much skin with nothing to fill it – even the bones themselves seemed to have shrunk.

'I'm sorry,' Gaby whispered, 'it's not one of her good days.' She felt deeply disappointed. Sometimes Catherine was so lucid and, when she was, she was wonderful. 'I regret nothing, Gaby,' she would say. 'I know you feel angry, I know you blame the drugs. But don't. I've led my life the way I chose – I've been selfish and indulgent and I've possibly cheated us of some of our years together, but don't make me regret that, my darling.' Then she would attempt to wipe away Gaby's tears. And they would laugh about the fact that, even on her deathbed, Catherine was laying down the law. 'Rather like father,' Catherine said.

172

And now, with Franklin by her side, Catherine was in her drug-induced twilight world. Gaby wondered, vaguely, whether it might be deliberate.

Nevertheless, Gaby chatted on. Mainly about Franklin's impending wedding and Franklin, awkwardly, nodded agreement and performed the way he thought Gaby wanted him to perform, all the while wishing he could get out.

Then, just as they were about to leave, Catherine's eyes found their focus. 'Be kind to your wife, Franklin.' The voice was weak and rasping but the strength of purpose was undeniable.

It came as a surprise to him and he simply stared back.

'It's not her fault that you don't like women.'

Franklin continued to stare and Gaby felt the prickle of tears she'd long thought had dried up.

'It's my one regret,' Catherine said. 'That day.'

There was a moment when nobody said anything. Franklin supposed it was his turn to speak, but he felt angry. What was he expected to say? He didn't want to think of that hideous day. How dare the woman remind him? Even on her deathbed she had to taunt him. How dare she?

It was Gaby who broke the silence. 'You have nothing to regret, Catherine. Nothing at all.' She turned to go. 'Come along, Franklin, Catherine needs her rest.'

They said little at the door. Gaby wished him bon voyage and promised to attend the wedding when he returned. She felt glad. She knew that Catherine, in acknowledging her regret, had relieved herself of a long-standing guilt. It was a pity that Franklin hadn't been able to openly absolve his aunt but that was, after all, his tragedy, wasn't it? Gaby felt happy for Catherine.

The nine-day flight to America with Frederick Howell was terrifying – terrifying, exhilarating and exhausting. Infected by the madness of aviation, Franklin loved every minute of it. They flew via Brisbane, New Caledonia, Fiji, Western Samoa and the Hawaiian Islands and landed in California at lunchtime on New Year's Eve.

Word had got out and members of the press were there to meet them but the indomitable Howell refused to stay any length of time. He had meetings in Sacramento with his business associates, he said, and the Governor of California, and a representative of the US Mail Service.

Franklin stood with the others on the airstrip and watched the Avro Ten climb its way back into the sky, turn, and head north.

The following day, the American newspapers carried the full story of the amazing flight made by the two Australians. They also carried the latest reports on the murder of Thelma Todd, even though it had been over a fortnight since her body had been found slumped in her car.

There was much talk about a row she'd had with her lover after leaving the Trocadero late on the night of her murder but, although the press insinuated and although friends assumed, there

174

was not one shred of evidence. Police statements insisted that 'an early conviction was expected', but days went by, and then weeks. Thelma Todd's murder was destined to remain one of the great Hollywood mysteries.

Penelope was deeply upset and, to Franklin's relief, more than happy to quit the country for a while. She'd been heavily questioned by the police and had found the whole business extremely sordid. The thought of pretty, blonde, fun-loving Thelma coming to such a grisly end had horrified her. More horrifying had been the memory of Lucky Jim Lonetti and that night in the garden. Could he have been the one? Penelope wondered. Could she herself have been under a similar threat? It didn't bear contemplation.

Penelope wanted to be somewhere safe and good. She wanted to marry someone strong and reliable. Her relief at seeing Franklin again was overwhelming and a great pleasure to Franklin.

Of course there was the bitter blow to her career to be considered but Penelope had the answer to that. 'We can come back to Hollywood in six months or a year, can't we, darling? After all this horridness has died down?' She showed him the press folio Minotaur had given her. It included the comprehensive publicity campaign for *True Blonde* and the stills they'd used of Penelope for *Harlequin Horror*. She felt a first step had most definitely been taken in her quest for movie stardom.

'We'll get your career up and going, my dear, I assure you of that,' Franklin said. And to a certain extent he meant it. He would take back to

Australia with him Sam's introductions to the Sydney film world and he would buy Penelope into the home industry. Until the children came and the family took over, it would be far more comfortable conducting Penelope's career from Australia – away from the sordidness of Hollywood.

The sea voyage home did Penelope good and, when they were met at the Sydney terminal by the chauffeur-driven Bentley Franklin had arranged via Solly, any misgivings she'd had about the return visit started to fade. When she laid eyes on The Colony House, they disappeared altogether.

'Oh, Franklin!' She gasped in genuine admiration as the car turned off the road and into the main circular drive. 'It's the most beautiful house I've ever seen.'

Franklin agreed with her. He'd been out of the country for most of the year and, although he was still determined to conquer the world, he knew that he'd be happiest conquering it from Australia. This was his home, where his roots were. And now he could start his dynasty. His sons could travel further afield and carry the banner of the Ross family on a global crusade.

It wasn't an autumn wedding. It was mid-winter before Penelope decided that everything was organised to her satisfaction. 'You mustn't rush me, Franklin – these things have to be done properly.'

Franklin was more than happy to let her have her way. So long as they married before the end of the year, he didn't care how they did it. He was only too delighted at the way Penelope fitted in. He had met her parents and they were exactly as he'd envisaged. Middle class, stolid, respectable. Good stock.

They were married in the oldest church in Australia – the Garrison church at The Rocks. The choice had been mutual – Franklin thought it was fitting and Penelope thought it was fashionable.

Penelope's family was well respresented but apart from Franklin, there wasn't a Ross in sight. He didn't even inform the South Australian sector. He would let them know after the event, he thought – they'd been out of contact with each other for so long that it surely wouldn't matter. The fact was that Franklin couldn't care less about his family. They were not necessary to him. He was, after all, about to start his own.

Gustave Lumet was there, of course. And The Colony House regulars, including the heavy gambling set – Paddy Conway, Robert Mitchell and Peter Lynell, who'd made a special trip from London.

Sam Crockett and Lucy-Mae were unable to attend, Lucy-Mae considering it a little premature to be travelling their new baby, so Sam had a massive present delivered in lieu. It was an impressively sculpted life-size bronze statue of a man, holding a duelling pistol, his right arm extended. The accompanying message read: 'As I can't be there in person, I am sending this substitute. Place him on the grass to mark the spot and point him towards the Bridge. May the pair of you always win in the game of life, with deepest affection from Samuel David Crocket', and there was a less melodramatic but equally sincere message from Lucy-Mae.

Franklin thought the statue was a little ostentatious, but Penelope loved it so, Sam's wishes were complied with and a place was found for The Dueller down on the grass frontage, his pistol pointing towards the Sydney Harbour Bridge.

Solomon Mankowski was thrilled to be Franklin's best man. 'Me, Boss?' he said incredulously when Franklin asked him. 'Me? You sure?'

'Yes, I'm sure, Solly,' Franklin laughed. 'Stop acting humble.'

Penelope was secretly disappointed that Franklin had asked Solly. Surely it should have been Viscount Peter Lynell. Or Gustave Lumet at the very least. Someone with more style than Solomon Mankowski. But she wisely recognised that it was a little early to be questioning Franklin's friendships.

Solly was quite aware of Penelope's misgivings about him, but they didn't bother him at all. He had a few of his own about her but so long as she made Franklin happy, who cared? Solly himself was far too happy to care about anything – he and Zofia were to be married themselves in two months.

The only member of Franklin's family to have been invited was sadly absent. Catherine had died in February while Franklin was mid-Atlantic. Gaby called around to give him the news shortly after his arrival.

'She tried to stay alive for your wedding, Franklin, but it was not meant to be. She left you something . . . a present.' Gaby gestured towards the large square object in brown paper which the house butler had carried upstairs for her. 'I thought of keeping it as her wedding present to you, but with all the other gifts and the excitement . . . ' She gave a tired shrug. Catherine's death had exhausted her. 'I thought you might enjoy it a little more at your leisure.' She nodded for him to open the parcel.

It was the painting of the bright orange wheat fields. 'Catherine was quite right,' Gaby said proudly. 'The piece is worth a lot of money. After only five years Margaret's work is very much sought after.'

There was a note inside: 'Franklin, my dear, Never forget – things are not always as they seem.'

Franklin smiled at Gaby. 'She always had to have the last word, didn't she?'

'Yes,' Gaby smiled back. 'Always.'

Franklin and Penelope honeymooned at the fashionable Hydro Majestic Hotel in the Blue Mountains, famous for its spa baths. They both agreed that they'd made enough sea voyages for a while. Besides which, Franklin was by now deeply ensconced in his many businesses, including the acquisition of shares in a movie company, and he wanted to get back to work within the fortnight.

'Would you turn the light off?' she asked. Franklin

paused for a moment, disappointed. He wanted to see her body. 'Please, Franklin,' Penelope insisted.

He obliged and, as he did so, he found himself inwardly agreeing with her. It's the way it should be, he told himself. It was the correct request from a woman of virtue on her wedding night. He must put aside the memory of his hot, passionate couplings with Millie, he told himself. For the moment anyway. Tonight he must be kind and gentle, there would be time later . . . He kissed her.

Penelope had been a little apprehensive of their first night together but she'd looked forward to it nonetheless. After years of safe flirtation, she was about to discover the depths of her own sexuality. The memory of the couple in the garden remained vivid in her mind – most of all, the animal sounds the woman had made. The sounds which had both disgusted and excited Penelope.

Now, in the dark, Franklin kissed her neck and fed his hand through the opening of her satin nightgown to gently caress her breasts. He was longing to lift the gown and run his other hand up her leg, over her belly, between her thighs. But, when he'd taken her into his embrace, he'd been aware that she'd flinched at the feel of him hard against her thigh.

It was an instinctive reaction of Penelope's to flinch at erections. She'd avoided so many on dance floors and in quiet corners while repaying a favour with a kiss and a discreet caress. But now she was married. Now it was fitting for her to discover such mysteries. In the dark, of course. She waited for Franklin to take off his pyjama trousers and to lift her nightgown so that she could feel their flesh together. Then, maybe, she would have the audacity to part her legs, just a little, as she wanted to do.

But Franklin carefully avoided contact with any area of Penelope's anatomy that he felt might be too confronting for her. As he did, his excitement mounted. The shadowy profile on the pillow before him. The woman he'd wanted for so long. The shape and warmth of her breast in his cupped hand. The feel of the satin nightgown through the open top of his pyjamas, rubbing silkily against his chest. He longed to rip their clothes off, to feel the full contact of their bodies against each other. But he daren't. He must be gentle, he must . . .

'Oh, God, Penelope . . . ' He lost control so suddenly that he was barely aware of the ferocity with which he ripped away his pyjamas and dragged her nightgown up to her waist. Then he was fumbling between her legs, forcing her thighs apart.

No, I don't want it to be like this, Penelope thought, although she did nothing to halt him. Distasteful as she found it, it was, after all, his right. Any prudery she'd felt at the prospect of opening her legs disappeared. In his excitement he was aware of nothing but his pleasure and she was performing as every good wife should – where was the shame? As she felt him start to push his way inside her, any desire of her own disappeared. It hurt. Penelope felt as though she was being ripped apart, but she clenched her teeth, determined not to cry out.

For a moment, Franklin seemed to realise his brutality and he slowed down. 'I'm sorry, my darling, I don't want to hurt you. I'm sorry.' And he pulled back, trying to ease himself into her more slowly, more delicately. 'That's it,' he whispered. 'Gently, gently.' But, considerate as Franklin was trying to be, each thrust, which was like a knife to Penelope, was driving him mad and within minutes he was forced to give in to his desire.

The last few seconds as he pounded at her like a battering ram and growled with the torment of his desire was an agonising lifetime to Penelope, but still she didn't cry out.

When it was over, Franklin held her close against him and stroked her hair. 'I'm sorry. I meant to be gentle.'

'I know.' There was a burning pain between Penelope's legs.

'It will get better.' Franklin kissed her gently. 'I promise.'

'I know, Franklin.' She returned his kiss and then awkwardly climbed out of the bed. 'I'd better clean myself up.'

While she was washing the blood from her nightgown, Franklin lay back, contented. Penelope had been a virgin and now she was his wife. There would be plenty of time for them to explore each other sexually. He would teach her the tricks that Millie had taught him. The tricks that pleasured a woman. Everything was perfect, Franklin thought.

CHAPTER SIX

Penelope

NEW YEAR 1938 came and went and still Penelope wasn't pregnant, despite the fact that she'd been married for nearly eighteen months. Franklin decided he wasn't going to let it worry him. A visit to the doctor proved there was nothing inherently wrong with either of them. 'These things take time,' the doctor said comfortingly and Franklin had to be satisfied with that. Besides, he was far too busy to be preoccupied with something which was beyond his control.

Franklin had never been so busy. In fact, he'd appointed a manager, one recommended by Gustave Lumet, to take over the running of The Colony House. Apart from refurbishing his suite there upon Penelope's insistence, Franklin had very little to do with The Colony House these days.

The expansion of Franklin's business had started in the spring of '36. That was when Solly had insisted upon taking Zofia to Poland.

'I must meet your family, ma petite,' he stipulated, 'it is only right.' Gustave Lumet had once jokingly referred to the buxom Zofia as 'ma petite Sophie' and Solly had adopted it as his personal term of endearment ever since. She was his little treasure. It seemed to escape Solly's attention that the young, healthy peasant girl from Central Poland was as big as he was and had the strength of a horse.

Zofia didn't care whether she saw her parents or not. When she and her elder brother had emigrated to Australia five years earlier it had been a relief to all concerned. Her background, like Solly's, had been one of poverty – too many children and not enough money.

She didn't confess to Solly that she also didn't care whether she ever saw Poland again. Zofia realised that Solly was using the excuse of meeting her parents in order to visit his beloved homeland so she meekly agreed.

'Yes, Solly, it is only right,' she said and she kissed him.

The trip brought out the wanderlust in Solly and they travelled throughout Europe, returning to Sydney in the autumn of 1937. Solly couldn't wait to tell Franklin everything he'd seen.

'This man is evil, Boss. This man is mad. He incites the people. They call him "the Fuhrer". This man is going to want more than Germany. More than Europe even. This man is going to want the world!'

Solly was pacing about the smoking lounge of

184

The Colony House in such a state of excitement that he'd forgotten his large glass of iced vodka on the corner table. The several guests who were quietly relaxing kept giving him odd looks.

'And he is going to want the world his way – his people only. You see what happen at the Berlin Olympics?'

Franklin nodded. He had seen the newsreels of Hitler leaving the stadium during the gold medal presentation to the black athlete Jessie Owens.

'And Germany,' Solly continued. 'You should see Germany! She is a war machine, Boss, I tell you!'

'Relax, Solly,' Franklin said finally. 'Sit down. Have your vodka.' Solly drew breath, looked about, noticed the curious glances and sat down to attend to his vodka.

Franklin sat quietly for several moments. Then he said, 'We must expand.'

Two months later, Franklin bought a cannery and began preparing it for the production of tinned beef. Army rations. It would only be a matter of time before the military would be heavily demanding 'bully beef'.

He also expanded the small leathergoods factory that he and Solly had acquired shortly after his return from America. Their army contract had not yet included the supply of boots. But it would shortly. Franklin would make sure of that.

Then he travelled north to Mandinulla for discussions with Kevin Never-Never Everard. An offer was made, and accepted, for the adjoining property. 'We must expand, Never-Never,' he said. 'We must expand.'

Despite the excitement of expansion, Franklin had not forgotten his commitment to Penelope and, while he was conducting his business transactions, he extended his bank credit yet further to include the funding of a mid-budget feature-length film which, given the limited overseas distribution available to Australian producers, would hopefully help launch its star, Penelope Greenway.

By 1938 there was certainly no time to ponder the fact that his marriage was not yet fruitful. Penelope was, after all, only twenty-four, time was on his side. And, although she wasn't as voracious or as adventurous as Millie had been, their sex life was good. In fact, Franklin was convinced that a preoccupation with sex dissipated one's energies and that he was accomplishing far more with Penelope by his side than he ever would have with someone like Millie. It was the correct relationship for a man to have with his wife and, on the occasions when they did make love, always in the dark, Penelope certainly seemed to be satisfied.

Penelope was not satisfied, but she quickly discovered how to dissemble. All she had to do was recall the moans of the woman in the garden and imitate them – an edited, genteel form of her own. It not only discouraged Franklin from experimenting but it excited him to the point where he climaxed earlier and he seemed quite happy with her response.

She didn't feel cheated. She too had decided that

theirs was the correct marriage relationship and she told herself it would have been wrong of her to seek a greater excitement – that was for loose women.

As usual, Penelope was managing, very successfully, to delude herself. It was convenient for her to play the proper woman, the respectable wife, and to ignore the urge deep down to feel what the woman in the garden had felt. There was no point in dwelling upon that, anyway. Franklin was fulfilling his promise to her and she was starring in her first feature film.

They were exciting times for Penelope. The role of Ruth, a strong, independent career woman, was the perfect vehicle for her and she loved the script. She loved the script and she loved the director and she loved the writer and, above all, she loved being a star.

Much of *A Woman of Today* was shot on location around Sydney. 'Identifiable places only,' Rick, the director, had insisted. 'This film is for international release. We must have locations people recognise.' Richard Lang was a very intense young man who desperately wanted to work in America. He'd directed meaningful, well-received documentaries and one successful low-budget film and this was his big chance for overseas recognition.

So they filmed around the various tourist haunts. The Sydney Harbour Bridge, Bondi Beach, the ninety-foot cliff known as 'The Gap' at the south harbour headland, a favourite suicide spot. Penelope was in her element when the tourists gathered around to watch. There was something about a movie camera which attracted crowds and she basked in the constant attention.

The writer wasn't too happy about the relentless glamour of the locations. 'Ruth came from a working-class background. We have to have *some* squalid locations, for God's sake.' But Rick and the producer didn't listen to him.

The producer agreed to ban the writer from the set if he upset Richard any further. They had, after all, bought the script outright and allowing the writer any further input was only a courtesy.

Franklin was in Queensland at Mandinulla during most of the filming. Penelope was so busy that she didn't really have time to miss him. But throughout the postproduction stage when she wasn't required, she felt lonely and restless and hoped fervently that he would be back in time for the premiere.

He was. 'As if I would miss your moment of triumph, my darling,' he said and she loved him for it.

So, on a Wednesday evening in early March, 1938, the Bentley pulled up outside the theatre and Penelope, radiantly beautiful, stepped out to acknowledge her newfound status in the film world. She was disappointed that there weren't crowds being held back in the streets but this was, after all, Australia. When the movie became a huge success in America things would be different.

Franklin didn't like the film very much – he found it a little too posed and self-conscious. But at the party afterwards, when everyone was telling Penelope that her performance was nothing short of brilliant, he reminded himself that he knew nothing of film. And of course he had no intention of bursting her bubble.

'You are the most beautiful woman in the world,' he said. It was a very safe comment. It satisfied her and he meant it.

Penelope was on a giddy high. She could indeed have been the most beautiful woman in the world that night.

They wined and dined and partied till nearly dawn and Penelope drank too much champagne, which was very unlike her. She always liked to be in command of the situation.

Not tonight. When they arrived home her defences were well and truly down. Penny Green from Brighton-Le-Sands was loving being Penelope Greenway, star . . .

'That was the most glorious night of my life, Franklin,' she said. 'And you were the one who made it happen.'

She was overwhelmed with love and gratitude. When Franklin kissed her tenderly and told her he was very proud of her as his hand caressed her thighs, she wanted him. She had never felt so desirable and she had never felt such desire. She even ignored the fact that the corner lamp was still on as he eased her back upon the bed and started gently to undress her.

As she lay there, naked, watching him disrobe, there was the vague knowledge in the recesses of her mind that this was one of the nights when she should avoid sex. This was her fertile time and she had assiduously evaded Franklin's advances during her fertile times for the past eighteen months. Penelope didn't want to have a child. Not when her career was moving at such a pace. One day, she told herself. One day – but not yet.

Tonight it didn't seem to matter. Tonight there was nothing but the feel of Franklin beside her. The first touch of their nakedness. Skin upon skin. Together.

Penelope felt an indescribable ache between her legs and she desperately wanted him to touch her there. Her nipples responded eagerly to the caress of his fingertips and a quivering sensation went through her entire body. Then his hand was travelling down over her hip, her belly and she wanted to part her legs.

'Yes, my darling, yes,' Franklin murmured encouragingly. Her response was exciting him to fever pitch but he knew he had to retain control. He mustn't rush her. 'You are truly beautiful, Penelope,' he whispered as his hand finally sought between her thighs, 'truly beautiful.' And she opened herself to him, gasping at his touch.

When he slowly entered her, their bodies were both shuddering with an unbearable desire. She thrust herself back at him as Franklin, fighting to control his excitement, kept withdrawing, teasing her to an exquisite pain.

Finally, when he felt she was ready, he drove himself into her steadily and rhythmically, their bodies responding in perfect unison.

The scene in the garden flashed through Penelope's brain. The woman's moans, the man's pounding buttocks. But these weren't the woman's moans, these were her moans. Then the image disappeared and she was gasping, desperately.

'I love you, Franklin. I love you, I love you, I

love you,' she said, over and over. And then another image. A cliff. She had to go over the cliff. She had to travel down the other side. 'Yes,' she cried out. 'Yes! Yes! Yes!' Still Franklin managed to keep control. And, finally, the image of waves. Waves of sensation. No sound. Time stood still as she was engulfed in a sea of pleasure so intense she could no longer cry out.

A groan from deep within Franklin's chest as he allowed himself the ultimate release. And then Penelope was airborne, fluttering. Fluttering over the other side of the cliff and she clung closely to him as they shared their final shudders of fulfilment.

The first rays of the early morning sun knifed through the curtains of the french windows as they slept, exhausted, in each other's arms. It was midday before they awoke. Franklin rose on one elbow to look at Penelope curled up beside him, naked, vulnerable, and very lovely. She stirred, opened her eyes and looked up at him.

'Good morning, my darling,' he said and, brushing the hair from her face, he kissed her tenderly, his hand sliding down the long curve of her neck. Before it reached her breast, she sat up and pulled the sheet around herself.

'What time is it?' she asked.

'Just after midday.'

'Good heavens, I have a press interview in an hour. The publicist is picking me up at a quarter to one.'

She obviously wanted to jump out of bed but he

sensed that she was self-conscious about her nakedness. Franklin was briefly disappointed. She was behaving as though the night before had never happened. Surely everything had changed between them now. Surely the abandonment of last night had expelled her inhibitions.

He chastised himself. It was only natural for her to be self-conscious in the cold light of day. There would be other nights and gradually her reserve would disappear and she would become at ease with her sexuality.

Overnight, it would seem, Franklin had reassessed his views on sex dissipating one's energies. Now his whole body ached for her. But he knew he must be careful. He mustn't ask too much too soon.

He got out of bed and gathered up his clothes. 'I'll leave you to get ready then, my dear.'

Penelope tried to avert her eyes from his naked body but it was difficult. She could plainly see his erection and it fascinated her. She felt that same slight ache between her legs and, as she watched him leave the room, she knew that she desired him. She wanted last night all over again, which appalled her. Was this the control Franklin was destined to have over her?

As Penelope bathed herself, she looked down at her body and her hand lingered upon her genitals. No. No, she told herself, she was no one's slave. That moment of pleasure, exquisite as it might be, was not worth the price of domination. She must suppress her desire, she told herself. She must suppress her desire at all costs. She had her career to think of.

Penelope washed her hair and towelled it vigorously. There certainly wasn't time now for such contemplation.

Three-quarters of an hour later, impeccably groomed, she left The Colony House in the company of her publicist for her interview with the feature writer of the *Sydney Morning Herald*.

For the following week, Franklin and Penelope abstained from sex. 'It's "that time", my darling,' she said as she kissed him deeply. 'Only a few days, be patient.'

Franklin had to accept it. He would certainly never make overtures to her during 'her time' and it didn't occur to him for one moment that she might be lying. She had abandoned herself and he had felt her pleasure – why would she deny herself the repetition of such an experience?

A week later, when she could evade the issue no longer, Penelope steeled herself. She would allow him her body but she would not allow him control over her. She would not give in to her own pleasure.

It was possibly the greatest test of her life. She responded warmly to his kiss and returned his embrace with equal affection, but when he started to lift her nightgown . . .

'Would you turn the light off, Franklin. Please.'

He looked at her. The steel-blue eyes seemed to bore into her skull. For a moment Penelope was unnerved. Did he know she was planning to cheat? Of course not, how could he? He was puzzled by her modesty, that was all.

'Please, my darling. Please, I'd prefer it.'

And Franklin could do nothing else but oblige. Penelope was right – he was puzzled. But he wasn't going to challenge her. They never discussed sex, which was only correct. It was not, after all, a subject one should discuss – and certainly not with women. But he hoped the return of her modesty didn't mean the return of her sexual inhibition.

In the dark, she allowed him to fully undress her and, as she undressed him back, Franklin started to relax. It didn't matter that she was too shy to let him watch her. It didn't matter that it had been the alcohol which had liberated her that night. Nothing mattered. She wanted him.

He felt her hand glide tentatively across his stomach, tracing the muscles of his belly, then, as if by accident, brushing against his erect penis. Yes, she wanted him.

Penelope was aware of the thin line she was treading. The touch of his penis, the silky skin with the rock hardness beneath, shocked and thrilled her but her mind was made up. The more she excited him and the more she feigned her own excitement, the less time he would take exploring her. But she mustn't be too adventurous, or behave too out of character.

When he entered her, Penelope steeled herself against the first ripplings of her own excitement. But she moaned and thrust her body back at him as she had that night. She timed her moans and her thrusts perfectly, recognising where the stages would be if she wished to abandon herself to them.

Her moans became louder as Franklin's passion grew stronger. Now the waves would be engulfing her. She cried out and arched her back as he drove himself into her in a frenzy of fulfilment. Then, as his strangled cry rang out, she clung to him fiercely. 'My darling,' she panted, 'my darling, my darling.'

It was the best performance Penelope had ever given. The first of many such performances.

Penelope's performance in *A Woman of Today* was not so well received. Neither was the film itself.

'Edited by one hour *A Woman of Today* would qualify as an impressive travelogue,' one major critic commented. He went on to say that 'Penelope Greenway may have the beauty and style of Katharine Hepburn but Miss Hepburn does it better.'

There were cutting comments from other reviewers: 'A one-dimensional performance lacking warmth' ... 'A hackneyed story which has already been done to death by Hollywood' ... 'Pretentious direction'.

The heavy criticism was aimed at all levels of the film but Penelope took it as a personal attack and was deeply hurt. Franklin did all he could to raise her spirits. He even offered to take her away on a holiday although he could ill afford the time.

Then came the thrilling news which propelled the film into total insignificance. Penelope was pregnant.

'You see, my darling? Nothing else matters.' Franklin was delighted.

Penelope was aghast. How had it happened?

That night, of course. It had been that night.

There was very little Penelope could do but accept her lot. For Franklin's sake, and for the sake of peace and quiet as much as anything, she feigned joy at the prospect and, during her confinement, took all the correct precautions in preparing herself for motherhood.

Shortly before the baby was due, Franklin's father died. Despite entreaties from his brother Kenneth and his Aunt Mary, however, Franklin declined to go to South Australia for the funeral. His place was at his wife's side, he said. And that was that.

In December 1938, Penelope Ross gave birth to a son. Terence George Franklin.

Franklin was overjoyed. For the first time in his life he was unable to control his emotions and there was a definite glisten in his eyes as he embraced Solly.

'A son, my dear friend!' he said. 'A son!'

Solly, as the elected godfather, was also pacing the floors of the waiting room of the Royal Hospital for Women when the doctor came out to announce the news.

Now a married man, Solly had openly wept a month earlier when Zofia had announced that she was with child. To Solly, Franklin's display of emotion was quite understated. Nevertheless he recognised it as uncharacteristic and was moved. He fervently returned the embrace.

'Cognac and cigars, Boss. That's what we need. Cognac and cigars.' And they went home to The Colony House, where they sat up till all hours drinking cognac, which Solly disliked, and smoking cigars, which Franklin loathed, and discussing the magic of birth and the future of the Ross empire.

Penelope had detested being pregnant. She'd loathed her swollen belly and thickened ankles and the pain in her lower back. As soon as she was able, she exercised rigorously to regain her former shape.

There had been one compensation during her pregnancy, however. Franklin had made no demands upon her sexually and she was thankful for that. She had denied herself pleasure with such regularity that the faking of her enjoyment was no longer a test of strength and character, it was a chore.

Although she resigned herself to being a mother, and determined to be a good one, Penelope had not yet relinquished her career plans. Certainly she realised they would have to be deferred for several years, but she had a long-term strategy that was a satisfactory alternative. Indeed, given the disaster of *A Woman of Today*, it might be to her advantage to keep a low profile for a while.

Penelope convinced herself that she would, after all, be in her prime around the age of thirty and that the roles would be far better then – she'd never been a lightweight juvenile actress, anyway. Undaunted, she once again determined to make the best of the situation.

Her plans did not altogether exclude Franklin. She didn't relish the prospect of another pregnancy but she recognised the fact that she must give him another son. She'd take a year's break, she decided, then plan a second conception. And she prayed fervently that it would be a boy. She didn't dare contemplate what she'd do if it was a girl – the thought of a third pregnancy was more than she could bear. Besides which, her career had to be back on course within three years. That was her plan.

Franklin was puzzled by Penelope's reluctance to have sex. For the first several months after the birth of Terence it was to be expected, of course, but when she finally did allow him to make love to her, and then only rarely, she didn't seem to display the same enjoyment she had in the past.

With some regret, Franklin supposed it was only natural. Women changed when they became mothers, he decided – it was to be expected. So he poured his energies into his work. As the year rolled by, he demanded less of Penelope sexually, while he delighted in her as a mother to his son. And Penelope made sure she played the role to perfection.

'Fellow Australians, it is my melancholy duty to inform you officially that, in consequence of the persistence of Germany in her invasion of Poland, Great Britain has declared war upon her, and that as a result, Australia is also at war . . .'

Franklin, Penelope and the guests and staff of The Colony House were gathered around the lounge-room wireless, like so many others across

198

the nation, listening to the live broadcast by the Prime Minister, Robert Menzies.

'May God in His mercy and compassion grant that the world will soon be free from this agony.'

There was silence after the announcement and then people broke away into families and groups and talked quietly in various corners of the lounge.

That night Franklin and Penelope made love. It seemed right, somehow. She knew it was her fertile time but she didn't care. She wanted to be loved and to feel his closeness. For Penelope, like many, many others, it was a vulnerable time.

She didn't conceive, as it turned out. In fact, she didn't fall pregnant for nearly a year. Franklin was often away at Mandinulla and, when he was in town, he worked sixteen hours a day at their offices. He'd acquired an entire inner-city office block from which to administer his burgeoning businesses. Ross Industries had become a massive concern.

Things didn't change much in the spring of 1940 when Penelope discovered she was pregnant. If she'd expected Franklin to drop everything and tend to her confinement, she was sadly mistaken. Thrilled as he was by the news of her pregnancy, the need to expand his factories to meet the army requisitions for beef and boots and leathergoods demanded his full attention.

He hired a live-in nanny for Terence and instructed Penelope to rely upon Zofia for companionship.

'Solly is working as hard as I am,' he said. 'Zofia is also in need of company.'

It was an idea which didn't altogether thrill Penelope. Baby Terence was nearly two years old and, despite the capable care of the nanny, he was a demanding infant. Penelope found him exhausting. Zofia had her own eighteen-month-old son, Karol, constantly by her side and her six-week-old baby daughter constantly at her breast and yet she never seemed to tire. She was a born mother and, as such, a constant source of irritation to Penelope. Furthermore, the woman seemed to delight in pregnancy and the prospect of childbirth. Penelope felt fat and bloated and unattractive – the glorification of motherhood was the last thing she wanted. If Franklin couldn't be with her to spoil her and pamper her, then she wanted to be left alone.

Franklin had planned to be with Penelope when her time came, but things went wrong. She was rushed to hospital with a fever four weeks before the baby was due. They wired Franklin, who did all he could to get there but, by the time he arrived, it was too late. A week after her hospitalisation, on April 4, 1941, Penelope gave birth to a stillborn child, a daughter.

The months which followed were terrible. Penelope sank into a deep depression and Franklin was unable to get through to her. She would sit staring into space, refusing all food except for the chicken broth constantly and painstakingly supplied by Zofia. Strangely enough, Zofia was the only person with whom Penelope allowed herself any contact, occasionally even smiling a 'thank you' as she accepted the broth. When Franklin approached her she became sullen, refusing to speak or even to look at him.

The one and only time he managed to communicate with her, she hurled recriminations at him. He was totally taken aback. He'd done his best to convey his sorrow at the loss of their baby and he'd tried to convince her that she would get over it in time and that they would have another child.

'For God's sake, don't be such a hypocrite, Franklin.' The eyes that had been staring dully at the wall suddenly turned on him and he could see the flash of hatred in their depths. 'You don't care a damn about the baby,' she spat. Franklin was dumb with amazement.

'You don't care a damn about the baby and you don't care a damn about me,' she continued. 'All you care about is sons. So spare me your sympathy. Please. It's sickening.' Her anger vanished as quickly as it had erupted and Penelope turned and stared at the wall, retreating again into her torpor.

Franklin didn't dare make another approach for fear of upsetting her but he discussed her condition in depth with her doctor.

'Such irrational behaviour is perfectly normal,' the doctor assured him. 'Many women suffer deeply traumatic reactions to the birth of a stillborn. You must be patient.'

The doctor advised him to take her away somewhere and, although Penelope didn't seem particularly enamoured of the idea, he eventually persuaded her to go with him to Mandinulla. Six months after the stillbirth they set off, together with baby Terence and Marie the nanny.

Mandinulla was 30,000 square miles of arid scrubland in central Queensland. It was a large property, certainly, but there were larger throughout the huge northern and western sections of Australia. They needed to be vast. Size was necessary for their sheer survival. The head of cattle allotted to each square mile of territory was kept to a minimum to ensure the grazing lands remained adequate for their existence. The other necessity for their survival was the ability of the overseers and the stockmen to police such a vast territory. And Mandinulla had the best.

Kevin Never-Never Everard was an expert. And so was Jacky, the half-caste Aborigine who led the team of stockmen. Never-Never lived in his quarters at the homestead and Jacky lived with the rest of the stockmen, all of whom were full or part Aboriginal, at the stockmen's quarters half a mile away, but the two men were firm friends. When Sam Crockett bought the property and discovered that Never-Never regularly entertained Jacky in his quarters and regularly dined with Jacky and his family in theirs, he tried to forbid it.

'Good God, man, they're niggers,' he said. 'You have a position to maintain here.'

Never-Never didn't deny that segregation was certainly the accepted policy on cattle stations throughout the country, but if he chose to do things differently, that was his business and his alone. He and Jacky had been running the property way before Sam Crockett had come on the scene, and Never-Never resented the American's intrusion.

'If that's the way you want to run things, Mr Crockett, fine,' he said. 'But I'll take off, if you don't mind.'

Sam had done his homework and knew the value of the man. Reluctantly, he gave in, making it apparent that he deeply disapproved of the situation, which didn't bother Never-Never one bit.

When Franklin took over the reins he didn't rock the boat. It wasn't that he particularly approved of Everard's methods, but if a thing was working well, why change it?

Penelope's first impression of Mandinulla was not favourable. She liked the homestead itself with its wide verandahs, large airy rooms and high ceilings designed to take advantage of the slightest breeze to help alleviate the oppressive heat. But the countryside itself horrified her. There was nothing but scrub. Dry, arid scrub as far as the eye could see. Why on earth had she allowed Franklin to bring her to this wasteland?

And then she talked to Never-Never. It was several days after they'd arrived and Franklin had invited the overseer to dine with them. Penelope picked at her food while Franklin and Never-Never talked business. She still hadn't regained her appetite. Her face was gaunt and her body too thin and there were dark circles under her eyes.

Never-Never felt sorry for her. She was obviously unhappy and Franklin was making no effort to include her in the conversation. Rarely one to observe niceties, Never-Never surprised himself as well as Franklin and Penelope.

'How do you like Mandinulla, Mrs Ross?'

Penelope looked up from her plate, slightly taken back. She realised that the enquiry was uncharacteristic of him and wondered whether or not she should reply with honesty. What the hell, she thought, why try to be nice? She couldn't be bothered.

'I hate it,' she said.

Never-Never appreciated her honesty. 'Why?' he asked.

She shrugged. 'The homestead's pretty. I don't mind the homestead. But the country ... ' She started toying with her food again. 'The country's vile. It's ugly and it's dead.'

There was a moment's pause. 'No, it isn't. It's magnificent and it's very much alive.'

She looked up and met his eyes. They were strange eyes in a strange face. Years of harsh Queensland sun had weathered his skin and reduced his eyes to slits. Never-Never could have been any age, but he was somewhere in his forties – he wasn't exactly sure where himself. He was lean and wiry and looked like the scrubland itself, she thought, sparse and brown and dry.

Her initial interest at his reaction died away and she gave another indifferent shrug. 'Maybe I haven't been looking in the right places.'

'Maybe,' he said. 'And maybe you haven't been looking in the right way.' Something in Never-Never was demanding that he get the woman's attention. He didn't for the life of him know why. But a face as beautiful as hers had no right to be devoid of animation. He wanted to kindle some interest in her, wanted to see a light in her eyes.

'If you look at this land in the right way you'll see colours you've never seen before. You'll see orange earth and silver trees . . . '

Franklin hadn't been paying much attention to the exchange. He appreciated Never-Never's attempts to engage Penelope in conversation but he didn't expect it to achieve much. He'd given up trying to get through to her himself. Then he heard 'orange earth' and 'silver trees', and the image of Catherine flashed through his mind. Catherine and the wheat fields. He heard her voice. Something about learning to use his peripheral vision: ' . . . and you'll find . . . that the earth is red and the mountains purple, and . . . '

'And when you look at them through a heat haze,' Never-Never was continuing, 'they shimmer like magic. And then, beyond the shimmer, you can see mirages. Sometimes a whole lake.'

It was surprising to see Never-Never so animated, thought Franklin, and he turned to watch Penelope. Was the man having any effect?

'And the wildlife,' Never-Never continued. 'You've never seen anything like the wildlife out here.' Aware that he'd gained a flicker of interest, Never-Never pressed on yet further and he was surprised to hear himself say, 'I could show you, if you like.'

Penelope looked briefly in Franklin's direction and he jumped in quickly before she could answer. 'I think that's an excellent idea, darling.' He turned to Never-Never. 'How about tomorrow?'

'Fine by me.'

Late the following morning Penelope returned
from her two-hour drive with Never-Never in his
battered utility. Franklin hadn't seen her so alive
in six months.

'Have you seen the termite mounds, Franklin?'
she asked. He had, but she didn't wait for an
answer. 'They're ten foot high. And there's so
many of them! They look like the columns of a
ruined temple. And the wedge-tailed eagles!
They're huge. Never-Never says they can lift a calf
off the ground. And they climb up in the sky
without even moving their wings. So high until
you can't see them any more. Never-Never says
they drift up on the thermal drafts.'

Franklin had seen the wedge-tailed eagles too.
But they were just birds to him. It would never
have occurred to him to show Penelope the termite
mounds or to study the eagles with her. And yet
it was that simple. The change in her was mirac-
ulous. He was a little put out that it had been
Never-Never who had made the breakthrough but
he was grateful nonetheless. He certainly refused
to blame himself for not having hit upon the solution. Who could possibly have guessed that Penelope, of all people, would find interest in the
outback?

The following day, shortly after dark, Never-
Never took Penelope roo-spotting. 'You shine a

light on them,' he explained, 'and it hypnotises them.'

Sure enough, the kangaroos stood poised on their hind legs and stared back at the light Never-Never shone on them from the rear of the utility. Apart from an occasional quiver of the nose and twitch of the ears, they were frozen in time.

Never-Never told her that was the way they shot the animals. 'Always at night,' he said. 'When they're under the light you can take your time setting your sights.'

When Penelope expressed her horror, he patiently explained that it was necessary to cull them from time to time. 'If you let the 'roos take over, there'd be no grazing for the cattle,' he said.

'Do you ride, Mrs Ross?' he asked on the drive back.

'You mean horses?' And she felt a bit foolish when he merely nodded. 'No,' she said.

'Pity. There's yabbies in the creek a couple of miles from the station but you can't get in there by car.'

Penelope didn't know what a yabbie was. He explained that it was a freshwater crustacean, fun to catch and good to eat.

'Then you must show me how to catch them,' she said. 'But first you'll have to teach me how to ride.' And she laughed.

Never-Never opened the utility door for her when they got back to the homestead. 'Good night, Mrs Ross,' he said.

'Call me Penelope,' she insisted. 'Please.' He

nodded a little self-consciously. 'And please may I call you Kevin? Never-Never is such a ridiculous name.'

'Sure,' he shrugged. 'Doesn't make any difference to me.' But secretly he was pleased. Very pleased. Kevin Never-Never Everard was falling hopelessly in love with Penelope.

It wasn't long before Penelope's appetite returned and she lost her gaunt, haunted look. In fact, Franklin decided, he had never seen her so carefree and lacking in inhibitions. He leaned on the fence of the home paddock, with little Terence sitting on the top railing between his arms, watching as Never-Never and Jacky gave Penelope her first riding lesson. He wondered, briefly, whether he should feel jealous. Ridiculous. Never-Never was getting a crush on Penelope – so what; most men did. He was nothing but a novelty to her.

Franklin was right. Kevin Everard was merely someone with whom Penelope felt relaxed. She was fully aware of the effect she was having on him but there was little she could do about that. And, in the meantime, she was deeply grateful for the distraction he and Mandinulla were proving to be.

Penelope had recovered from the actual loss of her baby far sooner than her doctor and Franklin had realised. Her extended melancholy had been more for the loss of herself. Whatever had happened to Penelope Jane Greenway, star? Her dreams had been lost along the way and Penelope was deeply depressed at the prospect of what lay before her. A wife to one man and a mother to another. It wasn't what she'd planned at all. Where was the power and the glory and the glamour? She blamed Franklin for it. Franklin and his demand for sons.

Now, here at Mandinulla, under the adoring eyes of Never-Never, Penelope had rediscovered her feminine powers. Of course, she still had control over Franklin. As soon as they returned to Sydney she would insist he produce another picture for her. And this time the budget would be limitless and they would have the pick of the writers, directors and actors. Penelope relaxed and allowed a little of Penny Green to emerge every now and then. She knew how well Franklin responded when she appeared ingenuous. Besides, having made her plans, she could afford to relax and enjoy herself.

Little Terry laughed as the horse shied and Penelope nearly lost her seat.

'Easy, easy, easy.' Jacky, who was holding the bridle, stroked the horse's neck and the animal calmed down instantly. Jacky always had that effect on horses, Never-Never told her.

Penelope called over to Terry, who was still chortling, 'That's enough out of you, mister.' It was bravado to cover her nerves. She'd never been thrown from a horse before and the prospect frightened her.

Never-Never realised it. 'If you're out riding on the property and you fall,' he instructed, 'relax and go with it. Don't tense up or you might break something ... ' Wonderful, Penny thought.

'Whatever you do,' he continued, 'hang on to the reins.'

'Why? Aren't I supposed to let go of them and cover my head or something?' She'd read that somewhere.

Jacky and Never-Never looked at each other. 'Not out here you're not,' Never-Never said.

'Why?'

'Because out here it's a helluva long walk back,' Jacky grinned.

It was the end of November before they returned to Sydney. They'd spent a whole two months at Mandinulla and it was all the time Franklin could afford away from his other concerns.

Penelope was happy to return. Mandinulla had served its purpose. She was fully recovered. She could ride a horse passably well, she had explored the outback, she had caught and boiled and eaten yabbies and now it was time to get on with her life. She made Franklin promise that they would return to Mandinulla again for a family holiday and Franklin was more than willing to oblige. His Penelope was back again, strong, vibrant and beautiful, and he would do anything to keep her happy.

Once they had made plans to return, Penelope was excited at the prospect of being home in time for Terry's third birthday. She would throw a party for him and for Zofia's children. And then it would be Christmas and she would host a big dinner at The Colony House. For Zofia and Solly and Gustave and all of their friends. Not that she had many friends – they were more Franklin's really – but she enjoyed being hostess and soaking up the admiration afforded her beauty. It was strange, she mused, that the only two true friends she had made were Zofia and Never-Never.

'Goodbye, Kevin,' she said and she hugged him warmly. Never-Never was self-conscious of the embrace and he broke away as quickly as he could. He preferred to worship from afar. 'Thank you for everything.'

Never-Never muttered something, shook hands with Franklin and tousled Terry's hair. Then he stood back, Jacky at his side, and waved farewell as the car took off in a swirl of dust.

On December 8, 1941, Penelope's social plans were completely overturned.

It was Monday morning and she and Franklin were seated in the corner of the main lounge by the bay windows sipping their coffee. One of the housemaids presented them with the early edition newspapers. There were several Colony House guests also taking coffee but the maid delivered the newspapers to the guests in their rooms upstairs before looking after those within view of Franklin. It was the customary practice. Franklin hadn't ordered it but it pleased him nonetheless. It set him apart from the guests and he liked to keep that little bit of distance.

'My God!' He smacked his teacup down onto its saucer with such force that Penelope looked up sharply. One didn't treat Royal Doulton like that.

'My God!' he repeated, 'look at this!' His voice was loud and several of the guests looked in his direction. It wasn't customary for Franklin Ross to create a disturbance. There was obviously something alarming in the newspaper. They were dying to know what it was but propriety forbade enquiry – it might be something personal after all. They didn't have to wait long to find out.

'Japan has bombed Pearl Harbour,' Franklin announced to all and sundry as he dumped the newspaper in front of Penelope.

She looked down at it. 'PEARL HARBOUR ATTACKED,' the headlines screamed. 'US DECLARES WAR ON JAPAN.'

Early the following year, when America joined forces with the Allies, many said that the war was over, that it was only a matter of time. But the new fear for Australia lay with Japan. The enemy was no longer far distant Europe, the enemy was now on their front doorstep and people were frightened.

Penelope, however, still didn't seem to grasp the full impact of the war. It had always meant little to her, apart from the fact that it was making her husband very rich. When she approached Franklin with the suggestion that he relaunch her career, she couldn't understand his dismissive attitude.

'Don't be ridiculous, my darling, there's a war on.' Surely she couldn't be serious, he thought.

But she was. And she, in turn, couldn't understand why he wasn't amenable to her idea. She had

212

fulfilled his requirements, hadn't she? She had given him a son – God knows she'd tried to give him two – and she had put her career on hold for nearly four years. What's more, since their return from Mandinulla, they'd been as happy as they'd been during their first year of marriage. They made love regularly – except during her fertile times, of course; she made sure of that – and she'd even taken to faking her orgasms again to give him pleasure. She couldn't understand why he was being so disagreeable.

'The studio isn't even making feature films at the moment,' he said, exasperated by her insistence. 'We're making war documentaries and newsreels and we're barely breaking even. Any profit we make is donated to the war effort.'

'Why?' Penelope was dumbfounded. Franklin never allowed a business to run at a loss.

'For God's sake, woman, if I'm going to make money out of men going off to fight, I must in all conscience do something to support their cause.'

Penelope was shattered. Why had he ever led her to believe he would further her career? That had been his promise to her. How could he have forgotten?

To Franklin her disappointment was simply a piqued vanity. As far as he was concerned, her desire for a career had been merely a youthful whim. He tried to cajole her out of it. 'My darling, what's most important: making films or having our family? I'm thirty-seven years old; you'll be thirty this year. We're not getting any younger.'

Penelope cringed. Franklin was never subtle. As it was, he was trying his hardest not to say 'Give me sons'. He probably didn't dare after her outburst nearly a year ago, she thought with resentment, but that's exactly what he meant.

It took Penelope several sleepless nights to completely replan her life. So much for having Franklin under her control, she thought. He was adamant; she knew there would be no budging him. Very well, she finally decided, if she couldn't be a star on the screen, she would be a star in her own life. She would have power and glory and glamour and Franklin would pay for it all. Much as she loathed the prospect of another pregnancy she realised that the price she had to pay for what she wanted was to give him his second son.

Cuddling up beside him on the sofa whilst he read his journals one night, she said, 'Franklin, may we talk?'

'What is it, Penelope?' he asked warily. 'Do you want something?' She'd been sullen for days, so he was pleased that she was once more her alluring, affectionate self, but he hoped she wasn't about to reopen the argument.

'Yes I do,' she admitted and then added hastily, 'but it's nothing to do with the studios. I understand that we must contribute to the war effort.'

He put an arm around her and gave her his full attention.

'I want a home of my own.'

'But you love The Colony House,' he said, surprised.

'Yes.'

'So why do you want to live somewhere else?'

214

'I don't.' Penelope didn't believe in beating about the bush. Not when she held all the aces. 'I want The Colony House for my own. I want it to be our home.'

Franklin drew back and stared at her in amazement. 'But The Colony House has become an institution. We have regular guests. We hold business meetings and social functions for people from all over the world.'

'We could still do that, my darling, but it would be at our personal invitation.' She meant at *her* own personal invitation. She continued before he could interrupt. 'We need a family home, Franklin. There are too many strangers constantly around and when the second child comes ... ' She hesitated. It was her ace.

'You're not ... ' She gave an imperceptible nod. 'Oh Penelope, my dear.' Overwhelmed, Franklin hugged her but she broke free of his embrace.

'I'm not positive yet; I have to see the doctor next week, and then it'll be a little while before we get the results of the tests but, yes, I think I am.'

Penelope wasn't pregnant and she knew it, but it was only a small white lie ... It was just a matter of time.

'Don't be too disappointed, my darling, it's just a matter of time,' she assured him a fortnight later when she told him the pregnancy had been a false alarm.

Franklin was profoundly disappointed but he agreed with her that they needed a home of their own. He'd already set the wheels in motion. If Penelope wanted The Colony House, then she must have The Colony House. He bought out his partnership with Gustave and Solly and, three months later, started restoring the mansion to its former glory as a private home.

But, as luck would have it, Penelope found that she couldn't conceive. It was the perfect irony after years of avoidance. The doctors and specialists she consulted came to the conclusion that the fever she'd experienced prior to the birth of her stillborn child had been due to a pelvic infection. As a result, one of her fallopian tubes was swollen and chronically infected and was hindering the healthy tube from functioning normally.

It didn't occur to Franklin to enquire about the 'false pregnancy'. He believed Penelope when she said 'these things happen, my dear'. Women's problems were women's problems, after all, and he was only too relieved when Penelope, who loathed hospitals with a passion, agreed to surgery. The doctors assured him that the operation was not a complicated one and, once the infected tube was removed, there was no reason why Penelope should not conceive.

The operation was performed and was successful. But, by 1944, when Penelope found herself still unable to fall pregnant, she began to think that fate was on her side and perhaps it wasn't necessary to fulfil her obligation after all. She was thirty-two years old, at the height of her beauty, mistress of the Colony House and now a member of the international social set.

The Colony House and the name of Ross had

always assured Penelope of a certain social standing but her acceptance by the reigning queens of the international set had taken two years of hard work. Finally, her invitations were being reciprocated. A chalet in St Moritz, a villa in Alicante, a mansion in Acapulco – even at the height of the war, the rich retained their playgrounds. It was understood that it was impossible for Penelope to accept most offers due to the vast distances involved but, token or not, the invitations were there. She had made the list.

Penelope agonised over which invitations she would accept. Although Franklin wasn't too keen, he could hardly refuse her. He was extremely proud of the poise and style with which she graced the social side of his businesses. He was aware of how much his colleagues admired her and he felt it was only fitting that she should be rewarded.

If they could only have another son, everything would be perfect for Franklin. Penelope's unrealistic career notions were a thing of the past and she had proved herself the perfect partner, just as he'd known she would.

In March, Penelope accepted an invitation to Alicante for the whole of July. They would escape the winter and laze on a Spanish beach for a month while Franklin did business in London. Terry was at a perfect age to accompany them with his nanny. All was set in motion and she was very much looking forward to her exotic holiday.

In April, she discovered she was pregnant. Franklin's joy knew no bounds and Penelope

217

could have wept. Damn! It would take her another two years to get back on the invitation list.

There were no complications during Penelope's confinement or labour and, on the evening of January 17, 1945, Franklin and Solly drank cognac and smoked cigars until dawn to celebrate the birth of James Franklin Charles Ross.

Three months later, Sydney went mad, like the rest of the world. The streets thronged with people and streamers and tears and joy. The war in Europe was over.

Not long after VE Day, Penelope's doctor informed Franklin that his wife had carcinoma of the ovaries. She required an operation immediately.

'An oophorectomy, Mr Ross, in which we remove the ovaries. It's not a dangerous operation,' the doctor assured him. 'And you'll have her home again within the fortnight. But I'm afraid it will mean no more children.'

Franklin contained his bitter disappointment. With his help, Penelope made a speedy recovery from the operation.

The doctor appeared pleased with her progress. The carcinoma had been fully arrested, he said. But what he was really pleased about was the vast sum of money Penelope had transferred to his bank account.

There had been no cancer, just as there would be no more children. Penelope had paid her price. Now she would collect her payment as matriarch of the Ross dynasty.

BOOK THREE

The

Middle Years

(1966 - 1968)

CHAPTER SEVEN

James and Terry

WOOK-A, WOOK-A, WOOK-A, WOOK-A. The sound was deafening. The helicopter blades sliced the air crazily as the vast machine hung only feet above the ground like a giant bird of prey. It hovered for a moment and the men leapt from its open fusellage, rifles at the ready.

He was a conscriptee. He'd been stationed in Nui Dat for three months but this was the first time he'd come in contact with the enemy and he was frightened. So were all the others. Even the experienced ones, even the ones who used bravado as a mask back at camp. They were all frightened.

His ankles jarred as he hit the ground and he quickly rolled and rose to his knees. There was no enemy in sight. Nothing but thick, tangled bush surrounding the clearing as the helicopter settled behind him. Above the roar of the 'Huey', there was no sound of returning gunfire.

But the enemy was there, all right. 'Twang! Twang! Twang!' Although he couldn't hear the shots, he could hear the bullets ricocheting off the blades of the helicopter. He fired back crazily,

223

blindly, into the trees. So did the others.

He started to run for cover. They all did. But they could have been running directly into the enemy fire for all they knew – it was impossible to tell.

The man in front of him fell. He tripped over him. He picked himself up and ran three more steps. Only three. Then he was hit. A massive blow to the chest. No pain.

He didn't know how much later it was, but suddenly he was being lifted. A man held his shoulders, another his legs.

The man holding his legs nearly dropped him. 'Careful, careful,' he heard the other one say. And he was hoisted back into the helicopter. The pain was excruciating.

Other men were there, groaning, crying out. But he couldn't see them as he stared up at the ceiling of the helicopter.

He heard the terrified voice of the man who'd scrambled in after him, the one who'd nearly dropped him. 'Oh, Jesus, why doesn't he take off? Jesus Christ, why doesn't he take off?'

'Easy does it, son.' He recognised the voice as that of the sergeant in command. 'There's a couple more to collect – now get yourself back out here.' That was when he blacked out.

He came to briefly as the helicopter took off. He felt a vague soaring sensation. Relief. He was going home. Then nothing. Nothing at all.

Penelope knew what was in the telegram before she opened it. She'd done this many times before.

Regularly in her nightmares she'd opened telegrams from the Department of Defence. 'Private James Ross killed in action in Phuoc Tuy Province, South Vietnam, on February 12, 1966' ... But this wasn't a nightmare. This was real ... 'in the service of his country ... ' Penelope's eyes scanned ahead. The Brigadier went on to express his deepest sympathy, but she didn't read that far. She fell to the floor in a crumpled heap and the servants came rushing to her aid.

They called her doctor and Zofia, who arrived twenty minutes later. Zofia was always there when Penelope needed her. Not Franklin. Franklin was in New York.

The doctor prescribed sedatives, Zofia rang Franklin, and Penelope lay staring numbly at the ceiling, her mind wandering in a thousand directions.

Her James. Her darling. He was only twenty one years old. Why did he have to be one of the unlucky ones?

If only Franklin had bought off that man from the Department of Labour and National Service. Others had. Then James wouldn't have had to go to that ghastly war. Other men's sons had cheated conscription, why couldn't James? If only Franklin had ...

But for once Penelope couldn't altogether blame Franklin. He had at least tried. At her insistence he'd tried.

She remembered with great clarity the argument when Franklin announced that he'd arranged a deal so James wouldn't have to go to Vietnam.

Well, it hadn't been an argument really. James had simply stood firm. Dear, sweet-natured James had stood up to his father. It was such a surprise. James had always been so agreeable, so helpful, never any trouble, even as a baby. He'd always been Penelope's favourite.

'Well you'll just have to un-arrange it, Dad,' James had said.

'Don't be a fool, boy,' Franklin growled. 'What's the sense in going off and getting yourself killed in someone else's war? No one's going to thank you for it, I can tell you that now.'

'Dad . . . ' Although James felt that he'd never really known his father, he admired him enormously. ' . . . you've always said we must remain "men of honour". I remember once, when we were kids, Terry laughed about it. He laughed and called you pompous and old-fashioned. Do you remember?'

Franklin remembered. He hadn't been offended at the time. As a boy, Terry had been wayward and undisciplined, but he'd been a charmer and it had been impossible to take offence when he looked at you with that twinkle in his eyes.

Franklin didn't answer and Penelope watched as he stood looking at his son and saying nothing. Good God, her mind screamed, surely the man wasn't going to stick to his ridiculous principles at a time like this? Not when the life of their son was at stake!

She'd pleaded with him to demand obedience. 'The boy will do anything you say, Franklin, just tell him. Order him,' she'd begged. But Franklin did nothing.

And now James was dead, Penelope thought. The whirling ceiling fan became a blur as the sedatives took effect. Their son had been killed in a lottery. A lottery in which the numbers could have been changed. Franklin could have changed them. He could have insisted. But he hadn't. Beneath Penelope's grief was a bitter resentment.

Bound for Sydney on his private jet, Franklin was also recalling that night.

'How can I stand by and watch the others go off to war,' James had continued relentlessly, 'knowing that I got out of it just because my old man's stinking rich? How do I remain a "man of honour" after that, Dad?'

Franklin hadn't pursued it. Of course he hadn't. He had no answer. And that night, he developed a newfound respect for his youngest son.

He cursed himself for not having recognised and valued the boy's strength of character. He'd been too busy concentrating on Terry. Terry, his first-born, the heir to the Ross empire. Terry, with his quick charm and his winning ways and his talent for getting into trouble which Franklin had fondly put down to the foolhardiness of youth. Terry didn't have half the spine that James had, Franklin could see that now.

He remembered the family holidays at Mandinulla. Never-Never and Jacky teaching the boys to ride. There were the inevitable spills and Terry would always boast of his cuts and bruises and how he got them.

'I took old Nell over the western fence, Dad,' he'd announced one day. 'She was cranky and she didn't want to go and I had two falls before she'd jump but we did it.' And Franklin had been proud.

James, who was six years younger, never had as many falls as his brother had had at the same age. He didn't show off as much either and Franklin had assumed it was because he didn't have as much to show off about, that he wasn't as courageous as Terry.

It had proved to be a foolish assumption. James had become the far superior rider. Franklin remembered watching the boys in the saddling yard one afternoon. Jacky constantly criticised fifteen-year-old Terry for pulling too hard on the horse's mouth.

'Don't fight him,' he said. 'Don't fight him and don't hurt him. No good, a horse with a hard mouth.'

And, while Terry had been showing off in front of his father, trying to get the animal to buck, nine-year-old James had been quietly practising his dressage in the corner of the yard, concentrating on his knees and his hands and being at one with his horse.

As Franklin looked out of the jet's windows at the lights of Sydney below, he wondered whether the favouritism he'd shown his eldest son was simply due to the boy's daredevil charm or the fact that young James was obviously Penelope's darling.

'You pamper him,' he'd said on a number of occasions. 'No wonder he's so docile, no wonder he's got no spine.' Franklin cringed now as he recalled his words.

'How would you know?' Penelope had retorted. 'You're hardly ever here these days. If you can find the time to worry about one of your sons, worry about Terry. He's out on the town and drunk most nights and he's barely eighteen.'

'He's sowing his wild oats – it's normal in a boy of his age.' In his youth, Franklin had never been 'out on the town and drunk most nights', but he always defended Terry, convinced that Penelope victimised him simply because she couldn't handle the boy's high spirits. And, because she doted on James, Franklin had ignored his youngest son. He'd dismissed James as a 'mummy's boy'.

And now James was dead, killed in battle serving his country, without ever knowing his father's love and respect.

Then, as the wheels of the jet touched down, the image of James' face flashed into his mind. The light shining in his son's eyes as they shook hands that night. 'How do I remain "a man of honour" after that, Dad?' Franklin hadn't answered, but he'd nodded and offered his hand. And the boy had smiled as they shook hands. Yes, thank God, he knew. James had gone to his death knowing that his father respected him for it. It was no consolation, but it was of vast importance to Franklin.

Over the ensuing days, there was little comfort Franklin could offer Penelope. There was little comfort he could offer himself. He held his grief deep inside, refusing to respond to her recriminations.

'The boy died an honourable death,' was all he would say. But, deep inside, his heart ached. He longed to cry like Penelope, to berate the system for the loss of his son. Anything to purge the pain he felt.

Several days later, James' body was flown home and a private burial service was held at The Colony House. James was the second member of the family to be buried in the Ross mausoleum Franklin had had erected at Waverley Cemetery after the stillborn birth of his daughter twenty-five years ago.

The pallbearers were Franklin, twenty-seven-year-old Terry, Solomon Mankowski and his son Karol. That night the four men went out to a bar in Kings Cross and got drunk.

Solly, now in his mid-seventies, had recently retired from the corporation. Although he was white-haired and weathered and looked his age, he was still a strong, virile man who very much enjoyed his life with a wife nearly twenty years his junior. He and Zofia lived in a fine house near Bondi Beach and each day Solly would go to the little shop he'd always kept in Surry Hills to work on private orders for fine leathergoods. He enjoyed working with his hands, working with leather, but he no longer wanted to match Franklin's pace.

'I am a wealthy man,' he said. 'At my age, why work for more than one needs? I leave that to Karol.' And, indeed, his son had taken over his father's position as right-hand man to Franklin.

Although similar in appearance to his father as a young man – dark Polish looks and solid build, Karol was as unlike Solly as he could possibly be. He was a solemn young man, not given to frivolous conversation, gambling or heavy drinking, and he took his job as Franklin's personal assistant very seriously. Franklin liked to travel as inconspicuously as possible and Karol, physically able as he was, doubled as his minder and bodyguard, always carrying a revolver.

That night, as they drowned their sorrows, Terry got very drunk. As usual. These days Terry always got very drunk. It annoyed Franklin, who wished his son could practise a little more self-control. He wished his son could take life a little more seriously, as Karol did. Handsome and debonair, Terry seemed to think his charm was enough to get him by. Very often it was. It was still difficult to bear a grudge when Terry flashed that disarming grin of his and said, 'I made a mistake, I'm terribly sorry.' He was always prepared to admit his mistakes, Franklin observed, but apparently he was unable to learn from them.

'Take him home, Karol,' he said as he watched Terry at the other end of the bar chatting to two attractive young women. It was his brother's wake, for God's sake – couldn't he leave the women alone for one night?

Three years ago Franklin had had to pay off the father of a pregnant factory girl and now he was biding his time for the next 'mistake', which was inevitable. Terry's sexual appetite was voracious and indiscriminate. Franklin had given up on the boy and his choice of women. He could damn well marry the next mistake, he swore to himself.

'Take him home,' he said.

The women didn't know how drunk Terry was and they were loath to see him leave, both finding him immensely attractive.

When the two younger men had gone, Solly turned to Franklin. 'And now, Boss . . . now we get seriously drunk, okay?'

Franklin nodded. They went into the back room of the bar and Solly ordered a bottle of vodka and a bucket of ice.

Two hours later, he called for a second bottle. Neither of them felt particularly drunk, but Franklin was talking. The best thing for him, Solly thought. He had only seen the Boss this voluble once before. It had been the vodka then too. He'd been twenty-five and had spoken with great passion about the vines, Solly remembered.

'I'm sixty years old, Solly, and I'm worth millions. What's it all for? Why did I do it? I did it for my two sons. For them and for their children and for their children's children.' Solly wisely didn't say a word. He could have said that Franklin did it for himself, to prove that he could. That's what Solly was thinking. But he didn't say it. The Boss was talking and that was good.

'And now what do I have?' Franklin asked. A rhetorical question. 'One son dead and the other a wastrel.'

Still Solly said nothing. He poured a glass for each of them from the fresh bottle.

It was a long time before Franklin spoke again and, when he did, his eyes demanded an answer.

'What was it, Solly? You know, don't you? You've always known.'

Solly looked at Franklin, genuinely mystified.

'Millie's child. What was it? A boy or a girl?'

Solly swallowed his vodka. He'd promised Millie years ago that he would keep everything a secret. Her child, her whereabouts, everything. It hadn't been a difficult promise to keep. Franklin had never asked. But now he was. Surely the promise wasn't one that he had to take to his deathbed? Surely not, Solly thought. It had happened over thirty years ago. Surely the death of a man's son was reason enough to talk freely?

'It was a girl,' he said, knowing that it would alleviate Franklin's suffering just a little. Although for the life of him, Solly couldn't understand why. His own daughter was the most precious thing in his life.

Solly was right. It helped Franklin to know that he had not denied himself a son, albeit a bastard.

'Is she well?' he asked and when Solly looked confused he added, 'Millie – is she well?' Solly nodded. 'I'd like to see her,' Franklin said.

Solly didn't know why he did it, but there seemed no reason not to. They were old, for God's sake. Well, he and Millie were, Franklin never seemed to change. Where was the harm?

It was closing time when they walked into the Surry Hills pub. The bar was deserted and a large woman was wiping down the tables. 'Sorry, fellas,' she said amiably, 'bar's closed.'

'Hello, Millie,' Solly said and the woman looked up.

'Solly,' she smiled. Then she saw the man standing beside him. The same ramrod back, the same stern face and steel-blue eyes. The hair was silver-grey now and the lines in the cheeks were deep, but there was no mistaking him.

'Franklin,' she said and she looked at Solly, who shrugged an apology. What the hell, she thought, and she smiled her forgiveness. We're old now. At least Sollly and I are – damn you, Franklin, why haven't you changed?

'It's good to see you, Millie,' Franklin said. And it was. Millie was over seventy and obese. The once luscious body was lost in a fat, old woman but, when she smiled, the years dropped away and there was the Millie he remembered. The dimples danced and the eyes were warm and inviting.

'It's good to see you too, Franklin,' she said and she kissed him on the cheek. 'Come on and sit down. Vodka?' No need to ask Solly, the query was directed to Franklin. He nodded.

They sat at a table and chatted. The conversation was easy and relaxed but impersonal. They talked about Franklin's business, his travels, and then he inquired about her job at the bar.

'Why are you still working? Surely you don't need to?' The inference was indirectly aimed at Solly. Solly had been instructed years ago to make sure that Millie and her child were never to want for anything.

Millie laughed. 'No, Franklin, I don't need to work. I do it because I love it. I own this place. It's my life.'

'This hotel? You own it?' She nodded. Franklin was impressed. He supposed she was widowed but he wasn't quite sure if he should ask. 'Your husband . . . ?' he said tentatively.

Millie laughed again and this time it was a boisterous laugh, full-bodied and throaty. 'Bless you, Franklin, I did it myself,' she said finally. 'Started out as a barmaid and fifteen years later I bought the pub.' Millie couldn't resist the gentle dig. 'Such success stories can happen, you know. Even to a woman.'

An hour later the men went home and Millie was left wondering why Franklin hadn't once inquired about his daughter. She was sure Solly must have told him. Just as she was sure Franklin would have displayed some interest if it had been a son. She also wondered briefly whether she should have told him that he had a two-year-old grandson. No, she would never tell him that. Franklin Ross was a powerful man who, if he wished, would have no trouble in taking over his grandson's life.

She was grateful that she'd never told Solly about the boy. Millie sighed as she cleared up the glasses. Dear, garrulous Solly. It was a miracle that he'd stayed silent for so long. But then it was quite likely that Franklin had shown no interest all these years. She wondered why he'd wanted to see her tonight. Mere curiosity? But she'd sensed a great sadness in him. It was strange. She'd read about his vast success, of course, and of his marriage years ago to the beautiful Penelope Jane Greenway. So why, all of a sudden, had he wanted to go back in time?

Several days later Millie read a newspaper article on the death of young James Ross, son of prominent citizen and businessman Franklin Ross. James had become one of the early Australian casualties in the Vietnam War. So that's why, she thought. Still, she didn't regret keeping the knowledge of her grandson a secret. Maybe when the boy was old enough to decide for himself, he might wish to trace his antecedents. But by then she would probably be dead and it would no longer be her problem. What will be will be, she told herself. She was too old to be bothered with that now.

Penelope's disapproval of Franklin's binge with Solly was evident the following day. She'd heard them come in after midnight and her bedside clock told her it was three in the morning when she heard Franklin come upstairs to his bedroom. (She and Franklin had long since had separate bedrooms.)

'It doesn't look good for a man in your position to be out drinking, Franklin,' she said. She meant 'with someone like Solly'. For all of his success and despite her bizarre friendship with Zofia, Penelope had never been able to approve of Solly. In her eyes, he had never acquired the style a man of his wealth and circumstances should have, and she simply could not understand the regard Franklin had for him.

'The evening of your son's funeral people would surely expect you to be at home mourning with your family,' she continued when he refused to answer. 'It's not correct for you to be seen . . . '

236

'You're nagging, Penelope,' he said and he poured himself another cup of tea.

It was Saturday and they were breakfasting on the terrace as they always did during the summer weekends when Franklin was at home. The harbour sparkled in front of them and small sailing craft glided across the waters.

Penelope kept quiet, but she was furious. How dare he? He always knew how to make her feel unattractive. She never 'nagged'. She merely tried, as any decent wife would for a man in his position, to safeguard his image. She picked up the newspaper and nodded curtly as he offered to pour her another cup of tea.

Franklin knew he had hurt her. He hadn't wanted to, but it was the only way to keep her quiet and he needed to think. God only knew why she was so insecure anyway; she was still one of the most beautiful women he'd ever seen.

At fifty-two years of age, Penelope could well have passed for thirty-five. She'd insisted on a facelift three years earlier, although Franklin hadn't been able to understand at all why she'd felt she needed it. She was an extremely handsome woman, he told her, why was she so preoccupied with her fading youth? But Penelope had merely laughed and said men didn't understand these things.

It was a good relationship in many ways. Penelope had made a career out of Franklin's business and position. Or rather, her position as the wife of so prominent a man. And with the exception of her refusal to accompany him to America, her refusal to have the knife twisted in the wounds of her thwarted career, she was a perfect ally for him.

He, in turn, had resigned himself to the fact that there were only to be two sons in his marriage. He would have liked five, but that was hardly Penelope's fault. She had been a good wife, a good mother, and now she was a good business partner.

They had even come to a tacit understanding about their sex life which maintained the status quo.

'It's so much better for one's health to sleep alone,' Penelope had insisted when he had been taken aback by her suggestion they have separate bedrooms. 'It's better for one's spine, therefore better for one's breathing, therefore better for one's skin. All the books say so.' Penelope was in her mid-forties at the time and paranoid about the loss of her beauty. She tried every treatment which professed to magic youth-enhancing ingredients and she read every book on the subject and she was already insisting she must have a facelift in the next couple of years.

Franklin took her insistence upon the separate bedrooms for exactly what it was, a healthier night's sleep, but he also assumed that it meant her beauty was of more importance to her than her sexual desires.

He hadn't been too disappointed by her decision at the time. He'd been spending several months of the year in New York anyway. In those days, Franklin had been devoting as much time as he possibly could to the amalgamation of Ross Entertainments and Minotaur Movies, which he and Sam Crockett had formed. Ross Industries, the major arm of the Corporation, he'd been happy to leave alone, as it had stood the test of time, but the production of television and movies for the world market demanded his personal attention.

Penelope loathed New York and the reminder that this had been the life she had originally planned for herself. Franklin had had no interest in the entertainment industry before he'd met her, but now his was one of the major international production companies. It was a bitter twist of the knife and Penelope always refused to accompany him on his trips to America.

Penelope's insistence upon separate bedrooms had not only failed to disappoint, it had signalled a certain freedom for Franklin. It meant he could now, in all conscience, set up an apartment for Helen so that they could live together during his New York visits.

Helen Bohan was an attractive thirty-year-old career woman, one of the junior directors of Minotaur Movies. Franklin had been having an affair with her for several years.

By Penelope's standards, Franklin supposed, Helen was no classic beauty, but he'd been attracted to her from the moment of their first meeting.

'You're the formidable Franklin Ross – how do you do? Helen Bohan.' The handshake had been firm, no-nonsense, and the expression in the eyes bold but not challenging. Friendly more than anything. 'I think this amalgamation's an excellent idea. Minotaur needs an injection of fresh blood and new ideas.'

They were at the cocktail party held specifically

for the directors of both companies to acquaint themselves with each other and Helen was making sure she did just that. It wasn't a flirtatious introduction. Franklin watched her as she continued on her rounds and each fresh handshake was just as open, just as friendly.

She wasn't slim and svelte like Penelope; her body was a little too thickset to wear clothes elegantly. Her face was not fine-boned and patrician but a little too square and almost devoid of make-up. Her hair was not styled fashionably but practically. This was a woman who couldn't be bothered spending hours each morning making herself beautiful.

Franklin had always been an admirer of cultivated feminine beauty. He liked women who went to great pains to look elegant. So why did he find Helen Bohan so attractive? He didn't for the life of him know, but there was something in the woman's directness, soemthing honest in her eyes, something warm and humorous in the curve of her mouth that made him want to get to know her.

'You appear to be without a drink, Miss Bohan,' he said, approaching her with two glasses of champagne he'd taken from a waiter's tray.

'Helen, please,' she smiled, 'and no, thank you, no champagne. It goes straight to my head.'

'But you'll have to have a drink,' he insisted. 'This is an introductory party, after all, we have to toast the amalgamation with something. What will it be?'

Helen was taken aback by the man's friendliness. She'd been told that Franklin Ross was a hard man, usually brusque and not one for social niceties. 'Well, I drink the occasional scotch and ice but . . . '

'A scotch and ice it is then.' Franklin signalled to a waiter. 'Noisy, isn't it? Cocktail chat always is. Like hens at feeding time. Shall we find a quiet spot?'

He found them some seats in a corner away from the mass of people and, when the waiter had delivered her scotch, they drank to the amalgamation.

'A toast, Helen,' he said. 'To Ross and Minotaur. Long may they reign.'

'Yes, Franklin, to Ross and Minotaur.' She studied him as she sipped her drink. There it was, she told herself, she'd been right, just the barest trace of surprise. He'd expected her to call him Mr Ross and wait to be invited onto a first-name basis. Helen was all for equality. Not that she didn't believe in mutual respect as well. If, being an older man and therefore possibly old-fashioned in his business etiquette, Franklin had insisted upon calling her Miss Bohan then she most certainly would have stuck to Mr Ross. She decided that, as his reaction had been infinitesimal, he'd passed the test. She smiled at him.

Although he'd covered well, Franklin was far more than a little surprised, he was startled. It wasn't the proper practice at all for a junior director, particularly a female, to assume a first-name basis with the president of the company.

Under normal circumstances, Franklin would have put the subordinate in his or her place. But the moment Helen smiled, he realised that this was what he liked about her. Not only her honesty, but her nerve. Helen Bohan had guts.

'How long have you been with Minotaur?' he asked.

During the rest of Franklin's stay in New York, he saw quite a bit of Helen Bohan. Board meetings followed by lunches, always at his suggestion and always under the pretext of necessary business discussions, although they both knew there was no earthly reason for the company president to take a junior director to lunch. Then, finally, just before he returned to Australia, Helen accepted his invitation to dinner. She knew she shouldn't. She knew he was married. She also knew she was in love with him.

They didn't sleep together that night but, on Franklin's return to New York the following year, Helen was the first person he phoned. And when, after dinner, they went back to her apartment, it seemed like the most natural thing in the world.

'I'd like to stay, Helen,' he'd said.

'Yes, I'd like you to,' she'd answered.

Their affair continued for the next several years, Franklin always staying in his rooms at the Broughton Arms – one of the luxury hotels owned by the Ross Corporation – and spending several nights a week at Helen's apartment. Helen accepted the fact that theirs was a relationship which existed for only three months of the year.

Then one day Franklin suggested that he find her a larger apartment. 'I spend so much time in

New York, my dear, we might as well be comfortable together,' he said.

Helen wondered at the reason for the change in their arrangements. Franklin had openly stated from the outset of their affair that he would never leave his wife. But he offered no reason. He didn't tell her that his guilt had been assuaged when Penelope had insisted upon separate bedrooms.

Helen accepted the offer and life progressed smoothly for Franklin. He didn't realise that, against her better judgement, Helen was desperately in love with him and that, although she wouldn't admit it even to herself, she lived in the delusion that one day he might leave his wife.

Penelope suspected that Franklin might have a mistress in New York but she never confronted him. It wasn't wise to rock the boat, she told herself, and she felt in no way threatened. Penelope was fully confident of her place in the scheme of things, secure in the knowledge that she was the co-ruler of the Ross Empire.

The maid came to clear away the breakfast things and Penelope continued to read the paper, still smarting at Franklin's comment about nagging. But he appeared oblivious, staring out over the harbour, his mind on other things.

He hadn't asked Millie about her daughter, he realised. But Millie had seemed so much her own person that he hadn't wished to intrude. Besides, if she'd wanted to talk about the daughter she would have, wouldn't she? No, it was safer to leave things as they were. And, with a tinge of sadness, Franklin realised that he would never see Millie again.

He looked over at Penelope and noticed that her eyes were not scanning the page. She was sulking.

'How would you like to go to Mandinulla?' he asked. 'I can afford a month off.'

'It'll be boiling at this time of the year.'

'So? That's never bothered you before. What do you say? Just the two of us.'

Penelope recognised the suggestion as a peace-making offer, and smiled. 'Very well.' It would be nice to see Never-Never. It would be nice to ride out to the creek, to catch yabbies and to pretend she was a girl again.

But they didn't go to Mandinulla. Several days later, Terry came to Franklin with the news his father had been dreading.

'How far gone is she?' Franklin asked, so annoyed he scarcely dared speak.

Terry could hear the anger in his father's voice and he started to feel a little nervous. It was obvious his charm wouldn't get him far this time. As a child, his father's anger had always terrified him. Franklin never shouted, never swore, never even raised his voice, but the tone was so threatening and the eyes so menacing that they instilled a genuine fear in the boy.

'She's not sure. She thinks about two months,' he said.

'And what does she do?'

'She works at the cannery.' Before his father could say anything, Terry continued hastily. 'But she's not a factory worker, she's a receptionist in the delivery office.' That sounded a lot better, he thought.

'I don't give a damn what she is. This time you'll marry her.'

For once Terry was at an utter loss for words. Vonnie was a nice little thing, and madly in love with him, but she was mousy – not his type at all. And they'd only done it a few times. Surely his father couldn't mean it? Not marriage. An allowance for the baby, if Vonnie wished to have it, or he could buy her out like he had the last girl ... But not marriage, surely?

'You can't be serious,' he said. 'Dad, you can't be.' Franklin still didn't answer. 'But she's a receptionist,' Terry insisted. How could his father force him to marry one of his factory employees? 'At the cannery,' he stammered.

'I don't care if she licks the labels,' Franklin said, his voice like ice. He could feel his right hand clench into a fist and he knew he would dearly love to hit his son. 'You will marry her. That is, if she's fool enough to have you. And then you will set up a decent home for her and the child, and you will give her more children and you will give her an honourable life.'

'Oh, come on, Dad.' Terry's mouth was dry but he tried to smile. Nine times out of ten the smile did the trick. 'You don't mean it ... '

'You'll do as you're told, boy,' Franklin snarled. 'You'll do as you're told or you'll be disinherited. Now get out.'

When Penelope met Veronica, she expressed her

concern to Franklin. The girl was definitely mousy and, Penelope suspected, not very bright. Certainly not the stylish, well-bred young lady one would have hoped Terry might marry.

'The boy should have thought of that,' Franklin growled and Penelope realised she would have to make the best of the situation.

As usual, it didn't take her long. Vonnie's lack of vivacity was to her advantage, she decided. A dowdy daughter-in-law would be no competition at all.

Penelope quickly befriended little Vonnie. And Vonnie, who was overwhelmed by the Ross household, was only too grateful for the support. Mrs Ross – 'Penelope, you must call me Penelope' – was the nicest person she had ever met.

Terence George Franklin Ross and Veronica Mary Slater were married on April 12, 1966 at St Mark's Church in Darling Point and there followed a grand reception at The Colony House. Twenty-two-year-old Vonnie felt like a princess. It was more than a dream come true – she would never have had the temerity (or the imagination) to dream that such a thing could be possible.

Six months later, Michael Terence Franklin Ross was born.

The birth of his grandson appeased Franklin. He'd been dismissive of his daughter-in-law. Not deliberately – she was simply invisible to him. Now that she had presented him with a grandson,

246

he instinctively offered her more attention. And she was a good mother. Terry, too, was a good father who enjoyed his baby far more than Franklin had his own children when they were infants.

As he watched Terry dandle little Michael on his knee, Franklin was prepared to forgive his son all his previous misdemeanours. Everything had worked out for the best, Franklin thought, and there would be more grandchildren. He was content.

It was Vonnie who realised that things hadn't really changed that much. At least not as far as Terry was concerned. She knew he still had affairs. Well, not so much affairs as conquests. She was aware that Terry couldn't resist a pretty woman. He couldn't resist the drink either but, when he came home, barely able to walk, and cried drunkenly on her breast, she had to forgive him. He was gentle and kind and he never abused her. Not the way her drunken father had abused her mother. He was a good provider and a good father and Vonnie supposed that his infidelity was her lot to bear. This was the price she was expected to pay for the elevated position she now held as wife to the heir of the Ross empire and mother to his son.

Barely a year after the birth of his grandson, Franklin was shocked out of his complacency. He'd just returned from New York and the successful conclusion of a television network deal between CBS, Ross Entertainments and Minotaur Movies. Things had gone extremely well.

'Mr Ross?' the girl said the moment he walked

in the door. But she knew she didn't need to ask. She knew it was him. Terry had told her all about him.

'Yes?' he said warily. The girl was in her twenties, fair-haired and physically quite attractive but there was a tough tilt to the chin and a glint in her eye which said she meant business. Penelope had told him she'd been waiting for two hours. Something to do with Terry, the girl had said, but she would speak to no one but Franklin. Penelope, frustrated, had been able to do nothing but wait with her.

The girl didn't beat about the bush. 'I'm carrying your son's child,' she said and she waited for the stunned reaction. She got it. Then she continued. 'I thought you might like to do something about it.'

'And what exactly do you expect me to do about it?'

'Give me money.' She stared back at him, unashamed. 'Quite a lot of money.'

Penelope wondered whether she should feign a fainting attack but she didn't think the girl would be impressed. It would be more effective to slap the brazen little slut hard across the face, she thought, and her palm itched. But of course she controlled herself.

'What does my son have to say about this?' Franklin asked.

'Oh, Terry's denying it's his, of course.'

Penelope felt a surge of relief. 'Well, he's probably right,' she said. 'You certainly can't prove it is.'

'Oh, it's his all right,' the girl continued

248

undaunted. 'He knows it's his. But he's scared. Not of me, not of the kid.' She turned again to Franklin. 'It's you he's scared of.' The girl dropped a touch of her bravado. 'If it wasn't for you, Mr Ross, your son would admit this kid was his and he'd set me up, look after me. Terry's not mean – he's just scared.' The girl was being reasonable now, and Franklin recognised it. 'But it's not fair to shut me out just because he's scared. I'll leave him alone. I don't want to wreck his life.' She raised her chin and the bravado was back. 'But it's going to cost money to have this kid and some-body has to fork out, so I thought it might just as well be you.'

'Good heavens, girl.' Penelope couldn't resist interrupting. 'If Terry isn't going to acknowledge the child as his own, why on earth should we?'

The girl barely glanced at her. 'Because you know I'm right, don't you, Mr Ross?' The chal-lenge was once again in her eyes but Franklin recognised something else. A sadness. 'You know your son's as weak as piss.'

What a pity the girl hadn't come on the scene a little earlier, Franklin thought. She was good daughter-in-law material. If Terry had been forced to marry this one instead of Vonnie the mouse, she might have toughened him up a little. Franklin despaired of Terry. The girl was right. He was as weak as piss.

'How much did you have in mind?' he asked.

'Franklin!' Penelope was shocked, but the look he flashed her brooked no argument so she kept quiet.

'I personally think you'd be far wiser not having

the child,' he continued. 'I could arrange – '

'That's really up to me to decide, isn't it?'

Franklin's eyes warned the girl that she was coming close to overstepping the mark. 'Whatever your decision,' he said coldly, 'there will be only one payment and that is for your silence. We do not recognise bastards in this family.'

She nodded and Franklin took out his cheque-book. 'I shall not expect to see you again,' he said as he wrote out the cheque. 'Ever.' She watched as he ripped it from the book. Yes, you're a tough old bugger, she thought. Everything that Terry said you were. He handed it to her. 'Agreed?'

She looked at the cheque. Fifty thousand dollars. She'd been hoping she might get ten. 'Agreed,' she said.

'I'm sending you to Mandinulla,' Franklin told Terry that night. 'You and Veronica and the baby. You'll work on the property for one year and when you return I expect to see a bit of common sense and maturity.'

Terry stood in front of his father's huge wooden desk in the study feeling like a ten-year-old. Franklin always did that to him. He always made him feel like a child.

As a child, though, Terry could remember, he'd always been able to get around the old man with his charm and his daredevil ways. Now he received nothing but scorn and contempt from his father, particulary since James' death. Whenever Franklin spoke of his youngest son it was with respect. 'A young man of honour and integrity',

Terry had heard him say. Is that what one had to do to win the old man's respect, he wondered, go out and get killed in some bloody stupid war? Jesus Christ, the old bastard had had little enough respect for James before he'd died. He'd paid the boy no attention at all.

Poor James, Terry often thought, all he ever wanted was his father's respect and he had to die to get it. But then he'd had his mother's love, hadn't he? Terry had always been envious of the love Penelope showered on James. He wondered whether that was why he vied so strongly for his father's affection. Probably. There was a strange sense of competition between Franklin and Penelope. God only knew what they were competing for – power, a hold over each other? – but it was bound to transfer itself to their children.

Not that it had ever interfered with the relationship between James and Terry. Despite their age difference, they'd been good friends and allies and Terry missed his brother desperately.

Maybe if he was here now, Terry thought, staring at the wooden desk top, he could help take a bit of the pressure off. The old man sure was mad about something. What could it be? he wondered. And why the hell is he sending me to Mandinulla? Jesus Christ, what am I going to do there? he thought, it's a million miles from anywhere.

'And while you're working on the property,' Franklin continued, 'you might work on giving me another grandchild. A legitimate one this time.'

Oh. Terry finally understood.

'Yes,' Franklin said. 'She's been here.'

'Julia.' Terry was starting to feel a little ill.

'She didn't give her name and I didn't ask. She's been paid off – we won't see her again.' Franklin leaned back in his chair. 'I'm warning you, Terry, this is your last chance. You want to be my son? You want to inherit the Ross empire? Then be a man. Stop drinking your life away, and stop bedding every woman you see. For Christ's sake, grow up, boy!'

At first Mandinulla looked as though it might be the answer. Terry tried hard to adjust to the culture shock. He tried to concentrate on the work involved, and there was plenty of it. The patrol and repair of fencing alone was a continuous job on a station the size of Mandinulla.

The days took care of themselves as his body tanned and toughened and he came to enjoy the physical labour. But the evenings were interminable. Terry desperately missed his racy Sydney set.

At least there was alcohol. Mandinulla Station was kept well-stocked. Indeed it was a rare night when Terry didn't go to bed at least halfway inebriated. But it was morose drinking – there was no longer the companionship and the good times he'd so enjoyed in Sydney.

The odd beer on a hot afternoon was the limit of Never-Never's alcohol consumption. Terry had asked him to dinner several times hoping for a soulmate, but he soon concluded that getting drunk was no fun when the other bloke gazed at you over the rim of a coffee mug for hours.

As for Vonnie, it was painful to see her bravely attempting to sip at a glass of wine to keep him company when he knew she loathed the very smell of it.

Baby Michael was a welcome distraction to start with but one couldn't fill in hour after hour of endless evenings playing with a fourteen-month-old-infant. And anyway, Vonnie would quietly whisk Michael off to bed when she saw the alcohol taking over. It wasn't that she was frightened. In the drink, Terry was either loving or maudlin, never violent, but he was clumsy and uncoordinated and not wise company for a baby.

The weekly excursions to nearby Quilpie or Charleville became inevitable. They were both tough outback towns with tough outback pubs and both were half a day's drive from the homestead.

Terry would take off at midday on Friday and he wouldn't reappear till Sunday afternoon. Then he would work hard during the week, get drunk – but not hopelessly so – each evening and simply bide his time till next weekend's binge.

Never-Never recognised that Terry was an alcoholic and at first he felt sorry for the wife. He made a habit of calling on Vonnie during the weekends to see if there was anything he could do for her – until he realised that there wasn't. The woman wasn't lonely at all. She was more than content with her baby and her radio and her books – in fact, she seemed at her happiest left alone. Left alone to live in her own world, somewhere – wherever that was.

Never-Never transferred his feelings of pity to Terry. Poor, desperate bastard. He wondered if Franklin Ross knew what a hopeless case his son was. Probably not. Although Franklin Ross was a tough, good, honest boss, when it came to personal relationships the man couldn't see the wood for the trees.

Penelope might know, the exquisite Penelope, although frankly Never-Never also doubted her powers of perception. He had long since become aware of Penelope's self-obsession.

As a young man, Never-Never had made it a policy not to get involved in other people's problems and he was certainly getting too old now to start changing his ways. It wasn't any of his business and, alcoholic or not, Terry pulled his weight around the place. When Franklin rang for regular reports on his son's progress, Never-Never said, 'Fine. He's doing fine.'

Christmas came and went. The cook baked a turkey and a plum pudding and Vonnie made mince pies and they ate their absurdly impractical meal in the evening to escape the worst of the searing heat. They pulled their Christmas bonbons and gave each other presents but, to Terry, the evening was as interminable as any other. He'd hoped they might make a trip to Sydney for the festive season and the New Year but Franklin was unyielding. 'I said one year and I meant one year, Terry. You're to stay at Mandinulla until next October.'

Franklin and Penelope were off to spend a fortnight in Acapulco with Sam and Lucy-Mae Crockett and there was no way that Franklin was going to let Terry loose in Sydney with his decadent friends in his absence. 'Never-Never tells me you're doing well,' he relented a little. 'Keep up the good work – only nine months to go.'

And then it was the 31st of December. New Year's Eve. The thought of New Year's Eve at Mandinulla was more than Terry could bear. At midday he got in the car and headed for Quilpie.

He pushed open the doors to the main bar, walked straight up to Ginger the barmaid and smiled his most engaging smile. 'Want to see in the new year with me?'

'Oh, hello, Terry, we haven't seen you for a while.' Like most women, Ginger found Terry Ross fatally attractive but she was no fool. He was not the sort you allowed yourself to fall in love with. Nevertheless she hadn't been able to resist sleeping with him twice.

Ginger was a divorcee of about thirty and an unusual kind of woman to find in the outback. She was soft and plumpish, with very fair skin: the worst complexion to weather the heat. She wore loose long-sleeved shirts and huge hats whenever she stepped outside. She was quick to correct people when they assumed that her head of thick coppery hair was how she'd got her name. 'Oh, no,' she'd say, 'my mum was mad about Fred Astaire and Ginger Rogers. I'm glad I wasn't a boy – isn't Fred an awful name?'

'Gee, give a girl some notice, why don't you?' she grinned at Terry. 'Actually the boss is having a party out the back for the regulars starting around nine. He's putting on a few kegs and after that you buy your grog – want to come along?'

'Sure. I guess I qualify as a regular, don't I?'

'Too right you do. See you in a couple of hours.'

Terry bought a bottle of scotch and booked into the small boarding house over the road which specialised in lodgings for itinerant workers. It was where he usually shacked up for the nights he spent in town when he was too drunk to drive.

He'd consumed most of the bottle of scotch by the time he arrived at the party and he was already looking a little the worse for wear.

'Take it easy, love, or you'll never make midnight,' Ginger laughed as she linked her arm in his.

It was a wild party, the kind one expected of the outback. Predominantly male. Unattached women stuck together to start with, then left early or latched onto a man of their choice so that they wouldn't be fair game later in the evening. Not that doing so solved the problem in every case. The night was hot, the grog was plentiful, the men were lonely and inevitably there was the odd young stud who wanted to fight for some other man's woman.

Terry was fairly safe with Ginger. She was held in high regard by the men of Quilpie. Besides, if they offended her, she could well have them barred from the pub, Mack the owner being particularly protective of his favourite barmaid.

There were jealous mutterings from some about the rich young bastard from the city walking in and taking over the hot favourite but it was more or less to be expected anyway. The rich always got the pick of the crop.

All in all, Terry was accepted by the locals.

Many of the townspeople wanted to curry favour with the heir to Mandinulla and Terry Ross was always very free with his money.

Tonight was no exception. Well before the kegs had run out, Terry was buying spirits for everyone.

'My shout,' he insisted, trying to sound like a bushie and feeling he was one of them. 'Crack open another four bottles, Mack.'

Terry was having the time of his life. And, when midnight came and they sang 'Auld Lang Syne', everyone in the pub was his best friend. At two o'clock in the morning he could barely walk.

'Come on,' Ginger said, fed up, slinging an arm over his shoulder. 'I'm going to put you to bed.' Ginger had had her fair share of alcohol too and it was making her randy. Damn it, she thought, she should have partnered up with young Scottie as she'd originally intended. Terry was going to be useless. But she could hardly leave him to pass out.

'Bed. Good idea.' He leered at her.

They managed to stumble across the street to the boarding house and Ginger fumbled in his pocket for the key.

'Yeah, good idea.' Terry leered again and started undoing his trousers. 'Let's do it here in the street. Give the town something to look at.'

She managed to get him into his bedroom and he slumped onto the bed.

'Shoes off, there's the boy, you'll be all right in the morning.' Hell, Ginger cursed, how many drunks had she played mother to over the years?

But something in Terry clicked and he pushed her away. 'Don't you talk down to me,' he mumbled, staggering to his feet. 'I'm not a child.'

He pressed her up against the wall. 'I'm not a child.' He took her hand and thrust it inside his open trousers, rubbing it against his flaccid penis. 'You feel that,' he said. 'You feel that. I'm not a child.'

'Oh, cut it out, Terry, for God's sake.' Ginger was starting to get cross. He was ruining her New Year's Eve and his breath was foul.

'Grab a hold of that baby,' he slobbered, grinding her hand into his crotch. 'Grab a hold of that and make it hard.'

'I said *cut it out*!' She wrenched her hand away and struck him as forcefully as she could across the face. For a moment he seemed to come to his senses. He looked at her, a mixture of shock and self-disgust in his eyes.

'I'm sorry, Terry,' she said, 'but you asked for it.'

And then his face crumpled and he bent over and threw up. Copiously. All over the wall. All over the floor.

'Oh, shit,' Ginger cursed. She tried to dodge out of the way but vomit poured out of him all over her bare legs and into her open sandals. 'Oh, shit. You pig.'

Terry dropped to his knees, still vomiting. 'You filthy pig!' Ginger yelled and she ran out of the room.

Surprisingly enough, he didn't pass out. He lost his balance and fell forward into his vomit but he cracked his head against the wall as he did and it shocked him vaguely into his senses. At least enough to be aware of what had happened, enough to be aware of his mortification.

258

He had to get out of this room, he told himself, out of town, back to Mandinulla. If he woke up in his own bed he might be able to pretend tonight had never happened. If he woke up in his own vomit it would be the end of him.

As he dragged himself to his feet, Terry even had the presence of mind to pull out a couple of crumpled twenty dollar notes from his pocket. He threw them on the bed for the land-lady who would have to clean up the mess in the morning.

In the car, his mind started to focus quite clearly as the hot night air rushed through the open windows. The movement of the air gave the impression it was cooler even though it still had to be all of thirty degrees. Perhaps if he drove faster, he thought, it would get cooler still. He pressed down on the accelerator.

He drove for hours and as he drove, he thought. What was wrong with his life? Why did his father treat him like a child? Where was Julia? He missed her. Julia was the only one he'd ever cared for. And she'd loved him. But she'd been right. He was as weak as piss. That's what she'd told him.

Christ, it was hot. Faster. Go faster, he thought, that'll cool you down. And he pressed the accel-erator to the floor.

It was late in the afternoon of New Year's Day, 1968, that the body of Terence George Franklin Ross was discovered in the mangled wreck of his new Ford Mustang barely five miles from Man-dinulla. The vehicle had obviously been driven off

259

the road at high speed and had tumbled a hundred yards down the gully to land in the creek below. It was the creek where his mother had taught him to catch yabbies as a child.

Terry was buried in the Ross mausoleum, the third and last of the children of Franklin and Penelope Ross. As Franklin watched the funeral procession, he saw the disintegration of his dreams. Where was the dynasty he'd planned? An eighteen-month-old grandson alone remained to carry the Franklin Ross name into the future.

After the grief, however, came the anger. He'd been cheated. But he was damned if he'd give in. His dream would survive. And Franklin swore that he would remain alive and strong and powerful until young Michael Terence Franklin Ross was of an age to inherit his empire.

The

New Generation

(1977 - 1984)

Book Four

The

New Generation

(1977 - 1984)

CHAPTER EIGHT

Michael

MICHAEL ROSS WAS AN engaging child. Physically, he was very like his father, with a ready grin and a cheeky charm. But Franklin was heartened to observe that the boy had far more ambition than his father had ever possessed. At ten, Michael had not only a vivid imagination and a spirit of adventure, but he had a fierce desire to achieve. The boy's a winner, Franklin thought with pride and satisfaction.

Michael, in turn, recognised very early in his life that his grandfather was not only a rich and powerful man but that he instilled fear in most people who knew him. At ten years of age Michael couldn't understand why. He would sit at the old man's feet and demand stories about New York and Hollywood and the movie idols his grandfather knew. He was too young to be impressed by the industrial empire Franklin Ross had built and the international renown of the Ross Corporation, but the magic world of the cinema never ceased to fascinate him.

Following Terry's death, Franklin had insisted

that Vonnie and her child move into The Colony House. Despite the fact that his business schedule was as hectic as ever and that, at seventy, he showed no signs of easing up, he always made time for his grandson.

Michael loved The Colony House. From his bedroom window he could see the old bronze statue of the dueller pointing across the water to the Sydney Harbour Bridge. Time and time again he begged his grandfather to tell him the story of that night and the duel with Samuel Crockett.

Michael had met old Sam Crockett once. When he was six, Sam and Lucy-Mae had visited The Colony House. The boy had been in awe of the giant American. Between his crippling bouts of gout, Sam was as big and as boisterous as ever.

There were many influences on young Michael. Grandpa Franklin was the most awesome, certainly, but there was Penelope too. Penelope, who always refused to be called Grandma, was, to the boy, the epitome of glamour.

In her sixties, Penelope had acquired a regality which was charismatic. Heads turned when she walked into a room. It was her carriage and assurance which created the effect as much as her beauty which, although as arresting as ever, now had a slightly hard quality to it, the skin being a little taut after her second facelift.

Penelope's added confidence was a direct result of her elevated social position and her role as chairman of Ross (Australia) Productions. After Terry's death, it had been Franklin's idea that she play an active part in the administration of their Australian film and television interests.

His offer had been by way of compensation or to keep the peace – Franklin was never quite sure which. Compensation for the loss of her sons or a gesture to keep the peace following the scene they'd had which had nearly escalated into a heated argument. Franklin and Penelope never argued. On occasion Franklin was brusque or remote, depending on his mood, and Penelope was at times acid or sulky, depending on hers, but they never raised their voices at each other. Both detested any display of temper in themselves or others.

It had happened the week after Terry's funeral. One night, at dinner, Penelope had more than her customary single glass of wine to aid the digestion and became morose. She'd been depressed since the accident and Franklin hadn't inquired too deeply, putting it down to mourning whilst he sorted out his own feelings about his son's death.

'What is there to live for, Franklin?' she'd asked as she stared at the dregs of her fourth glass of wine. She was obviously affected by the alcohol and Franklin assumed the question was rhetorical, so he didn't answer. She didn't expect him to. 'We killed our sons – you know that, don't you?' This time she looked at him, obviously expecting a reply. He said nothing. 'You know that, don't you?' she persisted. 'We killed them, you and I, we killed them.'

'You've had a little too much wine, my dear,' he said gently. 'You're distressing yourself unnecessarily. Perhaps you should go to bed.'

Penelope ignored him and poured herself another glass. 'You never loved James and you

265

sent him to his death.' Several drops of wine spilled onto the tablecloth and she covered them with a linen napkin. 'And I didn't pay enough attention to Terry and he killed himself.'

Her tone was maudlin. Franklin looked at her and felt a surge of irritation. She was wallowing in the drama of it all and whitewashing herself at the same time. Her guilt was a mere oversight and his was murder.

'I did love James,' he answered stiffly. 'And I most certainly did not send the boy to his death. He died a hero in the service of his country.'

'Rubbish and you know it!' Penelope raised her voice and the sound was grating to Franklin. 'He only went to war to prove to you that he was a man. And when he died you made him a hero and then Terry couldn't do anything right. He tried. I watched him try.'

Franklin's irritation was rapidly becoming anger. So now he was responsible for Terry's death too. He'd thought about whether there was anything he could have done to prevent the deaths of his sons and he'd come to the conclusion that there was nothing. He was absolved. James had been conscripted into the army and had died in battle. Heartbreaking but simple. And Terry? Terry had been weak, a loser. His own deficiency of character had been his undoing. Indeed, Franklin had been a fool not to see the weakness in the boy from the very beginning.

As he looked at his wife, Franklin felt a white-hot fury growing. How dare she? He had nurtured his anger at fate and the hand he'd been dealt. He'd kept it raging inside him and he'd be damned if he'd let Penelope undermine his belief.

'Go to bed, woman, you're drunk.' He tried not to raise his voice but there was such a venomous edge to it that he might as well have. Penelope recognised his anger and realised that she'd gone too far. She hadn't really meant to goad him, but it was all so unfair. There was nothing left in her life. It was empty. Someone had to be to blame.

'It's not fair,' she said, putting down her glass. 'It's not fair.' Tears welled in her eyes.

'Of course it isn't.' Franklin recognised that the danger was over and his fury abated. She was unhappy and lashing out at him, that was understandable. 'It isn't fair and it isn't anyone's fault.' He put his arm around her, gently easing her out of the chair. 'Now go to bed like a good girl and we'll talk about things in the morning when you feel better.'

They hadn't talked about things the following morning but Franklin had suggested that she take on a full-time administrative role with Ross (Australia) Productions and Penelope allowed herself to be persuaded.

It wasn't long before Penelope regained her love of power and position. Franklin was delighted with the result. Now, years later, she was literally running the business and Franklin was left free to concentrate on his American studios and production company.

His trips to the States were now more important than ever to Franklin. Penelope had long since refused to have sexual intercourse. In retrospect, he'd realised that it was around the time of James' death that she'd started to lose interest in sex, and he'd supposed it was understandable. But as a result, the convenient affair he'd been having in New York with Helen Bohan had become a far more significant feature in his life.

He hadn't intended it to be that way. He'd always been honest with Helen. He'd told her from the outset that theirs was an expedient affair, that he would never leave his wife. Helen chose to accept the conditions.

Then, years later, when his feelings for her deepened, he worried that he might be ruining her life. 'You're nearly thirty years younger than I am, my dear,' he said. 'You need someone close to your age. You need children.' Still Helen chose to stay with him.

Her love and loyalty gradually took effect and Franklin's annual three months in New York became four and then five. His only regret was seeing less of the grandson upon whom he doted, but time would rectify that. In eight or nine years the boy would be old enough for a position in the company and then they would work and travel together. Such were Franklin's plans for Michael.

Michael had his own plans, which didn't particularly conflict with Franklin's. At ten he'd decided he was going to make movies. He didn't want to act in them, he wanted to create them. Fantasies. His head swarmed with stories and visions and characters who belonged to a special world.

His glamorous grandmother, who had once been a Hollywood movie star and who had the photos to prove it, was more than encouraging.

268

Penelope was proud of her creative, imaginative grandson and she, too, had plans for Michael.

Everyone had plans for Michael, it appeared, except his mother. Vonnie seemed to have disappeared in the scheme of things, and yet it was she who, in reality, was the greatest influence of all upon the boy. Quiet, colourless Vonnie, 'the mouse', was the one responsible for Michael's private world of fantasy and the belief that, through it, he could achieve anything.

Ever since she'd been absorbed by the Ross household – absorbed to the point of oblivion – Vonnie had retreated into her own world. In that world she was important. In her own world she was beautiful, she was deeply loved and she could do anything she wanted. It had started with books and radio and television – they'd been enough of an escape for her in the beginning. But after Terry had died and they'd moved into The Colony House, she needed more.

One day she had overheard Penelope referring to her as 'the mouse'. Vonnie supposed a comment like that was to be expected from someone as glamorous as Penelope. But Penelope had always professed to be her friend. That was when Vonnie finally disappeared. She retreated into her magic world where anything was possible, and she took her baby with her.

Little Michael loved it. He loved the endless possibilities of the fantasy land she built for them and, by the time he was ten, something that had begun as an escape for Vonnie had become an extension of the real world to Michael. He couldn't wait for the day when he would bring his

269

visions to life, when he would create happenings, control the lives of the people in his mind.

In the meantime, he wrote plays and stories and made puppets and scenery and even a makeshift theatre in which to perform his inventions.

Franklin was so impressed that he had an extravagant marionette theatre made for the boy, complete with electronic curtains and backdrops and scenery changes. He also purchased a dozen hugely expensive handmade marionettes in an assortment of characters both classical and modern.

Michael was happy to use the theatre and its attendant equipment, but he left the marionettes alone. He only wanted to play with the puppets he had made. To Michael it was important that the characters in his plays and stories, and what happened to them, were of his creation. And one day, he told himself, those puppets would be real people. One day he would create and control the lives of real people.

Michael's was an idyllic childhood. Although he was spoilt by his wealthy grandparents, it didn't seem to tarnish his amiable disposition. A generous-natured boy to whom money and possessions meant little, he loved giving presents, which made him very popular at school. His natural exuberance and sense of mischief led him into trouble now and then but even the teachers who punished him realised that his behaviour was a natural extension of the child's creative imagination. Everyone liked Michael. And Michael liked everyone.

Everyone, that is, except Karol. Michael was unsure of Karol, even a little frightened of him. But then everyone was a little frightened of Karol Mankowski.

Karol Mankowski was his grandfather's personal assistant but even Michael knew that he was really Franklin's personal bodyguard and that the man was an expert in the martial arts and always carried a gun.

It wasn't that there was anything particularly violent about Karol. To the contrary, he rarely spoke and, when he did, his voice was so quiet that Michael could barely hear it. But there was no vitality in him, no humour.

Even Grandpa Franklin told the odd joke, Michael thought. Karol never did. And when Grandpa Franklin said something funny everyone laughed. Everyone except Karol. Michael wondered if he knew how.

As a young man, Karol Mankowski had always been of a serious disposition. Now, in his late thirties, he had reason to be. His wife and only child had been killed in a car crash three years before. A crazy, meaningless car crash. Police chasing two youths in a stolen car. An innocent mother and child waiting at an intersection. The youths had been unhurt, one policeman had an arm broken, the mother and child . . .

Karol was a bitter man. He'd always been a private person to everyone but his family. He'd never had friends but that didn't worry him. He had his parents and his wife and child. And, of course, Franklin. Franklin Ross was a second father to Karol. Then came the terrible accident and, a year after that, the death of his father.

Solly Mankowski died peacefully in his sleep of a heart attack when he was in his eighties. But Karol was convinced that his father would have lived another ten years had it not been for the accident. Solly grew old in the year that followed. Then he let himself die.

In Karol's life now there was only his mother and Franklin. Zofia was strong. She loved her son but she didn't need him. She devoted herself to her daughter and her two grandchildren. That left Franklin. Only Franklin needed Karol, and Karol's whole existence now revolved around the protection of Franklin Ross. Franklin Ross and his sole heir.

Karol was always watching Michael. Quietly . . . furtively. Michael hated it. It gave him the shivers. When his grandfather left for the States, and took Karol with him, Michael breathed a sigh of relief. Of course there were the general security guards who patrolled The Colony House – he knew they'd been told to keep an eye on him and one of them usually tagged along when he went out – but they were good fun and he could share a joke with them. When he went to the studios with Penelope or to the zoo with Zofia and her grandchildren, there was always a security man in attendance but he didn't spoil the outing – he managed to disappear into the background.

Not Karol. Michael could never get Karol out of his line of vision. Wherever he looked, there was Karol, somewhere in the corner of his eye. Stolid, immovable, except for the eyes beneath the heavy Polish brow. The piercing black eyes which missed nothing.

One day, shortly after his twelfth birthday, Michael decided that it was time to stop being frightened of Karol. The man was probably a fool anyway, he told himself, and he invented a convenient character.

Karol was really all show. That was it. A moron. Hired by his grandfather because of Franklin's close friendship with Solly. And Franklin had agreed years ago to disguise the fact that his friend's son was a halfwit by having him serve in a position as bodyguard. His appearance suited the purpose and nobody would question his wits. Perfect. It was a good scenario, Michael decided, and he persuaded himself that it was fact. Of course there was only one way to prove it.

'Can I come to the studios with you, Penelope?' he asked his grandmother one day. It was school holidays and he knew she'd say yes. Just as he knew that Karol would accompany them, Franklin having called an all-day conference at The Colony House. During the long, hot summers, Franklin regularly called meetings for his senior administrators at The Colony House rather than the city offices. It was cooler and more comfortable for all concerned.

'Of course, darling,' Penelope said. 'I'll be leaving in half an hour. It's "Family Love" script conference day too; I'm sure Reg won't mind you sitting in.'

Michael knew full well it was 'Family Love' script conference day, just as he knew Reg wouldn't mind him sitting in. He intended spending his usual hour observing the writers – it was all part of his plan.

'Family Love' was a successful television situation comedy which Ross (Australia) Productions had been producing for the home market for three years. Michael loved observing the monthly script conferences. And the weekly storylining sessions, and the writers' meetings – and anything else in which he could be included. During the storyline sessions his opinion was quite often sought. 'How do you think the younger viewers will take that, Michael?' they'd ask, and he always had a ready answer. He was careful not to venture an opinion without its being sought, though. Heir to the throne he might be, but if Grandpa Franklin found he was becoming a nuisance, he would quickly be banned from the studios.

As usual, Karol sat in the corridor outside the conference room. Michael could see him through the plate glass windows. He simply sat there. He never read a paper or had a cup of coffee, although the table beside him was strewn with magazines and the girl at the nearby reception desk always asked if she could get him 'a cup of something'. He simply sat. Michael found it infuriating. Today he'd get his own back, he told himself. Today he'd prove that the man was a halfwit.

'How the hell can we kill her off? It's a comedy, for God's sake!' One of the writers had taken offence at Reg's suggestion they get rid of a major actress. 'And Dolly's the most popular character in the show.' The writer had been with the series since its inception and Dolly was his invention.

'Our market research shows us that she's not,' Reg explained patiently. Reg was the executive script editor and he never lost his temper. 'The public's getting sick of the stereotype dumb blonde who messes things up but it always comes out right in the end. The plots are predictable. After three years we need to give the viewers a fresh approach.'

The writer was about to interrupt but Reg continued. 'What's more, Sal's become a pain in the arse. The directors are complaining that she's temperamental and also her contract's up soon and the casting department's warning me she's going to ask for a hell of a lot more money.'

The writer didn't have an answer to that. Budget ruled everything. 'So what happens if the viewers don't like it?' he said sulkily. 'What happens if they want her back but we've killed her off? This isn't a soap; it's a family sitcom, damn it. We can't rope in a lookalike and call her Dolly – they won't accept it.'

'Then we bring her back in the other characters' minds,' Reg argued. 'We can have Dolly storylines for weeks while everyone thinks about her and fantasises about her. And we'll bring in a new character at the same time. We phase Dolly out and after a month the viewers won't even notice she's gone.' Reg turned to Michael. 'What do you think, Michael? How do you feel about Dolly?'

'I'm a bit sick of her,' Michael agreed. 'She's funny but she's too dumb and you always know what's going to happen next.'

He loved discussions like this, particularly when

275

they made him a part of them. But they'd been talking for half an hour and he had his plan to adhere to.

'There you are,' Reg countered triumphantly, 'the instinctive response of the younger viewer.'

Michael excused himself to go to the lavatory. He could feel Karol's eyes on him as he walked down to the end of the corridor and into the men's.

Once inside, he knew he had all of five minutes before Karol would pretend the need to urinate and join him. The man would say nothing. He'd go into the adjoining cubicle and there'd be the sound of pissing (he could obviously urinate at will) but Michael knew that all the time Karol was listening and watching.

In less than three minutes, Michael had wriggled out of the tiny window and was running down the narrow lane and into the adjoining park.

His plan was simple. He'd stay away just long enough to make them confused, not angry. His intention was to prove Karol's inadequacy, not get himself into trouble. The last thing Michael wanted to do was incur the wrath of Franklin. He'd simply say he'd gone for a walk and had assumed that Karol had seen him leave.

Michael could hear himself: 'But, Grandpa, I walked right past him. He could have followed me if he'd wanted to.' (No one would be able to prove that he'd climbed out the toilet window.)

Penelope's board meetings usually lasted about two hours and the normal procedure was for Michael to go to the canteen after his hour with the writers. Or he'd watch some filming in one of the studios – all the time observed by Karol – and then report to reception to wait for the driver to collect them.

Michael walked through the park. What would he do for the next hour and a half, he wondered. He would dearly love to catch a bus into the city and go to a movie but that would take too long and clearly be seen as an act of rebellion.

The studios were in Randwick, not far from Bondi Beach, and it was a boiling hot day. That was it, he decided, he'd go to the beach.

He heard himself: 'It was really stuffy at the studios, Grandpa, I just went for a walk to the beach, that's all ... ' And why not? he asked himself. Perfectly reasonable.

It was school holidays and Bondi Beach was crowded. People in droves, sunbaking and surfing. The waves looked so enticing Michael wished he had his bathing costume with him. He bought an ice cream at the pavilion and sat on the stone steps looking out over the blue bay and the crowds wallowing in the surf. Karol would be searching the studios for him by now. He looked at his watch. Another half an hour and the driver would arrive to collect Penelope. That was when they would expect him to be waiting in reception. Only another half hour to go, he thought, and wondered what to do next.

He strolled up to the expanse of lawns which overlooked the beach. A blue heeler cross was insanely trying to round up the seagulls. Michael stopped and observed the mayhem as the dog charged like a mad thing through the groups picnicking on the grass. People dropped their milkshakes and fish and chips as hundreds of gulls screeched their annoyance and took to the air.

Michael laughed and was about to sit on the grass to watch the dog's antics when a figure appeared beside him.

'Time to go, wouldn't you say?'

He turned, startled. It was Karol. Michael stared back at him, dumbfounded. The man had appeared from nowhere.

'Come on.' Karol turned to go. 'We wouldn't want to keep your grandmother waiting.'

And Michael had no option but to follow.

They walked back to the studios together in silence. Karol demanded no explanation and he gave none in return. He didn't tell Michael that he'd been expecting this for a whole year. He'd sensed the boy's growing irritation and had been fully prepared.

For the past twelve months, each time Michael had gone to the men's, Karol had wandered a little further down the corridor and had watched the tiny lavatory window through the plate glass reception doors. After a five-minute lapse, he knew it was safe to visit the toilets and relieve himself. By then he usually needed to, and by then he knew it was safe – if the boy was going to make his bid it would be within the first few minutes of his disappearance.

It was only when they were waiting comfortably in reception that Karol finally spoke.

'It's not fair to play games, Michael,' he said.

Michael felt a tiny stab of fear. Was the man

threatening him? Was he angry because the prank might have jeopardised his job? But since Solly's death, Karol didn't need a job – he was a wealthy man; he owned massive shares in the Ross Corporation. Was he angry because Michael had tried to make him look bad in Franklin's eyes? No, that wasn't it either.

'It's not fair to play games on your grandfather,' Karol continued. 'He has a big stake in you.'

Then Michael realised that Karol wasn't angry at all. And that there was no threat. Karol was simply devoted to Franklin Ross.

An unspoken truce was declared after that. Michael never again attempted to goad Karol and Karol, in turn, stopped crowding the boy.

Thankful as he was for the extra space, Michael's opinion of the man hadn't radically changed. Admittedly Karol had a certain cunning, but he was still thick and humourless and Michael preferred to ignore him – until two years later, when something happened that rendered it impossible for him to ever again ignore Karol Mankowski.

It was barely a week before Michael's fourteenth birthday, a Saturday, and he was playing in his school rugby union semifinals. Michael was a fine sportsman. For the past two seasons he'd represented the Junior 1st XV as a winger and he invariably picked up the award for best and fairest player.

It was a fine spring day and, despite the fact that it was only a semifinal, the grandstand at Waverley Oval was packed with spectators.

Michael had been thrilled when Franklin had decided to come along at the last minute.

'Are you sure, Grandpa? It's only a semi,' he said, trying to sound nonchalant. On the rare occasion that Franklin had been in Sydney for the season and had attended the finals, Michael had basked in the reflected glow which always surrounded his grandfather. Franklin Ross was an eminent man whose picture had been on the covers of *Time* magazine and the *Bulletin* and everybody wanted to meet him. Michael was very proud of his grandfather.

'Of course I want to come,' Franklin said, gratified by the boy's obvious delight. 'I wouldn't miss it for the world. Now hurry up and get ready and you can come with Karol and me, we'll even watch the warm-ups.'

Phil, the security man who'd been assigned to accompany Michael to the game, was waiting by his car in the main drive when Franklin and Karol stepped outside.

Franklin's pesonal driver pulled up in the Bentley and Phil opened the door for Franklin, then he returned to his own vehicle and opened the passenger door in readiness for Michael.

'It's all right, Phil,' Franklin said, getting into the Bentley, 'Michael's coming with us. You can go on ahead – we'll meet you there.'

'You're going to the game, sir?' Phil looked a little taken aback.

'Yes, yes,' Franklin said with a touch of irritation, 'hurry up, boy,' he called, 'or you'll be late for the warm-up.'

Michael raced out, stuffing his football boots

280

into his sportsbag. Karol opened the back door of the Bentley for him and he jumped in. 'Sorry, Grandpa, I nearly forgot my boots.'

'Hell of a lot of good that'd do you.' Franklin couldn't resist the lecture. 'You should have packed them last night.' Much as he adored the boy, Michael's lack of attention to detail and his lack of punctuality always irritated the old man.

Karol stood watching Phil for a moment before he joined Michael in the back seat and he continued to watch Phil's car ahead as they drove to Waverley Oval.

It was a good match. Michael's team won and he played well. Franklin felt proud. He barely followed the game, his eyes on his grandson the whole time. What a fine figure of youth and health the boy was.

Karol didn't watch any of the game. His eyes were on Phil the whole time. The man was nervous, he thought. Why?

At halftime Phil went to the lavatory. Karol went too. It was unusual for Karol to take a toilet break at the same time as another security operator. And Phil knew it.

'Good game, eh?' he said, as they stood beside each other at the urinal.

Karol nodded and watched the beads of sweat on the man's brow.

At the end of the match Karol left the grandstand. He stood among the spectators who had gathered to congratulate the winning team on their way to the change rooms. From his position he was able to watch both Phil in the grandstand, and the boy as he left the field. That was when it happened.

A man came out of the crowd and gently took Michael's arm. He appeared to be shaking him by the hand but, as he did, he was edging him away from the team and away from the door to the change rooms. Then, suddenly, he pulled the boy around the side of the grandstand and out of sight.

Michael was so taken by surprise that, for a moment, it didn't occur to him to fight back. And he couldn't yell. The man was strong, his hand was over Michael's mouth. He was virtually lifted from the ground and carried towards the waiting car. By the time he realised what was happening and started to kick and struggle, he'd been bundled into the back, the man was beside him holding him down, and the car was taking off.

The driver slid into second gear. It was a woman. Michael could see her blonde hair. Then, through the windscreen, standing in the road only yards ahead, he saw Karol. Both arms extended. A 9 mm Beretta in his hands.

There was a flash from the barrel of the gun, the windscreen shattered and the woman slumped back. Her blood splattered Michael in the back seat and her blonde hair dripped red.

The car slowly veered to the left, hit the curb and came to a halt. The man beside Michael opened the back door in a bid to escape but there was no time. He had one foot out on the curb and Karol was there.

Michael couldn't see what happened next, but he heard a muffled crack and the man's head jerked back. He slid into the gutter, face up, one foot still in the car and a bullet hole through his forehead.

Michael remained frozen. He saw Karol put his gun back in his shoulder holster and take a switch-blade from his pocket. He pressed a button on the side, the blade flicked open, and he placed it in the man's right hand.

'Don't forget, Michael, there was a knife,' he said as he leaned forward and pulled the boy from the car.

For Michael, everything after that was a blur. He was in a state of shock. They took him home and washed the blood from him. There were the police. The questions. Was there a knife? 'Yes,' he said. 'Yes, the man had a knife.'

He said it over and over. It appeared he couldn't remember anything else.

There was an inquest. The verdict was justifiable homicide by a man licensed to carry a firearm. Franklin's lawyers even managed to minimise the fact that the dead man had been left-handed. He'd used his left hand to open the car door, they said.

A week after the incident, the body of Phillip Godden, security guard in the employ of Ross Industries, was found in an alley behind a gambling den in Chinatown. His throat had been cut. The case was never solved.

For quite a time after the killings, Michael had recurring nightmares but over the years and with the help of intensive therapy, they receded to an ugly blur and Franklin was informed that the boy had made a good recovery and would not be emotionally scarred for life.

A lesson had been learned, though, and for the next four years Franklin assigned a personal bodyguard for the protection of his grandson. He held himself responsible for the near success of the attempted kidnap. Of course his grandson was worth a king's ransom, of course he should have personally screened each of his security team. If Karol hadn't been there . . . If . . . Franklin cursed himself and swore that it would never happen again. After a painstaking search, he engaged a thirty-five-year-old ex-policeman as Michael's personal minder.

Daniel Pendennis was an ex-detective and a former member of the elite VIP Protection Unit. Franklin was pleased; he'd been fully aware that Michael had been inhibited by the dour Karol Mankowski who was hardly ideal company for a teenager. Daniel Pendennis not only had an impressive list of credentials, he had a sense of fun.

Dan was originally from Cornwall, a fishing village called Mousehole. 'But you don't say the "hole",' he insisted in his rough Cornish brogue. 'It's pronounced "Mouzle".'

The entire village had been taken aback when young Dan had applied for entry to the London Metropolitan Police. But then he'd always been an unpredictable boy, and they were all proud of him when he was accepted for training. Especially his father who had three other sons who were only too happy to follow in their dad's footsteps and become fishermen. A copper in the family would certainly be something to boast about.

So Dan went to London and became a policeman. And then he became a detective with the VIP Protection Unit. But he never forgot Mousehole and, whenever he could, he returned to the tiny fishing village with its quaint houses and its narrow streets.

'Some of them are so narrow that if you meet another car one of you has to back up the hill and out of town,' he told Michael. 'I haven't been there for four years now, not since I came out to Australia – longest time ever without a visit to the home town. It's my sanity, you know. I reckon one day I'll retire there.'

Daniel was an uncomplicated man. Life for him was simple. Which was why he'd left the police force after ten years. He'd shot a man in the line of duty and, when they took his gun from him, treated him like a criminal and demanded a full investigation, Dan was left in a state of utter confusion. He'd done what they'd trained him to do. The man had been armed with a knife, he'd refused to surrender and Dan had shot him neatly in the thigh. All very simple.

The investigation cleared him, of course, but by then Dan was so disillusioned that he decided to opt for a less complicated existence.

Personal protection was easier than being a policeman, he found. And, if the people he was personally protecting were wealthy like Franklin Ross, the pay was a damn sight better into the bargain.

* * *

Dan fitted in well with the Ross household. Michael took an instant liking to him and he, in turn, recognised the boy's good nature – surprising for an only child from such a wealthy home, he thought. The mischievous games the boy played were without malice; they merely stemmed from an adventurous spirit. Dan could identify with that. So rather than laying down the law and exercising discipline, he decided to join in the games whenever possible and he and Michael became firm friends.

Which was just as well for Michael – it made things a great deal easier for him when he lost his virginity.

Natalie Sinclair was nearly twenty-seven and it was quite obvious to Dan that she strongly fancied young Michael, despite the fact that the lad was barely sixteen.

It was also obvious to Dan that Michael lusted after the bosomy brunette with all the passion he himself had felt at sixteen for Dezmeldar Lee, daughter of the Mousehole postmistress.

Something had to be done, Dan thought. The lad was torturing himself and there was no one in whom he could confide. Michael got on well with his grandfather and, old as Franklin Ross was, he was still a virile man, Dan recognised that. Franklin could have helped, except that Franklin was in New York, as usual. That left Penelope. And nobody, Dan thought, could possibly share sexual confidences with the untouchable Penelope. The Ice Queen herself.

Penelope Ross was an extremely beautiful woman but Dan had great difficulty imagining her with her legs apart. It seemed sacrilegious to even think it. He didn't much like her, if the truth be known; she had a habit of making him feel out of his depth. Not that he took it too personally – it was fairly evident that Penelope made a habit of doing that to most people.

So it was up to Dan.

Although he was childless, unmarried and with two broken engagements behind him – to women he hadn't really loved anyway – Daniel Pendennis felt a strong paternal responsibility for the first time in his life.

'Want to go to Hardy's Bay next week for a few days' fishing?' he asked Michael.

'Yeah, fantastic!'

'Reckon she'll agree?' Dan had long since stopped referring to Penelope as Michael's grandmother. He'd suffered the withering looks when he'd inadvertently used the term in her presence.

'I don't see why not. She was pleased with the exam results.'

Michael had indeed breezed through his penultimate year at school. He'd decided it wasn't worth the hassle of endless lectures so he'd stopped playing games, put his fantasy world on hold for a while and paid attention. It had all been incredibly easy. Nevertheless, he couldn't wait to be out in the real world. One more year to go and he could take the first step towards converting his magic world into a reality. One more year to go and he would be working at the studios. Penelope had promised him.

'Can I go to Hardy's Bay next week with Daniel?' Michael asked, convinced she'd say yes. He'd been on holidays for three weeks and, fond as she was of him, he knew she preferred it when he was out of the house a little more.

'*May* I, darling – not *can*,' Penelope said automatically. 'I don't see why not. So long as it's convenient for Daniel, of course.' She smiled graciously at Dan, relieved by the thought that the two of them would be out of her hair for a while. Daniel Pendennis was a nice man but he was rather simple. And of course Michael was so young – neither of them understood the pressure she was under with Franklin gone so much of the time. Neither of them understood the demands placed upon her by her social responsibilities and her duties at the studios.

'Fine by me, Mrs Ross.'

The following week, they left for 'the shack' at Hardy's Bay.

It wasn't a shack at all, but a comfortable three-bedroom weatherboard house right on the water with a huge open verandah and views across the sleepy little inlet. But by Penelope's standards it was a shack. God forbid that people should presume this was their 'holiday home' – their holidays were spent in their London townhouse or their seaside flat at Menton on the French Riviera.

Franklin had bought the shack the year before to assuage his guilt at the fact that he didn't spend more time with his grandson.

'Take him fishing, Dan,' he'd said. 'I've got a

288

boat there, penned at the local marina. And teach him to shoot and defend himself too. He's got a lot of growing up to do.'

Hardy's Bay was only a couple of hours from the city but it was a world apart, a sleepy little post-war holiday town lost in the forties and fifties. Materials for the early cottages had been ferried across the massive waterways by barge until The Rip Bridge was built in the seventies. As a result, Hardy's Bay had escaped the hideous building boom of the sixties, investors choosing towns more accessible by road in which to construct their ugly, square red-brick monsters.

Now the few modern buildings erected in Hardy's Bay were of pleasing design, private owners choosing to maintain the aspect of the place. The shack itself was a renovated two-bedroom weatherboard built in 1948. A third bedroom, huge living area and verandah had been added in the style of the original.

Michael loved Hardy's Bay. He loved its 'lost in time' aura. The perfect place for a movie location, he thought, and straight away he could see the whole movie in his mind.

Sydney, 1945. VE Day. People crowded around their wirelesses listening to Menzies' announcement – victory in Europe. Celebrations in the streets, the whole of Sydney alive with joy. The return of the soldiers.

That was where Hardy's Bay came in. Couples fleeing to the little holiday towns up the Central Coast. In wooden shacks by sleepy inlets making love desperately, frantically. Forget the war, it couldn't touch them here. Then the recognition that it wasn't over yet. There was still the Pacific. Finally, the Japanese surrender, total victory. Once more, couples fleeing to the coastal havens to lose themselves in each other's bodies, grateful to be alive. (There was a lot of lovemaking in Michael's fantasies lately.)

'Why don't you invite Natalie to Hardy's Bay?' Dan asked casually. They were driving home from the studio Christmas party the night after they'd decided to go up the coast. It was early December, the start of the non-ratings period, and studio production went into recess while networks aired movies and re-runs of old shows. Ross Productions always held their Christmas party on the last taping day of the year.

'Natalie?' Michael gave a guilty start. 'Natalie Sinclair?'

'Sure.' Dan concentrated on the street ahead. 'She's on holiday as of tonight. Her show doesn't go back into production until the middle of January.'

Michael's pulse raced at the mere thought of Natalie Sinclair at the shack and the balmy summer nights overlooking Hardy's Bay. It was everything his fantasy movie was, and more. But his mind was in a state of shock. Had Dan seen him kiss Natalie in the studio car park tonight? He'd put his hand on her breast too. It was the first time he'd done either. Natalie had been a bit drunk and she'd used that as an excuse, but then he'd been a bit drunk himself and that had given him the courage.

She'd laughed when they stopped to draw

breath. 'Talk about a cradle-snatcher,' she'd said breathlessly. 'Thanks for walking me to my car, Michael.' And she climbed in the car and drove off. Had Dan been watching?

Dan hadn't been watching as such. He'd certainly observed them leave via the staff entrance and he'd observed them walking through the car park. That was his job. But, when they came to a halt at her car, he'd observed the surrounding area instead while he waited for Michael to return to the party.

'Hell, Dan, Natalie Sinclair's famous. She's a national television identity. Why would she want to come up the coast with us?' Michael was serious. To score a kiss in the car park from Natalie Sinclair was quite a major achievement – to contemplate a weekend away with the woman was sheer fantasy. And fantasy of such magnitude that not even he could envisage it as reality.

Dan pulled the car over to the side of the road and turned off the engine. Now for the moment of truth. 'She fancies you, Michael. Just as much as you fancy her. She'll come along if you ask her.' He allowed a couple of seconds for it to sink in. 'And I think it's time you found out what it's all about, don't you?'

Michael nodded, hardly daring to speak. When he did open his mouth to say something, Dan stopped him.

'It's all right. Penelope doesn't need to know.' Again Michael tried to say something and again Dan interrupted. 'Do it, Michael. Just do it.'

'I don't have her phone number,' Michael finally managed to blurt out.

'I do.' Dan handed him a slip of paper. 'It was in the studio files.'

Natalie lived only twenty minutes' drive from The Colony House. Michael opened the front car door for her so that she could sit next to Dan. Then he piled into the back.

'I've been looking forward to this, Dan. I hear the fishing's great and I believe you're quite an expert.'

Natalie was beautiful, charming, animated and normally self-assured. If she chattered a little more than was necessary during the two-hour drive it was because, for once, she was feeling rather self-conscious. What on earth had made her accept the offer from young Michael Ross? 'Dan'll take us out in the boat,' he'd promised over the phone. 'He's an expert fisherman and there are mudcrabs in the bay . . . ' Before she could answer, he'd continued ' . . . and blue swimmer crabs too, and prawns and oysters and . . . '

'Yes, all right, Michael,' she'd found herself saying. 'It sounds like fun. I adore fishing.'

But they both knew what was really being said. And now Natalie was wondering why she'd agreed. If anyone at the studio was to find out she'd been to bed with a sixteen-year-old she'd be a laughing stock. More importantly, though, the sixteen-year-old was none other than Michael Ross. If the Ice Queen were to find out that Natalie Sinclair, anchorwoman of the highly rating 'Weekend World Roundup', had screwed her precious grandson then Natalie would most

292

certainly be out of a job and possibly out of the industry. Penelope's power was such that, if she chose, she could easily have Natalie blacklisted.

What the hell am I doing here? Natalie asked herself again and decided that she'd invent an urgent forgotten appointment and return by train the following day.

But it didn't work out that way.

Natalie adored Hardy's Bay. She'd never been there before and it was every bit as picturesque as Michael had described it.

That afternoon Dan took them out in the boat for a sightseeing tour. 'We'll leave the fishing for tomorrow. Then we'll go out at dawn and fish on the flood tide.'

So they spent a pleasant several hours motoring across the bay to Ettalong, Umina and Pearl Beach, where they dropped anchor and dived overboard for a swim.

Natalie was aware that both Michael and Dan were trying as tactfully as they could to ignore her body in its lime-green one-piece. They weren't altogether successful, and she was thankful that she'd packed her tasteful bathing costume rather than her skimpy pink bikini. She, in turn, was a little ashamed of herself for her lecherous feelings towards Michael. In his bathing costume he looked like the gawky schoolboy he was. How could you? she scolded herself: he's a baby. If she wanted a torrid affair, she thought, she should be checking out the minder.

Dan's body was indeed impressive. If anything, he was a little shorter than Michael, who stood just under six feet, but his well-muscled body was that of an athlete, finely honed and conditioned. Next to it, Michael's bony form, yet to fill out, with too-long arms and too-big feet, looked a touch ludicrous.

Then Michael, who was sunbaking up the bow of the boat, suddenly turned to her and smiled that captivating smile. 'Hey, Natalie,' he called, 'some pretty high profile TV personalities have bought up here recently – you want to swim ashore and say hello?' The eyes twinkled mischievously.

'No thank you, Michael,' she called back. 'We work for different outfits.' He's irresistible, she thought, utterly irresistible.

The evening was also pleasant and Natalie started wondering whether she may have been overreacting. They had a good meal, played cards, listened to music and finally Dan announced it was bedtime.

'Early night,' he said. 'The alarm's set for five.' And Natalie retired to her comfortable bedroom with its view of the bay and slept like a log.

At dawn, when Dan woke her, all her plans for an urgent return to Sydney had vanished. A few innocent days' fishing, pleasant company, no strings attached – it was exactly the break she needed. And she packed the Esky with their picnic lunch, excited and feeling like a twelve-year-old.

It was a successful day. They fished off the reefs outside Point Barrenjoey and caught a number of decent-sized snapper, then put trawling lines out from the stern of the boat and chased the flocks of birds which signalled a feeding frenzy.

'It's probably tuna,' Dan explained. 'The birds are after the small school fish the tuna are chasing.' He was right, and they hauled in a half dozen albacore which had been feeding on a shoal of tiny squid.

They dropped anchor at pretty little Lobster Bay and picnicked on chicken and champagne and Natalie loved every minute of it.

It was mid-afternoon when they returned to Hardy's Bay and the marina. Dan suggested they go on ahead of him while he cleaned the fish.

'Saves the mess at home if I do it aboard,' he said. 'Besides, Michael's lousy at cleaning fish. You take the gear and I'll walk back.'

When they arrived at the shack, they were still chattering about which had been the most exciting catch.

'Bags first shower,' she said as they walked in the back door. 'I stink of fish.'

'Sure. Want a cold beer when you're finished?'

'I'd die for one,' she laughed.

She sat on the verandah in a sarong and sipped her beer while Michael had his shower. And then he joined her and they sat together watching the boats as they returned from the day's fishing.

Although it was late in the afternoon, there was no cooling breeze. The air was still and the sun was fierce.

'That was one of the loveliest days of my life, Michael,' she said and meant it.

'Yes,' he nodded. Although he'd had a cold shower, the beads of sweat were starting to form on Michael's chest and forehead. 'I think we're in for a heatwave.'

Neither of them knew who initiated it, but at that moment it seemed the most natural thing to kiss. Gently at first. Then the kiss became deeper, their mouths opening hungrily, their bodies responding urgently to each other.

Michael struggled with the knot of her sarong. Natalie's reservations disappeared completely. There was no point in fighting it, no point at all. She wanted the boy as much as he wanted her.

'Let's go inside,' she whispered.

They didn't make it to the bedroom. They undressed each other feverishly and made love on the hearth rug in the lounge room. She tried to slow him down in the initial stages, sensing this was probably his first time, feeling that, as the older woman, she should be teaching him the pleasures of foreplay. But within seconds she'd surrendered to her own excitement and, as she felt the vigour of his thrusts, she could do little but respond in kind.

Michael was aware of nothing but the feel of her surrounding him, the clashing of their loins and the knowledge that his months of fantasies were being realised and that any minute he was about to explode. And then he did, and it was over and he was lying on top of her gasping for breath.

'Hey,' Natalie said after a few moments, 'give us a bit of air down here.'

'Oh.' He came to his senses and rolled off her. 'I'm sorry,' he said breathlessly. 'I'm sorry.' He propped himself on one elbow and looked at her. For the first time he became aware that he'd left her far behind. 'I really am sorry, I got carried away and I . . . I know I should have . . . '

'Ssshh,' she said and she stroked the unruly lock

of hair from his brow. 'You were fine.' Oh, shit, Natalie, she told herself, you can't fall in love with a sixteen-year-old, for God's sake. But he looked so earnest, so naive, and she couldn't resist a surge of tenderness. 'Your first time, right?' He nodded. 'Believe me, you were fine.'

'Really?'

'Really.'

Michael felt suddenly and gloriously happy. He grinned at her. 'Wow,' he said.

And the grin was Natalie's undoing. What the hell, she thought, she was going to have an affair with a schoolboy. She couldn't resist him.

'You could do with a little tuition,' she smiled.

Michael was a quick learner. They made love twice that night and again in the morning and each time he found it easier to maintain his control. As a result, his own pleasure was not only prolonged, it was intensified by Natalie's. When her sensual moans became demanding grunts and the languid writhing of her hips became urgent pelvic thrusts, he didn't allow himself to surrender. He waited until her back was arched and her hands were clawing his buttocks trying to pull him deeper and deeper inside her. Then, his own passion at screaming pitch, he thrust back at her with equal fervour and they fed each other's passion until, together, they lost themselves.

'Hell, no more lessons,' Natalie panted finally as he once again took her breast in his mouth and she once again felt him harden. She pushed him away. 'Give a girl a break,' she said.

* * *

297

Their affair continued for a full two years. Secretly. They would meet at Natalie's flat several nights a week. Sometimes they would spend the whole weekend locked up there together.

It was Natalie who introduced Michael to drugs. Innocently. 'Just for an added sexual buzz,' she said. It started with amyl nitrate. 'Gives a whole new meaning to oral sex,' she promised.

And she was right. Then they graduated to cocaine. 'You can go all night,' she promised. And again she was right.

But it was more than the added sustaining power which excited Michael. By now he was so practised at restraining himself he could go half the night anyway. It was the trip itself which excited him.

As he surrendered his body to carnal pleasure, Michael's mind journeyed into areas he'd never known existed. But then, he wondered vaguely, perhaps he had. As a child he'd dreamed of power. The power to create a fantasy land. A magic place where the time and the people were of his own invention. And now, as his body writhed with Natalie's, he created that place, that time, those people.

The place was soaring somewhere in the sky. The time was any time. All time. Time was suddenly insignificant. And the people were controlled by him. All of them. Fond as he was of her, Natalie had ceased to be Natalie. She embodied all people and Michael was the controlling power. He was omnipotent.

Natalie persuaded him that there was no harm in what they were doing. After all, they only used the drugs as a sexual stimulant. Michael agreed, but to him the sating of desire was the least important aspect of their coupling. After each time, he couldn't wait for the next journey into his magic kingdom.

The only person who knew of their affair was Dan, and he began to wonder what he'd started. 'Don't you think you should be going out with girls your own age,' he suggested tentatively, but Michael just grinned and shook his head and there was nothing Dan could do.

After excellent passes in his final examinations, Michael dropped the bombshell on Franklin.

'I don't want to work in administration, Grandpa,' he said when Franklin started making plans for his training as a corporate director. 'I want to create.'

'Create what?' To Franklin nothing could be more creative than opening new markets, embarking on new fields of endeavour, or conquering new opponents.

'Movies', Michael answered. 'Movies with a difference. I have this idea, Grandpa. I want to make movies based around an actuality. They become real, you see? Not an actual happening from the past, but from the moment and from the future ... ' He was warming to his theme. Michael had told no one of his idea yet.

But Franklin interrupted. He'd heard many a director and producer expound their latest theme and he wasn't interested. It was enough that the lad wanted to make films, he wouldn't stand in his way. Besides, it could be good training for him. In ten years' time Michael would no doubt be sick of the superficiality of the entertainment industry and would be interested in a position of greater power. Franklin recognised ambition when he saw it.

'Very well,' he said. 'But you'll start from the bottom and learn your trade. You can't come to New York with me until you're ready. I'm sure Penelope could find you a position here at the studios.'

'Yes, she's already said she will. In the story-lining department, working on the new series. She promised me ages ago.'

'Oh, she did, did she?' Franklin felt mildy irritated. So they'd been discussing the lad's future without consulting him. But he decided not to confront Penelope. She had too much ammunition to fire back at him – he'd been in New York for a full six months of the year, after all.

In January 1984, when the studios went back into production, a seventeen-year-old trainee storyliner joined the ranks of the 'Destiny' writing department.

'Destiny' was the new, highly successful big-budget series which had recently taken the country by storm: 'a powerful saga of money, power and corruption' was how the publicity department was pitching it. The series had been presold to Network 5 and was designed and programmed as direct competition against the glossy American series the other networks had imported.

Michael loved the work and his talent quickly became evident. It was the type of 'no-holds-barred' drama which suited his fertile imagination. And the budget allowed for aerial shots and cars over cliffs and high-powered boat chases.

Within a year, Michael was associate executive storyliner and not just because he was the boss's grandson.

The affair with Natalie continued. As far as Michael was concerned, it was really a matter of convenience more than anything else. He didn't meet other women – there was simply no time to socialise. His hours at the studios were long and during weekends he spent his time at home working on his movie script. Stimulating as it was, 'Destiny' was merely a stepping stone to him. As soon as he felt he was ready, he intended to make his movie based around an actual event. He'd chosen his event but had told no one about it. The film would be shot in 1986 – he had a year to go.

To Natalie, the affair was more than a matter of convenience. Michael was no longer the gawky schoolboy to whom she'd taught the art of love. He was a charismatic young man. There was the same electric mischief in the eyes and the smile, but his body had filled out and there was an assurance about him that drew people to him like a magnet.

But Natalie was wise. She knew that their affair was living on borrowed time and she prepared herself for the inevitable moment when Michael would meet a girl and fall head over heels in love.

* * *

'Hi, Penelope, I'm home.' Michael bounded across the main hall of The Colony House, through the arch and into the main lounge, where he could see Penelope sipping a cup of her specially imported herbal tea. He dumped his briefcase on a chair and then noticed the girl seated on the sofa beside her. 'Oh, hello,' he said.

Penelope looked a little disconcerted. 'What are you doing back at this hour? It's Tuesday.'

'Reg and I had an argument so I walked out. Aren't you going to introduce me?'

'Of course, darling. This is Emma. Emma Clare, Michael Ross.'

What superb legs, Michael thought.

'Hi,' the girl said and, as she smiled a greeting at him, Michael found himself momentarily frozen to the spot. She was beautiful. She was tanned, even though it was not yet summer. A natural olive skin with blonde, sandy-coloured hair which she wore straight and to her shoulders. Her smile was warm and generous and her hazel eyes inviting. Everything about the girl was healthy and unaffected. Michael had rarely been exposed to such natural beauty – the glamorous actresses in 'Destiny' were highly manufactured – and it was like a breath of fresh air.

He finally found his voice. 'Hello,' he said. 'Where did you spring from?'

'Emma's doing some work for me for the Blind Society,' Penelope answered for her.

The Royal Blind Society was one of Penelope's pet charities. Besides the various functions she hosted, she regularly recorded book and poetry readings for their talking book library. It helped satisfy the thwarted actor in her and she very much enjoyed it.

'Oh, are you an actress?' Michael asked as he seated himself beside Penelope.

'No, I'm a writer,' the girl replied. 'Well, I'm trying to be. I've just finished school and I do a bit of reporting for the *North Shore Times* and Penelope kindly landed me a job writing synopses and book descriptions for the Blind Society.' She flashed a grateful smile in Penelope's direction.

'So what was the row with Reg about?' Penelope enquired.

'Oh, don't ask,' Michael said, jumping to press the servants' buzzer. 'We're finalising the end-of-season cliffhanger and Reg is too scared to kill off Ryan Clifford. He's happy to give him a hanggliding accident – you know, "Is he dead or is he not?" type of thing, he's happy with that. But when we come back to the new season he wants to resurrect him.'

'So what's the problem?' Penelope poured herself another herbal tea from the pot.

'Ryan's contract only goes till March, so why shouldn't we kill him off? Horrific death, massive funeral, a nervous breakdown for his mistress . . . it'll boost the ratings fantastically – far more than having him pack a suitcase and walk off into the sunset.'

Penelope offered the pot to Emma but she shook her head.

'Don't tell me you're drinking that filthy stuff of Penelope's,' Michael said. 'Don't worry, I'll get you a decent coffee in a minute.' Then he contin-

303

ued. 'Of course Reg is convinced that he'll recontract Ryan later in the year but I know for sure that he won't. The man's got two movies lined up in the States and once he gets over there we'll never see him again.'

The maid arrived. 'Coffee?' Michael queried and Emma nodded. 'Two thanks, Tina – that new stuff, the Kenyan blend. Anyway,' he continued when the maid had left, 'it's good riddance, if you ask me, the bloke's an arrogant shit.'

Penelope frowned her disapproval but Michael pretended not to notice. 'And we can always get another resident hunk; they're a dime a dozen.' He turned to the girl, who'd been listening spellbound. 'What do you think, Emma?'

'I think it all sounds fascinating,' she said. 'Ruthless but fascinating.'

'It is,' Michael nodded enthusiastically. 'Hey, you should come and sit through a few storylining sessions. We could arrange that, couldn't we, Penelope?'

Penelope looked a little dubious. 'Well, I'm not sure whether . . . '

But Michael carried on regardless. 'I'll look after it, don't you worry. They might even take you on as a trainee – I'll check if there's a vacancy on one of the other shows.'

The coffee arrived and they talked for a further twenty minutes before Emma rose to go. Penelope had looked pointedly at her watch and the girl didn't want to overstay her welcome.

'Where are you off to?' Michael asked, loath to see her leave.

'North Sydney.'

'I'll drive you there if you like.'

'Oh no, really, I couldn't possibly . . . '

'Yes, you could – I've got nothing else to do.' His car keys were in his hand and he was already crossing to the hall. 'Come on.'

Emma flashed an apologetic glance in Penelope's direction but Penelope nodded. 'Go on, dear, you might as well. He's not going to take no for an answer.'

Michael was proud of his Targa Porsche 911 sports car and, even though it was late afternoon and there was a spring chill in the air, he put the top down.

'You don't mind, do you?' he called above the wind as they drove down Edgecliff Road. 'Not too blowy for you?'

'No, I love it,' Emma called back, her hair blowing around wildly. Michael grinned at her, delighted by the disregard for her appearance.

He revved the engine up and darted around a car ahead. 'She's a beauty, isn't she? Grandpa's eighteenth birthday present.'

Emma had heard a lot about Franklin Ross. 'You get on well, do you, you and your grandfather?'

'Yeah, he's the greatest.'

Emma had never driven in a Porsche before and she couldn't help but be aware of the looks from other drivers as they sped across the Harbour Bridge. She also couldn't help but be aware of Michael's complete oblivion to their envy. He appeared totally unaffected by his wealth and it impressed her. He was confident, certainly, but he wasn't cocky and she decided she liked him.

When they pulled up outside the apartment where Emma shared a flat with two other students Michael was once more loath to say goodbye.

'Got time for a drink?' he asked. 'There's a pub up the road with a great beer garden.'

'Yes,' Emma smiled, 'I know the one.' Then, after a moment's hesitation, she added, 'I'd love to.'

Over the next hour and a half they had two beers each and talked endlessly. Well, Michael did. But Emma's way of listening was encouraging. She seemed genuinely interested in everything he had to say and Michael found himself telling her all about his movie ideas. Even his initial script which he'd sworn to himself he'd keep secret till the very last minute.

'People nick ideas, you know,' he explained. 'And this is one hot idea.' He looked around, then leaned forward in his chair and spoke conspiratorially. Emma wanted to laugh; he looked as though he expected spies to come out of the woodwork. But she felt a great warmth towards him. He was so genuinely charming, she decided, it was difficult not to.

'Halley's Comet,' he said. 'That's what my first movie is going to be about. Halley's Comet. Terrific, isn't it?'

She wasn't quite sure what to say but, as it turned out, she didn't need to say anything. Michael raved on excitedly. For the first time, he was voicing his idea out loud.

'Halley's Comet. Seen in the skies only once

every seventy-six years. Known as the harbinger of disaster. The last viewing was 1910, the death of King Edward. And its next appearance is due in 1986, less than two years from now. What disaster will it portend this time?' Michael couldn't resist the dramatic pause. Then he grinned. 'Great storylining stuff, eh? And it'll be best viewed from the southern hemisphere. We'll film the actual comet from the perfect vantage point – I've checked that out with the observatory – and build our story around the actual event. Fantastic, isn't it, the mixture of fact and fantasy? And the whole world will be talking about Halley's Comet, so the movie'll sell itself.'

His enthusiasm was contagious and Emma was enthralled. 'So what will be your disaster?' she asked.

'The pole shift,' Michael announced triumphantly. It was his coup. 'Nostradamus' prediction. The disaster the comet is portending is the Earth's pole shift.'

There was no stopping Michael now. 'A group of scientists and astronomers know the earth is about to shift on its axis but they don't announce it because there'd be a worldwide panic. The scientists are working frantically for a solution or at least a means to preserve areas of human life that might be least affected. In the meantime, there's a spy in their midst and he gives the news to the bad guys. Well, to one prime bad guy. A mega-rich, powerful businessman.'

'Someone like your grandfather,' Emma suggested with a smile.

'That's right,' Michael replied, deadly serious. 'And the businessman has a fleet of airbuses secretly designed and assembled. His idea is to take himself and his family and a few hundred other people wealthy enough to pay an exorbitant amount of money to the ionisphere where they wait out the cataclysm and the aftereffects. Then they come back to earth and rule the new race.'

Michael sat back in his chair and awaited the effect. He wasn't disapponted.

'Wow,' Emma breathed. 'It's fantastic.'

They talked for another hour after that. There were sub-plots and intricacies that Michael was still working out within his premise. 'I need another faction,' he said, 'a faction that finds out about the airships and threatens their destruction.' Excited by the idea, Emma proved tremendously helpful, even inspirational.

'Religious zealots,' she said. 'A following of religious zealots who worship the comet as the visitation of a wrathful God. They see the airships as the work of Satan and need to destroy them.'

'Perfect. Bloody perfect.' Michael stared at her in admiration. 'Give the arts course the flick,' he said. 'I can find a traineeship for you at the studios and you can work with me on the movie after hours, what do you reckon?'

Emma laughed. 'I reckon I have to go home, that's what I reckon,' and she stood up.

'I'm serious, Emma.' There was an intensity in his eyes. 'I'm deadly serious. I want to get to know you better and I want us to work together.'

308

'Perhaps,' she said, avoiding the issue. 'We'll talk about it later, Michael.'

It was early evening and he drove straight to Natalie's apartment.

'Hi.' Natalie was pleased to see him. 'I only just got home; I wasn't expecting you.' She embraced him warmly but Michael gently eased himself away.

'I'm sorry, Natalie,' he said. 'It's over.'

She stared at him for a moment. There was a sick feeling in her stomach and the quick sting of tears behind her eyes. But she didn't give in to it. 'You've met someone.'

'Yes.'

'You're having an affair?'

'Not yet. But I intend to.'

'I see.' She was grateful he'd told her in advance. She didn't think she could bear the thought of his having slept with someone else. But now she wanted him to go. She didn't want him to see her cry. 'Goodbye, Michael,' she smiled. 'It's been fun.'

'Yes, it has.' He kissed her very gently on the lips. 'You're terrific, Natalie. Good luck.'

He was gone. And Natalie let herself cry.

As Michael drove back to The Colony House, all he could think of was Emma. Her face, her body, her smile, her eyes. There was an electricity between them. She must have felt it. An electricity in mind, body and soul. They were meant for each other.

CHAPTER NINE

Emma

EMMA CLARE'S CHILDHOOD was a lonely one. She didn't know what she'd done wrong but it was evident to her from a very early age that her baby sister was the favourite of the family. Her mother and father both lavished love and attention upon little Vivien, one year Emma's junior, and it was a constant mystery to Emma why they didn't do the same for her.

She developed a strong defence mechanism, telling herself that it didn't matter, she was going to be a hugely successful novelist and she'd be so rich and famous that she wouldn't need their love. At nine years of age she started to write stories, inventing her own family and her own friends and her own world on paper.

But there were times when it did matter. Her imaginary world was a wonderful escape but you couldn't cuddle up to it and she would watch with envy as her mother sat Vivien on her knee and ran her fingers through the child's hair.

Emma had long since stopped trying to demand equal attention. 'Mummy, can I sit on your lap too?' ... 'Daddy, pick me up, pick me up too!' She knew what the answer would be. 'Don't be silly, you're too big for that.' 'So is Vivien,' she'd say. And the answer would always be ... 'Emma, you're a big, strong girl; Vivien isn't – she needs to be looked after, you know that.'

It was true her sister had been born asthmatic and the fact that she was a petite child and delicate in appearance always brought out the protective in grown-ups. But the asthma was controllable and, apart from the odd attack, Vivien had never had a day's illness in her life. Well, not to the best of Emma's knowledge. She hadn't had measles and mumps like Emma had. And she hadn't had a middle ear infection like the one Emma contracted the summer they went to Byron Bay for a holiday. Deep down, Emma didn't think that Vivien's physical condition in any way warranted the different degrees of affection they were allotted.

Vivien didn't seem to notice any inequality. She knew she received more cuddles than Emma, certainly, but that was only because Emma didn't ask for them – Emma didn't need them, Emma was so strong and clever. Emma wrote stories, wonderful stories which she read out loud.

Vivien adored Emma and the two girls had an excellent relationship, Emma successfully building her wall and concealing her jealousy from her good-natured little sister.

She built her wall so successfully that, by the time she was twelve, she'd even managed to persuade herself that maybe she was imagining the situation, that maybe her parents didn't pay her the attention they did to Vivien simply because she was the stronger of the two, just as they'd told her. That way it was easier to bear.

Then came Vivien's eleventh birthday party. It was a special day for Emma, even though it wasn't her birthday. It was special because Auntie Bea was there.

Emma hadn't seen Auntie Bea since she was nine years old. As a little girl, her mother's older sister Beatrice had always been Emma's favourite person. When Auntie Bea was visiting there had always been plenty of cuddles; in fact Auntie Bea cuddled her more than she did Vivien, which made Emma feel very special.

Then Beatrice went to live in Europe. Emma missed her sorely. That was when she'd started writing her stories and building her walls.

'Emma!' The arms were outstretched and Emma charged into them. Beatrice swept her off the ground in an almighty hug. 'My God, but how big you've grown, you're nearly as tall as I am.' She put the girl down but Emma remained clinging to her. 'I think I've wrecked my back,' Beatrice groaned. And Emma laughed with joy. Auntie Bea hadn't changed at all.

It was a wonderful party. There was a magician and lots of games and a huge birthday cake. But Emma didn't mingle with the other children – she chose to remain at Auntie Bea's side.

'Why don't you go and play with the others, darling?' Beatrice asked.

'I'd rather be with you,' Emma answered. And then, in case her aunt thought she was being a little

312

too clinging, she added airily, 'they're a bit young for me, Auntie Bea. I'm nearly twelve and a half.'

When the magician started his act, Beatrice insisted that Emma join the other children in the lounge room. 'Go along, darling,' she said, 'you mustn't miss him, he's supposed to be wonderful.' So Emma reluctantly joined the others.

Her mother introduced the magician and, just as he was about to start his act, Emma saw Beatrice signal her sister from the doorway and she watched as the two women walked out towards the back patio. Emma had noticed Auntie Bea's glance towards her and she knew in an instant that they were going to talk about her.

It wasn't normally in Emma's nature to spy or eavesdrop and she felt guilty as she quietly rose and sidled towards the door. But something told her she had to find out what they were saying.

She crept down the hall. It was a warm day and the back door was open to allow a breeze through the house. She could see them through the flywire screen door, seated close to each other on the patio only several yards away and, although they were talking quietly, she could clearly hear them.

'It's shocking, Jennifer,' Beatrice was saying to her sister. 'That child's entire personality has changed. She was an open, affectionate little girl. You've never given her enough attention. Can't you see what it's done to her?'

Emma's mother looked guilty but she was nevertheless very much on the defensive. 'She's as healthy as a horse, she always has been. Vivien's the weak one.'

'I'm not talking about her physical condition,

for God's sake – I'm talking about her emotional state, and you know it. That little girl is craving love. She plays it strong and remote and when you give her a crumb of affection she clings to you like a starving animal. What you and Bob have done is disgraceful.'

Jennifer stared at the patio pavement. She didn't say anything but blinked hard, trying to fight off the tears.

Beatrice didn't let up. 'You promised me when I left you'd try and give the girls equal attention. You promised. Both you and Bob.'

'I did try, I swear I did. And so did Bob.' Jennifer's voice was muffled. 'It's easy for him, he's away most of the time. I'm the one left trying to live a lie. How can you pretend to a love you don't feel, day in, day out?' Jennifer gave in to the tears. She sobbed quietly, racked with guilt. 'It's hard, Bea. So hard.'

Beatrice put an arm around her sister's shoulder and her voice softened. 'It shouldn't be, Jen. She's a little girl. It's easy to love a little girl.'

'But she's not *my* little girl,' Jennifer sobbed, 'and I can't change the way I feel about that.'

Emma stood rooted to the spot. Surely it couldn't be true? But the words rang in her head. *She's not my little girl.* Of course it was true. It explained everything.

'We would never have adopted her if we'd known we could have Vivien,' Jennifer said, fumbling for a tissue. 'Bob didn't want to adopt at all.'

'I know, I know,' Beatrice answered. 'But the fact is you did. And you're responsible for the child now. You owe it to her.'

314

Emma had heard enough. She crept back to the lounge room and sat down to watch the magician. But she didn't see him. Her mind was numb, but somewhere there was a sense of relief. It wasn't her fault that they didn't love her; there was nothing wrong with her after all. They didn't love her simply because she wasn't theirs.

After the party, when the other children were going home, Emma sought out her aunt.

'Auntie Bea, can I talk with you please?'

'Yes, of course, darling.' The girl looked so serious Beatrice hoped there was nothing wrong. They walked together out to the back patio.

'I'd like you to help me find my real mother,' Emma said.

Beatrice stared back at her, horrified. 'You heard,' she said. Emma nodded. 'Oh, my darling.' Beatrice gathered the girl in her arms but Emma didn't respond.

'It's all right,' she said, freeing herself from the hug. 'It explains a lot of things to me. But I want to meet my real mother.'

The child suddenly looked so grown up, Beatrice thought, and so resolved. 'Sit down for a moment, Emma, and let me explain a few things to you that I think you should know.'

They sat together on the patio for half an hour and Beatrice told Emma that her mother and father had tried for years to have a child. 'Medically there didn't seem to be anything wrong,' she explained, 'but they just couldn't conceive. For five years they tried. And then your mother was thirty and time was running out and they adopted you.'

Emma watched her aunt but she didn't say anything. 'Then, three months after your adoption, your mother fell pregnant,' Beatrice continued. 'I suppose, because they thought they could never have a child, that made Vivien extra special ... I don't know ... ' Beatrice's voice petered away lamely. It wasn't much of an excuse for a loveless childhood, she thought.

'I understand,' Emma said. She supposed she did but that wasn't the important issue to her at the moment. 'Will you help me find my mother?'

'Yes, Emma. Yes, I will.'

Beatrice devoted herself to the search for over two years. After a seemingly endless succession of stumbling blocks and blind alleys, she made her breakthrough.

It was a Saturday when she drove young Emma to the small duplex house in Redfern. There had been no telephone number listed so they'd been unable to ring.

Emma insisted upon going to the front door alone. 'Please, Auntie Bea,' she said gently, 'will you stay in the car?'

Beatrice nodded and she watched as the girl walked up to the shabby front door of the shabby little house. She watched as Emma rang the doorbell and the door opened. A woman stood there but Beatrice couldn't see her clearly. Emma said something and then she stepped inside and the flywire screen door flapped shut.

* * *

Emma stared at the woman. She was in her thirties, but looked older than her years. Worn out. But she'd once been pretty. She had fair, sandy-coloured hair in the process of turning grey and, beneath the fatigue, her hazel eyes were impressive.

'What are you after, kid?' she asked. 'If you're selling something I don't want it.'

'Are you Julia Bridges?'

'Yes.'

'My name's Emma. I'm your daughter.'

Julia stared at the girl. She knew it was true. The girl looked the way she herself had looked a very long time ago. She nodded. 'Would you like a cup of tea?'

Emma sat in the poky little kitchen while Julia busied herself making tea. The door to the adjoining room was open and a baby started to cry.

'How old are you?' Julia asked, taking no notice of the baby.

'I'll be fifteen next birthday.' Emma's birthday wasn't for another six months but she wanted to appear as grown up as possible.

'What do you want from me?' Julia looked the girl up and down briefly. 'You don't look as though you need money and I'm a bit short on maternal love – I've got three young kids who burn up most of that.' It was said good-naturedly – she didn't mean to be tough, but she was confused. The girl brought back so many memories.

'I just want to know about myself,' Emma said. 'Who is my father?'

'He's dead.' Julia poured the hot water into the

pot. 'Died about the time you were born. Terry Ross. Terence George Franklin Ross.'

She pushed the sugar bowl in Emma's direction. 'Do you take milk?' she asked, crossing to the refrigerator. Emma nodded. 'He was married and he didn't want to know about a baby, so ... ' Julia shrugged as she handed the cup to Emma. 'It wouldn't have worked out anyway.'

The look on the girl's face made her realise she'd sounded a little brutal. She hadn't meant to.

'Emma, isn't it?' she asked.

'Yes.'

'I loved him, Emma. And he loved me – I know he did. He was handsome and charming and ... ' Julia gave a rueful smile. ' ... and he was as weak as piss.' She sipped her tea for a moment. 'I seem to have a knack for picking the weak blokes, I fell for another one only a couple of months after Terry and I broke up. I suppose I was on the rebound, I know they say that happens, but I was mad about Steve.'

'I was five months pregnant by that time,' she continued, 'and, as it turned out, Steve didn't want to know about a baby either. Certainly not a baby that wasn't his, which is fair enough, I suppose. So I decided to give you up for adoption as soon as you were born.'

Julia stared into her teacup. The baby's cries from the next room were less urgent now. 'I'd had every intention of keeping you, you know.' There was nothing ingratiating in her tone, no plea for forgiveness, just a simple statement of fact.

'The Ross family paid me off,' she said, 'and I'll never forget that day when I walked out of their mansion with a fifty thousand dollar cheque in my pocket. We were going to conquer the world, you and me.'

She shrugged, picked up her cup and drained it. 'Want another one?' she asked, starting to pour herself a second cup.

'What happened?' Emma asked.

'Well I met Steve, didn't I, and he didn't want a baby and that was that. We got married about six months after you were adopted out and four years later we decided to start a family. Well, I did; I don't know if he was really all that keen. But I must say,' she admitted, 'whatever else he was, Steve was a good father to the girls.'

'Was?'

'We split up over a year ago. He fell in love with someone else.'

Emma glanced towards the adjoining room where the baby's cries had been reduced to the occasional sleepy whimper.

'Oh, the baby's his.' Julia answered the unspoken query. 'But I didn't tell him I was pregnant.'

'Why not?' Emma asked. 'Surely he would have . . .'

'Oh yes, he would have stayed all right. He wasn't a bad man, only a weak one.' Julia smiled. 'Rather like your father. It would only have been a matter of time before he left with the next young pretty girl. He couldn't resist them.'

'Emma . . . ?' There was a tap at the front door which Julia had left open. She started to rise but Emma jumped to her feet.

'No, it's all right. That's my aunt.' She'd completely forgotten that Beatrice was waiting in the car. 'I'll be out in a minute, Auntie Bea,' she called. Then she turned back to Julia. 'Can I come and see you again?'

Julia deliberated for a moment, then she nodded. 'Make it about the same time next week. The girls spend Saturdays with their father and the place is quieter then.'

Emma had found Julia's story so fascinating that she'd had little time to dwell on her own place in the scheme of things. She only knew that she liked this woman who was her natural mother and she wanted to get to know her. 'But the baby,' she said. 'If he's here each week he must know that the baby . . . '

'Yes, he knows about the baby now. And he knows it's his.' They started walking down the hall together. 'And he keeps feeling guilty and insisting that he has to come back and look after us. But it wouldn't work out.' Julia smiled at the girl. 'I'll see you next Saturday.'

The Saturday visits became a regular event which Emma and Julia both looked forward to. They didn't develop a mother-daughter relationship as such. Julia didn't want it, so Emma didn't seek it, but a bond was formed between them. A bond of mutual respect and a shared knowledge that they'd both been lonely and that they filled a gap in each other's lives. Emma and Julia became friends.

They talked occasionally about Terry Ross. Julia deliberately painted him in favourable colours – charming, debonair, handsome – it was the way she preferred to remember him, after all.

'A smile and eyes that could charm the devil' was the way she put it. But when Emma broached the subject of meeting her grandparents, Julia dismissed the Ross family altogether.

'Don't even think about it, love,' she said. 'You'd only give yourself pain; they're a hard lot and they'd refuse to recognise you. The old man told me so.' Julia could still remember Franklin's very words. 'We don't recognise bastards in this family,' he'd said.

One weekend, Julia had a surprise for her. 'Come in, love – there's someone I'd like you to meet.' An elderly woman was sitting in the front lounge. 'This is my mother, Grace,' she said. 'Your grandmother.'

The old lady rose and embraced Emma. There were tears in her eyes as she stood back and looked at her. 'You're just like Julia was when she was a girl,' she said. 'I'll put the kettle on, dear.' And she disappeared quickly into the kitchen.

After that, Grace too became quite a regular feature in Emma's life and the girl basked in her newfound affection. For the first time in her life, she felt that she had a family which was truly hers.

Julia and Grace encouraged Emma's writing and, in her final year at school, it was through a contact of Grace's that she landed a freelance job as a cadet reporter covering minor social occasions for the *North Shore Times*.

It was a period of growth for Emma and she blossomed into a strong, confident girl with an easy, outgoing nature.

She confided her burning ambition to Julia. 'I'm going to write a book one day,' she said. 'I'm going to write a book that'll take the world by storm. A best-seller. I want to see my name on the covers of thousands of copies in every bookshop in the country.'

'Good for you.'

Emma checked to see if maybe Julia was laughing at her. But she wasn't.

One day, she arrived at Julia's rather subdued and, for once, hoping that Grace wouldn't be there. She wasn't. Julia knew the moment she saw the girl that something had happened.

'I need to talk to you,' Emma said.

'I thought so. Come on, let's sit out on the back verandah. It's too nice a day to be inside.'

Julia opened a couple of cans of lemonade and they sat on the tiny back verandah looking out over the scruffy little back yard with its ugly Hills Hoist rotary clothes line. Emma studied the baby clothes flapping in the gentle breeze.

'Well?' Julia asked.

'I think I lost my virginity the other night.'

'What do you mean, you think?'

'Well I'm pretty sure I did, but I didn't mean to.'

Julia wanted to laugh but she didn't dare. Emma looked far too serious. 'What happened?'

'I went to the movies with Don. I've told you about him, remember? We've been going out for three months now and he wants to go steady.'

Julia nodded and Emma continued. 'We drove to the beach afterwards. And we got in the back of the car and started to fool around a bit.' She flashed a guilty look at Julia and then studied her lemonade can. 'We've been fooling around for a

322

while now. I mean, nearly all the girls I know have lost their virginity, I figured I should at least experiment. I mean, I've turned seventeen, for God's sake.'

Julia nodded understandingly and waited for the girl to finish justifying herself. It was all sounding so familiar. 'Go on,' she said.

Emma sighed. She might as well get it over and done with. 'Well we went a bit further than usual. I'd let him get my panties off and he had his jeans half down and we were feeling each other and then suddenly ... ' She paused. 'Suddenly he was trying to do it.'

Emma stopped studying her drink can and looked at Julia. 'Honestly, Julia, I didn't want to. I tried to stop him. And he called me a prickteaser and kept trying to shove himself into me. And it was hurting like hell. And finally I managed to get out from underneath and he gave up.'

Julia wanted to hug the girl but she didn't. 'What happened then?' she said.

'I put my panties back on and he said he was sorry. Well, he sort of said he was sorry, but he was in a rotten mood, I could tell. And then he drove me home and that was it.' Emma studied the drink can again. 'There was blood all over my panties, so I suppose that means I've gone and done it, haven't I?'

'Yep, you sure have.'

Emma looked up and was astonished to see that Julia was smiling broadly. 'I'm sorry, love,' she said and she burst out laughing, unable to contain herself any longer. 'I'm sorry, I really am, but I can't help it.'

Emma was amazed. It wasn't like Julia to laugh at her. And certainly not over something as serious as this.

'Stop looking at me like that,' Julia said when she eventually got herself under control. 'I'm not laughing at you, honestly.'

'What are you laughing at then?' Emma asked, a touch sullen.

'The story. The way it happened. I think just about every second woman I know lost her virginity like that. I sure as hell know I did.'

Emma started to relax. 'It was all so tacky,' she said.

'Yes, not exactly the true romance one hopes for, but cheer up, love, the next time'll be better. Oh dear ... ' Julia laughed again and there was sympathy in the laugh. 'That poor little bastard. He was quite right, you were behaving like a prickteaser. You'll have to put a stop to that, you know.'

'Yes, I know.'

'I tell you what we'll do.' Julia jumped up and went into the kitchen. 'We'll toast your womanhood, what do you say?'

She reappeared with a bottle of wine. 'It's only cheap stuff, I'm afraid, but it's got bubbles in it.'

Half an hour later, Emma was completely cheered up. The following week she took Julia's advice and visited a doctor for a contraceptive pill prescription.

Towards the middle of the year, the sub-editor of the *North Shore Times*, who had recognised

Emma's diligence from the outset, decided to give her a break.

'We're bringing out a magazine around Christmas,' she said. 'A "that-was-the-year-that-was" type of thing, and the boss wants a feature on women in power. If you were to write a submission on someone you admire, and if he were to like it, he might use it. What do you think?'

What did she think? 'Oh Meg, thank you! Thank you, thank you, thank you, thank ... '

'I thought you'd feel like that,' Meg smiled. She liked Emma. 'Here's a list of suggestions. Pick a person and see if she'll grant you an interview. That's half the test, getting your foot in the door.' And she left, calling 'good luck' over her shoulder.

There were at least twenty women on the list. Politicians, magazine editors, fashion designers, business people. Halfway down the page, under the heading *Entertainment Industry,* was the name Penelope Ross, Chairman, Ross (Australia) Productions.

Emma stood staring at the piece of paper. She wondered whether she dared. For two days she wondered whether she dared and then she decided.

'I'm going to interview Penelope Ross,' she announced to Julia that Saturday.

There was silence.

'For the paper,' Emma continued. 'They're doing an end-of-year feature on women in power.'

'Why Penelope Ross? Do you have an option?'

'Yes,' Emma answered.

Another silence. 'Then why Penelope Ross?' Julia asked again.

'I want to.'

'I see.'

Emma could tell Julia was angry and she didn't know why. 'I want to meet her, can't you understand that?'

'Are you going to tell her who you are?'

'I don't know. Maybe not.' Emma felt uncomfortable. She didn't want to anger Julia, but now that the opportunity had presented itself, she couldn't wait to meet her father's family. Not only Penelope, she wanted to meet the formidable Franklin Ross as well. Surely it was her right, after all.

Julia could sense the girl's determination and she knew that any attempt at dissuasion would be useless.

'You're a fool, Emma, you'll be hurt,' was all she said and the subject was closed. It was true she didn't want to see Emma hurt or humiliated but there was another reason altogether for her anger.

Julia had made a bargain with Franklin Ross and she'd read in the old man's face his acknowledgement that she would keep it. He was a hard old bastard and she hadn't liked him but there had been a flash of mutual respect between them which Julia had never forgotten. The thought that he would assume she'd reneged on their deal, that she'd sent her daughter to claim her place in the Ross family, was more than Julia's pride could bear.

She knew she was being selfish. It was Emma's life and she had a right to trace her antecedents –

326

it was a natural urge. But, to her dying day, Julia wanted no contact with any member of the Ross family.

'Mrs Ross? Emma Clare.'

'Ah yes, Miss Clare.' The voice on the other end of the phone was cultivated, cool and efficient. It definitely belonged to the image Penelope projected in the various articles Julia had read. 'You're the young lady from the *North Shore Times*. Rhonda's told me all about you.'

Emma had contacted Penelope through the correct channels, making an appointment with her personal press secretary, Rhonda Watkins. During the entire interview Emma had been aware that she was being carefully screened. But she got through. Not only had she observed protocol, she'd done her homework. She knew that Ross Productions were about to shoot the pilot of a series which would go to air at the start of the new season. Christmas would be a good time to promote it.

'And the special on the making of the Snowy Mountains mini-series,' she'd said. 'I'd like a still of that if it's possible.'

Rhonda smiled, aware that the kid had certainly studied up on the situation. 'That shouldn't present a problem. Mrs Ross doesn't like to be represented as self-seeking. Any interviews granted must be solely for the promotion of Ross Productions.'

Emma nodded. She knew that. She also knew that, privately, Penelope loved publicity. At least that's what her informer at the studios had told her.

'Would ten o'clock tomorrow morning be convenient?' Penelope asked. 'At the studios?'

'Yes, of course.' Emma said, her mouth suddenly dry at the prospect of meeting her grandmother. 'Ten o'clock would be perfect.'

'Fine. I shall see you then.' And Penelope hung up.

Emma didn't sleep soundly that night. Was she going to tell the woman of their relationship or wasn't she? If so, how would she break the news? Blurt it out – 'I'm your granddaughter'? Well, that's what she'd done with her mother, hadn't she, and everything had worked out fine? But something told Emma it wouldn't work the same way with Penelope.

'Mrs Ross will see you now,' the secretary said. And Emma, in her sensible beige reporter's suit, walked into the plush office with its original paintings, its objets d'art and its vases of orchids. Penelope liked to work in pleasant surrounds.

She was seated behind an elegant carved teak desk but she rose and offered her hand as Emma entered. 'Do come in, my dear,' she said. 'I'm sorry to have kept you waiting.' They shook hands and Penelope gestured towards one of the armchairs. 'Let's make ourselves comfortable, shall we?'

Emma was surprised and delighted by the

328

warmth of her reception. Her informer at the studios had told her that Penelope was a hard taskmaster. 'A right bitch at times,' the informer had said. But then a lot of employees, given the opportunity, would like to badmouth their bosses, Emma supposed. And what a beautiful woman, she thought.

Penelope wore her rich auburn hair (still rich and still auburn through the diligent attention of her personal hairdresser) swept away from her face and held in a loose but immaculate bun at the nape of her neck. She wore a jade-green silk suit which hung in elegant folds accentuating her slender figure. As she sat in the armchair opposite Emma and crossed her long slim legs, she was the epitome of sophistication.

'Jane will bring us tea soon,' she said. My God, the girl's a child, she thought. She can't be more than eighteen. Rhonda had warned her Emma Clare was young, but not this young.

Penelope heaved an inward sigh. She hoped she wasn't wasting her time, but Rhonda had also said the girl was smart and that she'd done her homework. And any good publicity was useful – for the company, of course. 'You're very young, my dear,' she smiled. Penelope was always charming to members of the press.

Emma nodded. 'I'm seventeen.'

'And you're a fully qualified journalist – that's rather unusual, isn't it?' Penelope's smile was warm and congratulatory but inside she was starting to feel angry. They'd sent her a cadet reporter. It was an insult.

'Well, I'm really only a trainee at the moment,'

Emma admitted. It was best to be honest, she decided. 'But they've been very kind to me at the paper and they're moving me through the ranks quickly.' Better not admit she'd just finished school, she thought. She smiled modestly. 'I suppose they must think I have something. Certainly to allow me an assignment like this.'

'I'm sure they do.' Penelope recognised the ploy. The girl was smart but she was still a cadet and Rhonda was going to get a swift rap over the knuckles for letting her through. 'Now, where would you like to start?' she asked, hoping the tea would arrive soon and they could get it over with quickly.

An hour later, Rhonda's reprimand was forgotten. The girl was impressive; her homework had obviously been extensive, her questions were intelligent and, furthermore, she was a very likeable and interesting young woman. Certainly attractive, Penelope thought. Although, with that ash-blonde hair, she should really wear brighter colours; beige was not her shade.

'Tell me a little about yourself,' she said as she poured them both another herbal tea.

Was now the time? Emma wondered. She was captivated by the woman's grace and charm but she sensed the strength beneath the elegant facade. Which way would she react?

'There's not very much to tell really,' she said, hedging. 'I want to be a writer, well, a novelist actually ... one day,' she added self-deprecatingly in case it sounded a little over ambitious.

'Excellent,' Penelope replied encouragingly. 'One needs to set one's sights high to get on in this

world. But tell me a little about your background.'
There was something about the girl, something strangely familiar, she thought.

'I was adopted as a baby,' Emma said. Suddenly she wanted to tell Penelope. She felt deceitful interviewing the woman under false pretences. She wanted her to know the truth.

'I traced my natural parents several years ago,' she continued. 'My mother's name is Julia Bridges and my father ... ' She hesitated for a moment, then took a deep breath. 'My father was Terence Ross.'

Penelope said nothing. She stared down at her teacup. That afternoon in the lounge room at The Colony House. That hideous scene with that young woman who swore she was carrying Terry's child. The girl wasn't lying, Penelope knew it. She looked exactly like her mother.

'I'm sorry,' Emma said. She couldn't bear the silence.

'No, it's I who should be apologising, my dear.' Penelope put down her teacup. What to do? Her mind was racing. 'It just came as such a shock, that's all.' She smiled at Emma, put her hands out and took the girl's in her own. 'So you're Terry's child.'

Emma's relief knew no bounds. 'Oh, Mrs Ross, I'm sorry. I really am doing the interview for the paper but I know I shouldn't have ... '

'I think, under the circumstances, we could make it Penelope, couldn't we?'

Emma felt tears threatening. Julia had been wrong. Her grandmother was welcoming her. The relief was overwhelming. 'Yes,' she said. 'Penelope. Thank you.'

'Here.' Penelope took a delicate lace handkerchief from the pocket of her suit and handed it to Emma. 'There's nothing to cry about.'

Emma dabbed at her eyes trying not to soil the pristine handkerchief.

'Blow your nose, there's a good girl,' Penelope insisted.

'No, it's all right, I've got some tissues somewhere.' She fumbled in her shoulder-bag.

'Go on, silly, you can keep it. It's a gift.'

'Oh.' Emma sniffed uncertainly.

'Go on, go on.'

'Thank you,' she said. Nevertheless she blew her nose on the tissues and put the lace handkerchief carefully into the side pocket of her bag.

'Now,' Penelope said when the girl had fully recovered, 'where do you think we go from here?' What does she want, Penelope was thinking. What is she after?

'I don't know,' Emma replied. 'I just wanted to meet you, and to talk about my father a little. Maybe if you have a picture of him ... ?'

'Of course. I have many.'

Encouraged, Emma continued. 'And I'd love to meet ... ' She couldn't bring herself to say 'my grandfather'. ' ... Mr Ross, if that's possible.'

Here was where Penelope drew the line. 'I'm afraid that's not possible at the moment; he's in New York.' Franklin didn't return to the States until the following week but Penelope needed space.

'Tell me, Emma,' she continued smoothly, 'how does your mother feel about your contacting us?' The woman had put her daughter up to it, Penelope was sure. But what did she want? More money? Not recognition, surely.

'Oh, Julia didn't want me to contact you at all. She said Mr Ross would disown me. She said he told her that he would.'

Penelope started to relax a little. The situation wasn't quite as threatening as it had first appeared. She smiled sympathetically. 'Sadly, my dear, that is the case. I was there when he said it. Mr Ross is an old-fashioned man in many ways and, in a situation like this, he's not one to change his views, I'm afraid.'

Emma nodded, disappointed.

'I think it's best if we keep our knowledge of each other a secret, don't you? For the time being anyway.'

'I suppose so.'

Penelope needed a firmer assurance than that. 'You see, I'd like us to meet from time to time and it would be most unfortunate if Mr Ross were to forbid me any contact with you. Which he most certainly would,' she assured the girl. In truth, Penelope wasn't at all sure what Franklin's reaction would be to the discovery of his granddaughter. Most likely he would stick to his principles and deny her, but Penelope couldn't afford to take any chances. Life was good for her now and she didn't want it in any way disrupted.

With Franklin away so often, Penelope had become the matriarchal symbol of the Ross empire. She knew they called her the Ice Maiden, which secretly pleased her. She was a star at long last. Admittedly, not a movie star and, deep down, that would always be a regret, but she held a position of power and she was the centre of attention wherever she went.

Then there was Michael. Penelope adored Michael. He'd grown into a charming, sophisticated young man, a perfect escort – and she was well aware that when he accompanied her to the theatre and gallery openings, people assumed he was her son at the very least, perhaps even her young lover, most certainly not her grandson.

Emma posed a potential threat in a number of directions. Should the story of a bastard granddaughter reach the press, the unpleasant stigma of illegitimacy would tarnish her image and (of far greater offence to Penelope) it would remind everyone of her true age. But above all, there was the feminine competition Emma could pose. Competition which could affect not only Penelope's relationship with her husband and grandson but her status within the Ross household itself.

Even colourless little Vonnie, who had always remained in the background, had been an annoyance to Penelope. 'But I believe young Mrs Ross doesn't fancy kidneys,' the cook might say as Penelope drew up the week's menu. Or, 'Young Mrs Ross has asked if breakfast might be served on the terrace,' the maid might say. The 'young' so rankled with Penelope that she wanted to snarl, 'Tell her to leave the kidneys on the side of her plate then', or 'Tell her she can breakfast in the billiard room or the bathroom for all I care.'

Penelope hadn't wished it upon poor Vonnie, who was definitely strange and lived in a world of her own, but it had been a relief when she was diagnosed with a mental illness which made it necessary for her to be transferred to a home where her condition could be properly monitored.

It was a comfortable home in pleasant surrounds an hour's drive out of the city. For the first six months, Penelope had visited her fortnightly, for appearances' sake. But Vonnie never seemed to know she was there – indeed she had never seemed happier – so eventually Penelope had stopped going.

Since then, no other woman had been in a position of command in the Ross household. Penelope reigned supreme and that was the way she intended to keep it.

The status quo must be maintained, she decided. She must keep the girl a secret. And to keep the girl a secret, she must keep her on side. They must become friends. If she dismissed her the girl might well approach Franklin or, God forbid, Michael.

'Perhaps you would like to visit The Colony House and see where your father grew up?' she offered. That would mollify her surely. 'And I can show you some photographs of him,' she added for good measure.

'Oh, Mrs Ross ... Penelope,' Emma corrected, 'that would be wonderful!' She was thrilled by Penelope's offer and the fact that her grandmother wanted to maintain contact. It was far more than Julia had led her to hope for.

'I have a rather full itinerary for the next week or so,' Penelope said, rising. 'Shall we say the Tuesday after next?' Franklin would be out of the country by then and Michael always worked late at the studios on Tuesdays.

'Yes, of course.' Emma jumped to her feet. 'What time?'

'Make it mid-afternoon and we'll have tea. Say around three? Here's my card.' She handed it to Emma and they walked to the door. 'In the meantime,' she continued, 'I'm sure I could find you a little more writing work if you're interested. I have many contacts.'

'You mean ... here, at the studio?' Emma couldn't believe her luck.'

'Oh no, dear, I'm afraid that would be quite impossible. Not only are there no openings but television scripting is very specialised work and we have a full team of highly qualified, experienced writers.

'However, I do a lot of readings for the Blind Society,' Penelope explained, 'and I'm sure there would be some freelance work available for you in the way of book precis and the like.' It would be a good idea to develop a neutral ground for them, Penelope thought, somewhere well away from any possible contact with Ross family or staff.

Emma nodded eagerly. 'That'd be fantastic.'

'Yes,' Penelope smiled. 'Very good training, I would think, for a future novelist. Ring me here at the studios tomorrow morning and I'll give you the contact name and phone number. I'll have had a chat with them by then – they're bound to have something for you.' Penelope would make sure they did; she was a generous benefactor of the Blind Society.

'Thank you, Penelope, thank you so much. I'm sorry for ... '

'Not at all, my dear. It's a delight to meet you.' Penelope kissed her lightly on the cheek. 'It's sad that we must keep our little secret but you understand, don't you, it's for your own good?'

'Yes, of course.'

'I'll speak to you tomorrow.' She opened the door. 'Goodbye, Miss Clare,' she said for the sake of the receptionist.

'Goodbye, Mrs Ross,' Emma replied.

On the morning of the designated appointment at The Colony House, Emma awoke a little nervous at the prospect. She didn't know why. Perhaps it was Julia's negativity. Julia hadn't been remotely impressed by Emma's ecstatic account of her first meeting with Penelope.

'Don't trust her, Emma,' she warned. 'The woman's up to something. She has her own motives for wanting to see you again and it has nothing whatsoever to do with grandmotherly affection. She's a hard bitch.'

Emma found her mother's venom unreasonable. Julia herself swore that Franklin would most certainly disown her, so what possible motive could Penelope have for their meeting other than a genuine desire to get to know her? Besides, when Emma had telephoned the following day, she'd received a warm and generous reception.

'The Blind Society has some work for you, dear. The head of the book reading department is waiting to hear from you,' Penelope had said. She gave Emma the details, wished her luck and told her not to hesitate to ring should she need any help or any further details for her article. Then, before hanging up, she reminded Emma of their appointment at The Colony House the following week.

Still Julia was not impressed. 'I don't care what she says. She's hard and cunning and she's up to something.'

'But you only ever met her once,' Emma argued.

'I only need to meet someone like Penelope Ross once to know that I wouldn't trust her as far as I could spit,' Julia said.

Emma decided not to push the matter further. Julia's dislike for the Ross family had become an obsession, she decided, and it was impossible for her mother to see reason.

Nevertheless, as she walked up the circular drive to the main doors of The Colony House at precisely five minutes to three on Tuesday afternoon, Emma felt a certain foreboding.

The maid showed her into the lounge room where Penelope was waiting.

'My dear, how lovely to see you.' Penelope rose and brushed her cheek against Emma's.

'Hallo, Mrs Ross,' she said, for the sake of the maid.

'Tea in ten minutes, thank you, Tina,' and the maid left. 'I think we can stick with Penelope in front of the staff, my dear,' she smiled. 'After all, we're associates in our work for the Blind Society now, aren't we? Come along and I'll show you the house.'

All of Emma's misgivings disappeared as Penelope gave her a personal tour of The Colony House.

'This is one of our major guest suites,' she said as she opened one of the upstairs doors. 'Rumour hath it that Mr Ross was challenged to a duel in this very room.' Penelope was rather enjoying herself. She liked playing queen of the manor and it was difficult not to warm to the wide-eyed girl who was obviously overwhelmed by the wealth and style of The Colony House.

'It's beautiful,' Emma breathed, looking about the elegant sitting room with its french windows leading off to the balcony. Through the open carved doors she could see the adjoining bedroom with its massive four-poster bed. 'Absolutely beautiful.'

'Yes, isn't it?' Penelope agreed. She led the way out onto the balcony. 'Look,' she pointed, 'you can just see the statue of the dueller from here.'

Emma looked out over the lawns to the harbour edge and saw the lifesize bronze in the distance, its arm outstretched, pistol pointing towards the Harbour Bridge.

'He's not frightfully pretty, I'm afraid,' Penelope laughed, 'but he's quite impressive and he does have a history. He was presented to my husband by the man with whom he had the duel. Samuel Crockett – still alive, although very old now. He's a movie producer,' she explained, 'a movie producer in Hollywood. I actually made several films for him.'

'How fascinating,' Emma said. It was.

'Yes. The duel caused a furore, I believe. Of course I was virtually a child at the time. I hadn't met my husband then.' She laughed girlishly, conspiratorially. 'Needless to say, Mr Ross won.'

Emma was overwhelmed by everything about her, The Colony House, the servants, the opulence. She didn't belong to this world. But she delighted in the communication with Penelope herself. This wasn't her grandmother at all. This was a woman sharing confidences and, to Emma, the relationship was precious.

Penelope was fully aware that she was playing the situation on exactly the right level and gaining the girl's personal trust. 'Come downstairs, dear, and we'll have some tea,' she said. 'The cook has made a batch of shortbread which is positively sinful.'

It was most pleasurable to have some feminine company, Penelope decided an hour later as she ordered more tea and showed Emma her collection of press clippings and photographs. Feminine company which posed no threat to her position. Pretty, young, feminine company which made her feel like a girl again.

'I do envy you, my dear,' she found herself admitting quite truthfully. 'You have a career ahead of you. A lifetime ambition to fight for. The struggle up each rung of the ladder will be such an exciting achievement for you.'

Emma recognised the regret in Penelope's voice and was surprised. 'But you had such a remarkable career yourself, Penelope – all those West End productions and Hollywood movies. Surely you achieved everything you wanted?'

'Oh yes, yes, I achieved my ambitions,' she agreed. 'But you see, I left at the height of my career.' (Penelope had convinced herself of this over the years). 'And I do so miss it at times.'

'Why did you give it up?' Emma asked.

'My husband,' Penelope answered. 'My husband needed me. You see Mr Ross is a great deal older than I and, when we met, he was already a highly successful businessman who needed a supportive wife at his side. There was no room for a young actress with a career of her own, so . . . ' She shrugged nobly. 'I suppose we all have our sacrifices to make.'

Emma felt privileged that Penelope had chosen to share such intimacies with her and she was moved by the woman's history of self-denial. Franklin certainly appeared every bit the ogre Julia had painted him.

'And then, of course, the children came along . . . ' That had been the end of it all, Penelope remembered, Franklin's lust for sons. She had moved herself almost to tears with the account of her lost career. And she'd told her story without bitterness or rancour. Hers had been a noble life.

Penelope had never had a female companion with whom to share her sacrifices and now here was Emma, obviously sympathetic. For a moment she had completely forgotten to whom she was talking. The look on Emma's face suddenly reminded her. 'Yes,' she said briskly, pulling herself together. 'Your father was the first-born. I promised to show you some photographs, didn't I.'

'Forgive my indulgence, my dear,' she said stiffly as she crossed to the corner cabinet, inwardly cursing herself. How could she have allowed herself to get so carried away?

'Oh, please don't apologise, Penelope,' Emma begged. 'It was fascinating, every word.'

Penelope paused and looked at Emma. The girl meant it. She had no ulterior motive. She'd been genuinely enthralled and sympathetic. Penelope couldn't help but like her.

They sat together on the couch and leafed through the old photo album. It had been a long time since Penelope had looked at the early family photographs and again she found herself moved. Terry and James at Mandinulla. Family holidays. She'd forgotten that once they'd been a family. It seemed a lifetime ago. If she'd known what was going to happen perhaps she wouldn't have allowed her bitterness to deprive her of those moments. Perhaps she might have enjoyed her young sons more. Perhaps ... Maudlin rubbish, she told herself, and turned her attention to Emma as the girl studied the photos of her father.

'He was a lovely looking boy,' she said as she watched Emma, mesmerised, slowly turning the pages. 'I don't have many pictures of him as an adult. We didn't seem to take so many photographs then. I suppose one doesn't when they grow up. There's one here, though ... ' She turned a couple of pages quickly and Emma wished she wouldn't. She wanted to study each one slowly. 'Ah, yes, here we are, this is one of my favourites.'

It was a young man in formal evening dress, probably only a few years older than herself, Emma thought, and incredibly handsome.

'The Hunt Club Ball,' Penelope said, 'Terry always looked good in black tie.'

Emma said nothing. Her eyes were glued to the photograph. 'A smile and eyes that could charm the devil', that's what Julia had said. This was him, her father, this was the man Julia had fallen in love with.

Penelope watched the girl studying the photograph, and she suddenly heard herself say, 'Would you like to have it?'

Emma turned to her, her eyes glowing. 'Really? But you said it's one of your favourites.'

'Of course, my dear,' Penelope answered briskly. It was time to draw an end to this conversation; things were becoming far too intimate. 'I have others.' Good grief, how long had it been since she'd looked at the damn album? And it would be a long time before she looked at it again. She withdrew the photograph and gave it to Emma.

Emma recognised the signs immediately. Their meeting was over and she mustn't overstay her welcome. As it was, she hoped that Penelope hadn't regretted the confidences she'd shared. Emma deeply admired her grandmother but she felt a surge of sympathy. Penelope was a lonely woman.

'It's been a lovely afternoon,' she said formally, preparing to take her leave. 'Thank you.'

But, before she could rise, a young man bounded through the hall and into the lounge room. 'Hi, Penelope, I'm home,' he called.

'What are you doing back at this hour? It's Tuesday.'

'Reg and I had an argument so I walked out,' the young man replied. 'Aren't you going to introduce me?'

343

'Of course, darling. This is Emma. Emma Clare, Michael Ross.'

'Hi,' Emma heard herself say.

'Where did you spring from?' he asked, but she found herself merely staring up at him. The eyes. The smile. She was looking at the photograph of her father. Fortunately Penelope answered for her.

'Emma's doing some work with me for the Blind Society,' she said.

For the next half an hour it was impossible for Emma to leave. Michael took over and his conversation was fascinating. Emma was riveted by the machinations of the television world and enthralled by the fact that she was listening to her half-brother.

When she was finally able to make her departure, Michael insisted upon driving her home. Emma was aware of the warning in Penelope's voice. 'Go on, dear, you might as well, he's not going to take no for an answer.'

Emma tried to signal a look of assurance in return. She had no intention of breaking her promise.

But she found herself unable to refuse the offer of a drink and further conversation with Michael when they arrived at her flat. Just half an hour, she told herself, half an hour of contact with her brother.

It was with reluctance that she managed to drag herself away nearly two hours later. What a fascinating mind, she thought. And she could hardly believe it when he said he wanted her to work with him. She'd dearly love to, but . . .

'Perhaps,' she heard herself say. 'We'll talk about it later, Michael.' It would be impossible, of course.

The following day, Emma telephoned Penelope to thank her for the afternoon.

'I think we should meet, my dear,' Penelope said. 'How about in the little coffee lounge down the road from the Blind Society?'

Emma arrived early and sat at a corner table overlooking the street for ten minutes before Penelope's car pulled up outside. She watched as Penelope gave her driver his instructions and the car drove off.

'Hello, my dear. Isn't it a glorious day?' Penelope signalled the waitress. 'Soon it'll be far too hot. Sydney summers – I do so loathe them.'

When the waitress had gone, Penelope got straight to the point. 'What did you think of Michael?' she asked.

'He's terrific,' Emma said enthusiastically, 'and very interesting. We talked for ages.'

'Yes, I know.' There was a wariness in Penelope's tone and Emma immediately sought to reassure her. 'I didn't tell him anything, Penelope, honestly. And I won't, for as long as you tell me not to. I don't want to spoil things and I couldn't bear it if Mr Ross . . . '

'Yes, yes, my dear, I believe you.' Penelope sipped her iced tea and there was a moment's silence. Then she said, 'He wants you to work with him.'

'Yes, I know. He said he – '

'He's going to offer you a job as a trainee script editor at the studios.'

'Oh.' Emma felt uncomfortable. 'He said he wanted to but I wasn't sure how serious he was.' Penelope said nothing, but her troubled look worried Emma. 'I'll turn the job down, I promise.' Still Penelope said nothing. 'Really I will. I swear.'

'I don't think it's going to be as easy as that, my dear.'

Penelope was in a genuine dilemma. Michael had come home raving about his 'meeting of the minds' with Emma Clare. 'Where did you meet her, Penelope?' he'd asked. 'For someone so young she has a stunningly creative brain. She'd be a perfect storyliner; I'm going to offer her a traineeship.'

Penelope had tried every ploy to dissuade him without appearing suspicious. 'But she's only seventeen.'

'So was I when I started.'

'Yes, my darling, but you were a sophisticated seventeen. Emma is really very young.'

'That's exactly what we need, some more young blood in the department. Reg is a real dinosaur.'

'But how do you know if the girl has talent?'

'We'll give her a try and find out, won't we? For Christ's sake, Penelope, what have you got against her? I thought you liked her.'

'I do, darling,' she said. 'Very much. That's why I'm being protective.'

'Protective of what?' There was a mischievous glint in Michael's eye. 'Her virginity? I'm hardly going to seduce her, am I? As you say, she's only a kid.'

346

Michael had never confided in his grandmother about his affairs of the heart. Indeed, the only person with whom he'd ever shared such confidences had been Daniel Pendennis, but Dan had gone. As arranged, his duties had ceased upon Michael's eighteenth birthday and Dan had returned to his beloved Mousehole to set up a martial arts school with the tidy cache he'd squirrelled away during his four years' employment with Ross Industries. Since then, there had been no one Michael wished to confide in and he'd grown to prefer it that way.

Penelope was forced to give in. Michael was obviously going to offer Emma the job with or without her approval. 'Don't be ridiculous, Michael. If you wish to employ the girl, then employ her.'

'No,' she said to Emma, shaking her head thoughtfully, 'it's not going to be that easy.'

'You mean I should accept the job?' Emma desperately hoped it was what her grandmother was saying. She longed to work at the studios. But surely Penelope couldn't be serious. 'You mean work alongside Michael without telling him who I am?'

'That's precisely what I mean.' The girl was staring back at her incredulously. 'For the moment anyway,' Penelope continued. 'You see, if Michael found out the truth, he would most definitely tell his grandfather – they're very close.' Penelope breathed a martyred sigh. 'And then, I'm afraid, we would both be forbidden any contact with you.'

Penelope had spent a sleepless night working out the details. Emma could get her training through the Ross Studios – there was little doubt that the girl was talented and Penelope herself would ensure that she moved quickly through the ranks – then, once she was qualified, one of Penelope's many contacts in another area of the industry would come up with an offer too good to refuse. An offer in another city. The girl was ambitious; she'd take it; and it would only be a matter of time before she was phased out of their lives altogether.

'We must bide our time, Emma,' she said, 'before we can let the truth be known. Mr Ross is a very forceful man and we must somehow mellow him before he can be told. But there will come a day, I'm certain of it.' Over my dead body, she said to herself.

For such a strong woman, Emma thought, Penelope was very much dictated to by her husband. But then, everything that was being said of Franklin Ross rang true of the tyrannical personality Julia had painted.

Emma nodded her agreement.

'In the meantime,' Penelope continued, 'I think it would be better if you didn't visit The Colony House, and if all contact with Michael was kept strictly to studio business.'

'We'll continue to see each other through our work at the Blind Society,' she added, when she noticed the disappointment in Emma's eyes. 'And ... ' she gave a comradely smile ' ... through our clandestine meetings in coffee houses.'

Emma smiled back, relieved that Penelope didn't want to relinquish their contact.

Two weeks later, Emma took up her official traineeship at Ross Productions.

Her first month was spent observing storylining sessions and script conferences of programmes currently in production, as well as the actual workings of the studio itself from marketing to publicity, from filming to editing and post-production.

She was kept extremely busy and she didn't see much of Michael except for the moments when he managed to corner her as she grabbed a quick takeaway sandwich and coffee at the canteen.

Michael himself was finding the situation very frustrating. He couldn't wait to get to know Emma but she seemed to avoid any personal contact with him.

'It was Penelope's idea to give you the full view of things,' he said one day while Emma waited for her sandwich. 'Are you getting fed up yet?'

'No way,' she answered enthusiastically. 'It's fascinating. I'm learning so much and it'll be a terrific advantage once I start working for the script department.'

'Yes, that's what Penelope thought. I must say she's certainly taken you under her wing.' Michael was a little peeved. Penelope had gone from one extreme to another. Having accepted the fact that he was going to offer the girl a job, she'd zealously taken over Emma's career to the point where he was denied any contact at all. 'Why don't you come to The Colony House after work and we'll put a few hours in on the movie?' he suggested.

It was the third time he'd asked her in the past fortnight and he received the same answer. 'Sorry, Michael, I can't tonight – I'm going out.'

'Okay, I'll give you a lift home, you can offer me a coffee and we'll chat about it before you have to leave.' Michael wasn't going to give up so easily this time around.

'Sorry, I can't. I'm going out straight from work.'

'Fine, I'll drive you. We can talk on the way. Where are you heading?'

Oh hell, she thought, where was she heading? 'Redfern,' she said off the top of her head. She'd go and see Julia.

'Fine. I'll pick you up at front reception. Five-thirty all right?'

'Yes, five-thirty's fine.' There wasn't much else she could do. Damn, she thought yet again, if she could only afford a car it would solve everything, but she was still a good month away from having enough money for a deposit. How could she keep steering clear of Michael's offers for another whole four weeks?

'Titles: what do you think? *Halley's Comet, Harbinger of Doom*, or just plain *Halley's*?' Michael was firing questions at her, talking very fast and driving very slowly. It was only a quarter of an hour from the studios to Redfern and he wanted to make every second count.

'*Halley's*,' Emma answered instinctively. 'I've

got a thing for one-word titles.' She knew he was working overtime on rekindling her interest in the movie theme and he was succeeding. It was impossible to be unaffected by Michael – by his intelligence and his enthusiasm and, above all, his imagination.

'Sabotage by the sect of religious zealots,' he was saying. 'They manage to blow up one of the airships, which alerts the media. The press realises something's going on, but at this stage, they don't know what. The astronomers won't tell them about the pole shift for fear of universal panic, and obviously the mega-businessman isn't going to tell them. So that leaves the religious zealots. Why aren't they going to alert the press and tell the world?'

'Good question,' Emma said. 'We'll have to think about that one.' Damn, the 'we' had slipped out. 'That's the place,' she pointed, 'next corner on the left.'

'Good.' Michael pulled up outside Julia's house. 'We'll think about it tomorrow evening after work. The Colony House. You can come over for dinner.'

Oh God, she thought, here we go. 'I can't,' she answered.

'The next night then?'

'No, Michael.'

'What is it, Emma?' It was time to confront her, Michael decided. He sensed that Emma liked him and she was certainly stimulated by the movie project – so why was she so wary of personal contact? If she was a virgin, and frightened that he was going to make sexual advances, then he was quite happy to bide his time. Despite the fact that he already fantasised about Emma, Michael was prepared to wait.

'Why am I threatening to you?' he insisted. 'I only want to work on the movie together, and I know you're interested in the project. Why are you so terrified of being alone with me?'

'I'm not, it's just ... ' Emma knew she must give some form of plausible answer. 'It's just that I don't want to abuse Penelope's kindness.'

'In what way?'

'She's been so good to me, getting me the work at the Blind Society and advancing my career at the studios and – '

'So?' Michael asked with a touch of impatience. 'So what?'

'So, The Colony House is her space. I don't want to crowd her.'

'Good grief, is that all?' He smiled, relieved. 'The Colony House is my space too, you know. I have virtually a whole wing of the place to myself – two double suites, even my own kitchen; it's bigger than a normal apartment ... '

'I don't care.' Emma refused to be cornered. 'I'd still feel uncomfortable. I'm not coming to The Colony House and that's that. Now, if you don't mind, I have to go.'

She opened the car door. Michael jumped out from the driver's side and was there in a flash to assist her. 'Okay, I promise, I won't hound you any more. No Colony House.' He gave her his most winning smile. 'But please, Emma, please ... work with me on this movie. Just a couple of nights a week. I'll drive you home and we can have a coffee at your place, or we can stay a bit later at the studios. Just say you'll work with me. We can inspire each other, you know we can.'

Emma looked at the eyes which shone into hers with all the eagerness of an excited ten-year-old. Yes, it would be a stimulating experience, she thought, and where was the harm? Just a couple of nights a week.

'All right,' she said, feeling guilty as she recalled Penelope's instructions that all contact with Michael was to be kept strictly to studio business. 'All right, you win.'

As she turned towards the house she saw that one of the lounge room curtains was pulled aside and she knew that Julia was watching.

'Starting when?' Michael asked.

'Starting Friday after work,' she called back as she walked up the path. 'Coffee, my place.'

'That was him, wasn't it?' Julia said as she opened the front door and they watched the Porsche speed off down the street.

'If you mean Michael Ross, yes it was. I'm sorry to arrive out of the blue but I needed an excuse.' Emma wasn't expected for another two weeks. Julia still didn't have a telephone so they arranged each successive meeting in advance. The meetings had dwindled from every Saturday to every alternate Saturday and, the last time they'd seen each other, they'd stretched it to three weeks.

Emma was saddened by the rift that had grown between them, but since she'd started working at the studios, Julia had never ceased to agonise to her over Penelope's ulterior motives. 'Why has she given you this job?' she asked. 'Why is she keeping you a secret? Why doesn't she simply tell Franklin about you and have you kicked out of the family? It's what she wants.'

'It's not what she wants,' Emma protested time and again. 'She knows that's exactly what he'd do and she doesn't want to risk it.'

'Bullshit. She's terrified that he might accept you after all. That's what it is, it must be.' On and on Julia went until Emma was worn out by her venom. Torn between her loyalty to her mother and her gratitude to Penelope, the strain was becoming unbearable.

'He's a good-looking bastard,' Julia commented as the Porsche rounded the corner. 'Just like his father.'

'So when the zealots find out about the pole shift, why don't they alert the press?' Michael asked. It was half-past six on Friday evening and they were at Emma's apartment. Both her flatmates were out, as she'd known they would be, and she and Michael had spent the previous hour going through the notes, characters and storylines that Michael had compiled. 'The million dollar question,' he challenged. 'The zealots were your idea, so what's the answer?'

'Easy,' Emma explained. She'd given it some thought. 'To the zealots, the pole shift is an act of God, an act intended to purge the planet.'

'So?'

'So the normal order of things must be observed.

The masses obliterated in the disaster are those who were destined to die in the cleansing and purification process.'

'Good, good,' Michael said, opening his briefcase and fumbling around in the lid pocket.

'If the news got out,' Emma continued, excited and pleased with herself, 'the populace would fight to preserve itself and the normal order would be – '

'In chaos,' Michael agreed. 'Exactly. The wrong people would be destroyed, etcetera . . . Now let's really get something happening here.'

He took a sachet of white substance and a crisp new one hundred dollar note from an envelope and knelt beside the glass-topped coffee table in the centre of the lounge room.

'What are you doing?' Emma asked as he gently tapped some of the substance onto the table top.

'Get us a knife, will you? Non-serrated.'

Emma did as she was told and watched as he held the knife by the blade and chopped the lumpy white granules to a fine powder.

'What the hell are you doing, Michael?' she asked. 'That's cocaine, isn't it?'

'Yeah,' he said. 'Great to work with. Really opens up the channels, makes you receptive. You'll love it.' For the past six months Michael had found that cocaine – used sensibly, of course – had far broader uses than mere sexual stimulation. Emma stared at the two neat white lines on top of the coffee table. 'It's good pure stuff, perfectly harmless,' he assured her. He was rolling the hundred dollar note into a tight cylinder. 'Just one little line each.'

'I couldn't,' Emma said. 'Honestly, I couldn't.'

'Of course you could. You're a writer – you're supposed to experience things. Look. This is all you do.'

He held the rolled-up hundred dollar note against his right nostril, leant over the coffee table and placed the other end against one of the lines of cocaine. 'Simple, you see? Just one big sniff.' He put the index finger of his other hand over his left nostril and fed the bill along the line, inhaling deeply.

Emma watched, riveted, as the white powder disappeared. She was mildly shocked, but enthralled.

'There you go,' he said, handing her the hundred dollar note. 'Your turn.'

She found herself automatically taking it from him. 'What will happen?' she asked.

'Just a bit of a buzz, that's all,' he assured her. 'It gives your mind a boost.' She hesitated. 'Go on, Emma. It's quite safe, really, everyone does it.'

Emma had never known anyone who snorted cocaine but she'd shared the occasional joint with friends and had allowed herself to get a little drunk on the odd occasion. What the hell, she thought, Michael was right – writers had to experience everything.

Here goes, she told herself, and she boldly sniffed along the line of powder until it had all but disappeared. Michael dabbed at the remaining white flecks with his finger and rubbed them over his front gums.

'Great,' he said, 'now let's get to work.'

* * *

Three hours later, they were still zooming. 'She wears a jellabah with a massive hood,' Emma said, 'and an ankh around her neck and she's always sipping a goblet of holy water.' They were discussing the leader of the brigade of zealots.

'Maybe she's an alcoholic and the holy water's really straight vodka,' Michael added jokingly.

'Why not? . . . No, seriously,' she insisted when he laughed. Emma was feeling giddy with inspiration. The whole thing was becoming wonderfully insane. 'In her drunken haze the zealot leader lets her fear take over, she decides she's only human after all and she opts to side with the businessman and save her own skin. She becomes a traitor to her people.'

Michael picked up on her excitement. 'Great conflict,' he agreed. 'She takes some of her followers with her and the zealots are actually divided in their midst.'

'And all the time she's betraying them,' Emma continued, 'she's quoting from the Old Testament threatening floods and plague and pestilence. You know the sort of thing . . . "he who is swift of foot shall not save himself" and "the mighty shall flee away naked".'

'I love it, I love it,' Michael said, scribbling away frantically. 'God, I wish you had a computer.'

It was after twelve o'clock when Emma decided to call a halt to the night. She was suddenly feeling tired and her flatmates would be back soon.

'I've had it, Michael,' she said. 'Home time – I'm totally brain-drained.' She grinned happily. 'I don't know how productive all that insanity was, but God I've had fun.' Weary as she was, Emma had never felt so exhilarated.

'Me too,' Michael agreed. He was feeling far from tired. He'd snorted a line before he'd come to Emma's and the effects of the cocaine hadn't yet worn off. All his fantasies about her were coming to the fore – coke always heightened his libido. He wondered whether tonight could be the night. He decided to throw caution to the winds.

'There are other exciting things we could do, Emma,' he said. They were sitting at the dining room table, papers strewn all about the place, and he leaned forward and took her hand in his. Nice and slowly does it, he told himself, don't alarm her.

Emma froze. Why hadn't she foreseen something like this? She had been so conscious of Michael as her sibling, feeling such an affection for him as the brother she'd never known, that it hadn't once occurred to her he might think of her sexually. What a fool she'd been.

She didn't blame him – it was only natural. They were in her flat, alone, at midnight; they'd snorted cocaine together. It was a nightmare come true, she thought, and she cursed herself.

'Michael,' she said slowly, letting her hand rest where it was. 'I'm sorry if I've misled you. But I'm not interested and I never will be and if you want to push things in that direction then I won't be able to see you again.' She withdrew her hand. 'I'm sorry.'

Michael was still on a high and his mind was working overtime. Despite the fact that Emma was rejecting him, he could sense a wealth of affection emanating from her. An affection far deeper than he'd dreamed possible. Could she actually be in love with him?

He felt elated. That was it! Emma was in love with him and she was rejecting him merely because she was frightened. She was a virgin, not ready for seduction, only just eighteen and, despite her intellectual maturity, very inexperienced. But she loved him. And one day she would want him. One day . . .

In the meantime, how should he play it? His mind was whirling at breakneck speed. Buy time, he told himself. Play it very low-key. Make a joke of it. Whatever you do, don't frighten her.

'Christ, I didn't know I was that unattractive,' he laughed.

'I'm serious, Michael.'

'So am I.' He took her hand in his once more and wouldn't let go when she tried to pull away. 'No, listen to me, Emma. I'm sorry I put the word on you and I want you to forget it happened. It's just the coke playing havoc with the hormones. It won't happen again, I promise.'

She smiled back, a little uncertain.

'I mean it,' he insisted. 'I wouldn't do anything to jeopardise our relationship. I want you as my friend and my workmate and my bloody inspiration. We're a great team, aren't we? What do you say?'

'I say terrific,' Emma replied and she smiled, relieved.

He leaned forward and kissed her gently on the cheek. Her hair smelt wonderful, her skin felt like velvet and the proximity of her mouth was tantalising.

She was tall and slim and attractive. An ash-blonde, not altogether unlike Emma in appearance.

Michael met her at a discotheque and took her home and made love to her. As he felt her writhing beneath him, he buried his face in her hair and told himself it was Emma. Emma's breasts, Emma's legs wrapped around him, Emma's moans. One day ... one day ... one day ...

BOOK FIVE

The

Years of Change

(1986 - 1994)

CHAPTER TEN

'BEHOLD, I WILL PRESS you down in your place as a cart full of sheaves presses down . . . ' She stood on the hill overlooking the valley, her jellabah flowing behind her in the breeze and she held aloft a goblet in her right hand. 'The strong shall not retain his strength, nor shall the mighty save his life . . . ' Her voice rang loud and clear, echoing among the surrounding hills. With her other hand, she raised the ankh which hung on a chain about her neck. 'He who is swift of foot shall not save himself . . . '

It was a surreal scene. In the valley below were ten gigantic airships, one of which was slowly lifting itself off the ground. Fifty people were crowded together watching the exercise; to one side, a cherry picker held a cameraman and director. Ten metres in the air, they were filming the bizarre spectacle. At the base of the crane, another group of a dozen or more were observing, among them Michael and Emma.

'He who is stout of heart among the mighty shall flee away naked in that day!' A concealed microphone made the voice reverberate.

The airship hovered three metres above the ground. Suddenly, there was a loud explosion and the watching crowd screamed in terror as it burst into flame. A man jumped from the cockpit. He was a ball of fire. A second man followed.

Emma looked on, enthralled. Michael had told her nothing about the stunt, wanting to surprise her. 'Come out and watch us blow up the airship,' he'd said. 'It's going to be massive.'

She felt a little anxious as she watched the flaming figure run from the airship and heard the man's screams of agony. Of course she'd seen similar stunts in the movies, and knew about the protective clothing and the perfect orchestration involved in such an exercise, but it was nevertheless a frightening thing to observe.

The second man who'd jumped out of the airship chased the ball of fire. He was wearing a short-sleeved shirt. Emma gasped as he grabbed the human bonfire and threw him to the ground. He covered him with his body and beat at the flames with his bare hands and arms. She felt sick with horror. Something had gone wrong, she thought, this wasn't meant to happen. She looked at Michael, who was standing beside her. His eyes were bright with excitement.

'Michael, for God's sake, something's gone – '

'Ssshh,' he said.

'Cut,' the director yelled through a megaphone.

There was a hushed silence. Obviously others in the group also thought that something had gone wrong – several people, Emma among them, rushed up to the two men apparently unconscious

364

on the ground. Michael followed behind at a leisurely pace. The cherry picker holding the cameraman and director lowered itself to the ground.

'Are you all right?' Emma asked but, even as she did, the men were sitting up and the onlookers were visibly relaxing.

'Great work, guys,' Michael called out to them, and he started to clap. Soon everyone was clapping and the men rose to their feet, grinning and acknowledging the applause.

'But how did you do it?' Emma asked. 'Your hands, your arms?'

The 'ball of fire' was being helped out of his specially treated overalls and Emma directed the question to the second man, who'd had so much of his skin exposed to the flames.

'Easy,' he said, and he peeled off a whole strip of what looked like thick, shiny skin from his biceps to the knuckles of his fingers. 'It's new fireproof latex – you spray it on. Safest thing for a stunt like this.' The man was about thirty, good-looking in a dark, brooding way, and he had an American accent. He turned his wrist over and continued to peel strips of fake skin from the inside of his forearm and his hands and fingers. 'I'm standing in for the chief pilot who burns his hands saving his buddy, so we needed to show the skin. Besides which,' the American grinned and gestured towards the handsome leading man who had cornered the director, 'he's the hero of the movie, so it had to look good.'

'Stan! Bob! Great stunt. Well done! Be with you in one second,' the director called, doing his best to get away from the self-obsessed actor.

'You don't have to tell her the story, Stanley, she's the co-writer,' Michael said as he joined Emma.

'Oh.' The American looked impressed. 'You're Emma Clare. Stanley Grahame – hi. I won't shake,' he laughed, holding up his scaly hands, 'and this is Bob.'

'Hello. Me neither,' Bob apologised and Emma noticed that minus his overalls his arms, hands and chest were covered in a thick gel. Bob, too, was American.

'Well, I insist,' Michael said and he shook hands effusively with both men. 'Great stunt, Emma, what do you reckon?'

'Terrific, but wasn't the chief pilot supposed to break his wrist when he jumped from the airship carrying his unconscious crewmate?'

Michael nodded. 'Yes, but we changed it. Stanley's idea.'

'The human torch stunt's always effective,' Stanley nodded. 'And now with this protective skin we can have a close-up of the hero burning his hands saving his buddy – more impressive than a broken wrist, wouldn't you say?'

'Oh yes, much more impressive.' Stanley Grahame was certainly not short on confidence, Emma thought.

'Stan the man! Bob! Well done, well done.' The director joined them, but he hadn't managed to escape the leading man who had followed him, continuing his one-sided conversation every step of the way.

'Stan,' the actor said, 'that moment of impact when you hit the ground . . . There was a second or so's pause before you ran after Bob. I was just saying ... perfect moment to cut in for a close-up, wouldn't you agree?'

'All right, Jack, all right,' the director finally snapped back. 'You've said your piece and I've told you I'll look after it.'

'I was just seeking a little extra input, that's all,' the actor replied peevishly. He wasn't used to being spoken to so sharply in public. 'There's certainly no harm in that; the more input the better, surely.' He turned tail. 'I'll be in my trailer.' There were derisive grins shared by all as he attempted a dignified exit. Jack was an American star with Latin good looks that drove women wild and he'd been imported to boost overseas sales. He considered himself above his antipodean counterparts and so wasn't at all popular.

A lunch break was called in the massive catering tent set up on the other side of the hill. As executive producer, Michael insisted on opening a crate of champagne to toast the successful airship explosion. After all, one of the highlights of the movie was successfully in the can, they were near the end of the entire shoot, they were well on schedule, and even the director agreed that the afternoon's itinerary was relatively simple.

''Course it is, it's a breeze,' Michael insisted. 'Just reaction shots and cutaways. Easy.'

Normally the director loathed producers who said things like 'Easy', and 'It's a breeze'. They were usually the same producers who said things like 'Yes, I know there's a car chase in the script here and aerial shots there but we're over budget – you'll have to cheat it. You can do it; simple.' But

Michael was a different producer altogether. He not only understood the world of movies on both a practical and artistic level, he was exciting and innovative and, if he appeared a little cocky every now and then, the director was prepared to wear it.

After lunch, Michael took Emma on a guided tour. They bounced around in the runners' jeep while he showed her the various movie locations. Yarramalong Valley was a beautiful part of the country, and remote, despite the fact that it was only a couple of hours' drive from Sydney. In the heart of the valley stood a hundred-and-fifty-year-old stone farmhouse which Michael had chosen as the location for the businessman's secret hideout.

'This is where they live while they oversee the building of their airships,' he explained to Emma. Then he drove her over the far side of the northern hill where the zealots had their camp. 'Impressive, isn't it?' They stood on the hill surveying the lines of tents in the neighbouring valley. 'We've got fifty zealots. Twenty of them are speaking roles – good character actors, all hand-picked.'

'Now,' he said as they got back in the jeep, 'I'll show you the true stars of the movie. Come and look at my babies.' And he drove her back to the first in the line of massive airships.

'She flies like a bird,' he said, helping her aboard the huge craft, 'and she comfortably holds a hundred and fifty people and supplies to last them for months.'

He showed her the cockpit with its complicated array of control panels. 'Fully operational,' he boasted. 'If a pole shift actually does happen, I'm keeping this little baby for my personal use.'

'But wait till you see the pride and joy of the fleet,' he said, and he called to Stanley Grahame as they climbed out of the airship. 'Hey, Stan, come and give Emma a demonstration.'

For a moment, Emma barely recognised Stanley Grahame.

Certainly his face had been grimed up for the stunt but what had happened to his black hair and brooding brow? A wig, of course. He was doubling for the star. It hadn't even occurred to her at the time.

'Well, that's certainly an improvement,' Emma said, taking in the unruly light brown hair and the shaggy sandy eyebrows.

'Don't let Jack hear you say that,' Stanley answered.

With Michael leading the way, the three of them walked along the line to the very last of the airships. With the exception of the burnt-out hull of the exploded ship, all remaining nine appeared identical, but as it turned out, seven of them were fakes, dummies designed to merely sit there.

'There's the one you've just seen that actually flies,' Michael explained, 'and there's this one. Just take a look at this.' He nodded to the stage-hands standing by and they pushed an entire half of the airship to one side. The immense structure rolled easily apart in two segments like the halves of a giant split walnut. The interior of each half was identical in appearance to the inside of the functional ship.

'All fake, of course, nothing actually operates,

but this is where we shoot our interiors. Much easier to get camera angles here than trying to line up shots in the real thing. And Stan's got a few clever little inventions hanging around that we couldn't possibly put in the real thing.'

'Ready for the demonstration?' Stanley asked. Emma nodded and he sat down at the controls, pushing buttons and operating switches on a dashboard which looked very complicated. Suddenly, the whole panel started to spark and hiss alarmingly. Emma backed away, startled, as flashes of electricity stabbed the air like miniature lightning bolts.

Stanley switched a button and everything stopped. 'A minute later in the sequence and the whole thing's designed to go up in flames,' he explained. 'That's when Bob and I make a jump for it – we're filming the interiors leading up to the explosion tomorrow.'

'You mean you're going to destroy this whole set?' Emma asked incredulously.

'Oh no,' he answered. 'It's just a special effect. The entire panel will appear to go up but, if we cut out of it quick enough, there shouldn't even be a scorch mark left. All an illusion.'

'Stanley's own invention,' Michael said. 'Impressive, eh?'

'But I thought you were . . . a stunt man.' Emma stopped herself saying 'only' just in time. Stanley was such an athletic looking fellow it was difficult to equate him with anything that wasn't purely physical.

'No, special effects. But sometimes I throw in a stunt or two if I like the director.' He flashed a comradely smile at Michael. 'Or, on very rare occasions, the producer.'

'Let's go to the executive van and have a drink,' Michael suggested.

Stanley's services weren't required and, as the remainder of the day's filming was going to be fairly mundane, they spent the next several hours pleasantly chatting together and drinking spiked coffees in the producer's Winnebago, one of two vans stationed barely a hundred metres from the old stone farmhouse.

Michael pointed to the other van. 'Jack's,' he said. 'The pompous shit insisted on the full star treatment – demanded the biggest Winnebago closest to the main location – so I lined up one for myself and plonked it here. There's bugger all he can do about it.' He laughed. 'Poor old Jack, if he bothered to get out a tape measure he'd find I'm actually three feet closer. Anyone for a joint?' And he pulled a leather pouch from his pocket.

The others declined and Emma gave him a warning glance. 'No nagging,' Michael said. 'I don't do it in front of the crew and Stanley's perfectly safe – he even shares the odd one with me, don't you, Stan?'

'Only late at night when I can go to bed,' Stanley replied. 'The damn stuff puts me to sleep.'

Emma had long ago stopped nagging Michael about his drug abuse. 'You snort too much coke and you smoke too much dope,' she'd said time and again.

'Rubbish,' he answered. 'A bit of this and that to get the juices flowing – it's just a little creative stimulation.'

'It's just a lot of indulgence.' But she stopped nagging and was glad to see that he wasn't making a public display of his habits, which would certainly be bad for his image as a responsible producer.

'So how long have you been working in special effects, Stanley?' Emma asked. 'It's a fascinating area.'

'Been a stuntie all my life, since I was a kid,' he said. 'Family business. But I only started specialising in effects about seven years ago.' He grinned. 'Probably because I got sick of being called Stan the stunt man and Stuntie Stan and all that.'

'Stanley is very big news in Hollywood,' Michael boasted, dragging heavily on the joint. 'The Grahame family has one of the oldest established businesses in town – his grandfather, Old Man Gus, started out as a stuntie with John Wayne in the early thirties.'

'Really?' Emma asked, intrigued.

'Yeah,' Stanley nodded. 'Amazing guy. He was still doing stunts when he was seventy. Mainly horseback stuff,' he conceded, 'that was always his speciality. Gus said his bones had grown crooked by then and he was more comfortable in a saddle anyway. Died in his sleep of a heart attack. My mother and two brothers run the business now and I stick mainly to special effects.'

'Your mother?'

'Sure. She met my dad when they were working stunts on *The Robe* in the fifties but he was killed five years later filming a car chase that went wrong so she took over the business with Old Gus.'

'And they're the best, believe me,' Michael said.

'It was my grandfather himself who personally recommended Stanley. Couldn't speak highly enough of him.' Michael was feeling very laid-back. He started rolling another joint. It was good to unwind. He'd taken an upper in anticipation of the morning's filming and the excitement of the explosion stunt and he needed something to bring him down a little.

'Stanley's done a lot of work for Minotaur Movies and Ross Entertainments. He's one of the few people who actually gets on with grandpa Franklin. Apart from me, of course.'

Emma couldn't resist the question. 'What's he like, Stanley? Franklin Ross?'

'Oh, he's a tough old guy, all right,' Stanley nodded, 'but I like working for him. If you give him your best you get a fair deal.'

While Emma and Stanley continued chatting, Michael put the joint out and sat back in his chair relaxing before lighting the next one.

Yes, Stanley was right, Franklin gave a fair deal, but then he was prepared to pay for the best. That's what he'd always said.

'Stanley Grahame's the best, Michael,' he'd said. 'He doesn't come cheap and hiring him'll boost your budget, but if you're going to do something as ambitious as this, you might as well do it properly.'

That was all Michael needed. If Franklin wasn't going to complain about an increase in the budget then the other investors sure as hell weren't. Franklin himself was the prime money man and the others had invested on the strength of his name alone.

'You'd better not blow it, boy,' he'd warned. 'You're getting your big chance here.' But Franklin wasn't investing for nepotistical reasons alone. If he hadn't loved the originality of the concept – the idea of shooting the actual comet, visible only once every seventy-six years – and if he hadn't loved the script itself, he wouldn't have invested a cent.

'This Emma Clare, your writing partner, who is she?' he'd asked after he'd read the script.

'Hell, grandpa,' Michael grinned, 'she worked for Ross Productions for eighteen months.'

'Really?'

'She took over as executive storyliner on the Snowy series.'

'Good series; very impressive.'

'Don't you ever look at the credits of your own shows?'

Franklin refused to be baited and he was far too fond of Michael to be irritated. 'Not the Australian productions, no. That's Penelope's area. So where is she now, this Emma Clare?'

'She got an offer from Richmond's. They're shooting a mini-series around the Great Barrier Reef and they wanted her there on location. She left three months ago.'

'I'm surprised Penelope didn't put in a higher bid,' Franklin said. 'Good writers are hard to come by. She should fight to keep them'. Franklin actually wondered whether he should say something to Penelope about it but he decided not to. The Australian side of the entertainment business was her concern, after all. 'Well, I'll look forward to meeting Miss Clare at the *Halley's* premiere,' he said.

'I did two years of a science course at UCLA,' Stanley was saying. Michael shook himself out of his reverie. 'But I got bored with the company of academics and I figured by then I knew enough for special effects work.' He grinned. 'I have to admit, ego was never my problem.'

Emma was finding Stanley Grahame an extremely interesting man. Certainly he was confident but he wasn't arrogant as she'd first supposed. He was simply a man who knew what he wanted and set about achieving it. And the world of special effects was most certainly an interesting one.

Michael was aware of Emma's intrigue and he didn't like it. Was she interested in the man's conversation or in the man himself? 'What's on the agenda for tomorrow, Stan?' he asked, although he knew the schedule full well. His interruption was a little rude but Stanley didn't seem to mind and Emma had long since grown accustomed to Michael's swift mood changes. The conversation was successfully changed and they spent the rest of the afternoon chatting about the film.

Emma stayed for a further week to watch the filming of the comet itself which, to her, was the most exciting part of the whole process. The first night they filmed it from the location site. Michael's research proved correct: Yarramalong Valley was a perfect viewing choice. The night was clear and still, a chill was in the air, and Halley's was clearly visible as it snaked its way across the black velvet sky.

The following night, when they returned to Sydney and filmed from Observatory Hill with the special equipment loaned by the Observatory itself, the comet was positively awe-inspiring. A mammoth fireball with an endless streaking tail, it looked for all the world like a demon wreaking havoc in the heavens. A demon with no regard for anything in its path.

Emma had seen many pictures of the comet in all its glory but the actual phenomenon, viewed through the special lens, was something altogether different. It really was the harbinger of doom. And the prospect of its heralding the planet's pole shift and cataclysmic aftereffects on the Earth's inhabitants was chillingly believable.

'The rushes are fantastic, Michael. The whole thing is utterly fantastic.'

It was the night before Emma was due to return to her miniseries on the Great Barrier Reef and they were dining out at a beachside seafood restaurant overlooking the harbour at Watson's Bay.

'And you did it,' she said. 'You finally did it.'

'We did it, Emma. You and me.'

Emma laughed. It was true; their months of work together on the script had paid off. And, as he'd promised, Michael had never again propositioned her. They'd become the best of friends and Emma loved him. She longed for the day when she could tell him she was his sister. It was the ultimate bond they could share.

'Yes,' she smiled, 'we did it. With the help of your grandfather's money.'

'He wants to meet you, by the way.'

'Oh.' Her smile faded. She wondered how Penelope would feel about that. Emma was fully aware that it had been Penelope's influence at work in gaining her the miniseries job in Queensland. And she'd been equally aware that Penelope's motives had been twofold. Penelope herself had been quite open about it.

'It's an excellent opportunity for you, my dear,' she'd said. 'And I think it's best if we keep a little distance between you and Mr Ross until the time is right to tell him, don't you?'

Emma wondered when on earth the time would be right to tell Mr Ross, but she didn't say anything. She knew that Penelope had her best interests at heart. Her grandmother was a wise woman.

'You'll meet him at the premiere,' Michael said. 'He's promised to be there.'

'Great, I'll look forward to it.' She raised her glass and changed the conversation. 'Here's to the most exciting world premiere of the biggest breakthrough movie made in cinematic history,' she announced dramatically and they clinked champagne flutes.

'Four months from now,' he said when he'd drained his glass. 'I'm going to miss you.'

'Rubbish,' Emma scoffed. 'You're going to be far too busy. Only four months for post-production? You'll be going like a bat out of hell.'

'True,' Michael agreed. 'It's going to be a nightmare, but we have to release the movie while Halley's is still hot. What a publicist's dream, eh?'

He was going to miss her. He missed her every day they were apart.

Michael had snorted two lines of coke before he'd called at Emma's to collect her and now, as the evening progressed, his senses were becoming more and more responsive to her, just as they always did when he was coked up.

He was aware of the warm, heady scent of Oscar de la Renta. She always wore Oscar de la Renta. He was aware of the swell of her breasts beneath the jade-green mohair sweater. And when the neckline slipped every now and then, he couldn't help staring at the exposed brown shoulder, until Emma unconsciously hefted the sweater back into position. To Michael everything about Emma was erotic. But the greatest aphrodisiac of all was the love which emanated from her. Over the past eighteen months it had become even stronger and he had no doubt whatsoever that she was in love with him and that it was merely a matter of time before their love would be fully realised. Just as long as he didn't push her, he warned himself. Although she was nearly twenty, she wasn't aware of the depths of her passion and yet again he told himself that he mustn't frighten her.

'Let's go for a walk,' he suggested, and he called for the bill. 'I want to discuss the next concept with you. It's a ball-tearer.' He'd hinted at another project on the phone and Emma couldn't wait to toss around ideas. She had never worked with anyone as stimulating as Michael.

'We'll have another bottle to take with us, thanks,' he said to the waiter, who took no notice as Michael slipped the champagne flutes into his pockets. Mr Ross was always good for a fifty dollar tip, after all.

Ten minutes later they were walking along the beach with their shoes off, the chill harbour water lapping at their bare feet. A late spring bite was in the air but it didn't bother them. They were sipping a fresh glass of Moet et Chandon Vintage and, as usual, the conversation was running riot.

'The America's Cup, Emma. Probably the greatest historical sporting trophy in the world. Originated by Lord Lipton over a hundred years ago. It hasn't been out of the States since then and the first non-American challenger to win it was Bondy.'

'And it comes to Australia next year and the challenge is in Perth,' Emma said excitedly. 'Great. So that's the theme, is it?'

'Yes. We'll film the actual race. Imagine it! Twelve-metre yachts in full sail battling the Indian Ocean off the coast of Western Australia. The intrigue, the dirty play – everything that goes with the lust to win. But the major premise is the political effect it has on the country.'

Michael was firing. 'Look at what happened when the Australians took it off the Yanks at Newport three years ago. No matter what the populace might have thought of Bondy as a shonky businessman, everyone knew that it had become a personal challenge of his to win the Cup. He'd been trying for over fifteen years and he'd spent a fortune. And then when he did it, when he created blue water history, the country claimed it as its own victory. Ticker-tape parades, screams of "We won the Cup", people chanting "We come from the land down under": the entire nation took a holiday and the prime minister himself said that any employer who didn't give his workers the day off was a bum. It was a farce. The whole country went apeshit over not only a mere sporting trophy, but a conquest to which they hadn't contributed at all.'

Emma was way ahead of him. 'And when the next Cup challenge is held in Perth small business will be encouraged by the government to provide for the tourist trade. Which means everybody will put themselves in hock to make the big buck. Chaos. If the Australians keep the Cup, small businesses are left with a hugely competitive cutthroat market, and if the Australians lose the Cup, the majority of those businesses will go bankrupt. What an indictment. It's a great controversial issue.'

'Spot on,' Michael said approvingly. 'That's the meat of the movie. That's what the critics will call "good comment", etc. But that's not the movie we're actually going to make. We're going to make something much simpler.'

Emma shook her head. 'You've lost me.'

'It's a heist movie. They're out to steal the Cup itself.'

They'd walked to the end of the beach and back and they were at Watson's Bay Jetty once again. 'Now listen to me,' he said as he sat her down on the jetty beside him. 'This is the good part. It's a movie within a movie, you see. We open with a film unit making a movie based on the challenge for the America's Cup. Their intent is to portray all the personal dirty intrigue, the political and economic competition, but, in the meantime, the core of the film unit itself is a group of internationally accomplished masterminds – the whole thing is a well-orchestrated plan to steal the Cup. A multimillionaire's behind it all – he simply wants to own the bloody thing, to put it in the back room and look at it. The film production is an entire cover-up. But the audience doesn't know that until three-quarters of the way through the movie. And of course, it's all intercut with the reality of the race itself and the real Cup.'

Michael poured the last drops of champagne into his glass. 'Mr Big is an oil billionaire, say, an Arab sheik or a Texan, so funds are – '

'I'd go with the Texan,' Emma suggested. 'Better for the American market – then we can import a legend: Lancaster, Douglas, Peck . . . '

'Or stay with the Arab and bring in Sharif. Now stop interrupting and let me get on with the storyline.'

'Sorry, sorry. Go on, go on.'

'Mr Big's funds are unlimited so the international crooks have millions available to bribe cops, yacht club officials, security guys, you name it. They bribe them in order to gain access to the Cup. Access to use the Cup in their film, of course – no one has any idea there's a genuine plot afoot.'

'Including the audience.'

'Right. Until the actual theft the audience is watching the making of a semidocumentary-style drama based around the America's Cup challenge with footage of the actual race and fictional char-

381

acters caught up in the competition and politics of it all.'

'What about subplot action for the actors in the "movie"?' Emma asked. 'We could have an off-screen love affair between the leading lady and the skipper of one of the challengers or the near-death of a stuntie in a rigged yacht collision. That'd keep the audience occupied and make the disclosure of the film crew's plot more of a shock.'

'Exactly! That's the sort of stuff I want you to start work on as soon as possible. Actors' characters, relationships, storylines – the lives of the innocents caught up in the centre of the intrigue. Because the bogus film crew really only consists of half a dozen people. The rest of the cast and crew all believe they're making a heist movie.'

It was a wonderful idea, Emma thought. Like all Michael's ideas, it was original, again mirroring his fascination for the marriage of fact and fiction.

'How are they going to do it?' she asked. 'The actual theft?'

'I knew you'd come up with something as practical as that,' he smiled. 'Trust Emma Clare to bring me back to earth from my flights of fancy. It's one aspect I haven't figured out yet, but I'm sending Stanley off to Perth next week to work on it. It's more up his alley anyway. He's going to case the Royal Perth Yacht Club for me, their layout and burglar alarm systems. That's probably where they'll house the Cup during the Challenge.'

They sat on the jetty for a further hour until Emma was chilled to the bone, although she barely noticed in her excitement. They talked plots, characters and finally titles. Endless titles.

'I've got it!' she said suddenly. 'Michael, I've got it. You said it yourself, and when you said it I thought it had a magic ring. Why didn't we think of it earlier? It's perfect.'

'What, for Christ's sake, what?'

'*Blue Water History*.'

A pause. He stared at her, then grinned. 'Perfect. Says it all without giving away the heist angle. *Blue Water History* it is.'

Emma worked hard on *Blue Water History*. For the next three months, stationed in Queensland, she devoted far more of her time to the Cup movie than she did to the Great Barrier Reef series, writing well into the night each time she returned from the production studios. With all the frustrating parameters set by commercial producers making formula material for the masses, the series had become tedious to her. And, because she was the youngest writer Richmonds had ever employed (purely upon the personal request of Penelope Ross) she wasn't assigned original scripts. Her job was to work on endless rewrites and to edit other writers' scripts which had come in under time or over time or simply not up to scratch. Then there were the boring production meetings and the budget discussions at which all she was required to do was sit and take notes. She was grateful to Richmonds for the experience, but Emma needed a greater challenge. And now she had one. To go home each night and lose herself in Michael's crazy movie was a great release for her.

'Go mad with it, Emma,' he'd told her. 'And

bugger the budget. My grandfather has promised me that if *Halley's* is half the success I've told him it's going to be, then Ross Productions will make *Blue Water*, no holds barred.'

Michael was thrilled that Franklin was prepared to place such faith in him but, secretly, he knew that whether or not his grandfather came to the party, *Blue Water History* would still be made. The following year, when he turned twenty-one, the massive personal trust account Franklin had set up on the birth of his grandson would be turned over to Michael. He would be worth millions.

Emma's first draft of *Blue Water History* (minus the actual heist scenes) was completed within two months. The second draft was completed a month later and then there was only a month to go before her return to Sydney and the *Halley's* premiere. A month to edit and polish the *Blue Water* script. A month of excitement at the thought of seeing the final cut of *Halley's*. A month of tense anticipation at the prospect of finally meeting the fabled Franklin Ross. And a month of something else. Something totally unexpected. A month to fall in love.

Malcolm O'Brien came from the Gold Coast and was twenty-seven years old. He'd made his first fortune in Queensland coastal real estate when he was twenty-two and had never looked back. His contacts and dealings were shady but no one could put a finger on anything actually illegal, although his competitors had tried.

384

Emma knew little of his background but she wouldn't have cared even if she had. She was too busy being swept off her feet by the suave, sophisticated young businessman who looked like a Greek god and treated her like a princess.

Malcolm had pursued her from the moment she'd arrived in Townsville. He owned the nearby marina which the film unit had hired as one of the locations for the series and they'd met on the first day of filming. He rarely visited his marina and had only flown up to watch the film crew work as a matter of interest.

'You're an actress, are you?' he asked. Well, obviously she'd have to be, he thought. She was without a doubt the most beautiful woman there and there were a number of lookers around. He'd checked them out.

'An actress? Good God, no,' she answered. 'I'd run a mile if they pointed a camera at me – not much talent in that direction, I'm afraid.'

The day's shoot was over and the company had laid on drinks and refreshments as an introductory goodwill gesture. Although the production staff and the key crew personnel had been setting up for a week, many cast and crew members had arrived just the previous day.

'Wrap drinks will only be provided on Fridays in future,' the producer was swift to point out. 'But, in the meantime, get to know each other, gang – there's a heavy week's workload ahead.'

'Oh.' Malcolm was surprised. 'You're one of the crew then, are you?' What a waste, he thought. She should be in front of the cameras, not behind them.

'No, I'm a writer,' Emma smiled. 'Well, they've employed me as a writer, but I'm a glorified secretary more than anything. No thanks,' she shook her head as he offered to top up her glass, 'it's a bit too hot for bubbly, isn't it?'

They were standing by the catering tent overlooking the marina. Although it was late afternoon, there was little breeze, the day was sticky and humid and the bulk 'champagne' and beer supplied by the production company was turning warm.

'How about a freezing gin and tonic in my air-conditioned office?' Malcolm asked. When Emma hesitated, he added, 'Your producer's already agreed,' and nodded at the dumpy dark-haired woman who was marching towards them.

'Thanks,' Emma smiled. 'I'd love to.'

As they walked down to the marina Emma was aware of Monica's disapproval but she didn't care. Monica was a martinet at the best of times and a bully at the worst. Obviously she'd presumed her invitation had been exclusive. Not that her sights would be in any way set on Malcolm – she was a confirmed lesbian – but Monica liked people to know and to keep their place and Emma was not part of the company hierarchy. Emma, however, believed in equality. Besides, a gin and tonic and air-conditioning was too good to resist.

As she looked out at the first glow of sunset over the water and the millions of dollars worth of boats bobbing gently in their pens, Emma thought what a charming host Malcolm was. He was telling a tale about an arrogant American multimillionaire who kept his boat penned at the marina and used it just once a year for a week's game fishing.

'He's utterly useless,' Malcolm laughed. 'Motherless drunk the whole time. We skipper and crew the boat for him and catch the fish and then prop him up and take photos of him with a spanish mackerel in each hand so he can go home and boast about his exploits "down under".'

Emma laughed. How refreshing it was to be listening to someone talk about something other than the television and movie business. Movie people could be such an indulgent lot. Many of them took themselves and their business so seriously when really they had no right to. Not Michael, of course. Michael was a constant source of challenge and stimulation. He was also witty and amusing and Emma sorely missed his company. Yes, she thought, Malcolm O'Brien was a welcome relief. Charming, humorous and, she concluded, stealing another quick glance at him before returning to the sunset, devilishly handsome.

Half an hour later, when the sunset was at its gaudy, glorious peak, Malcolm offered to take the two women to dinner. Emma immediately declined. She used the film shoot and its gruelling schedule as her excuse but it was really *Blue Water History* which was claiming her.

Before Monica could accept the invitation, Malcolm rose to his feet nodding in agreement. 'Yes, of course, you're quite right. "A heavy week's workload ahead", that's what the producer said.' He flashed a winning smile at Monica. 'Perhaps we'd better leave it till the weekend.'

'Yes, I think so.' Monica had no option but to agree, though she would have liked to dine with Malcolm O'Brien. Not only did she enjoy fine food, it would have been good for her image to be seen with such a powerful, high-profile man.

That night, Malcolm decided to stay in Townsville for the duration of the filming and the following morning he booked the penthouse at a nearby resort for three months.

It took him seven weeks to bed Emma. Not only was she playing hard to get, he thought, but she always seemed to be working. Undaunted, he persevered, never pushing too hard, never making too much of a nuisance of himself, until finally, what had started out as a bit of a challenge became a fixation.

He sent her red roses every day until she agreed to dine with him and, when she did, it was quite obvious she enjoyed his company. 'So what's wrong with dinner again tomorrow or the night after?' he asked. 'You're not filming, are you?' She shook her head and he concluded triumphantly, 'Exactly! And you have to eat.' But she continued to shake her head. 'We'll make it a sandwich, for God's sake, Emma – what's the problem?'

'I've set myself a deadline on the script I'm writing. If I have a sandwich at all it'll be while I'm belting away at a word processor.'

'Then I'll sit quietly in the background and serve you coffee.'

But she just laughed and accepted another glass of wine. And, the next day, more red roses arrived. Eventually he wore her down and they dined together several nights a week. Emma still met her

Blue Water History deadline. It simply meant that she had to work through till five in the morning on occasions.

Then came the expensive gifts. When he first presented her with a gold bracelet Emma tried to refuse but he took her hand gently in his. 'Please, Emma, it gives me pleasure.' Normally Malcolm's deep brown eyes were crinkled with laughter and the white teeth gleamed in a continual smile. Life never appeared to present much of a problem for Malcolm O'Brien. But now, as he looked down at her hand, his eyes were solemn and his voice was ardent. 'Don't deny me that pleasure. I love you.' He looked up. 'You must know that I love you, Emma.' And, as his lips gently touched hers, Emma felt herself start to melt.

They didn't make love that night. They didn't make love for another fortnight. The expensive gifts continued, but Emma didn't wear them – she wore very little jewellery. And Malcolm had the good taste never to press her on the issue: it seemed to be enough for him merely to have his gifts accepted.

But gradually Emma was weakening and they both knew it. From the outset, she'd felt fond of Malcolm and, deep down, a little guilty about the attention and presents he lavished upon her. It was still no reason to go to bed with someone, she told herself over and over, until finally she asked herself 'Why not?' She was nineteen years old and all she'd experienced was a messy tumble in the back of a car – so why not? Her capitulation to the seduction was a very conscious act on Emma's behalf.

But from the moment Malcolm started to

undress her, gently caressing every inch of her skin, Emma lost all conscious thought. At last she had stopped denying her sexuality and her body was making up for lost time. Her entire being was on fire at his touch. His hands, his mouth, his tongue seemed to be everywhere, more and more insistent. His lips surrounded one hardened nipple, his fingers caressed the other. His hand gently played along the line of her hip, slowly making its way between her thighs.

'You're beautiful, Emma,' he murmured. 'So beautiful.' And she moaned as she opened her thighs for him.

Emma's awakening had been a long time coming but it didn't disappoint her. The feeling in the very core of her being when he entered her was what she knew she'd been yearning for and she clasped him to her, wanting more and more of him.

She lost herself in her passion for him and, when she called out his name in climax, she felt wholeheartedly, achingly fulfilled. It was at that moment that Emma decided she was in love.

Malcolm was surprised to discover that Emma was so inexperienced – and even more so when he realised that she'd fallen in love with him. But, as she gave herself to him so completely, he realised with far greater surprise that he'd fallen in love with her. Despite his numerous affairs, Malcolm had never been in love before and it was a mystifying experience.

Malcolm returned to Sydney with Emma after the shoot. A month's holiday, he said, before he had

390

to go back to the Gold Coast. He booked into a hotel, although he would have preferred it if Emma had invited him to stay with her in her newly acquired Neutral Bay flat. But she didn't. Not to worry, Malcolm thought. Before the month was out he intended to persuade her to move north with him. He'd even marry her, he decided, if that was what it would take.

Emma was aware that Malcolm would have liked to stay with her and, indeed, she was tempted to suggest it. But she needed space. Things were moving too fast.

Michael was feeling a little peeved. Three whole days she'd been back and still he hadn't seen her. She'd couriered the *Blue Water History* script to him and he'd loved it.

'Fantastic,' he'd said, phoning her immediately he'd finished it. 'Let's meet right now. We've got a lot to talk about.' He couldn't wait to see her.

'I can't,' she'd said. 'This is my first day back and I have to hunt for a flat.'

'Fine. I'll hunt with you.'

'No, Michael, really. There's such a lot of things I have to catch up with since I've been away and I'll get more done on my own.' (Why was she loath to tell him about Malcolm, she wondered?) 'I'll see you at the premiere next week.'

And then the bombshell . . . 'Would it be all right if I brought a friend along?'

'Yes, of course.' What else could he say? he thought, trying to sound pleasant. 'What friend?'

'You'll meet him on Friday. See you on the big night,' she said and hung up.

Michael didn't like the sound of it at all.

By Friday, however, he had all but forgotten about Emma's 'friend'. This was going to be the greatest night of his life.

He snorted two lines of cocaine before he left for the theatre – the right amount to keep him zooming for the next six or seven hours, and he had his small glass phial for back-up and a good supply of speed if the party went all night. He intended to make a late entrance with Franklin and Penelope. Arriving in their chauffeur-driven Silver Cloud would look good. The photographers would have a field day, and it would be excellent promotion for the film.

The guests had been invited to the theatre at six-thirty. Champagne was to be served in the foyer for an hour, then there would be speeches in the cinema and the movie was scheduled to be screened at eight. Franklin loathed crowds so he was more than happy with Michael's suggestion that they arrive just in time to lead the troops into the theatre, where Michael would be introduced to make his speech.

'For God's sake, boy, hurry up.' Franklin's voice boomed through the main hall of The Colony House as Michael bounded down the stairs from his apartments.

'Sorry, Grandpa,' he said when he saw Penelope and Franklin seated waiting for him in the lounge room. They'd been there ten minutes. Michael belted through the hall and out the main doors. 'Come on, you guys,' he called back. 'We can't hang around here all night.'

Franklin helped Penelope to her feet. 'Incorrigible,' he muttered good-humouredly as they walked outside. 'Tonight had better be good.'

Michael was standing on the front verandah staring at the stretch limousine and the chauffeur standing beside it. 'Where's the Rolls?' he asked. 'I thought we were going in the Rolls.'

'Don't be ridiculous, Michael,' Penelope said dismissively, 'you know I detest travelling three in the back.'

'What do you mean, three in the back? Who – ?' Then he stopped as he saw Karol Mankowski quietly waiting beside the main doors.

As the chauffeur opened the rear door of the limousine, Karol briskly walked down the verandah steps and opened the front passenger side.

'Why the hell does he have to come with us?' Michael muttered to his grandfather. 'There won't be any bloody assassins at the theatre, for Christ's sake.'

'Any cheek out of you, boy, and none of us will go,' Franklin growled as he escorted Penelope towards the car.

Damn, Michael thought. Why hadn't it occurred to him? Of course Karol would be going. Karol went everywhere Franklin went. Joined at the bloody hip, they were. Michael felt intensely irritated. Not just because it meant they weren't going in the Silver Cloud. It was Karol himself. Sure, the man had possibly saved his life as a child.

393

Sure, the man would lay down his own life for any member of the Ross family. But Michael just didn't like him. He always felt uneasy around him.

'The back or the front, Boss?' Karol quietly asked as the chauffeur assisted Penelope into the car.

'You take the front,' Franklin nodded and Karol got into the passenger seat, fully aware of Michael's displeasure at his presence.

Franklin and Penelope sat beside each other with Michael facing them. During the entire trip he was aware of Karol's back on the other side of the partition behind him and he felt unreasonably angry. The outset of the evening was spoiled.

As soon as they arrived at the theatre, however, his misgivings were dispelled and the night was once again his own. Michael was aware that speed dramatically exaggerated his mood changes. He must control it, he thought, he must stay on his high and not let things affect him so.

The publicists had done a wonderful job. Pin spots arced across the sky simulating comets in the dusky night, a huge red carpet stretched from the pavement into the foyer of the magnificent State Theatre with all its ornate gold trimmings, and massive replicas of Halley's Comet hung from high in the vaulted ceilings.

Dozens of flashlights popped and hand-held news cameras swooped in on the limousine as it pulled up outside the theatre. The chauffeur opened the door, Franklin alighted and helped Penelope. And then Michael stepped out. He felt like a god. This was about as high as one could get, he thought, and he barely noticed Karol as

394

they started up the red carpet, the crowds threatening to break the barricades on either side.

Among the hundreds sipping champagne in the foyer of the theatre, Emma watched the procession. From the moment her grandfather stepped from the car she found herself unable to take her eyes from him. She was aware that Penelope looked as beautiful as ever and that Michael cut a dashing figure in his dinner suit, but all she could see was Franklin Ross.

It was impossible to guess his age although she supposed he would have to be eighty. Except for his head of pure silver hair, which was impressive, he wasn't a handsome man, but he was mesmeric. There was a set to the brow and the jaw and, although she couldn't see his eyes from where she was, she knew he was looking straight ahead as though the flashlights, the cameras and the crowds didn't exist. And his back was ramrod straight. He was everything she'd expected he would be.

Then Michael saw her. 'Emma,' he called. And he raced over. 'Come and meet Grandfather. Sit down the front next to me; I need to be able to see you during my speech.'

The moment the Ross family had arrived, the theatre bells had sounded, announcing to the guests that proceedings were about to start. 'Come on,' Michael said, dragging her over to Franklin and Penelope. 'We have to lead the brigade.' He didn't notice the man beside her – he'd completely forgotten about 'the friend'.

Suddenly Emma found herself staring into the eyes of Franklin Ross. They were shrouded in age. The epicanthic folds above, the bags below, the wrinkles to the side. But the eyes themselves were not old. They were unwavering and penetrating and the hardest steel-blue Emma had ever seen.

'Grandpa, this is Emma Clare – you wanted to meet her. Emma, my grandfather, Franklin Ross.'

'How do you do, Mr Ross,' Emma heard herself say, unaware that Malcolm had arrived beside her.

'Ah, yes, Emma Clare,' Franklin replied, 'the talented young writer Penelope allowed to get away.'

'Hello, my dear.' Penelope brushed the side of Emma's face with her cheek.

'Hello, Penelope.'

'The *Halley's* script was magnificent; I must congratulate you.' Franklin's eyes hadn't left Emma's face. 'I hope the cameras have done it justice. No, thank you.' He brushed aside a waiter attempting to offer him a glass of champagne. Still his eyes hadn't left her face.

'Thank you, Mr Ross. Oh . . . ' Emma dragged herself away from the eyes, suddenly aware of Malcolm at her side, 'this is my friend, Malcolm O'Brien, Mr and Mrs Ross.' Malcolm shook hands with Penelope and Franklin. 'And this is Michael,' she said. 'Michael Ross, Malcolm O'Brien.'

Michael didn't feel his hand being shaken. He was too busy staring at Emma. He'd seen her as she looked at Malcolm. He knew she was in love. He was sick with the realisation. Emma Clare was in love. But she was his. She belonged to him. She always had.

'Well, come along, you're the one who said we had to lead the way.' It was Franklin himself who

396

broke the moment and he started escorting Penelope towards the auditorium.

As Malcolm took Emma's arm she smiled up at him. Michael felt an almost overpowering urge to wrench her away. 'Mine,' he wanted to scream. 'She's mine!'

'You go ahead,' he said, 'I'll have a quick toilet break. See you in there.' Franklin frowned disapprovingly. 'It's all right for you, Grandpa, you don't have to make a speech.' He smiled winningly. 'Nerves. I'll see you in there.'

Behind the locked door of a cubicle in the men's lavatory, Michael snorted heavily from the small glass phial. She couldn't be in love, he told himself. Maybe he was imagining it. He always got a bit paranoid when he was speeding like this. He mustn't let it ruin his night. Emma loved him, he knew it. So what if she was having a bit of a fling? So what? She didn't have to be a virgin when she came to him. It didn't matter. Nothing mattered. He mustn't let anything matter. This was his night. He gathered himself together and went into the theatre to make his speech.

' . . . and without any further ado, it gives me great pleasure to introduce to you the mastermind behind tonight's extraordinary cinematic experience, Michael Ross . . . '

Michael talked for a full ten minutes but he had no idea what he was saying. The house lights were half up and he could see Emma quite clearly. Malcolm was seated in the centre aisle seat and he held her hand in his lap.

Michael could sense a restlessness in the audience. He knew he was rambling. He normally enjoyed public speaking and he was confident in front of a crowd but tonight he was distracted. What the hell was he talking about? Oh, who gave a shit anyway, he thought and he finished abruptly.

'So I'd like to say thanks to all those who contributed to the film and I hope you enjoy it tonight,' he said and he walked back to his seat.

Franklin, seated beside him, gave him a questioning look as the lights dimmed, but Michael didn't return it.

Halley's blazed across the screen. 'Produced by Michael Ross'. Michael started to relax. Fuck the lot of them, he thought. Including Emma. Fuck her too. This was his night.

Two hours later as the credits rolled and every member of the audience stood to their feet and applauded, Michael was back on his high. The movie had been magnificent – a breakthrough, an original, and everyone recognised it as such.

Emma hugged him and there were tears of joy in her eyes. 'You did it, Michael,' she said.

Her face was so close to his. 'We did it, Emma. It's us. Always us. And *Blue Water History* will be just the same.' And, for those several seconds, there was no one else there. No one else for him and, far more importantly, he knew there was no one else there for her either.

'Yes,' she whispered. '*Blue Water History* will be just as wonderful.' And she hugged him again.

A huge party at the Hilton followed the premiere. Hundreds of people straggled through the streets of Sydney, many still with champagne glasses in their hands.

Franklin and Penelope were not going to the party and when Michael had finally fought his way through the mass of congratulatory back-slappers, Franklin was waiting for him in the theatre foyer with Karol at his side, the chauffeur having safely escorted Penelope to the limousine.

'I want to see you when you get home,' was all he said and he turned to go.

'I might be late, Grandpa.' Michael was feeling bold. 'It's going to be a big night.'

'Fine. You've deserved it. Have a good time. I'll be waiting.'

At the party Michael watched Emma and Malcolm dancing, and again his mood swung. This time to utter depression.

Then she was by his side. She and Malcolm were leaving, she said. 'Do you want to come around to the flat tomorrow, Michael?'

'What for?' he asked sullenly.

'To go over the script, of course, stupid.'

'Sure you can spare the time?'

Emma put her hand through his arm and whispered in his ear. 'Go home, Michael. Please. You've snorted too much of that filthy stuff.' She pecked him on the cheek, sorry to see him down on such a triumphant night, but she recognised the signs and she wished there was some way she could help him stop his drug abuse. She whispered again. 'You're brilliant and I'm very, very proud of you and I'll see you at the flat tomorrow and you make sure you come along straight, you stupid bastard – we've got a lot of things to talk about.'

Then she was gone and Michael felt very alone among the hundreds of revellers. They were all dancing and drinking and talking and flirting and they seemed to have forgotten *Halley's* altogether. This was his night and there was no one special sharing it with him. Wrong, he told himself, wrong. Stay on the high.

He downed a quick three glasses of champagne and asked a very pretty girl to dance. For the next four hours he drank and danced wildly with numerous attractive young women, most of whom would have loved to go to bed with him, but he wasn't interested.

A crowd of them went on to a club in Kings Cross. And then another club and another, each one seedier than the last. And then it was five o'clock in the morning and Michael was suddenly weary. Very weary. It was time to go home.

He quietly closed the front door and started to walk through the main hall towards the staircase. Christ, he was tired. Not drunk. No longer high. Just burned out.

'Michael . . ?' The voice came from the lounge room. Franklin was seated in an armchair facing the archway with a full view of the main hall. He'd been sitting there since well before midnight, lightly dozing on and off. He rarely slept these days. Catnapping seemed to be all his body needed.

'Grandpa, you shouldn't have waited up. It's—'

'I told you I would. Come and sit down. Just a quick talk.'

'But it's five-thirty in the morning. Can't it . . . '

'Sit, boy.' Michael sat on the sofa opposite him. 'Just a quick talk, that's all.' Michael squirmed under Franklin's close scrutiny. What the hell was this all about?

'I didn't know you used drugs,' Franklin said finally.

Shit, so that was it. 'Hell, Grandpa, I don't, I . . . '

'What were you on tonight? Cocaine?'

Michael knew there was no way out. 'Just one little line, that's all.' A pause. The steel-blue eyes staring at him. 'Only every now and then.' Franklin said nothing. 'Everyone does it, Grandpa.'

'I don't like cocaine, Michael.' A flash. Franklin saw Catherine's face, white dust encrusted around her nostrils, saliva dribbling from the corner of her mouth. He remembered her radical mood changes, her seemingly endless energy. Michael's moods had vacillated of late, his energy had been boundless. Franklin asked himself whether it was his fault. Should he have read the signs? It was true he'd been away for half of the boy's life – he should have devoted more time to him, he should have . . . He hauled his mind back to the present. Self-recrimination solved nothing.

'You come of age next year. Next year your trust account is turned over to you.'

Michael could see it coming. He nodded.

'It will be withheld,' Franklin continued, 'if I see any further evidence of drug abuse, do you understand me?'

'Yes, Grandfather.'

'That will be all.' Michael rose to go. 'You did well tonight,' Franklin said. 'Ross Productions will most certainly fund *Blue Water History*.'

'Great,' Michael nodded. 'That's great. 'Night, Grandpa.'

'Goodnight, Michael.' Franklin sat in his armchair and watched his grandson as he walked upstairs. Such a fine figure of a young man. Hopefully the warning would be enough. If not, Franklin wondered, where could he go from here? Everything rested on Michael's shoulders. How had it come to this – what had gone wrong?

Franklin was tired. He felt old these days – except when he was with Helen. Helen made him feel young. No, that wasn't it exactly. She just didn't make him feel old. Well, she wasn't old herself, that was probably why. Not old and not young. Fifty something, wasn't she ... one or two. And she demanded nothing. She had a career and a life of her own, yet still she'd refused to leave him when he'd told her she should have children with a younger man. She'd refused to leave him when he'd insisted, only several years ago, that a younger man would surely give her more regular sexual satisfaction.

'I'm perfectly satisfied with the sex I have, Franklin,' she'd said. And it was true, they were still sexually active. Not frequently, but enough for Helen, whose passion was not demanding.

Strange, Franklin thought, as his mind strayed from Bronwyn in the upstairs servants' quarters, to Millie, then Penelope. Strange how one's sexual demands changed over the years. But even as his mind strayed, his thoughts kept returning to Millie. They always did. Millie was the one woman he'd ever truly loved. And now there was Helen. Helen, who'd stayed with him while he grew old.

'Why?' he'd asked her. 'Why do you stay?'

'Because I admire you, Franklin. I admire you more than any man I've ever known.'

He'd offered to marry her if that was what she wanted and she'd laughed.

'If you need to know what I want, Franklin, then forget it.' There'd been no venom in her voice. 'Leave things the way they are, I'm happy with that.'

It had been an easy escape for Franklin so he'd let things rest. Until recently. Recently he'd had a minor stroke. They'd rushed him to Mercy Hospital. He'd been fine. No aftereffects. And that's when Helen had said, 'I'll tell you what I want, Franklin. I want to be by your side when you die. You figure that one out. It can be here in New York or it can be in Australia. You figure it out.'

Which brought it all back to Penelope, to a marriage in name only. Surely Penelope was happy with her lot, Franklin thought. She was secure with her position in life, she saw him only several months a year – surely she wouldn't mind agreeing to a divorce? If he was to move to New York and live openly with Helen, then he wanted to marry her. If Helen was to be by his side when he died, he wanted them to be husband and wife.

Yes, he'd have to tell Penelope this time around, he decided. Maybe not tomorrow, maybe not next week, but it was a full two months before he was due to return to the States. He must tell her; it was only right for all concerned. Besides, he was running out of time.

Franklin hauled himself wearily out of the chair. Then there was Michael, of course. The boy must come to America. Living with Penelope had made him weak, spoiled, indulged. He was a brilliant film maker and there was a career waiting for him in America. Franklin could make a man out of him there.

He trudged upstairs, deliberately avoiding the railing even though his hip was aching. Franklin never held onto stair rails.

Besides, he told himself, he'd enjoy the boy's company. Since the death of old Sam Crockett five years ago, he'd had no male companionship outside of business. Except for Karol Mankowski, of course, and one didn't talk to Karol – one communicated. Telepathically at times. Karol often seemed to know what Franklin wanted before Franklin himself was aware of it.

Of course there was Sam's son Davy, who was now middle-aged. They worked closely together and they should have been friends – Davy was a replica of old Sam himself. But Franklin knew that Davy hated his guts.

'You're a bastard, Ross,' Davy had said. 'You shafted him. He was your lifelong buddy and you shafted him.'

'I merely agreed with the board that he had to go, Davy,' he'd replied. 'Sam himself knows he's too old – he doesn't have it in him any more.'

'He could have stayed on the board, for Christ's

sake. It'll kill him being out of the business – he'll die within a year.' And Sam had.

Franklin had no regrets. He'd done the right thing. The day he himself felt he was too old to take the pressure he'd resign. And that's what Sam should have done. He'd tried to hang on too long and if Davy didn't like Franklin and his methods then it was just too bad. One didn't have to like one's business associates. Respect was enough.

But Franklin had to admit that he missed old Sam. Yes, Michael would be good company, he thought. As soon as *Blue Water History* was in the can he'd make the boy an offer he couldn't refuse.

Exhausted as he was, Michael slept fitfully. Visions of Emma raged in his mind. Emma naked. Emma abandoned. Emma offering herself. The man to whom she was offering herself was not identifiable – a nameless, faceless, naked form revelling in her body and the pleasure he was giving her.

In his past fantasies, the man had always been Michael, but tonight, as he tossed and turned, he knew that the image was not his. He knew that the image was that of a real person.

Suddenly Michael was wide awake. Emma was doing it. Even now, as he thought of her, she was doing it. Malcolm O'Brien was tasting the delights of Emma Clare and the mere contemplation of that fact was enough to drive Michael mad.

* * *

405

'Michael, you look terrible.' She kissed him on the cheek and bustled him into the apartment. 'For God's sake, what on earth were you getting up to last night, you silly bugger? Of all times to go overboard with the coke, you pick the premiere. Honestly ... '

'Don't nag, Emma. I copped it all from Grandpa Franklin this morning. The old bastard's even threatened to withhold my trust account next year if I continue to muck up.'

'Well, I don't blame him. You have to cut it out – that bloody stuff'll kill you ... '

'I know, I know, and I'm going to stop, I swear.'

Poor Michael, she thought, he looked utterly worn out. 'Sit down and I'll get you a cup of coffee.'

Michael sat on the sofa. 'Where's whatsisname?' He couldn't resist asking although he tried to make it sound casual. 'I thought he'd be here.'

'Whatsisname's called Malcolm O'Brien,' she answered as she walked through into the open-plan kitchen area. 'And no, he doesn't stay here, he stays at a hotel.'

Michael was dying to ask whether she'd gone back to the hotel with him after the premiere but he knew that would be a huge mistake. 'Well, he seems a nice enough bloke but I hope he's not going to get in the way of our work.'

'How do you mean? How could he get in the way of our work?'

'He's a Queensland bigshot, isn't he?' Michael had made a point of asking around last night. 'Some shonky millionaire real estate whizz and he's bound to want to haul you off with him to

406

the Gold Coast and shove you in some ritzy pent-house and – '

'Shut up, Michael.' She stopped her coffee preparations and was staring at him frostily. 'You have absolutely no right to be jealous of Malcolm. He doesn't affect our friendship or our work in any way and if you're going to become possessive ... '

Michael realised in an instant that he'd gone too far. 'Oh, don't be ridiculous, Emma.' He smiled his easy, lazy grin and sat back comfortably on the sofa. You stupid bastard, he told himself. Don't scare her off. 'I couldn't give a shit about your love life, I just don't want you disappearing to Queensland when I need you in WA for *Blue Water History*, that's all. It's going to be a hands-on job, and I can't communicate across the entire continent when the script's going to change every half-hour.' The grin had disappeared and he leaned forward, the excitement of creation banishing his fatigue. 'Whatever happens during the filming of the actual race is going to affect the movie – we have to go with the flow, we have to – '

Emma relaxed. Was that all it was? How stupid for her to have overreacted. 'For God's sake, Michael,' she laughed, '*Blue Water History* is just as important to me as it is to you. I wouldn't miss out on one second of it. I'll be in Perth whenever you want me to be there.'

Michael felt a huge weight lift from his shoulders. She was his again. He could always excite her creatively. No one else could do that to her to the same degree. The physical was only an extension of that excitement. Perth. It would all happen in Perth.

407

'Good girl,' he said. 'Get the coffee, OK? I'm going to wash my face and get rid of this hangover – we've got work to do. Where's the bathroom? Any Berocca?' She pointed the way. 'Great flat,' he called as he walked through the bedroom to the en suite. 'Fantastic views.' He looked briefly at the double bed and wondered whether they'd done it there last night or at the hotel. Then he stopped himself.

He washed his face with cold water and took a Dexedrine. Just the one to get him going. Emma and Franklin were right, he decided. He snorted too much cocaine. He'd lay off for a while, just take the pills every now and then – they were harmless and easily accessible. He'd paid a doctor for a fake certificate stating he suffered from narcolepsy and was therefore legally qualified to obtain and carry amphetamines.

'Look at the subs,' he said coming back into the lounge room and gazing out the window. 'When I was a kid I used to love crossing the bridge and counting how many submarines were in the base.'

The flat was on the fourth floor and had magnificent views of the harbour. 'You know why it's called Neutral Bay?' he asked.

'No idea,' she answered. 'Tell me.'

'Because in the Colonial days ships of all nations were allowed to berth here regardless of their warring state with each other. This bay was declared a neutrality zone.'

'Look at that,' he said, leaning dangerously out of the window. 'Three subs – aren't they amazing? I always wanted to be a submarine commander when I was a kid. Amongst a million other things, of course,' he added.

'Michael,' Emma smiled. 'Shall we get on with the script?' She was pleased to see him looking so much better. His recuperative powers were truly amazing.

They worked for the next five hours and, once again, Emma thrilled to Michael's creative energy. It was like doing mental gymnastics as he ripped her script to shreds. 'It's great, Emma, but what say we do this ... ?' or 'Love it, yes, but what if this happens ... ? Where do we go from there ...?' He kept placing hurdles and obstacles in their path only to leap over them or mow them down.

Twice during the work session Malcolm telephoned. 'Can't talk, Malcolm, we're working.' Emma couldn't wait to get off the phone. 'Ring back later.'

The third time he called he was obviously insistent upon planning their evening. 'Well, yes, I suppose so,' she answered. Then to Michael, 'We'll be too burned out to work tonight, won't we?'

'I certainly won't,' he replied. 'We could have a final draft by tonight.'

'Great,' she said, 'we'll get takeaway.' Back to the phone. 'Sorry, Malcolm, not tonight.'

Michael's spirits soared. He took another speed pill in the late afternoon, and, by eleven o'clock that night, when they'd finished the script and read it through out loud, it was an utterly exhausted Emma who had to call a halt.

Michael gathered the script together. 'I'll have a

final shooting script typed up and a copy to you by the end of the week,' he said. 'We're off to Perth in a month, so get yourself prepared. We have to be there mid-January. Now go to bed; you were brilliant.' He hugged her and was gone, leaving Emma drained and happy and wondering how the hell he did it.

Michael slept well that night. No visions of Emma and the naked man. Malcolm was no threat. In a month he would have Emma entirely to himself.

The following day, a parcel arrived at The Colony House addressed to Franklin Ross. It was from the solicitors handling the estate of the late Kenneth Charles Ross.

Franklin's older brother had died six months earlier. Franklin hadn't bothered going to the funeral. He'd been busy in New York at the time; it would have been inconvenient and, furthermore, he felt it would have been hypocritical to do so.

The only time Franklin had returned to South Australia since he'd left the family property over fifty-five years ago had been a one-day courtesy trip to attend his mother's funeral. On that occasion, the members of the Ross family in attendance – Franklin's surviving cousins, their children and their grandchildren – had been strangers to him. He'd barely recognised his own brother, who'd grown fat and indolent and who did nothing at the funeral but complain of financial hardship and the struggle his son was having keeping Araluen out of debt.

'These are hard times for us on the land, Franklin,' Kenneth had whinged. But Franklin hadn't taken him seriously. 'On the land,' indeed. Franklin knew for a fact that Grandfather George had left not only Araluen, but vast property holdings and shares in a distillery and a bottling plant to his 'first-born'. Furthermore, Franklin had never once asked for a penny from the family estate, although it would have been perfectly within his rights to have made such a request. He'd earned his fortune, every cent of it, on his own, and if Kenneth and his son were looking for a hand-out because they'd squandered their inheritance then they could beg till doomsday as far as Franklin was concerned.

He didn't visit Araluen, although he would dearly have loved to walk through the old stone barn and to sit among the vines. There wasn't time, he told himself. Besides, he couldn't take any more of Kenneth's company.

The letter from the lawyers informed Franklin that Kenneth had expressly requested that upon the event of his death the enclosed journals be forwarded to his younger brother Franklin. The letter further informed him that Kenneth's first-born son, as chief beneficiary of the will and custodian of the estate, was being forced to sell Araluen.

Franklin wondered if it was a ploy intended to bring him galloping to the rescue, but, several telephone calls later, his solicitors informed him that the report was correct. Araluen was up for sale.

'Buy it,' Franklin barked.

Those stupid incompetent bastards, he thought. Obviously Kenneth's son was as piss-weak as his father.

Franklin ordered his solicitors to purchase the property under the name of one of his private subsidiary companies.

'They're not to know I'm the purchaser,' he instructed. 'Any member of the Ross family is welcome to stay and work on the property as an employee, but they must accept the total authority of the manager whom I shall appoint.'

Several hours later, in the study of his Colony House suite, Franklin opened the parcel which had accompanied the lawyer's letter. The journals his brother had bequeathed to him were two large logbooks whose pages were filled with the neat, precise hand of George Howard Ross.

Grandfather George's diaries! Franklin had never even known they existed. He skimmed through the pages, stopping every now and then to dwell upon a section that caught his attention.

I love this land. It claims me. We have cleared fifteen acres; the materials have been delivered, and tomorrow we start to build the stone barn. It will be an Herculean task and Richard thinks we are insane but I will finish it or I will die in the attempt. Poor Richard, his character leaves a lot to be desired and I feel sorry that there appears no goal he wishes to achieve ...

Franklin read on and on. For hours. He'd long since stopped skimming.

412

He never ceases to amaze me. He nurtures the vines as though they were his children. He is not well, yet he works like a dervish. My brother, whom I judged so harshly – the land has claimed him too. It may well kill him, but it has been the saviour of his spirit . . .

It was late in the afternoon, yet still Franklin read on.

Richard is dying. It is painful to watch. But it is noble also. He is gallant upon his deathbed. He knows that the end is near, I am sure of it, yet he is as engaging and as playful of wit as ever. I wonder now whether that is where his strength has always lain but I have failed to recognise it.

Father maintained that Richard inherited the weak Ross strain and, indeed, there have been times when I myself have doubted Richard as a man of honour. What judgements we make of others when perhaps we should look to ourselves. Richard is honourable in death and his strength is his charm.

What right have I had to judge? I have been harsh and unkind on occasions, characteristics I have never once witnessed in Richard . . .

Franklin rose and walked out onto the balcony for some air. The summer heat was oppressive and the ceiling fans afforded little relief. He could have retired to one of the air-conditioned lounges if he wished. But he didn't. He'd steadfastly refused to

413

allow an air-conditioning unit to be installed in his suite although he'd had to concede to its installation in other areas of The Colony House.

'You don't live here, Franklin,' Penelope had insisted. 'You have no right to demand the discomfort of those who do.' He couldn't really argue with that.

He gazed out over the harbour, but he didn't see the last of the white yachts skimming over the blue water and heading for home in the gathering dusk. He was thinking of Grandfather George – the man whom, above all others, he had always deeply admired. He had tried to live like Grandfather George, a man of honour and conviction. To learn now that George had questioned himself and his judgement of others was quite a revelation to Franklin.

His gaze rested on the statue of the dueller on the far edge of the expanse of lawn that swept down to the harbour. Had he, like George, been a little over-harsh in his actions and judgements? Had it really been necessary to get rid of Sam? Was that the action of a man of honour? He hadn't seen it as dishonourable at the time, but it certainly wasn't the act of a friend.

For the first time in his life Franklin recognised the price he'd had to pay in his struggle for power and success. It had cost him his friends. He'd turned his back on human contact when he should have been learning from people like Sam. And Gustave Lumet. And Solly. Above all, Solly.

Too late now, he told himself. Too late to have regrets and too late to make new friends. When you were over eighty there were no new friends to be made. There were only old friends, and he'd let those go.

There was something else he'd lost, though. Something else that it was not too late to regain. The land. He'd turned his back on the land. But it was waiting for him. The land and the vines.

He remembered that night with Solly when he'd spoken of the vines. 'They're timeless Solly,' he'd said. 'They're young and they're old. They're the past and the future. When you stand among them you, could be anywhere. In any place. In any civilisation.' How had he ever allowed himself to forget that?

Franklin returned to the study and the journals. Now Araluen was his again. It wasn't too late. He would go back. And he would take Helen.

He read on: . . . *the birth of my son. The first-born male heir to The Ross Estate* . . .

But his mind wasn't on the journals any more. He was making plans. He would have a civilised family Christmas with Penelope and Michael. Then Michael would go to Perth and *Blue Water History* and Franklin would inform Penelope that The Colony House and his entire Australian holdings were hers and that she must divorce him. He would then return to America and marry Helen. He would set Michael up in a career that would ensure the boy's success as the leading film maker he was obviously intended to be.

Michael was, Franklin decided, like Richard. His strength lay in his charm. He had a character defect, certainly, just like Richard. But this cocaine business was a momentary aberration. As soon as Franklin set him on the path to success, the boy would be strong and then when the time was right, Franklin would return to the vineyards. With Helen by his side, he would return to Araluen. It was all very simple.

Franklin went back inside, picked up the journal and read on:

> *Sarah is dead. Her death has shocked me. Women die in childbirth, I realise this, but neither the birth of Catherine nor Charles appeared to pose any complication and I had no reason to suspect the birth of the third child should do so.*
>
> *I am not only bereft, I am overwhelmed with guilt. I should have recognised the threat to her life from the outset of our parenthood. I should have placed more value upon Sarah herself, for I now realise that I have lost the dearest friend I ever had ...*

Again, Franklin was surprised that a man like George, whose actions had always been beyond reproach, should so question himself.

> *... My one comfort is that Sarah, in her wisdom, knew that I loved her. (Although, to my discredit, I rarely told her so.) It eases my remorse and my pain to know that she recognised my love and forgave me my selfishness ...*

Franklin closed the journal. It was time to dress for dinner.

Chapter Eleven

'YOU SELFISH BASTARD!' she hissed, her face white with fury. 'You selfish, greedy, egotistical bastard!'

In all their years together, Franklin couldn't remember ever having heard Penelope swear. And he'd certainly never seen her like this. Her beauty was distorted by rage. She was one of the most glamorous women he had ever known and now she looked positively ugly – it was very interesting. It was also very puzzling.

'But why should you object to a divorce?' he asked, genuinely bewildered. 'We haven't lived together as man and wife for over twenty years and you see me only three months a year anyway.'

Penelope fought to regain her control. Excessive emotional behaviour was not attractive, she knew that. She never laughed, cried or displayed anger to any great degree – it was too disfiguring.

She took several deep breaths before gracefully seating herself in her favourite writing chair beside the escritoire. These days she rigorously avoided direct sunlight, and the filtered glow through the rich red velvet drapes of the french windows

417

behind her was a flattering shade of rose.

'You are not only greedy, selfish and egotistical, Franklin,' she said when she'd regained her composure, 'you are ignorant. This action you propose is crass, vulgar and ill-mannered.'

'What? To marry the woman I love?'

'Oh, stop saying you're in love, for God's sake,' she snapped, intensely irritated. 'It's not at all becoming for a man of your age. And particularly not for a man of your type.'

She wasn't remotely offended by the fact that there was a mistress in his life – she'd suspected it for years and would have been surprised if there weren't. But to have the woman openly paraded was deeply offensive. She'd credited Franklin with more style than that.

'It is a crass and vulgar action to sacrifice a loyal wife and a marriage of fifty years in order to legitimise a grubby little affair with an employee,' she said. Franklin had given her the details and, to Penelope's horror, she vaguely remembered meeting Helen Bohan once many years ago. A young, efficient, no-nonsense woman. Extremely average-looking.

Franklin decided to skirt any discussion and get down to the practicalities. Penelope was choosing to overreact and it would be simpler to avoid questioning why. It was obviously a case of wounded vanity.

'The Colony House will be yours, of course,' he announced. 'And I am prepared to sign over to you all of my Australian holdings, except Araluen. I think that's more than generous.'

Penelope felt the muscles in her neck tighten and

a slow flush creep into her face. Generous! Generous to pay her off because her services were no longer required. Generous to toss her aside after she'd sacrificed a career for him, given him sons, maintained the perfect image of glamorous, loyal hostess-wife. Good God, she'd even been running his Sydney production company single-handed for the past ten years.

She couldn't trust herself to speak. Franklin continued, 'I shall take Michael to the States with me when he's finished this film in Perth. He's been developing some bad habits here and I'd like to keep an eye on him.'

Her mouth was dry. She tried to swallow but found it difficult. Franklin, unabashed, was telling her that he intended to leave her, quite openly, for a younger woman, and then was going to rob her of her grandson. Having stripped her of her dignity, he expected her to face the humiliating gossip and innuendo without Michael by her side.

Franklin appeared totally unaware of Penelope's growing outrage. He presumed that her silence was an indication of her compliance. Thank goodness she's calmed down, he thought – the initial overreaction must have been simply due to shock. He was glad. He didn't want to hurt Penelope. He was fond of Penelope. They'd been through so much together.

'Ours has always been a courteous relationship, my dear,' he said, 'and I see no reason why it shouldn't continue to be so. It has been a convenient marriage – for both of us – and it has served our mutual needs admirably.'

Penelope could take no more. She started

419

slowly, evenly, determined to maintain control. 'I have given you a great deal, Franklin ... ' she said.

'We have given each other a great deal, my dear,' he answered benignly. 'As I said, it has been a mutually satisfying experience ... '

'. . . my youth, my beauty, two sons ... '

Damn, Franklin thought, here she goes again. 'I realise that and I'm deeply grateful, but – '

Something snapped in her. Suddenly she could take no more of his patronising arrogance. She stood up so abruptly that the little writing chair toppled over behind her but she didn't notice. 'I sacrificed my career for you,' she snarled.

Franklin felt a surge of irritation. It should all have been so simple. He didn't want a scene. 'Oh, for God's sake, Penelope,' he snapped back, 'what career?'

'I could have been a star, damn you!'

'You could never have been a star, my dear.' He walked to the door. As far as he was concerned, their meeting was over. 'You simply didn't have the talent.'

'I suffered childbirth for you!' She was screaming now. 'I didn't want children but you had to have your precious sons, and I gave them to you!'

'You didn't give me my sons.' The irritation was turning to anger now. 'Curb your vanity, woman, my sons were God's choice not yours.'

In an instant, Penelope knew how to wreak her revenge. 'That's where you're wrong, Franklin. It was God's choice to take them from you. You could have had another five sons, another seven, but I chose not to give them to you.' The steel-blue eyes burned into hers but there was no stopping her now. 'You think God chose only two conceptions? Rubbish. *I* did! You could have had a son a year. Just imagine!'

Franklin said nothing. He wanted to strike her but did nothing while she continued her tirade.

'I timed my two conceptions and then I finished it. Do you understand? *I finished it*!' Still he said nothing. 'There was no cancer. There was no need for the removal of two perfectly healthy ovaries.' In her triumph, her voice was quieter now. 'I paid the doctor, Franklin. And I paid him with your money.' Her face was twisted with spite and revenge.

Franklin turned to leave the room. He knew if he remained for one more moment he would strike her.

'You chose to ruin my life, you bastard, and I chose to ruin yours. Your sons are gone now and you have one grandson left, just one . . . '

Her screams rang in his ears as he closed the door.

Michael had chosen to direct *Blue Water History* himself and he had been hard at work for a fortnight by the time Emma arrived in Perth. He'd filmed some general footage around the port of Fremantle and a lot of covering shots of the specific locations he'd chosen, and he and Stanley had set up the night shoot for the heist itself.

'I thought we'd get the theft of the Cup safely in the can before the race is under way,' he explained. 'Stan's done an amazing job. Just look at this.'

He crossed to a mysterious object, covered with

a sheet, which was sitting in the centre of the table. Emma had commented on it the moment she'd walked in but he'd refused to explain. 'All in good time,' he'd said, 'all in good time.'

Now he gestured impatiently to Stanley. 'Stan, my man, come on and show her our baby.'

The three of them were in the main lounge room of the luxury ten-bedroomed mansion Michael had rented in Birdswood Parade overlooking Melville Waters and the Royal Perth Yacht Club.

Between them, Michael and Stanley flung aside the sheet to reveal an impressive silver trophy, a metre high and ornately engraved.

'My God,' Emma gasped. 'Don't tell me they've loaned you the America's Cup.'

'No way,' Michael said. 'They wouldn't let us near the real thing for love or money. This is a replica Stan had made up by a mate of his in the States. It arrived three days ago.'

'And she's a gem,' Stanley said with pride. 'Lou's a genius, he's got it all down to the last detail. No one would pick this baby for anything but the genuine article, believe me.'

'The three actors playing the crooks arrived last week,' Michael explained, 'and Stan's been taking them through their paces, showing them the layout of the Yacht Club and its security system. The Club's been tremendously helpful . . .'

'Michael's "donated" them a fortune, needless to say,' Stanley added.

'. . . and the security guys are going to switch the real Cup for the dummy just before we start filming,' Michael continued, oblivious to the interruption. 'Once they've locked it away in a vault

422

or whatever, we have permission to use the display cabinet and the hall for the rest of the night. They've even agreed to release the locking system so our "burglars" can mime the cabinet break-in and they've agreed to switch off the alarms so they won't go off by mistake when the actors "deactivate" them.'

'That was the club's idea,' Stanley added. 'I don't think they want to risk calling attention to an action which would meet with disapproval from the visiting Cup officials. Of course they don't approve themselves, but Michael's made them an offer . . . '

'. . . too good to refuse. Right,' Michael grinned. 'One lesson I learned from my grandfather: anyone can be bought.'

That night, Emma and Michael dined at the Parmelia Hotel, where Emma was staying.

'Why on earth did you book in here?' Michael asked irritably. 'I told you I'd rented a bloody mansion for key personnel. The pace we're going to be working at we need to be close together.'

'Yes, I realise that,' Emma said apologetically. 'I can move in for the first couple of weeks, if you like, but I'll need a hotel for the rest of the time. Malcolm's coming over for the Cup.'

Michael tried to keep his disapproving frown strictly businesslike. 'Emma, our work on this movie is going to be very intense and if you're holidaying with your lover I don't see how – '

'I won't be holidaying with my lover,' she protested. 'I didn't even want him to come over. Hon-

423

estly. I told him so. But he said he was coming for the Cup.' Michael was obviously disbelieving. 'It's true,' she insisted. 'One of the yachts from his marina is racing and he has a share in it.'

'Well, I don't approve,' he said sternly. 'I find it totally unprofessional for you to shack up with your boyfriend in a hotel when the rest of the team is staying at the production headquarters on constant standby.'

Emma privately agreed with him and she was annoyed with Malcolm for placing her in such a position.

Malcolm had proposed to her before returning to Queensland. Well, first he'd proposed she come and live with him and then, when she'd refused, he'd proposed marriage. She'd refused that too. More or less. It was far too soon. She loved him, she said, but she was only twenty – she didn't want to marry anyone just yet.

'That's all right,' he'd answered. 'I'm prepared to wait.' Malcolm didn't actually care whether or not they married at all. Just so long as Emma remained his.

Emma looked at Michael's scowling face for only an instant before making a snap decision. 'Yes, you're quite right,' she said. 'I should be with the team. I'll move into the house for the duration and I'll tell Malcolm to keep his distance.'

Emma was immediately pleased she'd made the decision. Although she still loved Malcolm – well, she was fairly sure she did – lately she'd had the feeling that he was taking over her life. And, what's more, she'd been allowing him to. What had happened to the strong, self-reliant Emma Clare? She seemed to have disappeared.

Not any more, she answered herself. I'm back. She felt stimulated by her declaration of independence and thrilled to the impending battle of wits which lay ahead with Michael, the two of them locked together, creating *Blue Water History*. Malcolm would have to wait.

'I'll move in first thing tomorrow,' she said.

'No, not tomorrow. Make it the day after, the day of the nightshoot,' he answered.

Delighted as he was by Emma's acquiescence, Michael had his reasons for not wanting her around the following day. That evening he had plans, dangerous plans, and he didn't need the added distraction of Emma.

'You've only just arrived,' he continued. 'Give yourself twenty-four hours to loll around the swimming pool or see the sights or whatever. Then we can move your gear in during the afternoon and you can come along and watch us steal the America's Cup that night.'

'You're on.'

The following day, Emma took a taxi to Fremantle and wandered about the streets soaking up the Cup fever which was in the very air.

The city had tarted itself up beautifully to impress the influx of tourists. Old pubs had been restored to their former glory; new, trendy outdoor restaurants had opened; pokey cafes had expanded fashionably, spilling onto the footpath. The rough port town of Fremantle had become an outdoor city catering to an elegant sidewalk society.

She sat and sipped a cafe latte while she watched the fascinating potpourri of people from all over the globe who were already gathering for the Cup although the first of the trials wasn't due to start for a fortnight.

She wandered along the forefront and gazed at the magnificent yachts in the marina. She browsed through the fish markets, bought herself a steaming parcel of fish and chips and sat on a bench looking out at the trawlers anchored in the bay. As she ate she fed the seagulls and chatted to an animated American couple who'd come over for the Cup. Then she walked for another two hours, exploring the old women's asylum now converted to a maritime museum and the Roundhouse, once an army fortification, now also a museum. She had a delightful day.

When she arrived back at the Parmelia in the late afternoon Emma was exhausted. A hot bath, room service and television, she told herself. A bit of five-star hotel decadence to round off the evening, then tomorrow, the stimulation of Michael and his creative genius.

The following morning, when Michael picked her up, he was on a high. She knew he was. His eyes were dangerously bright and he seemed electrically charged.

Emma confronted him. 'You're back on the coke, aren't you?' she said accusingly. 'You stupid bastard, you promised to lay off it.'

'I'm not, Emma, honest,' he said.

'But look at you, you can't stay still – and look

426

at your eyes. Don't lie to me, Michael, I know the signs.'

'I swear to you I have not snorted coke,' he said, raising his hand. 'Word of honour.' And he hadn't. That morning. Of course, last night had been a different story. But, Christ alive, a night like last night demanded added stimulation; it was a once in a lifetime experience. 'It's a natural high, I promise.' And he wasn't lying. He couldn't wait to tell her.

'Oh Emma,' he said, elated. 'Last night we created history.'

'What?' she demanded. She'd never seen him so excited and she found it difficult to believe that it wasn't drug-induced. 'For God's sake, what?'

'No, not now. I don't want to spoil it. I'll tell you after the nightshoot. Come on, let's get you settled in.'

Michael introduced her to the rest of the team, besides Stanley and himself, who were staying at the mansion. The three members of the production department, the head of promotions, the caterer and the unit manager. The crew and the actors were staying at a hotel not far from the house.

Together with Stanley, Emma and Michael spent the afternoon sitting beside the swimming pool in the mansion's landscaped rear garden. It was a burning late-January day and every half-hour they dumped themselves into the water to cool off. Well, Emma and Stanley did. Michael was happy to sit under an umbrella on the terrace and sip away at the Dom Perignon he'd insisted on opening and drag on the joint he'd insisted on lighting up.

'For goodness' sake, Michael,' Emma scolded, 'you're working tonight.'

'All the more reason to relax this afternoon,' he said and then he laughed. 'I can't win with you, can I? This morning you tell me I'm too sped up and this afternoon you tell me I'm too relaxed. Besides,' he turned to Stanley, 'have I ever let the side down? Ever?'

Stanley shook his head. Emma decided not to remind Michael of the fiasco he'd made of his speech at the *Halley's* premiere. Better the booze and the joints than the cocaine after all, she thought. But she was relieved to see him surreptitiously put the marijuana away when the three actors arrived at four o'clock.

'I'd like you to meet our baddies, Emma,' he said. 'Of course you know Jonathan Kramer.'

'Yes, hello, Jonathan.' She kissed him warmly on the cheek. 'Lovely to see you.' Jonathan had played a leading role in *Halley's* and she had known of his casting as the chief criminal mastermind. One of the country's major character actors, Jonathan was heavily in demand, and it had been quite a coup to sign him up for *Blue Water History*, particularly as his role, although showy, was not a leading one.

'To work on a Ross-Clare collaboration again, dear boy?' he'd queried when Michael had approached him. 'One kills for such opportunities. Besides,' he'd added in a conspiratorial stage whisper that would reach the back row of any auditorium, 'it's a gift of a part and I might well steal the movie if you're not careful.'

'And this is Gussy and Ben Drummle – my co-

428

writer, Emma Clare.' Michael introduced the rather dowdy little English couple who looked more like domestic help rather than master criminals. Emma wondered at the strange choice but she said nothing until, having talked through the night's work ahead, the three actors left.

'Why Gussy and Ben?' she asked. 'They're straight out of *Upstairs, Downstairs,* not at all like the characters we conceived.'

'I changed it,' Michael said airily, rolling another joint. It's much more innovative if the mastermind's assistants are a colourless little married couple from the Midlands. I'm even calling them Gussy and Ben.'

'You're actually making the crooks a married couple?' Emma was astonished.

'Yes, original, isn't it?'

'Unbelievable, I'd say.'

'Rubbish. Adds colour. Too late to change it now anyway.'

Emma felt a surge of indignation. They always conferred on script changes and she found Michael's blasé attitude irritating. She was about to retaliate when Stanley, sensing a confrontation, wisely defused the situation.

'They're good, Emma. We've been rehearsing the scenes and the stunts and they're really good, believe me.'

Emma recognised Stanley's diplomacy and backed off. Michael was right, it was too late to change it now and he was the producer and director, after all. She would have liked to have been consulted though. 'I hope you're right, Stanley,' she said. 'I'm going to have a shower.

Dinner's at eight-thirty, right?'

'Right.'

'See you in the dining room then.'

Michael wasn't there at eight-thirty and when Emma phoned up to his room he told her that he wasn't hungry and that he'd meet them in the lounge at ten. The six-hour nightshoot was scheduled for ten-thirty.

'You're going to go right through till half-past four in the morning without any food?' she queried disapprovingly.

'There'll be caterers on location,' he said.

'Nevertheless . . . '

'All right, tell Tony to send me up a sandwich,' he interrupted. 'Now be a good girl and go and have your dinner, I'm taking a little rest just like you told me to.'

But Michael wasn't resting and he didn't eat the sandwich that the cook sent up to him. He opened another bottle of Dom Perignon instead and sat out on the balcony looking over the bay. Below him, he could see the lights of the Royal Perth Yacht Club in the early stillness of the evening and he recalled the excitement of last night. And he anticipated the excitement of tonight. His mind was buzzing.

The afternoon in the sun and the joints he'd smoked had left him a little weary so he'd taken two uppers when he'd returned to his room. Now he was feeling good.

At nine-thirty he snorted a couple of hefty lines and looked down once more at the lights of the

Yacht Club. Tonight held such promise. Tonight was the true test, the culmination of months of planning. He was exhilarated.

'Ready?' Let's go,' he swept into the lounge room where Emma and Stanley were waiting. 'Give us a hand, Stan.' Together the two men lifted the dummy trophy, still covered in its sheet, from the table and they made their way out the front door to the waiting car and driver.

As they drove the short distance to the Yacht Club, Emma was sure she could read the unmistakable signs of cocaine. Michael was talking a lot and loudly. He was jumpy, charged with energy. When they arrived, however, and he introduced her to the gathering of people, he was instantly calm, the professional, efficient director, and she could only suppose that she must have been wrong. He was on a natural 'high' just as he said he had been that morning. She shook off her misgivings – it wasn't for her to judge anyway.

Jonathan, Gussy and Ben were in the make-up van parked in the Yacht Club grounds and the rest of the crew were standing around outside waiting impatiently to set up the first shot of the evening. Several small-part players and extras dressed as security guards and policemen were also milling about. With the exception of Michael and Stanley, nobody was allowed inside the Club until the dummy Cup had been exchanged and the real one locked away.

'Emma, this is Geoff Neilson, head of security. It's all right if Emma comes in and watches the exchange, isn't it, Geoff?' Before the dour-faced guard could answer Michael continued, 'Emma's my co-writer and I'd be deeply grateful.' The look indicated that there would be something in it for him. Geoff had already accepted a little extra on the side, a little personal something above the generous donation Michael had openly made to the Club coffers. He nodded and Michael grinned to himself. As always, Grandpa Franklin was right: When you've bought them once, you can always buy them again.

Two policemen carried the dummy Cup into the small viewing hall where three security men were standing beside a locked glass cabinet. Inside the cabinet was the America's Cup.

Michael, Emma and Stanley stood to one side as Geoff unlocked the cabinet and nodded to the security men to remove the Cup. The policemen whisked the sheet off the dummy and stood by waiting to make the exchange.

There was something strangely ceremonial about it all, Emma thought, something reverent. As the Cups were exchanged in complete silence, she glanced at Stanley. The dummy was certainly magnificent – he'd been right: it was impossible to tell them apart. He caught her eye and gave her a returning wink of agreement.

As the dummy was placed in the cabinet and the security men carrying the real Cup slowly walked past Emma, she wanted to put out her hand and touch it. Silly, she thought, it's just a trophy. But it did symbolise man's struggle against the elements and there was something so solemn about the occasion that she felt she should pay homage to it. The America's Cup. She longed to touch it. One look at the intractable Geoff Neilson, though, and she knew she'd be out of line.

Once the Cup was safely locked away, the night's work started in earnest. There was a tedious hour or so while the lighting man set up the lights and Michael and the director of photography discussed their shots and the sound man rigged the actors with radio microphones.

Then they were ready to go. Emma heard the word 'Action', then she watched, spellbound in the dark, as Jonathan, Gussy and Ben, dressed in black and with blackened faces, crept down the corridor. Soundlessly, in single file, pressed against the wall, their masked torches affording them just the barest glimmer to see their way.

It was eerie. The lighting man had done a remarkable job. The rays of fake moonlight through the windows illuminated the burglars as they stopped at the entrance to the viewing hall. Ben and Gussy looked to Jonathan. He gave an imperceptible nod and they parted, Ben towards the alarm system and Gussy towards the cabinet.

'Cut,' Michael called. The first master shot was in the can.

They filmed the scene several more times from different angles. Then they changed the lens and the lighting and shot the close-ups.

A shaft of moonlight. Jonathan in command. The granite face, which Emma knew to be so impressive on camera, barely moved. The orders came through the eyes. And that one imperceptible nod.

Ben and Gussy. The close-ups of each of them

433

a study in utter concentration. Senses quivering. Animals, alert for predators, sensing their prey.

Then it was time to film the deactivating of the burglar alarm. Again Emma watched fascinated as, in the gleam of Jonathan's torch, Ben worked on the intricate alarm system. His fingers were dexterous. It was a surgeon's operation, she thought, or the defusing of a bomb – Stanley had certainly schooled him well. But despite his confidence, the tension was palpable as the beads of sweat the make-up artists had applied to his brow and upper lip caught the flickers of light.

The next shot was Gussy picking the lock of the cabinet in the shielded glow of Jonathan's torch. Obviously her research and rehearsal had been equally intense. She performed with utter concentration, deft and efficient and totally believable.

When Gussy was halfway there, Jonathan shone his torch onto his watch, then tapped her on the shoulder and nodded to Ben. In an instant, the torch went off and all three melted into the shadows. Ten seconds later, one of the extras playing a security guard wandered across the corridor and shone his torch briefly into the hall. The procedure was authentic. On the nightly rounds, at a quarter after and a quarter before each hour, a Yacht Club security man always checked the Cup.

They set up for the next shot. The security guard's 'point of view'. Emma remembered the script.

POV SHOT. TORCH BEAMS INTO HALLWAY, ARCS FROM CAMERA RIGHT TO LEFT, PAUSES, POINTS

434

DOWN TO THE FLOOR AND STARTS TO MOVE
BACK AS IF IT HAS SEEN SOMETHING. CUT TO:
CLOSE-UP. THE GLOW IN THE MOONLIGHT OF THE
TIP OF ONE OF BEN'S SHOES. HE HAS FORGOTTEN
TO DULL THEM. THE SHOE EDGES ITSELF OUT OF
SIGHT JUST AS THE TORCHLIGHT HITS THE SPOT.
CUT TO:
MID-SHOT. SECURITY GUARD. CONTENT THAT IT
WAS JUST A FLASH OF MOONLIGHT HE SAW, HE
STARTS TO MOVE OFF.

Once again, there was a change of lens and
lighting and more close-ups. Emma could see the
tension in the three faces as the sound of the
guard's footsteps receded, then stopped. Was he
coming back? Unbearable suspense. The guard
walked on. Jonathan's eyes darted to Gussy. She
stepped out of the shadows, he turned on his
torch, and she continued her work.

It was a long and tiring shoot with many different set-ups and lighting changes, but it all went
smoothly and Emma found every minute of it fascinating. So did Michael. In fact, Michael found it
exciting. He kept talking her through the plot,
whispering the script into her ear. As if she didn't
know it! She'd written the damn thing with him.
It had been her idea, the shoe shining in the moonlight. But, as usual, his excitement was contagious.
It fed her sense of involvement and she found
herself watching through the eyes of the camera.
Seeing it as it would appear up on the screen. Sus-
penseful. Real.

By two o'clock in the morning they'd finished
the interiors. They were nearly an hour ahead of

schedule and only the exterior shots of the beginning of the car chase remained.

'We're filming the entire chase sequence and the stunt stuff tomorrow night,' Michael explained to Emma while the crew set up. 'This is just where they're seen leaving the building and the security guard radios through to the police.'

Twenty minutes later Michael called 'Action' and Emma stood watching with the rest of the crew as the actors crept out of the building. Gussy appeared first, keeping watch, with Jonathan and Ben following behind carrying the Cup. Suddenly Gussy muttered something. Too late. A cry rang out. 'What the hell's going on there!'

In an instant, everything happened at top speed. No panic. Just action stations. Gussy raced forward, opened the door of the waiting van and was in the driver's seat with the engine revved up and ready to go by the time the men had reached the vehicle. They piled the Cup into the back, Ben with it, and Jonathan leapt into the front passenger seat. Before the doors were closed, Gussy had taken off. Behind them, the security guard fired a warning shot in the air and grabbed his walkie-talkie.

'My God, she can drive,' Emma muttered to Michael as they watched the car scream around the bend and head off down the road at breakneck speed. Michael nodded to the First Assistant Director, who was carrying a two-way radio.

'Thanks, guys, that's fine,' the First said into his walkie-talkie. In the distance, the car slowed down.

'You're not wrong she can drive,' Michael grinned. 'Now aren't they a pair, Gussy and Ben? Didn't I do right? Admit it.'

'OK, OK,' she smiled back. 'You did right. You're a genius.'

They set up for the reverse shots on the guard and by three-thirty all was completed. 'That's a wrap, boys and girls,' Michael called an hour ahead of time. 'Well done.'

The caterer put out a light supper and there were wrap drinks for all, but at four o'clock Michael suggested to Emma and Stanley that they come back to the house. 'I have an announcement to make,' he said eagerly. 'And there's a whole crate of Dom there – we can toast ourselves with the real stuff.' Michael had slipped into the men's lavatory for a quick snort and now the prospect of announcing his news, the thrill of anticipation, was becoming more than he could bear.

'To Jonathan, Gussy and Ben,' Michael announced when their glasses were charged. They were comfortably settled in the upstairs sitting room which had been allocated to Michael as his personal office. The dummy trophy had been placed in a position of honour on the large centre coffee table. Michael raised his glass in salute. 'They did a fantastic job.'

Stanley and Emma joined Michael in the toast. And then he continued. 'Particular congratulations to Gussy and Ben,' he said as he picked up the open bottle of champagne and poured the remaining half into the Cup, 'for doing it so well the second time around.'

As Emma and Stanley exchanged a puzzled glance, Michael leaned down, tilted the Cup to his lips and drank. Then he gestured for Emma to do the same. 'Drink from the America's Cup, Emma,' he said.

'What are you talking about?' she asked, puzzled. He was jumpy again, feverish in his excitement. Bloody cocaine, she thought.

'I'm talking about the fact that we have just stolen the America's Cup.'

For a moment they stared at him, dumbfounded. Then Stanley leapt up and grabbed at the Cup, the champagne spilling everywhere as he searched for Lou's distinguishing mark. It wasn't there. It should have been towards the bottom of the handle, on the inside of it – the distinctive looped 'L', the engraver's insignia Lou always incorporated in his imitations to ensure they could never be mistaken for genuine forgery attempts.

'Jesus Christ, Michael, what have you done?'

'I told you. I have stolen the America's Cup. Or, rather, we have. We three. We talented three. We band of brothers.' Michael's grin was one of sheer elation. 'Emma co-wrote the plot, you researched the feasibility and technique and we've done it.'

He started to open another bottle of champagne. 'With a little help from Gussy and Ben, of course.' Michael looked down at the drenched carpet and the pool of champagne on the coffee table. 'What a waste,' he said.

'He's serious, isn't he?' Emma asked. She pointed at the Cup. 'That's the real thing.'

'Yes,' Stanley answered. 'It is.' He turned to Michael, shocked. 'How the hell did you do it?'

'Exactly the way you told me to, Stan. I followed your instructions to the letter. Well, Ben and Gussy did. And there were no foul-ups like there were in the dramatised version. No shoe in the moonlight, no security guard seeing them leave the building. But of course they're pros – they wouldn't make such dumb mistakes. I was very proud of them. They're an odd little pair but they're bloody good at their job.'

'Ben and Gussy are the genuine article?' Stanley asked, astonished.

'Too right they are: the best in the business. Safe-cracking, lock-picking, cat-burglary, you name it – and they cost a fortune. Of course, Ben and Gussy aren't their real names.' Michael refilled the Cup from the freshly opened bottle. 'I watched the whole thing last night. Christ, it was exciting. They didn't want me to and I had to double the fee for the experience but it was worth it, I can tell you.'

'You mean, last night they exchanged the real Cup for the dummy?' Emma asked, still trying to figure it all out. 'Well, the night before last,' she added looking at her watch. It was half-past four in the morning. 'And the dummy trophy the security guys put in the case for the shoot was the real thing?'

'Yeah. Fantastic, isn't it?' Michael grinned. 'We stole it all over again. And the Cup they're carefully guarding at the Yacht Club is the fake. Isn't that hysterical?'

'It's insane,' Stanley said. 'And you're crazy,' He stared at the Cup, shaking his head. 'You're out of your fucking mind. That thing's the Holy Grail to the sporting world. They'll lock us up and throw away the key if we're caught with it.'

439

'So?' Michael giggled. He was enjoying himself immensely. 'We make sure we don't get caught with it. We're the only three who know about it except for Ben and Gussy and they're certainly not going to talk. They're on a plane to Mauritius in a couple of hours.' Stanley tried to interrupt but Michael continued. 'It was your idea to use stunties for the car chase, Stan, remember? "Can't use actors for car chases," you said. All of Ben and Gussy's stuff's in the can; Jonathan's the only one we need any more.'

'But why?' Emma asked. She stared at the trophy, fascinated. 'Why did you do it?' Stanley was right, Michael was crazy. But it was thrilling. Last night she'd wanted to touch the America's Cup and here it was sitting in front of her on a coffee table and it was filled with champagne and she was going to drink from it. Yes, it was insane. But it was also thrilling. Wildly thrilling.

To Michael, Emma's reaction was the most thrilling thing of all. He could sense her excitement and he delighted in it They were two of a kind. There was a madness in her too and he loved her for it.

'Why not?' he answered. 'I suppose I just wanted to see if it could be done to start with. But then it hit me ... if we really could do it, just imagine the hype! I could announce it at the New York premiere: "Hey, world, this is the real thing. You're about to watch the real live theft of the genuine America's Cup." Everybody and his dog is going to want to see this movie after that.'

'Did you plan it right from the beginning?' Stanley asked. He couldn't help himself. He didn't

440

approve but the insanity was contagious and, now that the initial shock had worn off, he was intrigued. 'Right from the initial script stage?'

'It was always in the back of my mind,' Michael nodded. 'But it was only when I saw how good the dummy was that I thought we could actually pull it off. You're right, Stan, Lou's a genius.'

'What are you going to do with the damn thing?'

'Oh, give it back, of course. They'd be bound to find out eventually.'

'You're just going to hand it back tomorrow?' Emma asked. ' "Here's your cup, sorry we stole it"?'

'Exactly. The Yacht Club'll be furious, but what can they do about it? It would be far too embarrassing if the news got out. I'll tell them we were testing their security system. Hey, that's a good idea,' he laughed. 'I've done them a favour – they should consider it a very valuable exercise. Now drink. Come on.' He tilted the cup in Emma's direction. 'We're the only people in the world who'll ever have a chance to do this, Emma. You first.'

Emma looked at Stanley, who shook his head, gave a wry smile and shrugged back at her. Then she leaned over, took the Cup in her hands, and drank deeply.

It became a ceremony. One by one they drank from the America's Cup. Two more bottles of Dom Perignon and two joints later, they started to get the giggles. Mildly hysterical giggles.

'Didn't you ever wonder why I made all those dialogue changes from the original script?'

Michael asked Emma. 'I gave Jonathan virtually all the vocal stuff in the baddies' scenes.'

'I didn't question it for a minute,' Emma replied. 'I thought it was because Jonathan's agent had demanded a larger role.'

'Nope.' Michael passed the joint to Stanley. 'Ben and Gussy's specialised training didn't include acting technique. I was playing it safe.'

Stanley threw back his head and roared with laughter. It was uncharacteristic of him but the marijuana and the champagne had gone right to his head. 'Poor Jonathan,' he said. 'Imagine the show he'd have put on if he'd known he was working with amateur actors – he's such an old queen.'

They all started laughing, very very loudly. 'Oh, I did the right thing,' Michael protested when they'd calmed down, 'I signed Ben and Gussy up as members of Actors' Equity.'

The three of them burst out laughing again. 'They were terribly good,' Emma said when things were once again under control. 'Both of them.' The booze and joints had gone to her head too and she felt awfully silly. 'You never know, they might win AFI awards for Best Support.' She'd meant it quite seriously but it started them all off again and eventually Michael, the first to recover, suggested they open another bottle and throw themselves in the pool to sober up.

It seemed a good idea. It was seven o'clock in the morning, they had a production meeting at midday and it would be wise to get a bit of sleep before then.

It would also be a good idea, Emma suggested,

442

as they started stripping by the side of the pool, to keep their underwear on. It was a bright summer's morning, the entire household would soon be awake and the landscaped garden was overlooked by two other houses. She jumped into the water in her bra and panties and the boys did as they were told and joined her in their underpants.

The shock of the cold water had a particularly sobering effect on Michael and he watched the other two as they splashed about childishly in the shallow end of the pool.

Emma had never looked more desirable. The white panties were stark against her lithe, tanned body and the lace bra accentuated the swell of her breasts. Without a trace of make-up and with her wet hair plastered back from her face she looked like a healthy, vibrant young animal at play.

Emma herself was completely oblivious of her appearance. She'd only been stoned twice in her life before and she'd certainly never drunk so much champagne in one sitting. The combination was a heady experience and she felt like a naughty, liberated ten-year-old.

Stanley too was feeling the effects. But he wasn't feeling like a ten-year-old. He was also aware of Emma's near-nakedness. God, she was a beautiful looking creature, he thought admiringly. But he didn't dwell on it. He never let himself dwell on the deep admiration and affection he felt for Emma. What was the point? She was unavailable and anyway, she obviously didn't feel the same way about him. Stanley had long since decided that any pursuit of Emma would be a useless, painful and destructive exercise. So he joined in the games and the two of them splashed each other and raced each other and ducked each other until they were thoroughly exhausted.

Michael was enjoying the sensation of the water caressing his body. He glided around the edges of the pool feeling the occasional contact of the smooth cold tiles against his skin and he basked in the sensuality of the moment.

He looked at Emma and longed to touch her. The thought of that firm flesh beneath his fingers. The nape of that neck. The curve of that back . . .

'I've had it.' With her last ounce of remaining energy, Emma hauled herself out of the pool. 'I'm going upstairs to pass out,' she said, gathering her clothes together.

Stanley also climbed out of the water and started drying himself with his T-shirt. 'Me too,' he agreed.

Michael floated on his back and looked up at the two of them.

Emma struggled into her shirt, still dripping wet. 'Well, that has to be the most wonderful and indulgent night of my life,' she grinned. 'You are wicked men the pair of you.' She blew a kiss to both of them as she turned to go. 'But most of all you, Michael,' she laughed as she disappeared inside, 'you're a danger to be near.'

When Stanley had gone inside, Michael floated for a few more minutes then collected his clothes and went up to his rooms. He had to be with Emma. Alone. It was the right time now. The time he'd planned for so long.

He dried off, donned a towelling robe and snorted a quick line to speed himself a little, then he went to Emma's room and knocked lightly on the door.

She opened it. She'd showered and washed her hair and she was wearing a light cream-coloured silk wrap. He knew she was naked underneath.

'No, no, no, Michael,' she said with mock severity. 'No more playing around. It's eight-thirty and we have a meeting at twelve and I'm going to bed.'

'A quick word, that's all,' he assured her. 'Without Stanley around. I just want to see you alone for a moment.'

'All right,' she agreed, opening the door. 'But no more joints and no more champagne, for God's sake. I'm about to pass out.'

He entered, closing the door behind him. She'd drawn the drapes preparatory to going to bed but a shaft of bright sunlight streamed in between them. It was going to be a hot day, he thought.

'Want a glass of mineral water?' she asked.

'Yeah, sure.'

He watched her as she took the bottle from the small bar fridge in the corner. The sunlight knifed through her robe and he could see the entire outline of her body. He crossed and stood behind her, his fingers aching to stroke the silk, to part the robe, to stroke the flesh beneath.

She put the bottle on top of the refrigerator and turned to get some glasses. Their bodies were practically touching. He was standing in her way but he didn't move and he didn't say anything.

'What is it?' she asked.

'I guess I just wanted to say . . . ' What did he want to say? He didn't want to say anything. His eyes travelled to her mouth. Her full, perfectly formed lips. He wanted to kiss her. That's what he wanted to do.

'I guess I just wanted to say, thank you . . . ' He put his hand on her shoulder. The silk was tissue-paper thin. A soft loose skin covering the firm flesh beneath. He put his other hand on her waist and started to draw her to him, his mouth travelling slowly, slowly towards hers.

No, Emma thought, oh please, God, no. 'Stop it, Michael.' She put her hands on his and tried to pull them from her but his fingers locked onto her body like talons. 'I said, stop it!'

His mouth was nearly upon hers. The hand on her shoulder slid to the small of her back and she was crushed against him while the other hand ripped her robe open. Then his lips were on hers, forcing them apart, and his hand was grasping her breasts, her buttocks. She could feel his erection hard against her. He tore open his own robe and now his naked flesh was upon her flesh, grinding, insistent.

She managed to tear her mouth away. 'No, Michael,' she cried, 'we can't! We can't!' Her hands on his shoulders, she pushed with all her might but she couldn't escape, she was locked to him.

'You love me, I know you do.' His mouth was on her neck. He could feel his groin on fire and he groaned as he thrust himself between her thighs. 'Say it, Emma. You love me. Say it.'

'Yes, I love you.' She stopped resisting. Michael in turn stopped forcing himself upon her. He raised his head and looked at her. It was true. She loved him. He'd known it all along. He took her face in his hands. 'You're my brother,' she said, 'and I love you.'

He heard the words but he was confused. What did they mean? For a moment his passion was arrested. Their mouths were only inches apart and he watched her lips as she whispered again. 'You're my brother.'

Confused, he drew back and looked into her eyes. 'My father was Terence Ross,' she said.

The words hung in the air and time stood still. Somehow Michael knew it was the awful truth. He was frozen there, holding her face in his hands. Emma thought she had never seen such pain.

Then he released her and turned away.

She did up her robe. 'I'm sorry. I'm really sorry. If I'd known you felt this way I would have kept out of your life. I should have known, I should have realised. I'm sorry, I'm so very sorry.'

His passion forgotten, Michael heard her words and a feeling of panic overcame him. Emma out of his life? He couldn't imagine his life without her. His mind raced. He couldn't lose her now.

'What do you mean, *you're* sorry,' he said. Keep it flippant, he told himself. He fastened his robe. 'I'm the one who was doing the raping. Shit, Emma, I'm sorry.' He turned to her, deeply contrite. 'It was the dope and the booze and the excitement and ... I'm sorry. It won't happen again, I ... '

'Michael, did you hear me? I'm your sister. You're my brother. Our father was – '

'Sure. I heard you. I believe you. So, it means we can't screw, for Christ's sake. What does that matter? I was out of line anyway.' He was getting

447

desperate now. 'I love you, Emma. It's wonderful that you're my sister. We can be together always ... '

Emma was looking at him curiously. 'Don't you want to know the details?' she asked. 'Don't you want to know who my mother is? Don't you want to know why I didn't tell you? Don't you want to know – '

'Of course I do. I want to know everything about you. Everything about us.' He knew he mustn't let his desperation show. 'Hell, it's not every day a bloke finds out he has a sister.' The smile was winning. Pure Michael Ross charm. 'Come on.' He sat on the bed. 'Sit down and tell me all about us.'

She stood, uncertain, disarmed.

'Emma,' he said gently. 'I do drugs. Too many, too much. You know that. I had a momentary aberration. I love you. You love me. The greatest gift you could give me is the knowledge that you're my sister. We have a bond, a blood bond. I will never abuse that again, I promise.'

She sat on the bed beside him. 'Now tell me all about us,' he said.

She did. They talked for an hour. She told him how Julia had been bought off by Franklin. She told him of her adoption as a baby and her determination as a child to trace her natural parents. She told him about Penelope and her oath of secrecy.

'But why?' he asked. 'Why did she want to keep you a secret?'

'She said Franklin would ban her from seeing me. She's been very good to me, Michael. And

448

then of course I worried that he'd ban you from seeing me as well and I couldn't bear the thought ... '

'Well there's no chance of that,' Michael assured her. He was trying to maintain a feeling of normalcy, trying to conduct a civilised conversation, but he was barely hearing her. Her words were jumbled in his head. All he could think was, 'Emma is my sister. Emma is my sister.'

He got up from the bed, unable to bear her closeness any longer. 'And there's no reason to keep you a secret now, is there? I must say I can't wait to see the old bastard's face when we tell him.'

'No.' Her voice was sharp. 'We can't tell him, Michael. You must promise me that.'

'Why not?'

'Because I gave my word to Penelope. Until she releases me from my promise, we don't say a thing.'

'Oh, for God's sake, Emma, what does that matter? You've kept quiet about it for three years. Surely ... '

'And I'll keep quiet about it for another three years if that's what Penelope wants. Don't you understand? I gave her my word, my word of honour.'

'Oh, bugger your word of honour.' Something in Michael snapped. Was he to be cheated of everything? If he was never to possess Emma was he to be denied the recognition of their blood ties? Was he expected to relate to her as an amiable writing partner and nothing more? 'You sound

like my grandfather. The bloody Ross honour –
I'm sick to death of it.'

She was studying him closely. Careful, he told
himself. He was letting his desperation show
again. 'I need a piss,' he said and he went into the
bathroom.

He stared into the mirror. His eyes were bright
and agitated. He put his hands to his cheeks,
spread his nostrils and inhaled deeply. He could
feel the residue of cocaine and he wished he'd
brought his dispenser with him – a quick snort
would do him the world of good. Play it down, he
told himself, she's getting suspicious, go back in
there, play it down and then get out quick. He
couldn't take much more.

She was still seated on the bed when he came out
of the bathroom and she was still watching him
carefully. He grinned. 'I give up. Like grandfather
like granddaughter. You're a Ross, all right, and if
we need to stand by your word of honour then that's
what we'll do. I won't say a word, I promise.'

An element of distrust remained in her eyes.
'Emma,' he said, sitting beside her and taking her
hand in his. Oh, the touch of her skin! He took a
deep breath, knowing he had to get out of the room.
'All this has come as a bit of a shock, you under-
stand. But you're my sister and I love you as such.
And you must trust in my love for you as a brother.'
He fought to stop himself from embracing her. 'And
I'll keep the secret, you have my word.'

He jumped up and gave her one of his magic
grins. 'Now, for God's sake, woman, let me get
some sleep – we have a production meeting in two
hours.' She smiled back at him and nodded and he

went to his room, grateful to be alone.

He didn't snort a line. He forgot. He went out onto the balcony instead, his mind on fire. Emma was his sister. Emma was his *sister*. For three years she'd been his obsession, the object of his passion. For three long years every woman he'd made love to had been Emma Clare. He wanted to scream, to let out a howl of anguish. It wasn't right! It wasn't fair! Emma was his sister!

He tried to lie down but he couldn't get the vision of Emma out of his mind. The cream-coloured silk robe, the touch of the flesh beneath, the feel of her breasts, her thighs.

He snorted two lines. Then, an hour later, freshly showered and changed, he bounded downstairs for the production meeting, a supply of uppers in his pocket to see him through the day. Life went on, after all. He forced the physical images of Emma out of his brain. As his sister there was an emotional bond between them, a lifetime connection that no one could break. He would have to school himself to live with the limitations of their relationship. It was one hell of a test, he thought, as he looked at her across the table. One hell of a test.

As far as Emma was concerned, Michael more than met the test over the next week's filming. He was his stimulating, creative, charismatic self. He was fun and exciting to be with. And he was something else. There was an added element to their relationship, an acknowledgement of love. Emma relaxed. She was finally relieved of the burden of her secret. Despite the awful circumstances of

Michael's discovery, she was glad, so glad, that they could share their knowledge.

But secretly, and at night, the images of Emma continued to burn in Michael's brain.

'Penelope and I are divorcing.' Franklin had arrived in Perth unannounced and, as usual, he came straight to the point. 'It's not altogether amicable,' he continued brusquely, 'so I shan't be returning to Sydney.'

It was early evening and they were seated on Michael's balcony watching the yachts return from their day's training. The first of the Cup trials was due to start the following day.

'I'm giving Penelope The Colony House and I think she expects you to remain there, but personally I don't think that's advisable.' He sipped at his Laphroaig and milk. These days his doctors advised him to add milk to his evening scotch. What a thing to do to a pure malt, he thought, but he obeyed instructions. Michael waited for him to go on.

'You've outgrown this country,' Franklin continued. 'There is a career for you in the States and I want you to come to New York with me. Just as soon as *Blue Water History* has finished filming.'

'What sort of offer?' Michael asked. It was a hell of a way for a man to say he wanted the company of his grandson but Michael was prepared to play it the old man's way if that's what Franklin wanted. 'Assembly line studio stuff, or would I work on my own projects?'

Damn it, Franklin thought, the boy should

be jumping at such an opportunity – not questioning the offer. 'Your own projects,' he growled after a moment's pause. 'Provided *Blue Water History* comes up to the standard of *Halley's*.'

'It will.' Beneath his facade, Michael felt a surge of excitement. It was a God-given opportunity. 'Can I take my co-writer with me?'

'This Emma Clare girl, you mean?'

Michael nodded. 'We're a great team. And Stanley too. I'd need to work with Stanley.'

Franklin pretended to consider the terms for a second or so but secretly he was delighted. He wanted the boy in New York with him. He wanted to share the last part of his life with his grandson. 'Done,' he said. 'Now bring me the bottle and a fresh glass. Skip the milk.' And they toasted the deal with Laphroaig, neat.

'It's a fantastic offer!' Michael had immediately called a meeting with Emma and Stanley. 'We're our own team, we call the tune – budgets like you wouldn't believe. Emma, start thinking ideas, projects. Stanley, start thinking stunts, the bigger and the showier the better.'

Stanley had caught Michael's enthusiasm and the two men started talking nineteen to the dozen. Emma didn't want to remind them about Malcolm. She was in a genuine quandary. She couldn't help but be excited by the opportunity, but was she prepared to terminate her relationship? Because if she agreed to go with Michael that's what it would amount to. She was sure

Malcolm wouldn't contemplate coming to America with her – his life was on the Gold Coast.

Emma didn't know what to think. Malcolm was her lover. She had even contemplated marriage with him – some time in the future, certainly, but she had accepted a commitment nevertheless.

He was due to arrive in two days' time. His yacht was sailing in the third day of the trials. She decided to postpone her decision until his arrival. She would talk it through with him. Perhaps she could go to America for a year only. Michael wouldn't like that of course, but . . .

'Well, say something, Emma.' Michael had suddenly noticed her silence. 'Isn't it the most stunning opportunity? Aren't you thrilled?'

'Yes Michael,' she smiled. 'It's stunning and I'm thrilled.' And she was. For him. She'd worry about her own position in the scheme of things after she'd spoken to Malcolm. And she leapt into the brainstorming session, as usual enjoying every minute of it.

But, as fate would have it, Emma's decision was made for her. In the most shocking way. Just two days later, on the morning of Malcolm's impending arrival.

'GOLD COAST LAND BARON FOUND SHOT TO DEATH' the newspaper headlines screamed. 'The body of real estate millionaire Malcolm O'Brien was discovered slumped over the steering wheel of his car in the early hours of this morning. The vehicle was parked outside his Surfers Paradise apartment block. O'Brien had been shot twice through the head at point-blank range with a .22 calibre weapon ... '

The article went on to infer political corruption, illegal land dealings and the involvement of several key figures from the underworld. Malcolm's dirty linen was on full public display but there were no clues whatsoever as to the identity of his killer.

The days that followed were a nightmare for Emma. The only thing that kept her going was the distraction of *Blue Water History* and she threw herself into her work with a vengeance. Despite the sympathy of those around her, there was really no one with whom she felt she could share her grief. None of them had known Malcolm.

But she felt most alone when she flew to Queensland for the funeral. Michael offered to accompany her but she knew it was something she must do on her own. It was then that she realised just how much Malcolm had kept her to himself. She knew no one there, and started to wonder, indeed, whether she had ever really known Malcolm himself.

When she arrived back in Perth later that same day, she was severely shaken. The shock had caught up with her and she could feel herself going under.

Michael was waiting for her at the airport. He helped her into the car and said nothing as she wept silently all through the drive home.

When they arrived at the door to her room he said, 'Give me your key', and when they walked inside, he sat her on the bed and took off her shoes.

'Would you like me to stay with you?' he asked. She didn't answer. She could feel the tears coming on again and she knew she wouldn't be able to control them this time. 'I know you're feeling alone, Emma,' he said. 'But you mustn't be. I'm here. I'll always be here.'

The emotion she'd been suppressing for days finally escaped and she sobbed uncontrollably. He sat beside her and put his arm around her and she clung to him as she wept.

'I'll always be with you, Emma,' he said. 'Never forget that.' He held her close to him. 'I'll always be with you.'

CHAPTER TWELVE

BLUE WATER HISTORY premiered in New York in the spring of '89 and, just as Michael had forecast, it was a runaway success.

During the actual filming, Michael had prayed that the Americans would reclaim the Cup and he was delighted when they did. He was aware that the United States would show little interest in a film depicting the defeat of their sportsmen. At the time, he had wondered idly whether the fifty thousand he'd paid to a particular crew member had had any effect on the result. But it didn't make any difference. Following his announcement that the heist had been real, that the America's Cup had indeed been 'stolen', the film world was agog with conjecture.

Was Michael Ross for real? everyone asked. Surely it was a publicity hoax. He'd not announced how the feat had been accomplished. Some believed it, others didn't, but everyone went to see the movie. Everyone talked about it. Then word filtered out. Members of the film crew swore they knew for a fact that a dummy had been

457

exchanged for the real Cup before the shoot. Had that been how he'd done it? No, surely it was just a scenario his publicist had spread around. But, whatever the actual story, it didn't ultimately matter. Audiences flocked to *Blue Water History*.

Franklin had generously allocated a whole section of his studios to Michael for use as a production headquarters.

The studios were in central Manhattan. They were a rabbit warren – similar, Emma thought, to the studios in Sydney where she'd started her television career. But bigger, much, much bigger. They produced concurrently several game shows, two sitcoms, a top-rating daytime soap and, from time to time, various miniseries. It took her a week to find her way around the place.

Michael immediately called Emma and Stanley together in the boardroom of Michael Ross Productions to start plotting their next creation. There was a new member of the team: Mandy Crockett ...

To appease his conscience, Franklin had promised Davy that he would find a senior position in a highly creative field for his daughter. No matter how hard Franklin explained it away as a business necessity, the dismissal and subsequent death of old Sam Crockett still rested heavily with him. It was the least he could do to look after the old man's granddaughter.

Although Michael had agreed to employ Mandy as a favour to Franklin, she proved to be very useful. She was only nineteen and not averse to the dogsbody work, taking notes during creative sessions and running errands. She was keen to learn the business and, as it turned out, she was great fun. A party girl – one of Michael's kind.

Davy was glad of the opportunity afforded his daughter, although he considered it the least Franklin could do. Mandy was the baby of the family, spoilt by her mother and father and two older brothers, and she had been a wayward child. She was Davy's favourite, he couldn't deny it, his little princess, and it had broken his heart when she'd insisted on moving into an apartment with a wild young bunch when she was barely seventeen. She was headed for trouble, he could see that. He knew she smoked marijuana and drank more than she should, but there was nothing he could do to control her.

The job with Michael Ross's production company appeared to have solved all that. She moved into an apartment of her own nearer the studios, which afforded her privacy so that she could bring her work home. She was totally committed to her new career; stimulated by the Michael Ross method of movie making.

'He's brilliant, Pop,' she raved. 'None of the bullshit about demographics and television ratings I copped when you gave me that work experience gig at Minotaur last year. He does his own thing and he's stunning. You just wait till you see the movie we're going to make.' Davy was pleased.

Mandy was an attractive girl. Fortunately her brothers had been the ones to inherit Davy's physical bulk and square jaw. She had simply inherited the generosity of his features and his nature. She was not beautiful, but the immediate impression was one of sexuality. She was of average height and average figure but her mouth was full and her eyes held a wicked twinkle. She had an abundance of unruly reddish hair which, when worn up, untidy tendrils escaping the pins, reminded Franklin vaguely of Millie.

Mandy wasn't the only one who was finding the work at Ross Entertainments stimulating. With a massive production headquarters and a whole studio at his beck and call, Michael could barely contain himself. His ideas were grander and wilder than ever. His first American feature was going to be a massive 'War of the Worlds' epic, he said, an alien invasion which was going to be frighteningly real. 'The Americans love that sort of thing,' he insisted. 'And whatever the Americans love, the world loves.'

Emma suggested that maybe Steven Spielberg had beaten them to it and they should try something a little less competitive and more original, but Michael wouldn't listen. 'Balls,' he said dismissively, 'Spielberg's stuff's been fanciful and commercial – this is going to be real and horrifying. I want people wondering if it is actually going on in the world. Aliens taking over from the inside.'

When she mentioned that it had been done in *Village of the Damned* and *The Boys from Brazil*, he again refused to listen and even started to get angry. Did she no longer trust in his originality? Why was she being so negative?

'I'm not talking clones, Emma,' he said impatiently, 'I'm talking breeding. The aliens have been selectively breeding with humans for the past thirty years without the humans realising. It's original – why don't you trust me?'

Eventually Emma realised that she had to let him go his own way and she hoped the whole thing was not going to be a ghastly mistake. Stanley and Lou were busy designing prosthetic faces, mechanised alien body suits and multitudinous special effects and, as Emma gave herself up to the plotting sessions with Michael, she found the old excitement once again returning. Many of his ideas were, as usual, original and exciting, and she told herself she must trust in his creative genius as she always had.

It took Emma a while to adjust to New York. At first, she was a little overwhelmed by the jungle of buildings and the people and the pace. But, gradually, the electricity of the city won her over and she came to love its very size and turmoil.

She would stand in the Avenue of the Americas, look up at the row of massive buildings and wonder at the fact that they were man-made. They were human termite mounds. And she marvelled at the steam that wafted up through the air vents in the pavement. The fact that a seething metropolis lay beneath the solid concrete and asphalt was a never-ending source of amazement.

And there were the simple things too. The squirrels that stared back at her in Central Park. The daring ones that stayed their ground until she was only a metre or so away before they scurried up the nearest tree to sit laughing at her from a fork in the branches.

After a month of searching, she found her ideal apartment. It was nothing to boast about, in a modest block on Jane Street, but it was the location which won Emma. She loved Greenwich Village. The little theatres and galleries and nightspots; coffee and bagels at Zabars and after-show singalongs with the showbiz crowd at Don't Tell Mama's. Yes, she decided, a month after she'd moved in, she felt at home in New York City.

She may have adjusted to New York, but Emma was finding it a great deal more difficult to adjust to Franklin Ross. Of course her parting scene with Penelope had not helped. She could still hear the bitterness in her grandmother's voice.

When Emma had returned to Sydney to organise her belongings in preparation for the move to New York, she had seen Penelope and had felt dutybound to tell her the truth.

'I'm sorry,' she admitted, 'but I've broken my word to you.' She waited for a reaction but there was none. 'Michael knows the truth,' she said.

Penelope didn't appear remotely interested. She was in a strange mood, Emma thought. Distracted. She sat there, staring out of the lounge room windows over the front lawns of The Colony House. 'I don't suppose it matters any more,' she said.

'But Mr Ross hasn't been told,' Emma insisted. 'And I've sworn Michael to secrecy – at least until you think the time is right.'

'The time will never be right.' The eyes Penelope turned upon Emma were cold and accusing. 'Michael has chosen to be with his grandfather.

462

He is no longer a part of my life. And as you have opted to join them you too are of no further concern to me.'

Emma was about to say something but Penelope continued regardless. 'I can assure you, though – if you tell my husband about your parentage he will do one of two things: he will either claim you as his, in which case he will own your very soul, or he will destroy you. Franklin Ross is a cruel man. A tyrant.'

Penelope rose to indicate their meeting was over. 'Either way, the outcome is immaterial to me.' She no longer looked beautiful. Her mouth was twisted with spite, her eyes narrowed and venomous and, for the first time, Emma could see the true age in the woman's face. 'The three of you can rot in hell as far as I'm concerned,' she snarled. Then she nodded to the maid to see Emma out.

At the hall archway, Emma turned. 'I'm so sorry, Penelope,' she said. She meant it; her heart ached for the woman. 'I'm truly sorry that you've been so hurt.' And she left, wondering if she would ever see her grandmother again.

After she'd gone, Penelope wept. She sat looking over the lawns at the statue of the dueller and wept for her life.

Now, whenever Emma saw Franklin, and she often did at the studios, she recalled the snarling, wounded animal Penelope had become and she heard the warning 'he will own your very soul, or he will destroy you'.

As a result, she tried to avoid Franklin whenever she could, but it was difficult. Particularly

463

when he insisted on a welcoming dinner at the penthouse apartment he shared with Helen on 57th Street.

'This is the gifted young writer who works with Michael, my dear. Emma Clare, Helen Bohan.'

'Hello, Emma, I've heard a lot about you,' she said, offering a firm handshake. Instinctively, Emma liked her. She knew she probably shouldn't. Helen was 'the other woman', after all, and presumably the major reason for Penelope's unhappiness. But something told Emma that Penelope had been unhappy for a long time before Helen Bohan came on the scene.

There were a dozen people at the dinner, most of whom Emma knew. Michael, of course, and Stanley, Lou, Mandy and several heads of studio departments to whom she'd been introduced when she'd first arrived. The evening was ostensibly a belated welcoming party for Michael but it was also good for business relationships. Franklin only ever threw dinner parties when there was a political purpose.

'And this is Mandy's father.' During pre-dinner cocktails in the sunken lounge Franklin had decided, for some unknown reason, to take Emma under his wing and introduce her around personally. She felt a little uncomfortable and wished Michael was by her side. He'd disappeared. He was probably in the bathroom hyping himself up for the night, she thought. For once she rather envied him; she wouldn't mind a little artificial stimulation herself to get through this evening. It was somewhat daunting, particularly with Franklin paying her so much attention.

'How do you do, Mr Crockett,' she said, shaking hands.

'Davy'll do just fine,' the jovial American pumped her hand effusively in reply. 'Mandy never lets up about your talents, yours and Michael's, and how great it is to be working with you two. I'm just so proud that you've taken her on, I surely am.'

Davy Crockett was as big and loud and unreal as Michael had painted him, but then Michael had said his childhood memories of Old Sam were just the same. Emma liked him but she winced as she felt her knuckles grind against each other and she wished he'd let her hand go.

She chatted to Davy and Franklin for a further five minutes then excused herself to talk to Mandy who was attacking the array of canapes in the open-plan dining room alongside the sunken lounge. But she didn't join Mandy. She drifted to the massive penthouse windows instead, and stood there for a moment, gazing at the sea of lights sixty storeys below before looking back at the surrounds and the assembled gathering.

The penthouse was fascinating. It was a reflection of wealth and taste as Emma had expected it would be, but it reflected only Franklin. With the exception of the massive floral display on the central hall table, there was no evidence whatsoever of a feminine presence. The lounge suite was large and leather with mahogany armrests, the dining suite was magnificent but similarly large and bulky. There was a strangely colonial feel to it, as if Franklin had brought his private quarters from The Colony House and set them up in central New York. But Penelope's touch had always been evident in The Colony House. Where did Helen feature here? Emma wondered if their bedroom would be the same. A massive wooden four-poster and a masculine chest of drawers? Or would there be a dressing table in the corner with an ornate mirror and a vanity set? Somehow she doubted it. Helen Bohan was not a vain woman. But she was not a weak woman either.

Emma looked across the room at Helen chatting with Michael, who had just emerged from the bathroom. She was a matronly woman – in her fifties, and she looked it. But she was confident, at ease with herself. She wasn't living in a man's shadow, but she was happy to allow him centre stage. Her clothes were sensible, but of the finest quality, her hair beautifully styled but practical, and she obviously saw no reason to disguise the iron grey. What an amazing change from Penelope, Emma thought, and wondered at the relationship between Franklin and Helen.

Suddenly she was aware that Franklin Ross was staring at her from across the room. The piercing eyes beneath the shaggy, lined brow had settled upon her and they refused to be distracted. Someone was talking to him but he wasn't noticing. His gaze was fixed upon Emma.

She felt her cheeks flush. It was ridiculous. The man couldn't read thoughts, for God's sake. So why was he staring at her? She turned and concentrated on the view.

Far below and to her left was the blackness of

the Hudson River. In the centre, the massive square of the park, outlined by the endless lights of upper Manhattan. And, to the right, the unbroken blaze of Fifth Avenue.

'Impressive, isn't it? She turned. Franklin was at her side. 'I bought the apartment for the view. The lights are spectacular but I prefer it in the daytime. On a clear morning one can see right up to the top of the island. Although personally, I think nothing quite matches Sydney Harbour.' Despite the fact that he was talking about the view, he wasn't looking out of the windows. His eyes hadn't left hers. And she had the feeling that he wasn't so much looking at her, he was looking inside her. He was trying to read her thoughts. Why? What was his interest?

She smiled politely and turned her attention once more to the view. 'Yes, it's most impressive,' she answered.

Franklin was indeed trying to see inside her head. There was something about the girl that he couldn't quite fathom and it annoyed him. Despite her youth, she was strong and resilient; he could sense that. Yet she avoided him. He knew he could be a little daunting to the younger ones, but not to this girl. This girl wasn't frightened by him, she didn't like him. He sensed an animosity which both intrigued and irritated him.

He smiled as amiably as his stern features would allow. 'Michael tells me the movie is coming along famously.' His tone was as jovial as he could make it.

Emma turned back to him but again her smile

was remote, polite. 'Yes, Mr Ross, you should be extremely proud of your grandson, he's very clever.'

Franklin felt a flash of annoyance. He was doing his best and the girl was closing him out. He didn't like social games, and was never comfortable playing them. He preferred people who called a spade a spade. He wanted to ask her straight out, 'What is it you don't like about me, girl?' He wanted to bark, 'Spit it out.' But he decided to try another tack instead.

'Franklin. Please,' he smiled. 'And I have a favour to ask.'

'Of course. Franklin,' Emma replied. Charm didn't sit well on Franklin Ross, she decided. She could sense the tyrant beneath the pleasant social exterior and she felt awkward calling him Franklin. 'What can I do for you?'

'It's Michael.' She was relieved when Franklin finally turned his attention to the windows and the view. 'Of course I'm proud of him, but I'm a little worried also.' Franklin was no longer smiling. This girl was the closest person to Michael and he needed her as an ally. He dropped the social pretence and made a genuine plea. 'I know he uses drugs and I'm worried about him. I wondered if you might help me.'

Emma could see the concern in the old man's face and for the first time she felt a stab of sympathy. But what could she do? What did he expect of her? She herself had nagged Michael constantly about his drug abuse but, until he himself recognised it as a problem, there was nothing anyone else could do about it. She'd even discussed it with Stanley, the only person she could trust, and he agreed with her. 'Michael has to clean up his own act, Emma,' he'd said. 'You can't do it for him.' She was, however, certain of one thing. Threats from Franklin Ross would not solve the dilemma.

'I only *work* with Michael, Mr Ross ... Franklin,' she answered. 'I don't know what he does in his spare time.'

'Oh, come on, girl – of course you do,' Franklin snapped. 'If the boy's a bloody junkie, I want to be told.' The genuine fear for his grandson brought out the harshness in Franklin. Why were they pussyfooting around about such an issue? Enough niceties, he decided. 'I'll have none of my kin using the filthy stuff. I'll have his guts for garters. I'll have him signed into a clinic so fast his eyes'll water.' Franklin sensed her withdrawal and he knew he'd sounded overharsh. He didn't want to frighten her off. He tried to soften his tone. 'Don't you see, it'll be the best thing for him? Tell me the truth.'

'I don't know. I seriously don't,' Emma answered, and she wasn't lying. She rarely went to the discotheques and nightclubs Michael frequented and he never openly took drugs when they were working. 'As I said, I only work with him. I don't socialise – '

'Then start.' It sounded like an order. 'Start socialising. You can tell me what, when, how much. How great a control these drugs appear to have over him. I need to know.'

She stared back at him. It was a confronting experience. The steel-blue eyes demanded obedience. After what seemed an age, she heard herself say, 'I'm sorry. I can't do that.'

'And why not?'

'It's a matter of honour, Mr Ross. Michael is my friend and my work partner. I can't spy on him.' Emma turned. 'Now, if you'll excuse me, I need to go to the bathroom.'

Emma's heart was pounding as she walked away. That was it. She'd probably just talked herself out of the greatest job opportunity of a lifetime. Not only would she be sacked from Ross Entertainments, Franklin would most likely have her blacklisted throughout the entire industry. 'He's a tyrant,' Penelope had said. 'He'll destroy you.' But it wasn't just the threat to her career that had set Emma's heart pounding. It was the man himself. Her grandfather. She had just felt the force of his power, and to deny such power was truly frightening.

Franklin had felt a similar force. 'It's a matter of honour, Mr Ross', she'd said. She'd met him blow for blow and he admired her for it.

When she returned from the bathroom, Helen was calling people to the table and Emma wondered whether she should stay for the dinner. The decision was made for her.

'Emma, you must sit by me – I insist.' Franklin was pulling her chair out for her and his expression was benign, welcoming. It was as if their exchange had never taken place.

Michael was sitting opposite her and he gave her a wink which said, 'How did you do it? How did you charm the old man?' She gave an imperceptible shrug back, the dinner party commenced, and the rest of the evening proved to be most enjoyable.

Franklin and Helen were excellent hosts. The food was superb and the wines, all Australian and all Ross Estate, were magnificent. It was one of the rare occasions when Franklin actually seemed to enjoy a social gathering. He spoke of the Ross wines and his pride in acquiring the old family vineyards and he even talked briefly about his childhood at Araluen.

'When you've made your movies and you decide to settle down one day, Michael,' he said, 'you should bring your children up on the land. Among the vines. At Araluen. It's the perfect childhood.'

The look of fondness on Helen's face as she looked at Franklin did not escape Emma. It was a look she had never seen on Penelope's face when she spoke of her husband. This woman truly loved Franklin Ross.

Helen was proud of Franklin that night. Proud that people could see the man she knew. He'd become cantankerous in his old age and he rarely displayed the side she knew best – the man from the land who loved the vines and wanted to share them with his family. She was the only one who saw that side.

'Oh, if we'd had children, my dear ... ' he'd say regretfully from time to time. Then he'd change the subject. 'It's not too late to return to the land though. As soon as the divorce comes through and we can marry ... '

It was his grandson's presence in New York that was bringing out the softer side of Franklin, Helen thought, and she smiled gratefully at Michael.

471

Franklin loved his only grandson with a passion which quite possibly Michael himself did not even realise.

Michael was having a wonderful evening. The ecstasy he'd taken before he left home was helping him find everyone interesting, and everyone seemed to find him interesting. He was the centre of attention as people talked about *Blue Water History* and asked him about the present script. He played it secretively, though, hinting at the convoluted plot and the wonderful special effects. 'A visual feast, that's what it will be,' he announced.

The only dampener was the presence of Karol Mankowski opposite him, seated beside Franklin. Every now and then, in one of his flights of fancy, Michael would catch Karol's eye. The dour, immovable, implacable shadow. Why the hell his grandfather had to invite the man to a private dinner party was beyond Michael. Christ, his presence was a downer. Michael tried to avoid eye contact whenever possible – it wasn't good to get paranoid when on a high.

Michael loved New York. From the moment he'd arrived he knew that this was his city. It fed his craving for excitement and stimulated his desire for adventure.

It also catered to the party animal in him and encouraged his drug habits. His wealth and newly acquired fame opened every door he wished to enter. Cocaine was plentiful, as were the designer drugs which often replaced his speed pills. He avoided heroin and any form of mainlining, persuading himself that, as he didn't use a needle, his indulgences were not addictive. He was confident that his drug abuse didn't affect his work but he nevertheless hid his habits from Emma. She'd only start nagging again, he knew.

In fact, he monitored his social behaviour in general. He knew how unwise it would be to appear totally bombed in public. Word got around quickly in this industry and he couldn't afford to have people misconstrue his drug use and assume that he had a genuine problem. Most of his heavy-duty partying was done in his hotel suite, either with a gang of similarly inclined friends, or with whichever girl he'd met earlier that evening at Doubles or Tatou or a late private gathering in a basement apartment at The Village.

'Let's party,' he'd say, lining up the coke on the special glass cutting board.

Michael was content for the moment in his hotel suite. He was taking his time finding an apartment. He knew exactly what he wanted and, until he found it, he wasn't going to settle for second best.

He wanted somewhere even more luxurious than Franklin's. Well, more luxurious by his standards. He didn't need Franklin's views of Central Park and he certainly didn't want colonial surrounds. Australia was a lifetime ago. He didn't care if he never went back. New York was his town.

Michael's idea of luxury was a party palace. He wanted an indoor pool and a spa and a circular bed with surrounding mirrors. And he hunted for a place he could convert to his fantasy.

In the meantime, he was happy enough with his hotel suite. He'd shifted the queen-sized bed in front of the two large mirrors on the built-in wardrobes and he'd set up a video on the top shelf in one of them so that, if he opened the door, he could film his bedtime activities. The girls always found it great fun and it was harmless enough. What they didn't realise was that, more often than not, Michael would mask their faces from the camera so that, when he watched the film the following day, he could fantasise that it was Emma he was making love to.

He saw no harm in it. He was happy to have Emma as his sister, his love for her was genuine. And if a little erotic fantasy helped keep his sexual yearning for her under control, then surely that was healthy.

Life was good for Michael. And in twelve months' time it was going to be even better. In twelve months' time, when *The Breeders* came out, he'd be the toast of New York City. He'd own this town.

CHAPTER THIRTEEN

BUT THE BREEDERS WAS not the massive success Michael had vowed it would be. Two years later, twelve months behind its planned schedule and three times over its original budget, *The Breeders* premiered in Hollywood to a lukewarm reaction. Over the next few weeks, it proved to be a monumental disaster. Stanley's and Lou's special effects were nominated for awards, certainly, but the film itself was labelled 'derivative', 'uncoordinated' and 'indulgent', just as Emma had first feared it might be. The 'moments of great flair and originality' the critics mentioned couldn't save it and Michael sank into a deep depression. Again and again he asked himself, how had he so totally lost the plot?

But he knew the answer. He'd tripped too far and too often. He had to clean up his act. He called a meeting – just Emma, Stanley and Mandy. He wasn't going to admit his errors to all and sundry – these were the three he needed on side.

'I fucked up,' he announced. 'It's my fault and I take full responsibility. You advised me against it, particularly you, Emma, and I wouldn't listen.'

'Oh, I think we all went off the rails a bit,' Emma said, and she looked at Stanley, who nodded in agreement. It was true. Stanley too had had his misgivings at the outset of the venture, but both he and Emma had allowed themselves to be caught up in Michael's madness, and had allowed their work to become inconsistent and indulgent.

Michael laughed. 'Bullshit,' he said. 'What egos you people have. I insist on taking full credit for the stuff-up.' Secretly he was delighted by their loyalty. 'Besides,' he added with an impish grin, 'that way I can take full credit for the mammoth success we're about to create.' He leaned over the huge boardroom desk which was strewn with notepads, pencils and jugs of water and glasses. A session was about to get under way. 'I have ideas, masses of them, and I need input. Everybody ready?' Emma and Stanley nodded and grabbed pencils and paper. 'Mandy, take notes,' Michael ordered and Mandy sat, poised, in front of the computer at the other end of the table.

'Stuff the glossy unlimited-budget crap,' he said excitedly. 'This one's going to rely on content. Original, topical content with a moral theme. And an actor who'll blow their tits off. Modest budget. We're going to show them that we can really make movies.'

Michael saw no reason to share Franklin's threat with them. 'You've got one more chance, boy,' Franklin had said. 'I know I gave you free rein to produce your own projects and I'll stand by my word. I shan't interfere with your next film, but I'll not have this company made a laughing stock, do you hear me?'

Franklin was in a genuine dilemma. He still worried about Michael's drug intake and he wondered whether it was responsible for the film's abysmal failure but, despite Karol Mankowski's continued surveillance, nothing could be proved. Michael's 'party' friends were loyal – after all, Michael was a very generous provider – and his creative associates assured Franklin that Michael was never drug-affected during working hours.

'Another monumental mistake like that last fiasco and you're out,' he growled. 'This is your second chance and you'd better make it count. And you'd better make it count on one-tenth of the budget – you understand me?'

'Yes, Grandfather.' Michael had understood him all right. And the prospect was strangely exciting. A movie free of tricks. No Halley's Comet to film. No America's Cup to steal. Not even a massive budget to impress. Yes, it was exciting. He'd prove to the world that he was a true movie maker. 'So we need a topic and we need an actor: let's start from there,' he said, jumping out of his chair and pacing around the boardroom. He always liked to move when he felt a creative surge.

'Let's look for the actor first.' It was a bizarre way to go, he knew, but he was warming to his theme and there was no stopping him. 'We'll pick an actor that this country loves – male or female, it doesn't matter – and we'll write the perfect vehicle to fit the star. An English actor. Or a European, with international appeal. Americans take the English and the Europeans so seriously. Emma, you first, what do you think?'

Emma was a little bemused. As usual Michael was moving at a pace that was very difficult to keep up with. 'Well, I think we need to at least have some idea of what sort of comment we're going to make before we start choosing an actor.'

'Rubbish. The choice of actor'll do that for us.' The others gazed back at him, bewildered. 'Look,' he explained, just a little impatiently, 'to the Americans, the English are aristocrats and the Europeans are lovers. If we pick an Italian star we head for a sexual comment. If we pick an English star we head for a class statement. Simple.'

Emma nodded. Yes, it was simple. Michael's basic ideas always were simple. Simple and clever. 'Excellent,' she said. 'What do you think, Stanley?'

'This is a bit out of my league,' Stanley smiled. 'Can you come back to me when you want a few stunts?'

But Michael wasn't in the mood for jokes. 'Call up the B-list star file, Mandy,' he instructed, 'and then go and get me the newspapers. We'll marry the star with the topic. Something current, something global.'

They studied the computer screen while Mandy fetched the papers. The B-list star file was a comprehensive record of actors who commanded top billing but didn't demand top dollar and a share in the profits. 'Can't afford the A-list – they're too commercial anyway,' Michael insisted. 'The bigger they are the bigger they can flop at the box office. We need someone the public takes seriously.'

It was Emma who came up with the ideal candidate. Well, Emma and Mandy together. Mandy was scouring the papers for issues. 'Hey, there's an editorial here on the French nuclear testings in the South Pacific. That's a helluva hot one.'

'Yes, but it's been going on for years,' Stanley said. 'Maybe we should head for something more current, more headline. . .'

'No,' Michael disagreed, 'if we go for something headline it might be yesterday's news by the time the movie comes out. It has to be an ongoing issue. Good one, Mandy.'

'Marcel Gireaux!' Emma yelled it out and they all jumped. She'd been rolling through the actors' names and biographies, starting with the Europeans. She'd done the Italians and was into the French. The name leapt at her from the screen. 'Marcel Gireaux,' she said again. 'You won't find a European actor the public will take more seriously than Gireaux and you get the two elements in the one bloke. Sex appeal and political commitment. He's one of Greenpeace's major spokespeople. We'd gain fantastic press from the fact that he's allied himself to the movie because he believes in the cause.'

'Bring us the composite file on Gireaux,' Michael ordered. As Mandy left, he started prowling the room again. He could feel the familiar buzz. It was an excellent idea. 'But could we get him? He's France's major classical actor, and he's shunned Hollywood for years. The only movie directors he'll work with are Truffaut and Zeffirelli and Malle and . . . '

'But we're not Hollywood,' Emma countered. 'We'll show him *Halley's* and *Blue Water History* and tell him that we're putting all of that original approach into a movie about the environment. A movie about a man committed to the welfare of the planet and his fellow man.'

'Yes, that's it,' Michael agreed. 'Appeal to his vanity and his ambition. He's probably after a career in politics – we tell him he can use this as his personal springboard – '

'Wrong,' Emma interrupted. 'Very wrong. He's an idealist, not personally motivated at all. What's more, he'd be deeply insulted if you inferred he was. He'd run a mile. Haven't you read anything at all about him?'

Mandy arrived with the file. 'Of course I have,' Michael answered, 'but it's bullshit. The man's protecting his image.' Emma was shaking her head in disagreement. 'Oh, come on, Emma,' he insisted, 'anyone can be bought.'

'Just look at him,' Mandy interrupted as she spread the photographs out on the table. 'That's what I call sex appeal. What a hunk!'

The photos showed a tall man in his mid-thirties with a granite face, a rather large nose and a head of thick, greying hair. It wasn't a conventionally handsome face but there was a sensitive curve to the lip and the eyes were enquiring. It was an intriguing blend of the patrician, the sensual and the intelligent.

'I agree,' Emma said. 'He's a hunk, all right. If we get Gireaux we get everything we want in the one actor.'

'What do you think, Stanley?' Michael asked.

'Does he do his own stunts?' Stanley was feeling a little out of his element. The plotting and scheming and conniving wasn't his area and he was more than happy to admit it.

The others laughed. 'Marcel Gireaux it is then,' Michael announced.

They started on a treatment that same afternoon, and a month later they had a first draft script. But, as they'd anticipated, the script was not the problem. The problem was the contracting of Marcel Gireaux. 'Monsieur Gireaux is not interested in making an American film' was the terse reply from his agent in Paris.

Michael responded by sending the agent tapes of *Halley's* and *Blue Water History* together with a synopsis of the newly titled *Earth Man* and the assurance that it would be shot primarily on location in the South Pacific by a European director mutually agreed upon by both parties. The response was a little less terse but predominantly the same. 'Monsieur Gireaux found your films well-made and the premise of *Earth Man* sound but he regrets he is not interested in making an American film.'

Emma was prepared to give up but Michael refused. 'We have to see him personally,' he insisted. 'He has to realise that we're not Hollywood producers, that we're not brash and materialistic and –' Emma couldn't resist a smile. 'OK,' Michael grinned back, 'so I'm brash and materialistic, but you're not. You're the one, Emma. You go to Paris and get the man on side.'

'Me?'

'You. Start packing, you're off to Paris.'

A fortnight later, having secured an agreement from the French agent that Monsieur Gireaux would at least grant an interview with Miss Clare, Emma was on her way.

It was business, she reminded herself as she boarded the plane. Purely business. She was to hand over the final script to Marcel Gireaux and she was to acquire the actor's services. But she couldn't deny the thrill of anticipation. Paris! She was going to Paris.

The day after she arrived, she booked out of the suite Michael had arranged for her at the Hilton – 'I know you want to mingle with the peasants, Emma, but it's not good for the image,' he'd insisted – and she found herself an attractive little bed and breakfast place which catered for four guests only. It was in the Latin Quarter, a minute's walk from the embankment and, through her bedroom window, if she leant out far enough, she could catch a glimpse of Notre Dame Cathedral. Emma was in seventh heaven.

She walked and walked until her feet ached. For a full two days she explored Paris by foot, both the tourist spots and the backstreet alleys. On the third day, she prepared herself for her appointment with Marcel Gireaux.

His agent's offices were on the second floor of a gloomy little house in a gloomy little lane behind the Rue Lafayette and they consisted of a tiny reception area with a tiny receptionist and the 'inner sanctum'. The inner sanctum was a room barely larger than the reception area with just enough space for a sizeable desk, an office chair and two rather uncomfortable seats for guests. It was fortunate, Emma thought, that the agent, a bony man called Jean-Pierre, was as petite as his receptionist.

'Miss Clare, come in, come in,' he said, gesturing toward one of the uncomfortable chairs and sidling his way around the desk. The walls were smothered with photos of actors and, dead centre, in pride of place, larger than all the other photographs, was a portrait of Marcel Gireaux. It was obvious he was the star attraction of the agency. Emma didn't know whether it was a good sign or not. In fact she didn't know what to make of the entire situation. She certainly hadn't expected such a seedy set-up for France's premier classical actor.

'Marcel has just telephoned,' Jean-Pierre said in his fractured English, 'he is on his way. Cafe?'

'Thank you, yes.' Ten minutes later, and several sips into a mug of lukewarm, muddy coffee (fancy a French person making bad coffee!' she thought) the door was flung open and Marcel Gireaux arrived.

He was too big for the office, she thought. Not that he was physically enormous. He was relatively tall, and his build was certainly in proportion to his height, but it was his presence which was too big for the office.

'Bonjour, Jean-Pierre. Miss Clare.' He shook her hand without waiting for an introduction. 'I am sorry. I have kept you waiting.' The voice, too, was big. Big and magnificent.

'That's perfectly all right.' She gestured to her coffee mug. 'Monsieur Marchand has been looking after me.'

'Hah. Filthy stuff, yes? Come. I shall buy you

483

some excellent coffee and croissants at my favourite patisserie.'

'No really, I'm ... ' She looked at Jean-Pierre to see if he was offended but he was nodding benignly. Meetings at the agency were only ever a ruse for Marcel. If Marcel sat down in the uncomfortable chair to chat it meant he wasn't interested and it was Jean-Pierre's signal to get rid of the other party as soon as was politely possible.

'I may call you Emma, yes?' Marcel was assisting her to her feet and she was at the door before she knew it.

'Yes, of course. Thank you for the coffee, Monsieur Marchand, I'm sorry to – '

'And you must call me Marcel.' He pointed at the briefcase she was carrying. 'You have the script?'

'Yes.' Three steps and they were through the reception area.

'Good, good.'

Marcel took her to his favourite sidewalk cafe in the Rue Lafayette and ordered croissants. Then he held out his hand. 'The script?'

'Oh. Yes, of course.' She opened the briefcase and handed him the script. He sat forward in his seat, hunched over the table, and buried himself in it, oblivious to all else.

Emma looked at him for a moment. He'd forgotten she was there, the concentration was so intense. She turned her attention to the passers-by. It was a beautiful autumn day. A clear blue sky and a nip in the air. And the Rue Lafayette was a passing parade. She could sit here forever, she thought.

'Croissants, M'sieur?' They'd been so tied up in themselves that they'd both failed to notice the waiter standing by, patiently, waiting for a space to be cleared on the table.

'Oui. Merci.' Unfazed, Marcel closed the script, pushed it to one side and sat back in his seat.

'You are very young,' he said and she wondered whether she should be offended by the accusation.

'I'm nearly twenty-four,' she answered. 'And I've been writing for television and film since I was seventeen.'

'Good, good.' He apparently failed to notice her defensive tone. Or if he did notice, he chose to ignore it. 'This is good.' He bit into a croissant. 'I like it.' He tapped the tabletop and she realised that he meant the script. She was about to reply. 'Tell me about yourself,' he said. And she changed tack. She was quickly realising that the way to get through to Marcel Gireaux was to be flexible. She was aware she was being tested and she was quite prepared to go with the punches.

The attention he'd previously directed to the script, Marcel now turned upon her. She was under scrutiny and was obviously expected to discuss her personal life in detail. With the exception of her relationship to Michael and Franklin Ross, she did. She even touched upon the death of her fiance, Malcolm O'Brien, four years ago. At which point, Emma decided to put an end to the examination.

'What about you, Marcel? You're married, aren't you? For how long? You have children, don't you? How old?'

He stared back at her and she wondered if she'd

overstepped the mark. Then he burst out laughing. 'Yes, fourteen years, two children, twelve and ten.' Despite the compulsion of the tabloid press to spread rumours and to insinuate affairs with leading ladies, it was known amongst the profession that Marcel was a happily married man, as deeply committed to his family as he was to his causes.

An hour later, he excused himself. 'I must have my rest before the evening performance,' he said. 'You will come and see me?'

'Yes, I'd love to.' Emma had done her homework. She knew he was playing the title role in *Tartuffe* and that all of Paris was raving about his performance.

'I will arrange tickets. You wish to bring someone?'

She shook her head. 'I don't know anybody in Paris.'

'Ah, in that case, Jean-Pierre will ... '

'No thanks. I'm quite happy to come along on my own.' He was about to insist. 'Really,' she assured him. 'I enjoy going to the theatre alone.'

What a peculiar thing for a woman to say, Marcel thought. Peculiar and very interesting. No French woman would say it. Well, she might say it, but she wouldn't mean it, and this young woman obviously meant it. The American women he'd known, and there had been many, wouldn't say it or mean it either. He supposed it must be because she was Australian. Very interesting.

'You know *Tartuffe*?' he asked.

'No,' she said. 'I know it's a Moliere play. I saw a production of *The Miser* once.' Marcel laughed out loud. The girl was truly delightful. 'Sorry,' she smiled. 'To be honest, I'm not that crash hot on the English classics either. Well, I'm fine on the literature side,' she added, aware that she mustn't sell herself too short. 'But the theatrical classics I'm afraid I . . . '

'No matter. You write a good movie.' He pushed the script across the table to her.

'But you haven't finished reading it.'

'My mind is in *Tartuffe* now. I will read it tomorrow.' He rose from the table. 'And I will see you after the performance, yes?'

'Yes. Thank you for the coffee and croissants . . . ' But he was gone.

Emma understood barely a word of *Tartuffe*. She tried to apply her schoolgirl French but the actors spoke at such speed it was impossible to discern anything more than the occasional phrase. She vaguely followed the plot and she bought a programme hoping that it would help her fathom the intricacies which clearly abounded, but it didn't. The words off the page were just as confusing to her as the words in the air. But there was one thing of which she was certain. One thing which transcended the language barrier. Marcel Gireaux. He was magnificent.

'You were magnificent,' she said as he poured her a glass of champagne in his dressing room. A group of admirers had just left and he'd insisted she stay with him while he take his make-up off.

487

He looked at her for several seconds. She meant it. Many people told him he was magnificent. The word was easy for them. But it wasn't a word which sat naturally with this young woman. And that made it valuable. 'Thank you,' he said. 'You will have croissants with me tomorrow? At noon?'

'Yes. Thank you, and I'll bring the script, you can – '

'I will make your film.'

'But you haven't finished the script, how can you – ?'

'I like it. I will make your film. Tomorrow? Noon?'

For three-quarters of an hour she watched the passers-by in the Rue Lafayette and cast surreptitious glances at Marcel as he gulped his coffee, bit into his croissants and assiduously studied the script of *Earth Man*.

'Yes, it's good, I like it,' he announced finally. 'What are your plans for the rest of the day?'

'Well, I thought I'd go to the Louvre. But don't you think we should discuss business? My partner and I – '

'The Louvre. An excellent idea. I shan't accompany you, I must rest for this evening's performance, but perhaps a walk in the Tuileries Gardens before you visit the galleries?'

'Yes, I'd enjoy that, but shouldn't we get the business – '

'I never discuss business. We leave that to your Mr Ross and Jean-Pierre. Shall we go?'

They did, however, discuss the film as they

walked through the Tuilleries Gardens. Emma was not only impressed by Marcel's comprehension of the script – he saw angles which even she and Michael had not envisaged – but by the man's perception as to his role in the casting of the film.

'You are obviously aware of my involvement with Greenpeace and other environmental organisations,' he said. 'That is good. It is clever: it will work in the selling of the film.' She gave him a quick sidelong glance. He was not offended by such a commercial aspect and she was rather surprised. He caught her glance and smiled back.

'I have to warn you,' he said, 'that not all your press will be necessarily good. There are factions, quite a number, I can tell you, who do not approve of me because I am so vocal about my causes. There are many critics who think actors should be dumb and pretty, yes?'

She laughed. 'Yes,' she agreed. 'And there are many producers who think there is no such thing as bad publicity. I'm afraid I should warn you that my partner is one of them.' Emma didn't even question the risk she might have taken. The man was being honest with her, he deserved honesty in return.

Marcel studied her shrewdly for a moment. No, it wasn't a trick. There was no conscious attempt on the girl's part to beguile him. But beguile him she did. 'I shall look forward to working with you, Emma.' He took her hand and pressed it gently to his lips. 'Very much.'

Emma didn't know whether to burst out laughing or to feel embarrassed. She wasn't sure whether the gesture of mock-chivalry was intended to be humorous or serious but fortunately Marcel's timing was as impeccable offstage as it was on and he didn't leave her time to ponder the question. 'Enjoy the Louvre,' he said. 'See you on location.' And he waved to her as he walked briskly off across the lawns of the Tuileries Gardens, neatly avoiding a 'Do Not Walk on the Grass' sign.

'We've got him. He's ours!' announced Emma's triumphant fax to Michael. She'd booked herself back into the Hilton for the last two days of her stay. Michael was right; it was easier for business. She started negotiations with Jean-Pierre Marchand and sent endless faxes to Michael.

'Paris is everything I'd hoped for, and more,' she wrote. 'All the things one expects will disappoint, don't. The Eiffel Tower is as outrageous and modern as it was over a hundred years ago and the Arc de Triomphe is as timeless and Sacre Coeur as awe-inspiring. And Notre Dame ... Strange, bald-spired Notre Dame. I'd always thought it was quite ugly on postcards. Mammoth certainly, but – those nasty cut-off towers that look as though they should have delicate spires on top. Well, you should see it! All around the building are the statues of the saints. And they're standing on the sinners. It's not fair – these pathetic, twisted little creatures with these hefty great saints perched self-righteously on top. You want to yell, "Get off!" But they're wonderful. So wonderful. I could look at them for hours.'

'Anyway, I had another meeting with Jean-

Pierre this afternoon. Evidently Marcel is mad keen to do the movie. Of course Jean-Pierre is insisting that he must have total choice of director, right of veto over any script changes, and he won't work in New York for more than a fortnight. All of which we'd anticipated, of course. And I don't think he'll cost nearly as much as we'd expected. Isn't that great?'

'We've got Marcel Gireaux,' Michael announced. 'Had a fax from Emma this morning.'

It was one of those occasional family dinners with Helen and Franklin in their apartment and Michael was delighted at the opportunity to steer the conversation into a positive business area. He knew only too well that Franklin was scrutinising him closely, assessing him all the while.

'How's your new project coming along?' the old man had asked. So Michael pulled Emma's fax out of his pocket and made the announcement.

'Marcel Gireaux, really?' Franklin was impressed.

'He's ours, Grandpa. Ours for the asking.' Michael handed Franklin the fax. 'Take a look. Emma's sure of it. And she never exaggerates. Not the facts, anyway.' He grinned at Helen. 'She waxes a bit poetic about Paris, mind you.'

As Franklin started to scan the three pages of fax paper, his attention was caught. He had heard this before. Where? Then he remembered. Catherine. He could hear Catherine. 'Paris is a glorious city, Franklin. A city designed for those who love beauty. There's space to stand back and admire the light on the buildings and the statues. And the churches. Ah! The churches. Notre Dame with its saints and sinners.'

Catherine had said that. He'd been ten years old and they'd sat looking over the valley and she'd sketched the vineyards in charcoal.

'I'm delighted to see things are progressing so well,' was all he said as he handed the fax back to Michael.

It proved to be a companionable evening. Just the three of them. Karol Mankowski was absent, Michael was at his entertaining best and Franklin, charmed by his grandson, was far less acerbic than usual. Helen was pleased to see the two men openly displaying the fondness they had for each other. Surely it meant Franklin's worry that Michael might be 'going off the rails', as he put it, was unfounded.

But two weeks later, news reached Franklin which confirmed his worries were far from groundless.

'What comment do you have on the allegations that your grandson is a rapist, Mr Ross?' the voice asked down the line.

'What allegations? What the hell are you talking about?'

'Oh, I'm so sorry.' The voice had a cockney accent and dripped hypocritical concern. It was a British tabloid journalist – the worst of the gutter press. 'I was sure you would have heard by now. You see, the victim, Miss Waverley, has granted me an exclusive and my story hits the stands next Tuesday, so I naturally assumed your grandson would have warned you. I mean, it's under just such unpleasant and upsetting circumstances that families like to stick together, isn't it?'

'Listen, you obsequious piece of shit,' Franklin snarled, 'you'll get nothing out of me. Not one cent.'

'I assure you, Mr Ross ... ' The voice was grovelling now, but not frightened. The journalist was unperturbed, obviously used to such reactions. 'I was merely after a comment from you regarding – '

'And if you attempt to print one word of such slander, you'll be hit with far more than a libel suit.'

'Mr Ross,' the voice sounded a little less sure of itself now. 'I've already started writing the article ... '

'Then stop. And start worrying about your health.' Franklin hung up. Then he telephoned Michael.

'What the hell's going on, boy?' he asked. 'What have you got yourself into? Do I need to pay this worm off or not?'

Michael assured him that he didn't, that it was pure tabloid fiction, and that there was nothing to worry about. But Franklin wasn't satisfied with that.

'Get yourself around here this instant and explain yourself,' he ordered.

It had happened at a basement party in The Village. Michael related the story as patiently as he could. A girl had been coming on strong to him, so he'd taken her into one of the bedrooms and obliged.

'Yes, I know, I should have been more discreet,' he added hastily before Franklin could interrupt, 'but it was one of those parties – everyone was playing up. Anyway,' he continued, 'the girl called rape on me. She raced out of the bedroom and started screaming that I'd attacked her. She was off her brain, of course.'

'Honestly, Grandpa,' he insisted as Franklin said nothing but scowled back at him, 'she's just after publicity, she's renowned for it. Rebel Waverley, that's her name – she's always in the papers for one thing or another. Trying to kiss Prince Charles, or arriving topless at a movie premiere. She's a weirdo.'

Franklin realised that he had to accept Michael's story at face value, there was nothing else he could do. 'Temper your behaviour from now on, boy,' he warned. 'You have the Ross name to think of.' And Michael left, relieved.

'Keep your eye on him, Karol,' Franklin instructed ten minutes later. 'And get me the girl's side of the story.'

As it turned out, Rebel Waverley's story backed Michael's word for word. 'So I was a bit bombed,' she shrugged. Michael had told her that his grandfather would have her investigated. 'I just thought it was a funny thing to do at the time. Then a journalist friend of mine decided to take it a bit further. No harm done.'

Michael had paid her off handsomely. And the

fact that her head still hurt where he'd ripped at her hair and that she still had a vivid bruise on her shoulder where he'd sunk his teeth into her was a fair enough price to pay for ten thousand dollars, she decided. But she'd certainly never set her sights on Michael Ross again.

Michael had shocked himself that night. When they'd gone into the bedroom together, giggling and teasing each other, he'd had no intention of being so rough with Rebel. But when they were actually doing it and she was moaning and begging for more, he couldn't help himself. Rebel Waverley looked so very like Emma. That's what had attracted him from the outset of the evening. When he was at the peak of his passion, he had wanted her to scream that she loved him. The woman he had worshipped for seven years. 'Love me, love me,' he said over and over as he tore at her hair and sank his teeth into her shoulder. That's when Rebel had pushed him from her and run screaming from the room.

The story never reached the press. The cockney journalist had indeed been after a pay-off, and Rebel's reputation was already as tarnished as Michael had painted to Franklin. But it was a sobering experience for all concerned.

Six months after Emma returned from Paris, an American film unit landed at Nadi Airport on Viti Levu, the main island of Fiji. Michael had decided to play it safe and had chosen Fiji as the major location for *Earth Man* rather than any of the French territories in the Pacific. Given the controversial subject matter of the film, he didn't want to risk incurring the wrath of the French government.

The unit stayed at the capital, Suva, for two days while final arrangements were made and then travelled by boat to Moala Atoll, the chosen location for the scenes depicting Mururoa Atoll prior to the nuclear testings.

As executive producer, Michael didn't accompany them but remained in New York controlling the project's finances. Emma, as associate producer, was put in command of the location shoot.

'You're the one Gireaux trusts,' Michael had instructed. 'You're the one to keep him on side.'

Although Michael had been delighted by Emma's coup in securing Gireaux for the movie, on their one meeting in Paris the two men hadn't got on particularly well. Purely a matter of egos, Emma supposed; they were both supremely confident and used to commanding the top roost.

'Besides,' Michael added when she looked a little dubious, 'you'll have Stanley to back you up and Derek doesn't seem a bad sort of bloke.'

Derek was the English director, approved by both Marcel and Michael. Strangely enough, it had been Marcel's idea to choose the Englishman over several French names which had been suggested. 'A French person may be too biased one way or another,' he said, 'either too guilty or too defensive – who can tell? Derek will be more objective. Besides,' Marcel shrugged a little dismissively, 'he is a typical Englishman, detached, remote. That will work to our advantage with such an emotive theme.' Marcel had made several films with Derek and deeply admired his talent and technique but he didn't particularly like the fellow. No matter, one didn't need to like the people one worked with.

Derek and the crew left for Moala Atoll and Emma and Stanley remained in Suva for a further two days awaiting the arrival of Marcel.

'Emma!' As he came through customs, Marcel spotted her immediately and was effusive in his greeting.

'Marcel,' she said as he kissed her on both cheeks, 'welcome to Fiji. This is Stanley Grahame, one of Ross Entertainments' associate directors – '

'And stunt man extraordinaire,' Marcel added, 'and special effects genius.' He shook Stanley heartily by the hand. 'Your work in *Halley's* and *Blue Water History* was remarkable, my friend.'

'Thank you.' Stanley was taken aback by the man's expansiveness. He'd expected something a little more aloof, a little more grand. But Gireaux obviously didn't intend playing 'star' at all.

During the interminable drive from the airport to Suva, Marcel was in excellent spirits and as engaging as a child on summer holidays.

'Look!' he said. 'Look! We are in paradise.' Palm trees and lush tropical growth flashed past as the cab zoomed along, narrowly avoiding stray cows and goats and dogs. 'I love Fiji. I have been here twice before. Paris is gloomy,' he said. 'Dank and gloomy and oppressive.'

'I'll bet it's not as bad as New York,' Emma

remarked. She was picking up on his mood – indeed, it was difficult not to feel abandoned in Fiji. 'It was snowing when we left. The first day of spring and it was still snowing.'

Marcel, seated beside the driver in the front seat, turned and grinned at Stanley. 'And here we are in Nirvana. And paid to be here! Ah, Mon Dieu,' he corrected himself with a grin, 'you are the producers – I am not supposed to say things like that.'

They laughed and waved out of the windows at the Fijians, who called 'Mbula' as they passed.

'Mbula,' the hotel staff said in welcome when they arrived.

'Mbula,' Marcel replied. He was having a wonderful time.

Marcel Gireaux was not as complex a man as many people perceived him to be. Admittedly he was intelligent, committed and his background was academic, but his very ideals and education were a result of his simple origins.

He came from peasant stock, the son of a fisherman. Although his childhood in Marseilles had been a happy one, he'd aspired to greater things. With the help of his family and a scholarship, he'd attended university, ultimately achieving a PhD in French literature, majoring in the seventeenth century poets and dramatists, and then he'd progressed to his status as a major classical actor. But the peasant boy was always there. The greater the hero he became to his people, the more he realised he could use his status to serve their cause.

He became quite a power in the fight for the rights of the lower classes and, from there, he progressed to the fight for human rights and then to the plight of the environment. They were heady times – particularly when, as a young man, he realised that leaders and politicians were vying for his support.

Marcel's image as a hero of the people was important to him. So was his reputation as France's premier classical actor. Inevitably, the roles became interwoven and there were occasions when he lost touch with reality a little. Just what was a role and what wasn't? It was sometimes difficult to tell.

Not for Annette, his wife. Annette was firmly in touch with reality.

Annette and Marcel had met at university, where she'd topped the law course. She'd seen him through all of his formative years. From an academic middle-class family herself (who had initially opposed her association with Gireaux), Annette was fully aware of the effects of fame upon the peasant boy she loved.

When she saw his roles as an actor and as a leader of the times had become interwoven, she didn't try to disillusion him. Why should she? He was happy, he was serving a purpose, and the fight was a good fight.

But when, after five years and two children, the adulation afforded Marcel posed a threat to her marriage, Annette took a stance. 'Grow up, Marcel,' she said. 'I don't mind if you play the hero off the screen but I will not have you play the lover.'

It was the first time she'd caught him out having an affair with his leading lady. She'd never believed the tabloid and film magazine rumours before but now she wondered whether she should have. Wisely, she didn't press the issue. What had happened had happened. She knew the depth of his love for her and she was prepared to believe that this was the first time.

'I won't have it, Marcel,' she warned. 'I won't have it, you understand me?' Marcel did and, for a year or so, he was terrified into submission. He worshipped Annette and the thought of life without her and his beloved children was more than he could bear. But, eventually, in a remote location, far away from the real world, the adulation of a beautiful young leading lady once again proved too much for him and he became infatuated.

Annette took the children and left him twice over the ensuing five years. Both times, when he begged her forgiveness, she succumbed and their marriage survived. It still survived after a fashion, but it was not the marriage they'd once had. Marcel loved Annette and Annette loved her children and her children loved their father. It was happier for all concerned, she decided, if she turned a blind eye to his odd dalliance. And he was very discreet; he never strayed when he was close to home – he never wanted to. Besides, the discipline of working in the Paris theatre reminded him of his craft and his dedication.

Annette called it 'la folie du filmage' – 'movie madness'. She was aware that it was the suspended reality of filming in exotic locations which affected

Marcel. For those several weeks or months, he genuinely became infatuated with the person and the situation that presented itself.

She remained loyal. She never undermined Marcel's public image, but Annette hardened herself to the fact that her marriage could never be what it once was.

'Have you ever seen anything more beautiful!' It was the following day and Emma, Stanley and Marcel were standing in the bow of the boat as it ploughed its way through the aqua waters of the Koro Sea towards Moala Atoll.

Marcel held his arms out wide and breathed in the balmy heat of the day. 'This is truly heaven on earth.'

Emma breathed in deeply too. He was right. The sea was so clear that she could see through the aquamarine of the water to the white sand below with its dark patches of weed and shimmering sea grasses. The tide was not yet full and, as the skipper skilfully manoeuvred the boat through the surrounding reefs, she marvelled at the vivid coral and neon-coloured fish darting amongst the rich vegetation. Such colours!

Gradually Viti Levu, with its towns and tourists and resorts, slipped away behind them until it was no more than a narrow strip of white sand with silhouettes of tiny palm trees in the distance.

It was a five-hour boat trip to Moala Atoll. Finally, they saw it, low on the horizon. A tiny, lush green outcrop surrounded by coral reef, beckoning to them in its wilderness.

'That would have been what Mururoa Atoll looked like before the testings,' Stanley mused. 'Pretty shocking, isn't it?'

'Shocking?' Marcel turned angrily on the two of them. 'It is obscene! Only man could commit such an atrocity. Do you know that the birds affected by the radiation are rendered infertile? That they make nests and tend eggs which will never hatch? Do you know that the giant sea turtle loses her sense of direction? That when she has laid her eggs and, exhausted, should return to the sea, she heads inland instead and slowly bakes to death?'

Stanley and Emma exchanged a glance. Marcel's eyes burned with all the passion of a zealot.

'I am sorry,' he said as he recovered himself. 'You have researched your film, of course you know all of this – it is just that such a crime makes me angry.' He relaxed and smiled, his mood having dissipated as quickly as it had appeared. 'I shall not lecture you any more, I promise.' He looked about again at the picture postcard surroundings. 'It is far too nice a day.'

The film unit was comfortably ensconced in a small village of prefabricated cabins which had been built on the southern side of the atoll. There were two larger cabins constructed for communal purposes. One was a dining hall and the other a general recreation area which doubled as a viewing room when the film rushes were shown.

There were men's and women's ablution blocks set up and no one complained about the lack of privacy or the fact that Marcel, Emma and Derek had cabins with private amenities. It was accepted that the star, the producer and the director should have superior accommodation. Indeed, Marcel was to be admired for the fact that he hadn't demanded a Winnebago or something equally unrealistic.

It was a happy shoot and a 'family' atmosphere prevailed. After the day's filming, in the heavy dusk while the heat still sat like a blanket over the island, people would 'party hop' from hut to hut. They'd sit together on the small front verandahs of the cabins, chatting about the day's shoot, sipping cold beer and looking out over the darkening Koro Sea.

They were idyllic days. The atmosphere amongst the unit was as peaceful as the surroundings. It was one of those 'magic' shoots, they all agreed, when making movies was a pure joy. Marcel's performance was electric and he was a pleasure to work with, Derek was a skilled director who knew exactly what he was after, and Emma was a thoughtful producer who didn't believe in playing power games or rocking the boat. What more could anyone want?

Every ten days, when the processed rushes arrived from the mainland, there was a flurry of excitement. Not only was it inspiring to see the result of their hard work on film, but it meant 'rage' time. Marcel, Emma, Stanley and Derek would view the rushes the evening they arrived, but the general cast and crew showing was reserved until the following Saturday so that they could really let their hair down and have the

Sunday free to nurse their hangovers. Despite the camaraderie amongst them, it was agreed that they needed an outlet every now and then. The place was so isolated they needed to party hard once in a while.

And party they did. Music blared around the island and they danced and drank and smoked until the early hours of Sunday morning.

Emma and Derek rarely stayed the full pace, often retiring to Emma's cabin where they'd discuss the following week's schedule in the none too sober light of early morning.

Emma liked Derek a great deal and deeply respected the fact that he didn't hold her youth and inexperience as a producer against her. She had expected a director of his calibre to be a little condescending, but he wasn't.

'Why should I be?' he'd asked her when she'd expressed her thanks. 'You're good at your job. Besides,' he'd continued in his clipped English tone, 'you keep Marcel in line.'

Derek was fully aware that Marcel didn't particularly like him, but then he didn't particularly like Marcel either, so what did it matter? So long as the work was done, and done well.

Personally, Derek believed that Marcel had a tendency to overindulge, which was certainly effective in the European films the actor made. For *Earth Man*, however, Derek demanded an economical performance. Marcel was basically in agreement but, on the odd occasion when he wanted to argue – and it was purely because of their temperamental differences, Derek was sure – it was always Emma who kept the peace.

'What do you think, Emma?' Derek had now taken to asking. And, invariably, Emma would find a diplomatic way to agree with his views without undermining those of Marcel. It appeared she had Marcel around her little finger, which certainly made Derek's life a lot easier.

Marcel Gireaux was in love with Emma. He was convinced of it. And it wasn't 'la folie du filmage'. If it were merely movie madness he wouldn't have been so drawn to her in Paris, would he?

He recalled their first meeting, when they'd sat and eaten croissants in the Rue Lafayette and she'd spoken about herself with such candour. He recalled her simple statement, 'I enjoy going to the theatre alone'. And then, that night, backstage, 'You were magnificent,' she'd said. And she'd meant it. Yes, Marcel thought, she had beguiled him then and she was beguiling him now.

He tried to be near her, alone with her, as often as he could. But she was invariably with Stanley or Derek. It was frustrating.

'Would you care to have a drink with me after filming today, Emma?' he would ask. 'Yes, I'd love to,' she'd answer, 'but shall we make it my place? Stanley's coming over.' Or, 'Yes, I'd love to drop in for a drink, Marcel — do you mind if Derek comes too? We have a bit of production business to discuss; I promise it won't take long.' Marcel didn't know what to make of it. Her answers were so ingenuous.

But they weren't ingenuous at all. Emma was fully aware that Marcel was attracted to her and that he wanted to be alone with her. She found it most disconcerting. Surely he didn't want to sleep with her? He was known to be a loyal, happily married man with children. She couldn't believe that he wanted to seduce her, and she didn't want her deep admiration for him to become tarnished. But there was another reason she was disconcerted, another reason she sought not to be alone with him. He was one of the most attractive men she had ever met.

There were only three more weeks to go in Fiji. Then it was back to New York and the city locations. Marcel watched Emma, deep in conversation with Stanley and a couple of others. He watched as Derek came up to them. And he watched as Derek quietly said goodnight and left. Alone.

Emma remained chatting for a while with Stanley. Marcel knew it wouldn't be long before she too left the party. Things were hotting up. The music was loud, the atmosphere was raucous and soon the crowd, exhausted with dance and drink, would gather around for the singalong. That was Marcel's favourite part of the evening. He would invariably lead the troops with his fine baritone voice. Not tonight, he decided, hoping that Stanley wouldn't leave with Emma.

Stanley usually stayed. He played guitar and he enjoyed the singalongs. There were two other guitar players and several excellent singers amongst the crew, and Stanley found that the harmony of voices and instruments and the vivid sunrise over the horizon was an excellent way to round off the night.

Marcel watched as one of the crew members started strumming his guitar in a corner. Several others gathered around him. And then he noticed Emma leave. Quietly he slipped out the rear door of the recreation hut.

She bumped into him accidentally. Or so it appeared.

'Marcel,' she said, surprised. 'Don't tell me you're going home? You're usually one of the stayers.'

'Not tonight,' he answered. 'Tonight I have decided that we must talk. Tonight I will not let you escape me.'

'I'm very tired, Marcel.' Emma's disappointment lent a brusqueness to her tone and she knew it. If she was being rude, then that was just too bad. She'd been right. He was brazenly trying to seduce her while posing as the blissfully happy family man and she didn't approve of his double standards.

She turned to go, but he stood in front of her with one hand upon her arm – not forcefully, but firmly. 'Why do you avoid me, Emma? What is it you think I want of you?'

Emma was in a state of confusion. She was conscious of their closeness. The touch of his hand upon her bare skin was confronting. And she was at an utter loss as to what she was expected to say. How did you tell a man that you thought he was trying to seduce you?

He said it for her. 'You think I wish to make love to you?' Her silence spoke for itself. 'Of course I do. The man who wouldn't wish to make love to you would have to be a fool.' He took his hand from her arm but remained standing in front of her, blocking her way on the narrow path. 'But that is not what I want from you, that is not what I am after. I wish to be your friend. I wish us to talk. Is that so bad?'

Emma was starting to feel a little foolish. Perhaps she had been overdramatic. It was just that the man was so damned attractive and so damned French and such a glamorous movie star and he made her feel so ... Australian, so ... ordinary ... Suddenly, she was angry with herself. Very angry. What the hell was wrong with being Australian and ordinary?

'I'm sorry, Marcel,' she said and boldly took his arm. 'Of course we can be friends. Now, come on, you can walk me home.'

Marcel was a little surprised, but he met her brisk pace as they started walking the several hundred yards towards her cabin. He was further surprised when, at the front door, she invited him in for a drink. He had anticipated asking her to his cabin; he was unaccustomed to women taking the lead. 'Thank you, I would like that,' he agreed.

When Emma had poured him a scotch, she sat back in the little hardbacked chair beside the desk and gestured to the sofa. 'Have a seat, please.' Marcel sat, wishing she would join him on the sofa. 'I'm sorry I insulted you by presuming you wished to seduce me, Marcel. I would like to be your friend, I truly would, I am a great admirer of you and your work.' She sipped her scotch. 'Tell me about your family.'

Marcel looked at her for a second or so before he laughed. She wasn't ridiculing him, she meant it. What an extraordinary young woman she was. He would have preferred to tell her how deeply he loved her, he would have preferred to touch her skin and kiss her lips and hear her moan. But he hadn't been lying when he'd said that seduction was not what he wanted from her, not what he was after. Marcel never seduced a woman who didn't desperately want him back. Her desire – indeed, her adulation – was his aphrodisiac.

Now, as he looked at Emma, he wanted her to like him. He wanted her to smile for him. He wanted her to be his friend. There would be time for her to know that he loved her.

'My family,' he said, 'you wish to know of my family?' And he told her. He spoke glowingly of his beautiful and accomplished wife, Annette. 'I doubt whether I would ever have graduated from university if it had not been for Annette,' he said. And he boasted of his children, the proud boast of a genuinely loving father. It was difficult not to warm to him, Emma thought as she got up to pour them another drink.

'Look, Emma, come and look.' When she turned with the drinks in her hand, he was standing beside the open door admiring the first dawn light to streak the sky. She joined him. 'Only three weeks to go,' he said with a touch of sadness. 'I shall never forget these dawns.'

'Me either,' she agreed as she handed him the drink.

He wanted to add, 'And I shall never forget you.' He longed to take her in his arms and kiss her. But he didn't. 'Tell me about your fiance,' he said, his tone was very gentle. 'He died four years ago?'

'Yes,' Emma answered.

'And there has been no one since?'

She shook her head, not quite trusting herself to speak. She knew the conversation was taking a dangerous turn. She knew she should turn brittle, change the subject, tell him it was time to go, but for some strange reason she wanted to cry. She was probably a bit drunk, she supposed, although she certainly didn't feel it.

'You loved him?' Marcel asked and she wished his voice wasn't quite so warm and attractive and concerned.

'Yes,' she nodded. 'Well, I thought I did at the time. I was very young.' She blinked hard, willing away the threat of tears. It was just the dawn light and the colour of the palm trees and the ocean and the sand, she told herself.

He took her glass from her and she remained staring out across the sea. She supposed she knew what was coming next. Had she been fooling herself? Was this what she'd been hoping for all along? She didn't know any more. His arms were suddenly around her and she didn't know. 'I am very much in love with you, Emma,' he said. And she didn't care. She knew she didn't love him but she knew she wanted him and as his arms encircled her and his mouth found hers, her body screamed to be touched. For four long years she'd denied her sexuality and now she ached with desire. She ached to be kissed and caressed and to feel their bodies become one. She opened her mouth and returned his kiss as hungrily as he gave it.

After Marcel had gently stroked her cheek and told her once again that he loved her, Emma watched him quietly slip out the back door to make his way, unobserved, through the palm trees and ferns to his own cabin higher up the hill.

She lay staring at the low wooden ceiling but not seeing it, aware of the gentle hum of the fan in the corner and the movement of the air it created, as the artificial breeze caressed her naked body. She tried to feel guilty, but she couldn't. Not just yet. She rolled over and let the fan caress her buttocks and back. She felt too sated, too content, to suffer guilt just yet. Marcel was a wonderful lover – she'd never experienced such a lack of inhibition in herself.

She recalled how she'd moaned as his mouth moved gently down from her breasts, to her belly, to her mound. How she'd parted her legs and watched as his head nuzzled between her thighs and how she'd tensed and held her breath as she felt his tongue, gentle at first, then persistent, then defiant, demanding her to lose control. And she had. On and on, the waves of pleasure had engulfed her. And just when she thought she could take no more, he entered her and the exquisite process started all over again until Marcel himself could take no more and they quivered on the brink together. Emma recalled her own cries of ecstasy mingling with his as she clung fiercely to him.

Had that really been her? she wondered as she listened to the hum of the fan. Her lovemaking with Malcolm O'Brien had never been so prolonged, so abandoned. Had she been starved for sex, or was it simply the fact that Marcel Gireaux was a superb lover?

The truth was, Marcel was only as good a lover as his partner wanted him to be. When a woman wholeheartedly gave herself to him, the exercise of his control was the greatest source of delight to Marcel. He had sensed it was the first time Emma had given herself so completely and her response had been inspiring. He had revelled in her sexuality as much as she had in his.

Marcel lay on the bunk in his cabin staring up at his own wooden ceiling and feeling the breeze from his own corner fan. He could think of nothing but Emma. The feel of her, the smell of her. He thought not only of her sexuality but of her voice, her laugh, her refreshing honesty. His love for her consumed him. And she loved him back, he knew she did.

So certain was he of their mutual love that he was puzzled by her reaction to him later that evening during the Sunday dinner in the recreation hut. He realised that they must keep their affair secret – it was the tasteful and considerate thing to do. But there were ways to flash hidden messages of love and lust, and Emma was doing none of these.

He looked at her across the table as she accepted

the glass of mineral water Derek poured for her before resuming her conversation with Stanley.

Sunday evening mealtimes were always a laid-back affair. Many were nursing hangovers and everyone went to bed early in preparation for the first of the week's dawn shoots.

Apart from her normal friendly greeting Emma had paid him virtually no attention during the meal. He understood, of course, but . . .

'You don't need to play it quite so cool,' he smiled.

He had once again bumped into her 'accidentally' as she left the recreation hut, and he started walking with her to her cabin.

Emma said nothing until they reached the front door.

'May I come in?' he asked.

'No, Marcel, you may not,' she answered. Not rudely, not even curtly, she hoped, but definitely. She didn't want any arguments.

Emma's lack of guilt had not lasted long. As the day had progressed, she'd thought of Marcel's wife and children and of the facade he presented to the world. Did he do this often? she wondered. No matter whether he did or not, she told herself, it was up to her to end it. Now. Now, while there was nothing more between them than an indulgent night of lust on a South Pacific island during a film shoot. Just a night of fantasy, that's all it had been, she told herself. And that was all it must remain. Marcel was an attractive and desirable man and a liaison between them was far too dangerous to contemplate. Not only dangerous in the hurt it could bring to his wife and family, but . . .

Exactly, she thought, don't kid yourself that you're being totally noble, Emma – face it, it's been a long time and you're vulnerable. Particularly to a world-famous sex symbol and movie idol.

That was when she was jolted back to reality. That was when, in an instant, her resolve was strengthened. She was the producer, for God's sake! What the hell did she think she was up to, screwing the star? It was grubby and tacky and, although many did it, she wasn't that sort of producer and she knew she'd feel utterly humiliated if word got out and the crew thought that she was.

'You may not come in,' she repeated firmly. 'I'm sorry.'

Marcel was staring at her, dumbfounded. 'But I love you,' he said. 'You love me.'

'No I don't,' she replied and now there was a curt edge to her tone. She needed to get rid of him as quickly as possible – her body was starting to respond to the nearness of him. 'And you don't love me.'

She continued quickly before he could interrupt. 'I'm happy to remain your friend – I'd like to remain your friend, Marcel – but that's all there is between us, you have to understand that.'

She didn't wait for an answer but stepped inside the cabin and closed the door behind her, leaning against it waiting to hear his departing footsteps. It was several minutes before she did and, when he finally started up the path towards his own cabin, she breathed a sigh of relief. Or was it a sigh of regret? she wondered momentarily.

Whatever – that was it. But she didn't sleep well that night as she remembered how his hands had caressed her body, and the way his tongue had driven her wild.

For the remaining weeks of the shoot, Marcel didn't appear to be himself. Everyone commented on it. He was moody and irritable, not at all the amenable, easy-going actor to whom they'd grown accustomed. He was behaving more like the star they'd expected in the first place. Oh well, it had been a long shoot and, despite the beauty of the location, everyone was beginning to miss home and family. It was to be expected, they supposed.

Marcel was in torment. He tried many times to talk privately with Emma but she always avoided him and, on the odd occasion when he did manage to find her alone, the answer was always the same: 'Leave it, Marcel. It's over.' He was teased beyond endurance. This had not happened to him before. Was she playing games with him?

He had never forced himself upon a woman and he had no intention of starting now, but on the last night of the shoot when the party was at its height, he left early and waited for Emma outside her front door.

He was sitting on the verandah, swinging his legs in the moonlight, when she walked up the path. The sound of the revellers was still loud in the night. It was close and humid, a tropical storm was threatening and the very air hung heavily upon her skin.

She knew the moment she saw him that she was going to weaken. She'd been so strong. Oh shit, she thought, don't do this to me, it's not fair. But it was the last night on the island and she knew she couldn't resist him.

Send him away, one part of her brain said, he'll go if you ask him.

Then the memories of their lovemaking flooded her mind and her body made the decision for her.

What the hell, she thought. This was their last night on a desert island together, a woman could only hold out so long, for God's sake.

'Emma, I had to see you. I – '

She threw caution to the wind. 'Come in, Marcel.' She opened the door, took him by the hand and, to his astonishment, all but dragged him inside the hut. He'd been prepared to get down on his bended knees, to beg her to let him love her. But before she'd even closed the door, she was kissing him and touching him and pulling off his clothes.

Emma abandoned herself completely. The very elements were on her side, she thought. The storm broke over the island and the wind lashed and the palm trees clashed and the ocean swept itself into a frenzy. And, all through the fury, sweat mingling and skin sliding wet against skin, Emma gave herself up to her pleasure.

When they returned to Viti Levu the next day, the air washed clean by the overnight storm, Marcel was in high spirits. He even told Derek that he was looking forward to working in New York. Marcel loathed New York, he always had. But Emma was going to be there. She loved him, he was sure of it – just as he loved her.

Everyone was pleased that Marcel's enthusiasm had returned. His ill-humour had infected the entire company but, in true good-natured style, they forgave him. He'd become bored with the island, that was all. After several months they all had; it was perfectly understandable.

Emma was aware of the reason for Marcel's buoyancy and her guilt returned tenfold. She cursed herself for her weakness. She didn't love him, she knew it. And, despite his protestations, she was convinced that he didn't love her. What was it he'd said to her? 'This is not la folie du filmage, Emma. I love you. I love you deeply.'

'Movie madness' – what a perfect term, she thought. And she tried to put her guilt behind her. New York would sort everything out, she told herself. Michael would be there and he was a hard taskmaster.

Ahead of them lay the final three-week shoot culminating in the scenes of the motorcade through the streets of the city. The orchestration of the motorcade would be the most intricate and difficult sequence of the entire film – the whole of New York celebrating the triumph of the 'Earth Man' and the redemption of the planet. Yes, it would be a busy time, Emma told herself. There would certainly be no place for movie madness.

* * *

517

'We have to rethink the end of the movie, the motorcade,' Michael said. 'It'll be limp, it'll wimp out, there'll be no finale. We need more dramatic impact.'

It was conference time. They were seated around the boardroom table. Michael, Emma, and Stanley. Mandy was taking notes as usual and the only stranger in their midst was Derek. They'd viewed the rushes shot on Moala Atoll, together with the fortnight of city scenes they'd just finished shooting on location in New York.

'We're running the risk of being too complacent,' Michael argued. 'So the "Earth Man's" won. So what? Too much the happy ending. Too smug.'

Derek was nodding. 'Yes, there is that danger,' he agreed. 'We're lacking conflict at the end of the film, but how do we combat that?'

'We martyr him, that's what we do,' Michael said. 'We kill him off.'

They stared at him. All four of them. 'We kill him?' Emma asked finally. 'We kill the "Earth Man"?'

Michael nodded. 'Yep,' was all he said.

'How? How the hell do we kill him?' Stanley queried.

'And why?' Derek added.

'I told you. Martyrdom. He's assassinated by an extremist group – he dies for his beliefs. Good stuff.'

'It's a total change of script.' Derek looked thoughtful. The idea was certainly intriguing.

'We'd better check it out with Marcel,' Emma added. 'He might not like it.'

518

'He'll love it,' Michael said scathingly. 'His ego won't be able to resist it.' He looked at Derek, who nodded in agreement.

'I think we should let Emma break the news though,' Derek suggested. 'Just in case. Marcel will do anything she says.'

'Yes, very well,' Michael answered curtly. 'You tell him, Emma. This afternoon.'

Michael had made it very apparent that he didn't approve of Marcel's obvious crush on Emma. 'God Almighty, Emma, you couldn't be interested in someone like Gireaux, surely!' he'd exploded when he'd sensed, to his horror, a chemistry between them. 'The man's a poseur and a womaniser.'

'I'm *not* interested in him,' Emma protested. Although she didn't agree with Michael's dismissive view of Marcel, she was taken aback by his perception. There was an element of the poseur and womaniser in Marcel, certainly, an element few people recognised. But he wasn't the fake that Michael thought he was. He was simply a man who took his passions very seriously. He embraced his women and his causes with equal fervour and, like a kid in a candy shop, he didn't know how to be selective or where to stop.

She had told him as much when he'd come up to her apartment late at night having threatened, through the intercom, to ring every apartment bell in the block if she didn't let him in.

'But I love you,' he'd said when she'd once again refused him. That was when she'd lost her temper.

'You're behaving like a spoilt child, Marcel,' she said, exasperated. 'Just because you want something, that doesn't mean to say it's yours. You don't love me.' Before he could launch into his protestations, she carried on. 'And if you do, you bloody well shouldn't. I don't love you,' she continued patiently. 'You're a beautiful man, but I don't love you. Practise a little self-restraint, Marcel. Grow up. This isn't Fiji any more, this is the real world.'

She seemed to get through to him that night. They sat and had a drink and he apologised for harassing her.

'It is not normal for me to make a nuisance of myself with a woman,' he said sadly with as much dignity as he could muster. Emma wanted to laugh but she didn't. She felt a genuine affection for Marcel. Beneath the talent and the sexuality and the charisma and everything that impressed his legions of fans, there really was an indulgent little boy.

She saw him down to the front door of the apartment block and couldn't resist a teasing whisper as he left.

'Starting tomorrow, we play grown-ups, all right?'

But he didn't smile back. 'I love you and you mock me,' he said. 'That is cruel.'

'No, it isn't,' she answered. 'A bit of mockery now and then does you the world of good. You don't get enough of it. Oh, cheer up, Marcel,' she said and she patted his cheek gently. 'Friends, remember? I'll always be your friend. And I'll always remember Fiji. I promise.' She kissed him lightly on the cheek. 'Now go home and go to bed.'

As Michael and Derek had anticipated, Marcel was in favour of the assassination of the 'Earth Man'. He was more than in favour, he was delighted with the suggestion. 'Excellent. What a scene we will have, eh? The death of a hero. A man who gives his life to save the world.'

Emma was pleased that the idea was appealing enough to distract Marcel from his melancholy. He'd been irritable and depressed since she'd convinced him that their shortlived affair was over. Now he could finish the movie on a high and, within a week, he would be back with Annette and the children.

Michael paid a fortune for the motorcade. Bugger Franklin's modest budget, he thought, and forked out his own money to cover the massive scale of the scene. He paid a huge amount to the New York Film and Television Office for location rights to vast areas of the inner city and, although Captain Matthew (Mac) Macfarlane, Commander in Charge of the Police and Citizens Liaison Unit, insisted that the PCLU was proud to be a part of such a worthy project, a sizeable amount ended up in his pocket as well.

'It's an epic scene,' Michael insisted. 'Historic.' And he showed old footage of John Glenn and the first American astronauts as they were paraded through the streets of New York. 'That's what I want,' he said. And that's what he was going to get.

The streets were to be closed off to traffic and

the scene shot in the dawn light but Michael gave the story to the press to ensure that there would be thousands of people lining the pavements to watch not only the pomp and ceremony, but 'the greatest European star of them all, Marcel Gireaux'.

And thousands there were bound to be. 'Mac' wasn't too happy about it. 'This wasn't part of the bargain,' he said when the story hit the papers. 'We'll need crowd control. I thought you just wanted the streets closed off.' But Michael made sure it was worth Mac's while.

The week before the actual parade, Derek filmed the segments of the scene involving the assassin.

The motorcade was to proceed from upper Manhattan down 5th Avenue on its way to the United Nations building. It would never get there, of course, because the assassination was to take place on central 5th Avenue. After a short search, Michael had decided that the ideal location for the assassin was the rooftop of the Frick Museum on the corner of 5th and 70th.

The Frick Collection was housed in the former residence of Henry Clay Frick, a gracious two-storey stone mansion built in 1913. There was a wide roof area with plenty of space to set up a film unit and, not only was it a perfect vantage spot for a would-be assassin, the building itself would look superb on film. It was without doubt the ideal location and, having gained permission and generously greased the right palms, Michael gave Derek the go-ahead.

Several days later, Michael sat back in the

viewing room and watched the rushes. Derek had done well, as had the director of photography and the actor. It was an effective sequence. The man on the Frick mansion rooftop. The perfect view overlooking 5th Avenue. The Heckler and Koch .308 sniper rifle, the military model, with bi-pod and Bisley 20x80 telescopic sight.

The man methodically and painstakingly setting up his equipment and making himself comfortable, very much the way a birdwatcher might. The man settling himself in for the long wait, everything prepared.

Then the man's reaction as the quarry came into view and he positioned himself for the kill. Then the careful sighting. No rush. Then the gentle easing back of the trigger. And then the man packing away his equipment as methodically as he had assembled it.

Cut in with the master shots and the close-ups of the parade it would look superb. Michael was pleased with the rushes. A member of the crew had paraded around the block a number of times standing up in an open car so that the eyeline of the actor playing the assassin would look correct in the editing. And of course there would be a marvellous soundtrack to accompany the suspense. It was all looking very good.

The day of the parade dawned bright and clear. It was going to be hot. But the light was perfect and they would finish filming well before the fierce heat of the New York summer hit.

The press announcements had served their

purpose. Despite the early hour, thousands of people lined 5th Avenue, a particularly dense crowd gathering around the Frick Gallery. And the media were everywhere – photographers, journalists and television crews from the various news and current affairs programmes. Michael was delighted. It was a publicity coup – the exposure was going to be fantastic.

They filmed the start of the procession at the top of 5th Avenue, Marcel looking resplendent as he stood in the open limousine waving to the crowds, occasionally making the victory sign and acknowledging the flowers that were thrown high in the air to land on the bonnet or in the vehicle itself. Every now and then he'd catch one and the crowd would roar its approval.

They stopped filming for half an hour while the cameras were set up by the Frick Gallery to cover the assassination. Derek was using five cameras, four to film the wide shot of the procession and one to concentrate on the close-ups of Marcel.

Michael, Emma and Mandy stood on one of the gallery balconies beside the cameraman covering the close-ups. They watched as Derek gave his final instructions through a two-way radio to his assistant director, who was with the waiting motorcade a block up the street. 'Standing by,' he said finally and signalled one by one to the cameramen covering the wide shots. One by one the cameramen signalled back. Derek looked towards the cameraman covering the close-ups. The cameraman nodded. 'Action,' Derek said into the walkie-talkie and the motorcade started its slow procession towards the Frick Gallery.

The extras amongst the crowd whipped the onlookers into a frenzy. People cheered energetically and waved the flags and threw the flowers and streamers that the film unit had handed around. Marcel saluted them, acknowledging the tribute. Stanley, in his role as bodyguard to the 'French Ambassador', was travelling in the vehicle behind Marcel's. When the shot rang out, he was to leap from his car into Marcel's and throw his body over that of the mortally wounded 'Earth Man'.

Closer and closer came the motorcade, led by four motorcycle police and two cars. They crossed 71st Street. The motorcyclists passed by the Frick Gallery and over 70th Street. The two cars passed by. Then the Earth Man. Marcel, smiling, waving, acknowledging the victory and the cheers of the crowd. The vehicle was directly in front of the Gallery. A shot rang out, clear in the early morning air. Marcel fell back onto the car seat.

To Emma it looked effective. It looked as if all had gone according to plan.

But then she heard the cameraman whose zoom lens was focused on Marcel. 'Oh my God, oh Jesus, oh my God!' She watched dumbfounded as he fell to his knees in a state of shock.

People in the crowd closest to the motorcade were screaming. Emma saw Stanley leap from the following vehicle into Marcel's car but it wasn't the way they'd rehearsed. He was yelling at nearby police and pointing up at the Frick building. He was also screaming at the driver to pull the vehicle out of the procession and up onto the footpath. Something's gone wrong, Emma thought. Something's gone terribly wrong.

It was on the news later that day. Marcel Gireaux had been shot through the head. Assassinated by a person or persons unknown while filming a sequence in his latest movie, *Earth Man.*

CHAPTER FOURTEEN

ON THE MORNING OF the procession, many of the people living in the block on the corner of 70th and 5th had invited friends up to their apartments. It was the perfect vantage spot – the newspapers had reported that the 'assassination' was to be filmed from the rooftop of the Frick Gallery.

The commissionaire had his time cut out buzzing up to everyone's apartment to get a clearance on each of the visitors. No names were recorded. 'A Mr Harris to see you, Mr Weinberg,' was one in dozens of requests.

'Thanks, Norman. Send him up.'

The man Judd let into his apartment was neatly dressed in a polo-necked sweater and sports jacket and carrying a briefcase. He could have been a business executive on a Saturday appointment when suit and tie were not mandatory.

'Mr Harris, isn't it?' Judd said jovially. 'Come – ' The man was inside the room and the door closed before Judd could offer the invitation. He thought it was rather rude. 'My name's Judd,' he beamed and he held out his

527

hand, expecting the man to offer his Christian name. The man offered neither name nor hand, but walked over to the front windows and looked down through the curtains at 5th Avenue. Then he walked through the door to the right, the room in the very corner of the apartment. It was the bathroom and it looked over 70th Street, the Frick Gallery and up 5th Avenue.

Well, if he wanted to go to the bathroom, Judd thought, why didn't he just say? He waited until the man came out of the bathroom, no longer carrying the briefcase, and was about to offer him a drink, but didn't get the chance. 'Thank you,' the man said curtly. 'That will be all – I don't need you.'

'Oh.' Judd wasn't due at Felicity's apartment, which was only one floor down, for another fifteen minutes or so. He'd expected to have a drink with the chap. It was only hospitable, after all. 'Are you sure you wouldn't. . .'

'You may go now.'

'Oh. Right.' Bloody rude, Judd thought. Still, it was a business arrangement, after all, and if leaving the chap the apartment for an hour meant clearing a fifty thousand dollar debt, who was he to argue? Besides, the man didn't look like the sort of person one would want to argue with. Eerie sort of guy. His speech was accentless; it was impossible to tell where he was from. He was of average height and weight, but obviously fit. He moved effortlessly, like a boxer or a dancer, with the lazy grace of a person whose body was prepared for anything. And, although the pale grey eyes didn't dart about, it was apparent he was taking in every detail of his surrounds.

'Well, I'll leave you to it then.'

'Take your key,' the man reminded him. Judd picked his keys up from the hall table and made as dignified an exit as he could.

An hour later, when the shot rang out and all hell broke loose, Judd felt sick. Could this have anything to do with the man in his apartment? All he could see from Felicity's window was pandemonium. 'Binoculars,' he snapped, 'give me your binoculars.' Felicity wasn't used to being snapped at and certainly not by Judd. 'Hurry it up, woman.' He snatched the binoculars she sulkily handed to him and focused on the car which had been driven up onto the pavement. Marcel Gireaux was slumped in the back seat and a man was beside him screaming orders to the police who were racing towards the Frick Gallery. He focused on Marcel Gireaux's head, but there didn't seem to be one. Just blood, masses and masses of blood and . . . Judd dropped the binoculars, turned away and started to vomit, all over one of Felicity's Persian rugs.

Judd's heart was pounding as he let himself into his apartment. Not with fear for his own safety – he knew the man wouldn't be there. It was pounding with horror at what he'd seen, and with terror at his involvement in the whole ghastly business.

He looked around the apartment. There was no trace of the man. He went into the bathroom. The window was open two inches just as he always left it and the chintz curtains were flapping gently in the breeze just as they always did.

He didn't dare look down at the street below. Could he just pretend that this had never happened? That's what he was expected to do, wasn't he? Of course he was. It had never happened; the man had never been there – he must put it out of his mind. He'd witnessed something horrific, certainly, but then so had many others. He'd had nothing to do with it. There had been no man in his apartment. That was the part he must forget.

He drank half a bottle of scotch that afternoon and had the presence of mind to ring Felicity and apologise for the rug. Then he read and listened to music. In the evening, he didn't send out for the paper or turn on the news as was his habit. He took two Nembutal instead.

The next morning he'd nearly convinced himself that it had all been a bad dream. Then he made the mistake of turning on the television. There it was, graphic footage of the horror he'd witnessed. He needed a brandy. He took the bottle of Hennessy XO from the cabinet, poured himself a healthy measure into a whisky glass and gulped it down greedily. He looked back at the television set. Oh God, the images were still there. He went into the bathroom, opened the window and looked out. It had happened from here, he told himself. It had happened from here.

It was then that he noticed the brandy balloon, rinsed and left to drain upside down on the bathroom shelf. And he remembered that the Hennessy XO had been unopened yesterday. Ready cash was short these days and he'd been saving it for a special occasion.

He picked up the brandy balloon and stood staring out of the window at the street below. This was what the man had done yesterday, he thought. The man had stood right where he was now, looked out of this same window, held this same brandy snifter in his hand. And he'd quietly sipped twenty-year-old cognac while he watched and waited. Judd wondered whether he'd finished the brandy and rinsed the glass before or after he'd . . .

He slammed the window shut. He took two tranquillisers and then he picked up the telephone receiver. He had to talk to someone. He looked back at the television set as he dialled. The ghastly pictures were no longer there but the news item was still on the murder of Marcel Gireaux. A reporter was harassing a senior police officer in the street outside police headquarters. 'Captain Mac-farlane, can you explain how. . .'

Come on, come on, Judd thought as he heard the bell ringing at the other end of the line. It took him three telephone calls over the period of an hour to get through. By then his nerves were strained beyond endurance. 'Wait there,' he was told. 'Just sit tight and everything'll be fine.'

It wasn't long before the parcel arrived, delivered by special courier. Judd opened it. Inside the heavy packaging was an hermetically sealed syringe and a small plastic bag containing one ounce of heroin.

He looked at it for a full ten minutes and started

to sweat. Judd had been off the hard stuff for over a year now. But it took him only ten minutes to make a decision. It was what he needed. Just one good hit to take his mind off things, to clear his brain of the awful images.

The death of Judd Weinberg III, only son of one of America's most prominent financiers, would have been news five years before. But Judd Senior had been in retirement for nearly six years now and, to those who knew his son, death by heroin overdose came as no great surprise. Judd had been flirting with hard drugs for so many years now that it had really only been a matter of time. There was a small byline in several of the papers, but that was all they could afford to run. Every centimetre of space was taken up by the murder of Marcel Gireaux. Even the coincidence of the apartment block on the corner of 70th and 5th barely rated a mention.

The assassination of Marcel Gireaux continued to make headlines and monopolise television screens all around the world. There was footage to cover every angle – from the gruesome impact of the bullet which had blown Marcel's head away to the crowd hysteria and the ghoulish news crews scrambling to film the bloody scene.

The police were in chaos. Where had the bullet come from? This hadn't been expected. They were there to govern crowd control. This was a movie, for Chrissakes. If an assassination had been even a remote possibility the secret service would have been there. And the intelligence division.

On Stanley's instructions, several officers had raced towards the Frick building while others tried to stem the spreading panic. The emergency squad was called in and the gallery was surrounded, but no trace of the assassin could be found.

Ballistic tests later showed that the shot could not have been fired from the rooftop of the Frick Gallery. The weapon had been aimed from a greater height and the bullet had entered Gireaux's head from more of a frontal angle. It was deduced that the assassin must have fired from one of the upper apartments or from the rooftop of the block on the opposite corner of 70th and 5th.

The newspapers, which were quick to publish the findings, further concluded that the assassin or assassins had been in the pay of some extremist group who opposed what Gireaux stood for. Marcel Gireaux had died the way he had lived, they announced dramatically. Playing a role. And his final role had been that of a martyr to his cause.

The inquest was two weeks later. They all attended: Michael, Emma, Stanley, Derek, Mandy, even Franklin Ross. And Annette Gireaux was there.

Emma watched her. She was a handsome woman, despite the fact that her face showed great fatigue. Her eyes mirrored the strain she was under but she was strong, obviously determined not to give in to her grief.

The findings of the inquest were just as the newspapers had hypothesised. Marcel Gireaux had been shot down by a person or persons unknown. There was no link with the film he had been making. But the judge was quick to voice his disapproval of the fact that the publicity surrounding the film had obviously afforded the assassin information and accessibility.

As they left the courtroom, Annette walked straight up to Emma and introduced herself.

'I am Annette Gireaux,' she said, but didn't offer her hand.

'How do you do,' Emma replied. 'I'm Emma Clare.'

'Yes, I know. The writer. Marcel spoke of you.'

'I'm so sorry,' Emma said. 'It's a terrible thing. I don't know what to – '

'There is no leading lady in *Earth Man*.'

Annette's eyes were drilling into hers and Emma had no idea what it was she was expected to say. 'No.'

'Marcel always worked opposite a leading lady. This time it was opposite sea turtles and gulls and terns. One wonders what he got up to during all that time on an island in the South Pacific.'

Still Emma didn't know what to say. But Annette saved her the trouble. 'Did you sleep with my husband?' she asked.

'No.' Nothing in Emma's face betrayed the lie. And yet she had never knowingly lied in her life before. Even the fibs, the 'white lies' of her childhood, had caught her out. She'd always become flustered and confused by deception. Now, all of a sudden, it was so easy. Why?

It was the pain inside Annette Gireaux which made it easy. Behind the bold challenge in the woman's eyes was the desperate plea to know that her husband had belonged to her at the end. And he had, Emma thought – so where was the lie? He'd always belonged to Annette. Annette and her children. What had two nights of lust meant in the scheme of things? What had Marcel's infatuation meant? 'La folie du filmage' – that's all it had been. And as soon as he'd returned to his home he would have recognised it himself.

'No, I didn't sleep with your husband,' she said. 'But we talked a great deal. A lot about work, but mainly about you and the children. He loved you very much.'

Annette held her gaze. It was a test. But Emma didn't flinch from it. Why should she? She was telling the truth. And Annette knew it.

'Yes, he did.' The smile was tight, strained. Maybe, deep inside, Annette sensed there had been something between Marcel and Emma, but she also sensed that this young woman was telling the truth and relief flooded through her. For the first time since she had received the news of Marcel's death, she wanted to weep. She wanted to cry for her dear peasant boy. Her dear foolish, self-deluding child of a man. If only he hadn't believed the roles he'd played – if only he hadn't let the world believe them – he'd be alive today. But then he wouldn't have been her Marcel, would he? Annette knew she had to leave. Before the tears.

She offered her hand. 'Thank you.' The handshake was firm, businesslike. 'I must be going,' she said and she turned and walked briskly down the marble-floored corridor before Emma could say another word.

'Irresponsible, Michael. The judge said as much.' Franklin had requested that Michael accompany him to his office after the inquest. It was more of an order than a request. 'The story should never have been given to the newspapers.'

'Why not, for Christ's sake?' Michael had found the inquest interminable despite the three uppers he'd taken that morning so he'd snorted a hefty line towards the end of the day's court proceedings. He was still on a high and not in the mood for a Franklin Ross lecture.

'One of the world's leading actors was placed in jeopardy, that's why not,' Franklin barked. 'And he was *murdered*, that's why not. The publicity surrounding the filming afforded the assassin accessibility – they were the judge's very words. It was damned irresponsible of you.'

'I don't agree, Grandfather. Surely I can't be held responsible for every crazy zealot running around New York City.'

Michael had continued to call Franklin 'Grandpa' well into his adult years – it was a measure of his affection. He no longer did so. His grandfather's constant disapproval had placed a strain on their relationship and Michael was tired of having to continually monitor his behaviour, tired of being treated like a child. The fondness he'd felt towards the old man was a thing of the past.

Franklin was aware of this, and it saddened

him. Apart from Helen, Michael was the most important thing in his life. Nevertheless he could not relax his authority over the boy. Michael had to learn to discipline his actions.

'The "crazy zealot" to whom you so glibly refer would never have been afforded such a perfect opportunity if you hadn't gone public,' he growled. 'It was – '

'I know: irresponsible – you've already said it twice. But the deed is done, Grandfather. It can't be undone.' Michael wasn't going to let the old man get away with it this time. He wasn't going to say 'Sorry, Grandfather' and look penitent. He knew it was what was expected of him. But not this time. This time he was going to come out on top.

'And just think of what it'll do for business,' he said eagerly. 'The movie will skyrocket.' He was rewarded by the look of sudden shock in Franklin's eyes. It took a lot to shock Franklin Ross. Michael felt a surge of power. 'It was a regrettable incident, I agree,' he added. 'But you've always said yourself, Grandfather – when an opportunity offers itself, it's foolish not to take advantage of it.'

Franklin stared at him, appalled. He said nothing. 'For the past two weeks,' Michael continued, with a glint of madness in his eyes, 'every news, current affairs and chat show has been airing footage of Marcel's murder. It's the death of the decade, the death that shocked a nation – as big as Kennedy's. If I can speed up post-production it'll still be headline news by the time we premiere Earth Man ... '

It was true the media exposure of Marcel's death had reached epic proportions. The gruesome footage had been shown so often that even the milder chat shows were cashing in on it under the guise of human kindness. Was it fair on the actor's family and friends, they debated, to show such horrific film? And then, to up their ratings, they themselves showed the same footage.

The whole thing had become a tasteless circus and even those closely connected and deeply committed to the making of *Earth Man* were shocked when Michael demanded they speed up post-production so the film could premiere while the topic was still hot.

'I think we should do exactly the opposite, Michael,' Emma argued. 'I think we should postpone the film a year as a gesture of respect.'

Stanley agreed. 'It's sick to cash in on it,' he said.

Even Derek, whose career would skyrocket with the movie's success, was in agreement.

Only Mandy was on Michael's side. 'I think Michael's right,' she said. 'This is a business, after all. We have to do what's best for the movie.' It was no secret that Mandy idolised Michael.

He grinned at her, pleased by the support. She was a feisty little thing. 'I respect your humanitarian instincts,' he said to the others, 'but we're speeding up post-production – and that's an order.' The smile vanished and the voice hardened. 'I want this movie released by March in time for the Academy Awards.'

Emma looked at Michael. What was happening to him? There was a madness in him these days.

It was no longer the craziness of creative genius, it was the destructive madness of a megalomaniac.

Now Franklin was looking at Michael in the same way. What had gone wrong with the boy? He was sick. Was it the drugs that had done it? 'I strongly disapprove of your using this tragic event to in any way promote your film,' he said evenly. 'But I take it my disapproval means nothing to you.'

'No, Grandfather, it doesn't.'

Franklin nodded curtly. End of interview. And when Michael had left the room he pressed the intercom buzzer. 'Get hold of Karol Mankowski,' he said to his secretary. 'I want him in here immediately.' Franklin did not intend to give up on Michael yet. Karol must intensify the surveillance, he must use every means at his disposal. If Michael's mind was becoming deranged through drug abuse then they must prove it and get him committed as soon as possible. It was the best thing for the boy. Franklin's only grandson was not going to go off the rails if there was any way he could prevent it.

Michael felt elated when he left Franklin's office. He'd stood up to the old man at long last. He'd even shocked him and he remembered with pleasure the revulsion in Franklin's eyes as he'd spoken of 'the death of the decade'.

The truth would have shocked the old bastard even more, Michael thought, and he could have laughed out loud. Jesus, the truth would probably kill him. Not that anybody would ever know it of course, which was a pity in a way. It had all been so very clever. Easy too. Surprisingly easy.

It had been easy for them to persuade Marcel that the 'Earth Man' should die a martyr's death. Well, they hadn't had to persuade him at all, had they? Emma had done it for them. Michael remembered Derek's words – 'Marcel will do anything she says'.

Of course Marcel would do anything Emma said, Michael had thought impatiently at the time, they were lovers, weren't they? At night, when Michael was lying awake thinking of Emma, or when he was driving himself into a woman's body fantasising it was Emma's, Marcel was doing the real thing. It was Marcel who was caressing Emma's breasts, it was Marcel for whom Emma was parting her thighs, it was Marcel's name Emma was crying out in the heat of her passion.

Michael had suspected it when they'd first come back from Fiji. He remembered the night he'd followed Marcel and seen him go up to Emma's apartment where he stayed for nearly two hours. When he'd seen her kiss him goodnight at the front door, he'd known it was true. And the knowledge had tormented him.

They were clever at keeping their assignations a secret; he hadn't been able to catch them out again, but he knew they were doing it. Emma denied the affair, of course, and he didn't dare force the issue for fear of alienating her but his mind screamed to him each night as the images of them together infected his brain with the demons of madness.

There was only one way out. Marcel had to die. Just as Malcolm O'Brien had had to die. If Michael couldn't possess Emma, then no one else could. And, once the decision was made, it was amazing how quickly the torment disappeared. Michael even felt sorry for Marcel. It was a pity and a waste, but it had to happen.

Even the way it had to happen was easy. Judd Weinberg III. Judd's widowered father had left him a luxury apartment in the block on the corner of 70th and 5th and Judd was very much in debt to Michael. Of course Judd was in debt to a lot of people, which was why his father had so totally given up on him. 'Good money after bad,' Judd Senior had said when he'd settled his son's debts for the third time. 'You can have the apartment on 70th and 5th, boy, and that's the last you'll get out of me.' And Judd Weinberg II had retired from the banking business and moved to Switzerland with his secretary who was thirty years his junior.

His wastrel son had continued to throw good money after bad, mainly in support of his drug habit. Which was how he'd got into debt with Michael.

When Michael had first arrived in New York, he'd been impressed by Judd's aristocratic lineage, the luxury apartment and the apparently endless supply of 'old money', and he'd believed Judd's request for a loan was perfectly valid. 'Just to tide me over for six months, old man. My money's all tied up till the end of the fiscal year.'

It was a hefty amount, but worth it to Michael. Judd Weinberg III was an excellent introduction to many an elite New York circle. Now, three years later, with accrued interest, the amount was even heftier and Judd was more than happy to grant a simple favour to Michael in order to cancel the debt.

'The key to your apartment for an hour, Judd, that's all,' he said. 'A friend of mine wants to watch the movie procession from a good vantage spot.'

'Anything to oblige, old man,' Judd had agreed hastily. 'I'll lay breakfast on if you like.'

'No, he wants to watch it on his own,' Michael said. 'It should be very impressive – why don't you watch it yourself? You'd have an excellent view from your girlfriend's apartment.' He knew Judd was screwing the middle-aged widow on the next floor down.

Judd didn't like Michael's tone and the sugges-tion sounded very much like an order to him, but there wasn't much he could do about it. 'Good idea,' he smiled.

Michael knew that, after the event, he could always pretend that he'd wanted Judd to have an alibi. 'I was looking after you, old man,' he could hear himself saying. But it wasn't that. He needed Judd to be aware of his own complicity. Judd was a coward and a wimp and if he knew he was involved in a murder there was no way he would ever come forward.

But Michael's assumption had been incorrect. Judd hadn't kept quiet. He'd telephoned the fol-lowing morning. Three times he'd telephoned. 'Tell him I'm in a meeting, Mandy,' he'd instructed.

And then, the third time, when Mandy had said,

'The guy sounds hysterical, really off the planet, he keeps saying "You should have told me" over and over', Michael started to worry.

'Tell him to hang up and I'll ring him back,' he snapped. And when Mandy had left, he dialled Judd's apartment on his private line.

'I believe you're trying to reach me, old man,' he said, his mind racing. It was a pity Judd was overreacting like this. Something would have to be done about it.

'We have to talk, Michael,' Judd said. 'We have to talk.'

'And we shall, we shall, just calm down, take it easy.'

'We have to talk – you should have told me – we have to talk.'

'Tell you what,' Michael said, 'I'll send you something over to calm you down and then we'll talk a bit later, all right?'

'No, Michael, please, don't hang up.' Judd sounded desperate. 'Talk to me, I need to – '

'I will, I will, I promise. You just sit tight for a while and everything'll be fine. You have my word.'

With Michael's contacts, organising the delivery wasn't difficult, but it was expensive. Very expensive. Pure heroin always was. But it would do the trick. The death of Judd Weinberg III hadn't been part of his plan. But it was necessary.

Michael worked around the clock on *Earth Man*, consumed by his plan to premiere the movie in early spring. Much as the others may have disliked

543

the notion, they could do little else but obey his orders.

Michael played as hard as he worked. He didn't want to give his mind a moment's respite. He didn't want thoughts to creep in like snakes in the quieter moments of the night, reminding him of his guilt about Judd Weinberg. Poor old Judd, all he'd had to do was lend a bloke his key.

For the first month after the shooting, Michael had felt no remorse over Judd's death. But when it became apparent that no connection was going to be made between a heroin overdose in the same block of apartments from which the assassin had fired, he had time to reflect. It had all been so easy. The police were now assuming the bullet had been fired from the rooftop of the building and that the assassin had made his or her escape via the connecting rooftops. Perhaps if Michael had seen Judd and simply calmed him down there would have been no necessity for his death after all.

Strangely enough, Michael never felt a shred of remorse for the deaths of Malcolm O'Brien and Marcel Gireaux. They had been violating his property, his shrine. They had known Emma. They had to die. But Judd? Judd had committed no crime. He was a party animal, like Michael. They had shared many a fun night together. It didn't bear too much contemplation, he decided. In the spring, when *Earth Man* hit the screens, all would be vindicated. He would have created a movie classic, an historic masterpiece to live forever. He had to focus solely upon that.

And so Michael worked. And when he didn't work he partied. Clandestine parties in his new home. He was fully aware that Karol Mankowski was watching his every move. He knew that, on his grandfather's instructions, Karol had been 'keeping an eye' on him ever since the Rebel Waverley rape allegation. He'd even seen the man openly observing him at the China Bar one night and asking questions of the barman. What the hell was Mankowski doing at the China Bar? He didn't drink, for Christ's sake.

Michael's new home became his haven. It was every bit as luxurious as he'd planned it would be. He'd acquired the three-storey brownstone terrace in uptown Manhattan while the unit was filming in Fiji and he'd started immediately on his massive renovations. The pool was completed by the time they returned and he'd proudly given Emma, Stanley and Mandy a guided tour.

'My God, I don't believe it,' Emma had said as he ushered them through the front door and into the living room where half the floor was carved away and lined with a marble balcony and columns over which one looked down on the indoor heated pool in the basement below.

Michael laughed, delighted by her reaction. 'I always said I'd have a place with a pool.'

'Well, you've certainly done just that,' Emma agreed. The pool dominated everything. To the left of the living room a large semi-circular staircase led to the two bedrooms on the first floor and there was an open landing at the top which also looked down over the pool two floors below. 'It's actually quite attractive,' she added. 'A bit over the top,' she laughed, 'but attractive.'

'It's wonderful,' Mandy breathed admiringly.

'It's goddamn decadent, that's what it is,' Stanley said, but there was a touch of grudging admiration in his voice as well. 'So when do we get to christen the thing?'

'I'm shifting in next week,' Michael said. 'They haven't finished upstairs yet.' The bedroom was going to be his true masterpiece. He'd promised himself the circular bed and the surrounding mirrors. 'And I'm having a security system installed. There'll be cameras covering the main entrances, the interiors, the works.' He didn't add that he was also having a camera installed in the air-conditioning vent of the master bedroom as well.

'Next week we'll christen the pool,' he said.

And they did. Many a party was held at the brownstone between 5th and Madison. Even as Michael agonised over the relationship between Emma and Marcel, he invited the crowd back to his home. He entertained them royally, all the while planning the inevitable. And after the crowd had gone, he'd party. Usually with the girl or girls he'd invited that night. And always with the video camera whirring. Always with the fantasy in his mind that Emma wasn't with Marcel. Emma was here with him. And the following night he'd play the video and relive the fantasy. The girl's face would be masked from the camera, and as he watched her writhing body and listened to her cries of pleasure he relived his night with Emma.

* * *

It was shortly after the new year, when they were well into post-production on *Earth Man*, that Franklin made his casual comment to Michael. 'When do Helen and I get an invitation?'

Michael was momentarily confused. He hadn't seen Franklin for over a fortnight. 'Invitation? To where?'

'The movie maker's palatial mansion, that's where.'

Michael smiled, aware that Franklin was attempting a reconciliation. Their argument after the inquest had left a feeling of animosity between them. 'A two-bedroom brownstone hardly constitutes a palatial mansion, Grandfather.'

'A brownstone with an indoor heated swimming pool sounds pretty palatial to me. So when do we get an invitation? I believe we're the only ones who haven't, as yet.'

'How about Friday week? We're viewing the rough cut and I'm going to ask the others over for supper.'

'What others?'

'Only Emma, Stan, Derek and Mandy.' Michael was fully aware that Franklin would have preferred a more exclusive invitation, just himself and Helen, but that would leave the evening wide open for another lecture, or more probing discussion, and Michael wanted to avoid that if it was at all possible. As it was, he'd have to be on his best behaviour and it would probably be wiser not to invite one of his girlfriends. Damn it, he thought, Franklin had successfully ruined his evening already. Michael wished he hadn't allowed himself to be pushed into making the invitation.

547

'Friday week it is,' Franklin said. 'Excellent. We'll look forward to it.'

'Michael has invited us to supper Friday week,' Franklin said to Helen later that evening.

'How lovely,' she replied, hoping it was a sign that the rift in Franklin's relationship with his grandson was on the mend.

'Only because I virtually told him to,' Franklin grumbled. 'And we'll have to put up with his cronies.'

'Who? Emma and Stanley?'

'Yes, and young Mandy Crockett and that director bloke, whats-his-name. Michael's determined not to be left alone with me.'

'Well, they're a nice crowd. It should be fun,' Helen said briskly, refusing to humour him. He grizzled a lot lately, she thought. Grizzled and whinged and played the cantankerous old man more than ever. But she knew it was directly because of his worry for Michael – it had become so intense that Helen was starting to feel concerned for Franklin's health. The indomitable spirit that was Franklin Ross was finally showing signs of tiring. He'd long since acknowledged the physical limitations of his age. He no longer refused to hold on to banister railings – indeed, these days he walked with the aid of a cane. But his fierce determination had never left him. Until now, Helen thought. Now, behind the steel-blue eyes which had clouded with age, she could detect indecision and uncertainty, two elements which had never been a part of Franklin Ross. It worried her.

Helen was right. It was Franklin's indecision that so exhausted him. His divorce had been finalised for nearly two years now and he wanted to go back to Australia. He wanted to take Helen to Araluen. He wanted to marry her among the vines.

Franklin was obsessed with his desire to return to the land of his childhood, to prepare for a peaceful death, just as Grandfather George had done. Over the years he had lost count of the number of times he'd read and re-read the journals of George Ross. It had been a nightly delight to read aloud segments of them to Helen, painting her new home to her, feeding her anticipation. She had resigned her company directorship shortly after the divorce came through and, although she sat on several boards and kept herself busy with charity work, she was looking forward to the activity of taking over the reins of a vineyard. It was an exciting prospect for both of them.

But although Franklin ached to stand on the soil of Araluen with every fibre of his being, his wife by his side, he refused to leave New York until he was satisfied that Michael was in a fit state to inherit his empire.

'I can't leave it all to a junkie and a madman, Helen,' he agonised. 'And that's exactly the way the boy seems to be heading.'

When Helen argued that he had dozens of directors perfectly capable of managing his interests, Franklin exploded. 'I didn't work my guts out for sixty years to hand it all over to a bunch of strangers, woman!' he roared. 'I built an empire to hand down to my son and my son's sons.'

'Don't shout at me, Franklin.' Helen refused to be bullied.

'All right, all right. I'm sorry,' he growled. 'But until I know that Michael can take over I will stay at the helm – and that means we both stay in New York.'

'Very well, we'll stay in New York.'

Helen refused to be ruffled. The woman's damn complacency was at once her most admirable and her most annoying trait, Franklin decided. He tried to persuade her to marry him in New York, thinking she would like that, but she refused. 'You've always said that you wanted us to marry at Araluen,' she argued, 'and that's exactly what we'll do.' He couldn't budge her and when he tried his bullying tactics she actually burst out laughing. 'For God's sake, Franklin, I don't even care if we marry at all,' she said, infuriatingly. 'You're the one who's so keen on the notion.'

Franklin was strangely shocked by her attitude. 'Of course I am,' he said. 'If you're going to be by my deathbed, you're going to be there as my wife.'

'Yes I am,' she said and kissed him gently. 'I think it's a lovely idea.'

And time dragged on while Franklin worried about Michael.

CHAPTER FIFTEEN

FRANKLIN AND HELEN were the last to arrive at Michael's for the Friday supper party. When Michael opened the door to discover Karol Mankowski with them, he was sorely tempted to slam it in their faces.

Franklin was fully aware of his grandson's displeasure but he didn't seem remotely fazed by it. 'My driver has the night off,' he said, 'so Karol very kindly offered to drive for me. You don't mind if he joins us, do you?'

'Yes!' Michael wanted to scream. 'I can't stand the man; get him out of here!' Michael had been exuberant after watching the rough cut of *Earth Man* and the thought of sitting at a table with Karol Mankowski was an instant downer.

'Hello, Karol,' he said. 'Come in.'

As he ushered them inside, Franklin murmured an aside to him. 'Don't be surly, Michael. I can hardly have him wait in the car outside – it's freezing. Besides which, the man's a business partner.'

'The man's a psycho, that's what he is,' Michael muttered churlishly.

551

Franklin ignored him. After exchanging greetings with the other guests, he accepted a drink from one of the two waiters in attendance and wandered over to the marble columns. 'Very impressive,' he said as he looked down at the pool. Personally he thought it was indulgent and ostentatious.

'It's beautifully designed,' Helen said. 'I think you've done a wonderful job – I adore the marble.'

'Thanks.' For such an ordinary looking woman Helen really was very modern in her outlook, Michael thought. He knew Franklin didn't like the place though, and it annoyed him. He watched Karol refuse the offer of a drink and he suddenly had the feeling that the entire evening was going to annoy him. Fuck you, Franklin, he thought. Fuck you, Mankowski. Michael's intentions to behave himself flew out the window. Fuck the lot of them, he thought. It was his home and he'd bloody well do what he liked.

'Hand around some hors d'oeuvres,' he ordered a waiter. 'I'll be back in a tick.' And he went to the bathroom to snort a quick line.

'So how was the rough cut?' Franklin asked the assembled company as he dug a wedge of toast into the bowl of caviar the waiter offered him. He wasn't supposed to eat caviar – too much salt – but he loved the stuff.

'Fantastic, Mr Ross,' Mandy answered enthusiastically. 'It's going to be a masterpiece. Your grandson's a genius.'

Emma, Stanley and Derek nodded their agreement. But they seemed a little subdued, Franklin thought. Perhaps they'd found the film upsetting.

They had. Even Derek, who'd been working with the editor for weeks now, had been deeply moved on watching the film in sequence. Despite the fact that it was only roughly cut together and there was no soundtrack, it was an emotional experience. And Emma, who'd made a point of keeping well away from the editing process, was visibly shaken.

'It's pretty shattering, Mr Ross,' she said. She still couldn't bring herself to call him Franklin. 'But the editing's tasteful. Derek's deliberately kept away from using the more graphic material.' Emma wished she hadn't come back for supper. It didn't seem right to be eating and drinking and discussing the film as if it were just another movie.

'I think it's bloody disgusting that Michael's bringing the film out so soon after the man's death,' Franklin barked. 'Bloody disgusting.'

Helen groaned inwardly. Not now, Franklin, she thought. Don't start. Please!

Emma's silence spoke her agreement but she didn't say anything. They were a team. She must stay loyal to Michael.

'Well,' Derek explained, 'as Emma said, Mr Ross, we're keeping the death scene very tasteful and before we roll the titles we're dedicating the film to Marcel Gireaux and his commitment to the environment . . . ' Michael was coming out of the downstairs bathroom ' . . . so I think . . . '

'People will still say that's a device to help sell the film,' Franklin argued. 'It's tasteless. Tasteless, irreverent and downright bloody immoral if you ask me.'

'We didn't, Grandfather.' Michael poured

himself a large straight iced vodka. 'We bloody well didn't.' He downed it in one hit and poured himself another.

'I believe the special effects are extraordinary, Stanley.' It was a desperate interruption from Helen and fortunately Stanley rose to the occasion.

'You're not wrong there. Dynamic stuff.' Stanley knew that he was being called upon to save the day but he didn't mind. He'd always got on well with Helen. Surprisingly enough, he'd always got on well with Franklin too, although the old man had certainly soured of late, he thought. 'Lou and the team did an amazing job,' he continued. 'We've got a nuclear explosion that's unbelievable. And the aftereffects, the devastation ... well, we used models of course but you'd never pick Lou's work from the real thing.'

Emma looked at him with affection. Dear Stanley. He was always good value when he was dealing with his own world of make-believe. Whether it was throwing himself into a fearsome stunt or constructing some unbelievable effect, he was at home then. She'd long ago realised that Stanley was not arrogant at all. He was merely confident of his abilities and, outside of his own sphere he was, if anything, on the shy side.

The conversation remained in safe territory for the next hour or so, although Franklin's silence was as conspicuous as Michael's drinking.

The supper itself was superb – Michael only ever used the best caterers – but everyone was aware of the growing tension. The more Franklin glowered his disapproval, the more Michael drank; although he was offering his guests fine wines, he himself stuck to vodka.

Towards the end of supper, when the waiters had packed up the warming ovens and departed, Michael rose from the table to open his second bottle. Franklin had only seen one person drink vodka like that. Solly Mankowski. But then Solly could handle it.

'Don't you think you've had enough, boy?' Helen's sidelong glance was palpable and Franklin knew he should have kept his mouth shut but he was finding the deliberateness of Michael's drinking and his slide into inebriation intensely annoying. The boy was consciously setting out to aggravate him, Franklin thought. Even when he'd opened the wine earlier in the evening, his dig had been malicious. 'No, Grandfather,' he'd said, 'no Ross Estate, only a rather good Bordeaux, I hope you won't find that too offensive.' But Franklin did. Not the wine of course. The comment. It was snide, unnecessary. Why was the boy needling him?

Michael himself didn't know. Perhaps it was the sight of Karol Mankowski drinking mineral water, eating sparingly and missing nothing. Perhaps it was his grandfather's silence which spoke volumes. But this was his house, he thought. His life.

'Yes, Grandfather,' he said, 'you're quite right.' He turned, the second bottle of vodka opened in his hand. 'I've had enough. More than enough.' He poured the drink, slopping it over his fingers. 'I've had enough of being treated like a child.' He knew he sounded childish as he said it and that infuriated him more. 'I've had enough of never being able to do anything right ...'

He was whining now and Franklin, disgusted, shot a quick glance towards Helen. Michael followed the glance and, in doing so, noticed that Karol was not seated beside her. When had he disappeared? What was the man doing? Looking for incriminating evidence? Yes, that was it. The bastard was probably going through the bathroom cupboards at that very moment. Not that he'd find anything; Michael kept his drug supply under lock and key. But the thought of being spied upon, the thought of his belongings being searched ... and by Karol Mankowski of all people ...

Karol Mankowski had spied on Michael as a child and now he was spying on him here. In his new and wonderful home. Karol Mankowski was desecrating the very symbol of his independence, his success, his achievement.

Something snapped inside Michael. 'Where is he?' he snarled. 'Where is the bastard?' And there was madness in his eyes.

Emma had been watching him closely all night. She'd seen the threat of madness from the moment Franklin had arrived. All night she'd been willing the old man to stop aggravating Michael. Couldn't he see that his grandson was at breaking point?

Franklin feigned innocence. 'Who?' he asked. 'Where's who?'

Michael didn't answer. He slammed his glass down on the table. It shattered and cut his hand but he didn't notice. He ran into the downstairs bathroom smashing open the door but Karol wasn't there.

'Mankowski!' he screamed, and when he came back into the lounge room he looked demented. Franklin rose from the table.

'Michael ... '

But Michael didn't even see him. He raced up the staircase still screaming. 'Mankowski, you bastard!'

As he disappeared into the upstairs master bedroom, Franklin remained standing, staring up at the landing. The others remained seated, silent. There was nothing anyone could do. Emma stared at the old man. His face was set and stern. Was there no compassion in him? Couldn't he see that Michael was sick?

In the upstairs bedroom, Michael was frozen to the spot. Karol Mankowski stood opposite him, as implacable as ever.

'It's a nice place you've got here, Michael,' he said quietly. Michael said nothing. His chest was heaving and his breath came in rasping gasps. 'Big bed,' Karol added.

Finally, Michael found his voice. 'What are you doing, Mankowski? Why are you spying on me? What is it you want?'

'Just taking a look around, Michael. The door was open. I didn't think you'd mind ... '

'Get out!' Michael screamed. 'Get out of my house!' Karol shrugged and nodded and walked towards the door. 'Get out! Get out of my house!' Michael kept screaming and he wanted to attack the man, to tear him to pieces. But Karol paused at the door and looked at him for a second and he didn't dare. Even in his madness, he could recognise the danger in Karol Mankowski.

Karol left and Michael stood for several seconds. He could hear himself sobbing with rage. He pulled open the top drawer of the dresser and took out the Walther .32 calibre pocket automatic. As he stood there, staring at it, a shred of reason returned. What was he going to do with the gun? Was he going to go downstairs and blow Karol Mankowski's brains out in front of his grandfather and the others? Gradually, his sobs subsided. No, he thought frantically. No. One day . . . One day . . .

The plans for revenge were clearing Michael's brain. His grandfather had sent Mankowski to spy on him. One day he'd send him again. One day Michael would find Mankowski in his home. And he'd shoot him. Justifiable homicide. 'I thought the man was a burglar,' he could hear himself say. No court would convict him. The fantasy was perfect and Michael finally felt himself enough in control to join the others. He must, he told himself. He must face them and somehow get through this hideous night.

He returned the gun to the drawer and, slowly, he walked out onto the landing. His guests were still seated, silently waiting for what was going to happen next. Franklin was still on his feet, staring at the landing. Beside him stood Karol Mankowski.

At the sight of Karol, Michael felt his rage returning. 'Get that man out of my house, Grandfather,' he said tightly as he walked down the stairs. 'I will not be spied upon in my own home.'

'Karol was merely looking around, Michael, there was no need for such an exhibition of . . . '

'*Get him out*!' Michael screamed as he clung tightly to the railing of the staircase, blood dripping from his cut hand.

Franklin's eyes were gleaming with his own madness. He was sickened and enraged by Michael's outburst. The boy was indeed insane, he thought. How had it gone this far without his knowledge? Beneath Franklin's rage was a deep and terrible grief. This was his grandson. His only male heir. The man who was to inherit the Ross empire. He'd worked for sixty years to hand the reins over to *this*! He maintained his control and made one last desperate bid.

'Karol, would you take Helen home, please,' he said, his eyes locked into Michael's. 'And I'd be grateful if the rest of you would leave now. My grandson and I need to talk.'

'No!' Michael let go of the railing and walked to face the old man across the table. '*You* go!' He was losing control again, he could feel it. '*You* go. You get out of my house and take that man with you!' He knew his voice was hysterical, he could feel himself shaking and he was spitting in his rage but he couldn't help it. 'Get out! Get out! Get *out*!' He slammed his fist on the table. A half-full bottle of wine fell on its side and several more glasses shattered.

At this final outburst, everyone rose from the table, galvanised into action. Stanley took a hold of Michael's arm, Emma, Mandy and Helen rose for sheer fear and Karol moved closer to Franklin. Only Franklin didn't budge. He remained staring back at Michael and the steel glint of old flashed in the faded blue eyes.

'Look at you, boy,' he said. 'Look at you. You're disgusting.'

Michael couldn't unlock his eyes from the old man's, but suddenly there was no attack left in him. His energy was spent and he didn't resist Stanley's restraining arm.

'You're sick,' Franklin said with revulsion. 'You're a junkie.' Michael's body started to sag. He felt himself cave in and allowed Stanley to ease him into a chair. 'An excuse for a human being,' Franklin continued relentlessly. 'You're no kin of mine.'

Michael started to sob. He couldn't help it. Things were going on in his brain. Grandpa Franklin. His hero. He saw The Colony House. He saw the main doors, the car waiting . . . 'Got your football boots?' . . . The pride when Grandpa Franklin came to a game.

'. . . You're no grandson of mine,' Franklin was saying.

Michael's sobs grew louder.

Suddenly, Emma could stand no more. 'Stop it!' she cried. 'Stop it! Can't you see he's ill?'

For the first time, Franklin's eyes left Michael's. 'Of course he is,' he said scathingly. 'He's sick, poisoned by his own diseased mind . . . '

'You don't know a thing about his mind,' she said and, as Michael bent his face to the table, she took his head in her hands and cradled him to her waist. 'You don't care about his mind and you don't care about him! All he's ever been to you is the next step in the Ross dynasty – he's never been a person at all.' Visions of Julia – 'He's an evil man' – and Penelope – 'All he wanted from me was sons' – flashed through Emma's brain as she held her brother close to her. 'You don't care, you've never cared,' she said. 'You're a tyrant!'

She waited for Franklin to fire back at her but he didn't so she turned her attention to Michael. She sat beside him and embraced him, his head on her shoulder and, for a moment, there was a deathly stillness.

'Apparently I've been unaware of a development here,' Franklin said quietly. 'You obviously feel you have some rights to interfere in a personal family matter.' His voice was scathing, patronising. 'As his lover surely you could have had a little more influence over his drug addiction – '

'I'm not his lover!' She shouted it. In the stillness, her voice was jarring. And she knew she couldn't stop herself. She knew she had to say it. She had to shock the old man out of his complacency, she had to prove to him that she knew him for the tyrant he was. 'I'm his sister,' she said.

The words hung in the air. And she was glad when they did. Glad that she'd halted the old man's venom. He looked at her for what seemed an eternity. Everyone did. Everyone except Michael, whose head was sunk against her breast. Like a child. He was no longer sobbing. He could have been sleeping. 'My father was Terence Ross,' she said. 'I'm your granddaughter.'

It seemed an eternity before Franklin spoke. And when he did his voice was strange, subdued. 'Yes,' he said. 'Yes, you are.'

He could see it as clearly as if it were yesterday. His mind played tricks on him lately. Sometimes he couldn't remember whether he'd kept an appointment that same morning. Sometimes he couldn't remember what he'd eaten for breakfast. But the long-ago yesterdays were vividly etched in his memory. And he recalled that afternoon, that hot summer afternoon when he'd come home to find a young woman waiting with Penelope.

'She won't say what it's about,' Penelope had announced, thin-lipped. And then the girl had told him. Even when they'd challenged her she'd sworn it was Terry's child she was carrying. And Franklin had believed her. Just as he now believed this girl who sat before him, holding his grandson in her arms. The defiance in Emma's eyes could not be ignored. It was the same defiance he'd seen in the girl that afternoon. And they were the same eyes.

After the initial shock, he wondered at the fact that the knowledge didn't come as a greater surprise. It explained Emma's strange belligerence towards him from the outset. But why had she kept her secret? To protect her mother? To protect herself? 'We do not recognise bastards in this family.' Yes, Franklin could still hear himself saying it.

So many questions to be answered. But he was tired. Too tired to ask them now.

'It's time we went home, Helen,' he said wearily.

While Mandy fetched their coats, grateful for an excuse to leave the room, Franklin once again addressed Emma.

'We need to talk. May I see you tomorrow?' Emma didn't reply, she wasn't sure what to say. 'Perhaps in the afternoon, at the studios, you and Michael together?' He glanced at his grandson.

'That is, if he's well enough by then.' There was no malice in his voice. He was too tired for malice.

Mandy returned with the coats, Stanley opened the main doors and Franklin, Helen and Karol left.

'Let's get him up to bed,' Stanley said when they'd gone and he heaved Michael over his shoulder in a fireman's lift. Michael groaned and started to gag slightly. 'Better grab a bucket or a bowl just in case,' Stanley instructed Emma. 'And Mandy, could you clear up some of that broken glass?'

Emma fetched a plastic basin from the laundry and followed Stanley up the stairs.

As Michael was unceremoniously dumped on the large circular bed, she looked around at the room. She'd never seen the master bedroom before. It was unashamedly designed for an orgy. What worlds of fantasy had Michael been weaving for himself in his nightly drug-induced state? She felt guilty that she hadn't spent more time with him, made more effort to protect him from himself. She'd known he still used drugs but, when he'd become irritable with her nagging, she'd done the easy thing. She'd stopped. She shouldn't have. He was her brother and she loved him. He deserved more from her.

Michael groaned again. 'I think he's going to sleep it off,' Stanley said, 'but you'd better get a couple of towels just in case.'

While Emma disappeared into the bathroom, Stanley loosened Michael's collar, took off his shoes and covered him with a doona. He needed to keep himself occupied, he needed time to absorb the truth. His mind was still in a state of shock. Emma was Michael's sister! He'd always thought they were lovers. No time to think about that now, he told himself. Later. He could think about it later.

'Thanks,' he said as he took the towels from her. He placed one underneath Michael's head. 'I don't think he's going to throw up but that'll help with the mess if he does.' He found himself avoiding her gaze. 'Want a lift home?' he asked.

'No. I'm going to stay with him.'

Stanley stopped being busy for a moment and looked at her. 'I think he'll be fine.'

'What if he does throw up?' she argued. 'He could choke on his own vomit – people have done it before. Besides,' she added, 'we know that it's more than a few drinks too many. He's had a bad trip and I don't think he should wake up on his own.'

Stanley wasn't at all sure that it was a good idea. 'Do you want me to stay with you?'

She shook her head. 'No thanks.' Then when he continued to look dubious, she smiled gently. 'I think I can look after my own brother, Stanley.'

He busied himself again, spreading the second towel over Michael's chest. She sensed his avoidance. 'You were pretty shocked by the news, weren't you?'

'Yeah, I guess so,' he nodded. There was an awkward pause. 'Well, I'll be off now. I'll drive Mandy home.'

'Stanley.' He stopped at the door. 'Thank you. For everything.'

'Call me if you need me.'

Emma bathed Michael's cut hand. Then she sat on the bed beside him and wondered at what she had done. And she wondered at what tomorrow would bring. Would she go and see Franklin as he'd requested? Why not? There was nothing she had to fear from him – he was a very old man. So why did she have such misgivings? She knew why. Old man or not, there was still fire left in Franklin Ross. Penelope's words still rang in Emma's ears ... 'He'll destroy you' ...

Oh no, he won't, she told herself. What could he do to hurt her? Nothing. There was nothing she wanted from him, so there was nothing for him to take. He would not destroy her. And, if there was any way Emma could prevent it, he would not destroy his grandson either, although for some perverse reason he seemed bent on doing so.

Beside her, Michael stirred. He opened his eyes. Although they looked a little bloodshot and weary, they were clearly focused. 'Emma,' he said.

'Hello, trouble,' she smiled. What was the point of being angry with him? He looked so vulnerable. She'd read him the riot act tomorrow. 'Feel all right?'

'Fine,' he answered. 'I'm fine.' He started to sit up but his head screamed at him. 'No, maybe I'm not.'

She eased him back onto the bed. 'Lie down, Michael. You've drunk a bottle and a half of vodka – no wonder you've got a headache.'

'Shit,' he said. Then he put his arm out across the bed. 'Lie down with me, Emma.' She did, nestling her head against his shoulder, and together they stared up at the ceiling. 'I made a fool of myself, didn't I?' Michael could remember confronting Karol Mankowski in the bedroom. And he could remember the gun and his plan to one day kill Mankowski ... yes, that was a good plan. Then he could remember glasses smashing and a screaming match with his grandfather across the dining table. But that was all.

'Yes,' she said, 'you made a fool of yourself.'

'Oh, bugger it,' he muttered. 'The old bastard'll be down on me like a ton of bricks now.'

'Go back to sleep,' Emma instructed. 'We'll talk about it in the morning.'

'Will you stay with me?'

'Yes,' she nodded.

Michael felt strangely peaceful. Emma was lying beside him. It was all he'd ever wanted. Well, there was more he would have wanted if things had been different, of course. Much more. But so long as she loved him and she was with him, that was enough. 'It was the booze, Emma, that's all,' he said apologetically. 'I'm not used to the booze.' It was true. Michael had stopped drinking hard liquor long ago. His body had built up a resistance to his drug intake, which had increased heavily over the years, but the addition of alcohol made the combination lethal and he'd learned to avoid it. Several glasses of wine over an evening was the extent of his intake.

'I know, I know,' she said, fully aware that he was deluding himself. She'd talk to him in the morning. Something must be done about his addiction and the first step was his admitting to it, but now was not the time. 'Go to sleep.'

She lay there beside him for over an hour.

Michael was aware of her presence as he slowly drifted off, and he couldn't stop the fantasies from crowding his mind. The fantasies that had been part of him for years. Emma's breasts, Emma's mouth, Emma's body beneath his ...

She looked at him as he slept. He had the face of a child. Close up she could see the ravages of drugs, the shadows beneath the eyes, the fine lines carved in the cheeks – close up Michael looked older than his twenty-seven years. But he was still a boyishly handsome man and the impression as he slept was one of childlike innocence. Emma so wanted to protect him. But how did one go about protecting someone from himself, she wondered.

He was sleeping soundly now and Emma herself was feeling tired. Gently, she eased her head from his shoulder. She rose from the bed and quietly slipped out into the spare room. She'd have to work on a plan of attack tomorrow, she decided. She was far too tired tonight.

'Yes, yes, I agree,' Michael insisted. 'You're quite right. I have a problem and I must do something about it.'

Mid-morning, over the toast and coffee she'd prepared him, Emma was amazed to hear Michael so readily agree to everything she said. His reaction in the past had always been, 'Stop nagging, Emma. If I like a touch of the good life, what business is it of yours?' This was a total turnaround. 'After the *Earth Man* premiere I'll sign myself into a clinic,' he said. 'I promise.'

* * *

567

'I promise, Grandfather. As soon as *Earth Man* is released.' Later that same day, Franklin was just as surprised as Emma had been by Michael's recognition of his problem. Franklin wasn't sure what he'd expected but he'd certainly been prepared to threaten his grandson with disinheritance unless he agreed to medical treatment. And here the boy was, offering the perfect solution himself. Franklin was mystified. Then it occurred to him. Of course. The girl – it was her doing. He turned to her gratefully but, before he could say anything, Emma shook her head.

'It wasn't me.' She knew what the old man was thinking. 'It was Michael's idea.'

They were seated opposite Franklin in his office. The light through the plate glass window behind him made a halo of his silver-white hair and put his face in shadow. Emma was aware that it was a deliberate device designed to put interviewees at a disadvantage. She looked at the vast mahogany desk separating them. It was as though she and Michael were being interviewed for a position, and she wondered at the fact that it hadn't occurred to Franklin Ross to seat them in the comfortable armchairs only a few feet away or to offer them a cup of coffee.

'Would you like a cup of coffee?' Franklin rose as he pressed the intercom button. 'Or tea, whichever you prefer. We'll make ourselves comfortable, shall we?' And he gestured to the armchairs.

Franklin's oversight had been deliberate. He never offered guests refreshments or comfortable seating until he was sure things were going satisfactorily to his advantage. He maintained his position of power until the last moment and only when the deal was done did he play the magnanimous host.

This time, sensing the antipathy in Emma, he decided to forgo the normal procedure. When they were settled and the secretary had taken their coffee orders, he once again turned his attention to Michael.

'When do you anticipate the release of *Earth Man*?'

'End of March. Two months at the outside.'

'And between now and then?' Franklin couldn't resist the enquiry. He knew he was courting an aggressive response but it was a fair question which demanded an honest answer. 'You really think you can keep yourself on the straight and narrow?'

Michael felt an insane rush of irritation. Again he was being treated like a child. What was he expected to answer to such a question, for Christ's sake, 'No, Grandfather, I think I'll probably bomb out altogether'?

'Yes, Grandfather, I'm quite sure I can stay on the straight and narrow.' Try as he might, Michael couldn't keep an edge of sarcasm out of his voice. What the hell did 'the straight and narrow' mean anyway? Did his grandfather seriously think that because of one night's fall from grace, Michael was now a cot case, unable to function as a human being? No, it was a dig – the old bugger wasn't that naive.

He saw the warning flash in Franklin's eyes and he knew he must tread carefully. It was four o'clock in the afternoon and Michael had only had two uppers during the entire day. It wasn't enough. He was tired and nervy and irritable, but he knew he had to play the game the way his grandfather wanted it. For the next two months he knew he had to monitor his drug intake more than ever and be on his very best behaviour. After that, he'd have to sign into a clinic and undergo some ridiculous form of rehabilitation programme. Why couldn't everyone just leave him alone? But he didn't dare display his annoyance, even to Emma. In her own way, she overreacted to his drug use as strongly as Franklin did. It was none of their bloody business! But ...

Michael dredged up one of his easy, lazy grins. 'Sorry to sound a bit irritable, Grandfather – a touch of a hangover, that's all.'

Nothing, Michael told himself, absolutely nothing was worth risking his inheritance. And the quicker he could lull the old man into a sense of security, the quicker Franklin Ross would hand over the lot and bugger off back to Australia.

'I'm not at all surprised,' Franklin's reply was acerbic.

'So which clinic do you suggest?' Michael asked. 'The Betty Ford? We'd better sign me in now, it's very popular and there's probably a waiting list.'

Franklin frowned. The boy was being smart with him, surely. But Michael's smile was so amiable, so willing to please, that it was impossible to be sure. Franklin decided not to push too hard. 'Very well, the Betty Ford Clinic it is.' And he turned to Emma. 'Now you, young lady. What about you? It would appear we have a great deal to talk about.'

'I don't think so,' Emma answered firmly. She'd been in a dilemma, wondering which tack she would take when Franklin inevitably turned the conversation to her and her parentage. But the old man simplified any decision by immediately putting her on the attack. He was treating her like a child, she thought. She didn't like being addressed as 'young lady', and certainly not in a tone which intimated she'd done something wrong. 'I don't think we have anything at all to talk about,' she repeated.

Franklin was taken aback. Why was the girl so aggressive towards him? He'd opened the conversation with a perfectly reasonable comment delivered in a perfectly reasonable tone. Indeed, his approach had been fatherly, he thought, considerate. Why was she on the defensive? Franklin didn't realise it but, these days, Helen had given up pointing out that even his most civil of tones was abrasive to the average person.

It was a pity the girl was choosing to be unpleasant, he thought, but so be it. 'Very well,' he said. 'If you don't wish to talk, perhaps you'd be kind enough to furnish me with the answers to several questions – '

'I don't really see why – '

'Questions to which I am owed an answer, damn it.' Franklin's voice hardened. He was starting to feel genuinely annoyed. The girl was strong and proud – he respected her for that. But he wanted answers. He was in a quandary. How was he supposed to play this?

'Emma,' he said reasonably, 'whether or not you like it, your mother and I made a bargain. An agreement was reached, money was exchanged and if either you or she are going to renege on the deal then I most certainly have a right to know the reasons why.'

Emma look back at him for a moment and then she nodded. 'Yes,' she said. 'Yes, that's fair enough.' She cleared some magazines from the coffee table as the secretary entered with a tray but the action was more to break eye contact with Franklin than anything else. 'Ask away,' she said when the secretary had gone.

'Very well. First of all, why? Why tell me now?'

'She was protecting me, Grandfather,' Michael interjected. Although he had no memory of the actual event, Emma had filled him in on all the details that morning. 'You demanded a reason why she was defending me and . . . '

'Yes, yes, I know, I know that,' Franklin snapped. What, did they think he was a fool? 'I mean, why now? Why wait all these years to tell me?'

'You said it yourself, Mr Ross,' Emma answered evenly. 'You and my mother made a deal.'

Franklin stared back at her. No, the answer was too simple somehow.

'Besides,' Michael added in the pause that followed, 'Emma gave her word to Penelope.'

Emma glanced sharply at him. She didn't know why, but she wished he hadn't told Franklin that part.

Franklin witnessed the exchange between them. He saw Michael's imperceptible shrug in return. A shrug that said, what's the harm, let the old bloke know the full truth. 'Seven years ago,' he continued with some relish. 'It must be all of seven years ago she promised Penelope.'

Penelope. Yes, of course it was Penelope. Franklin's mind seized upon several reasons as to why Penelope would demand secrecy. Primarily, of course, she wouldn't have wanted female competition; only one woman ruled the roost at The Colony House, Penelope had always made sure of that. She'd even got rid of poor Veronica, Terry's mousy little wife, Franklin recalled. But could there also be an element of revenge involved? Penelope had denied him sons and she had revelled in the fact. Had she also revelled in the fact that she was denying him a grandchild? Certainly he had said that he would suffer no bastards in the family but at the time he said it, he had a healthy young son who had already given him one grandchild and was expected to give him many more. Penelope would have been aware of that. If it were so, how she must hate him, Franklin thought. Then he forced himself back to the present.

'How long have you known that Emma was your half-sister?' he asked.

'Five years,' Michael answered.

'I see.' He paused and looked from one to the other before concentrating again on Michael. 'And why did *you* keep the secret? Did you promise Penelope too?'

Michael shook his head. 'Penelope and I have never spoken about Emma. But then Penelope hasn't spoken to me since I left Australia to be with you. She hasn't spoken to Emma either, for that matter.'

Franklin finally turned his attention to Emma.

'So you expect me to believe that this entire conspiracy is born of a promise you made to your grandmother seven years ago? And that for the past five years you haven't even seen or spoken to the woman?'

Emma merely nodded. But to Franklin it was incomprehensible. The girl had to have an ulterior motive. There was a plan afoot, he thought, there had to be. Were the two women in league? Was Penelope quietly biding her time in Australia waiting for him to die while her granddaughter stood by in New York watching Michael sink into the abyss? With Franklin dead and Michael destroyed they could take over his empire with ease. Was that the plan?

'I don't believe you,' he said.

'That's your prerogative,' Emma replied stiffly. 'But frankly, what you choose to believe or disbelieve is immaterial to me.'

Damn it, Franklin thought, the girl was determined to push him to his limits. The defiant flash in the eyes and the tilt of the chin reminded Franklin of her mother and that afternoon twenty-five years ago.

'What is it you want from me, girl?'

She rose. 'I want nothing from you, Mr Ross. Nothing at all.'

'You're lying,' Franklin said. And Emma walked out of the room.

Michael controlled his desire to laugh but he couldn't resist a mild smirk. 'I think you've offended her, Grandfather, Emma never lies.'

Franklin eased himself out of the armchair with the aid of his walking stick. 'I expect you to abide by your promise, boy. You may go now.'

Damn the girl, he thought as he watched Michael leave. Damn her. Given the circumstances she could at least stop calling him Mr Ross.

CHAPTER SIXTEEN

EMMA AVOIDED FRANKLIN ROSS like the plague over the next several weeks but their occasional meeting was inevitable. And, each time, he attempted affability. 'Under the circumstances you could call me Franklin, surely,' he suggested. But, although she found herself referring to him as Franklin in conversation to others, she found it impossible to do so to his face.

On their last chance meeting, Franklin dropped the affable act and got straight down to business. 'I realise the influence you have over the boy, Emma, and I'd like you to give him a warning.'

'The boy', Emma thought with irritation. Michael's twenty-seven years old, he's hardly a boy. Why does Franklin have to treat us all like half-witted children? Someone should tell him, she thought, but she certainly wasn't going to be the one.

'I want you to warn him that if he doesn't undergo the treatment as he's promised, I'll disinherit him,' Franklin continued. 'He won't get a penny – tell him.'

She did. And Michael scoffed. 'As if I didn't know that. He'd do it too, the vindictive old bastard.'

The premiere of *Earth Man* loomed near and the whole of New York was buzzing about the movie.

'The trade papers have been good to us, that's for sure,' Stanley remarked one day as he and Emma sorted through still shots of the stunts for a forthcoming article in *Time* magazine.

'It was Michael's interview with Oprah that got them all on side, though' Emma replied. 'He was brilliant. And the clips they aired from the Fiji shoot were stunning.'

'Yeah, and of course we all know why the Oprah show caused such a stir, don't we?' Stanley said. 'The whole goddamn interview was about Marcel's murder.'

Emma nodded, ignoring his tone. Stanley always spoke sharply these days. She couldn't help but notice that his attitude towards her seemed to have changed. He was surly and irritable. 'Stanley, what's the matter?' she asked time and again. 'Have I done something to offend you?'

'No,' he'd abruptly reply and then turn the conversation towards work. Lately she'd given up trying to communicate with him on a personal level.

'The Oprah show was pretty vulgar,' she admitted. 'For once I agree with Franklin. It's too soon and it's tasteless. But at least Michael's refusing to use any film footage of the assassination scene for publicity. All the networks have been asking for it.'

'You can bet your bottom dollar it's not due to

any finer feelings on his part,' Stanley snapped. 'He wants to make damn sure people realise they have to pay to see it.'

'Yes,' Emma had to agree, 'he's a bit of a monster when he's making a movie. Everything and everyone's fair game.'

'It didn't used to be people though – it used to be events. He's changed and it sure as hell isn't for the better.'

The subject of Michael also seemed to annoy Stanley these days and Emma usually tried to avoid talking about him.

'The guy's turned into a bastard,' Stanley continued. He was more than surly today, Emma thought. He was tense, on edge.

'Michael's not well,' she countered defensively, 'you know that. He's promised he'll undergo treatment and after that he'll be fine. He'll be the same – '

'Bullshit! He's doing it to appease the old man. He'll never change – he doesn't want to. He uses people and he always will.'

Emma felt her own anger start to burn. Stanley was talking like Franklin Ross. Franklin thought of drug addiction as a weakness, not as the evil disease it was. 'Michael's addiction is an illness,' she said evenly, 'it's not a crime.'

'Oh stop being so fucking self-righteous, Emma.' Stanley slammed a pile of photographs down on the table and turned on her. She'd never seen him so angry. 'He wants to be the way he is – can't you see that? Franklin's right, the man's diseased and it's all in his own brain. Why do you keep defending him?'

'Because he's my brother, that's why!' Her own voice rose in anger to match his. 'He's my brother and I love him!'

'And how do you love him? Like he loves you?' Stanley's face was close to hers now and she could see the rage in his eyes. 'Like a lover? Have you seen the way he looks at you? Is that the way you feel about him? Do you want him the way he wants you? Do you want to – '

She hit him. With all the force she could muster, she struck him across the face and her hand stung from the impact.

Neither of them said anything for a while. There was a red mark on Stanley's cheek; he didn't touch it, he didn't even seem to acknowledge the blow, but his anger had dissipated.

Emma's anger, too, had gone. She was appalled by his words. But she was more appalled by her own action. She had never struck anyone before, she had never thought it was in her to want to.

'I'm sorry,' she said.

He sat on the desk, photographs spilling onto the floor. 'You should have told me,' he said. 'You should have told me years ago.'

'Told you what?'

'That you were Michael's sister.'

'Why?'

'Oh for Chrissakes, Emma, why do you think! The way Michael looks at you is the way I've looked at you for five years, maybe seven, who can tell, maybe the first day I met you – I don't know and who cares. But the man's in love with you and if that offends you, then tough.'

Emma remembered the night Michael tried to

make love to her, the night she told him the truth. And she knew, if she was being honest with herself, that she had seen him looking at her occasionally. Special looks. Looks that she'd chosen to construe as brotherly love. But they weren't, and, deep down, she knew it.

'Yes,' she said, and her voice was a whisper. 'Yes, you're right.'

Stanley couldn't bear the fact that she'd absorbed only one half of what he'd said. He could see that Emma was appalled by the knowledge of her brother's incestuous desire but did Stanley's own admission of love mean nothing? Did the fact that he'd stood by for five years, never declaring himself, accepting a relationship that had never existed, did that mean nothing?

'So is this incest a two-way street?' he asked. He was goading her. He wanted her to strike him again. He wanted her to stop thinking of Michael. He wanted to force her into acknowledging his admission. It worked.

'Stop it, Stanley! Stop it!' He said nothing but sat glaring at her. 'Why are you tormenting me?' she asked. 'Why do you want to hurt me?'

'Because you've wasted five years of my life, that's why. Because when I tell you I love you, you don't even acknowledge me, that's why.'

'I'm sorry,' she murmured. 'I never knew.'

'Oh, come on, it must have crossed your mind once or twice, surely? Maybe when we were horsing around in a pool half-naked together,' he added sarcastically, 'or – '

'No,' she said, 'never.'

'Well, it should have,' he said impatiently.

'Jesus, you're a woman – where the hell's your female intuition?'

'I'm sorry,' she said again. 'If I'd known I would have. . .' Her voice tailed off wretchedly.

'You would have *what*, Emma?' He was demanding an answer. 'You would have what?'

'Oh Stanley, how do I know? I've always cared for you. You know that. How can I tell what I . . . ?'

'How much have you cared, Emma?' He rose and took her by the shoulders, his grip painful. 'How much?'

'Stanley, please . . . '

'This much?' And he kissed her. His mouth was rough and demanding and she was so completely taken by surprise that she didn't fight back. She accepted the kiss, brutal as it was. And when he'd finished, he took her face in his hands and said quietly, 'I didn't mean to hurt you, and I won't again, I promise. But if there's any chance of making up for lost time, I'd like to give it a try. Think about it, Emma, that's all I ask. Think about it.'

A week later, Stanley asked her out to dinner and Emma accepted. It was a pleasant evening, the conversation warm and comfortable, the companionship that of close friends. Neither of them mentioned the confrontation of the previous week. At least not until coffees at Emma's apartment.

She'd wondered about asking him in and whether he'd misconstrue the invitation but it seemed unbelievably rude not to offer coffee after he'd driven her home. Besides, she was enjoying his company, wasn't she? And she had to admit, when he refused a second coffee and took her in his arms instead, she enjoyed the kiss and the feel of him. Strange as it was.

But, somehow, it was too strange. She drew away from him. 'Stanley. . .'

He stopped her. 'It's okay, I don't expect a miracle after five years.' But, as he rose from the sofa, his grin was confident, happy. 'We know where we stand now though, don't we? And, believe me, I'll keep trying.'

She started to say something but he interrupted again. 'Don't worry, you can always tell me to butt out. See you.'

He left, quietly closing the door behind him, and Emma couldn't help smiling. The Stanley Grahame arrogance was back and it was very attractive.

Over the next fortnight, as the premiere drew near, there wasn't much time for Stanley to press his suit, but there was a special feeling between the two of them and he was content not to force the issue.

Everything was set for the big night. And the big night didn't disappoint. Michael's publicists had gone mad setting the stage. Red carpets and searchlights abounded and, in the foyer of the theatre, a sixteen-piece orchestra played the haunting theme music from *Earth Man*. Michael's special police contact, once more in the form of Captain Matthew 'Mac' Macfarlane, closed whole

582

inner-city blocks to all traffic apart from the stretch limos and the Rolls-Royce limousines which arrived bearing the star guests. Thousands of fans lined the pavements and screamed their approval as their favourites alighted, waving to the cameras and shielding their eyes from the glare of the flashlights.

Inside the theatre, when the guests were finally seated, Michael made his introductory speech. It was perfect. A touching tribute to Marcel Gireaux. 'What you are about to see tonight is a timeless record of one man's commitment to the planet and his fellow man. And we, as a team,' he looked at Emma and Stanley and Derek and Mandy, 'are proud that this film is proof of the fact that Marcel Gireaux did not die in vain and that, indeed, he and his ideals will live forever.'

He didn't acknowledge the applause as he returned to his seat – the applause was, after all, for Marcel Gireaux. Michael was pleased with himself. He hadn't built up to a high before the screening; the ecstasy and coke in his top pocket were for the all-night celebrations which would follow. Yes, he thought with satisfaction, his speech had gone down very well, with just the right degree of humility. He did indeed feel deeply grateful to Marcel.

As the lights dimmed, he caught Franklin's eye. The old man gave a curt nod of approval but Michael knew he'd found the speech hypocritical. So what? he thought. Too bad – the crowd had loved it.

The titles rolled, the theme music swelled to a crescendo and the audience sat, spellbound, for the

583

following two hours. There was a hushed silence in the build-up to the assassination scene and an audible gasp when the gunshot rang out.

The final credits were rolled in silence and, at the end of them, a tribute to Marcel Gireaux appeared on the screen. When the houselights were finally brought up, people were weeping. Some unashamedly, others surreptitiously, trying to repair their make-up. Silence continued to reign for a full minute, and then the applause began. It went on and on. People rose to their feet. And, finally, the entire audience was standing in tribute.

The reverence and awe didn't last long, of course. In the foyer, as they mingled, the guests once more reverted to their standard premiere behaviour. 'A masterpiece, my darling.' 'Brilliant, bound to carry off best film.' 'Got your Academy Award speech ready, Michael?'

He basked in it. He'd popped an ecstasy halfway through the screening and he was floating on a wonderful cloud. Life couldn't possibly be better.

He continued to bask in his glory all through the festivities that followed. A crowd of them went on to Au Bar and then Doubles. Then it was four o'clock in the morning and still the pace was furious. By this time it was mostly the hard-core film crowd. Those who'd worked on the movie were all on a high. It was their night. Most of them had taken ecstasy. Even Emma had been persuaded.

'Come on, Emma,' Mandy had urged, 'it's that

sort of night.' Mandy had been as high as a kite from the outset of the evening. 'The sort of night that might only happen once in your life.'

'But I've never taken one before – what's it like?' The champagne had gone to Emma's head and she was wondering whether she should go home before she made a fool of herself.

'Like coke, only it's gentler,' Mandy said. 'It'll keep you going all night – stop you getting drunk too.'

'Oh.' That sounded tempting.

'Come on, just a half'll do you.' Emma looked at Derek who was nodding his approval. Derek had surprised himself by accepting an ecstasy from Michael two hours ago and he was feeling no pain. Hell, Mandy was right, this was a once-in-a-life-time occasion.

It worked. Just half a pill and, an hour later, Emma wanted to dance until dawn. And she loved the feeling of Stanley's arms around her.

Stanley was enjoying the sensation too but he was getting tired of dancing. Emma was being so unashamedly sensual. He wanted to kiss her, to feel her, to make love to her. Was tonight the night? But then, he thought, he was pretty drunk – it was probably just wishful thinking.

'Let's go outside and get some fresh air,' he said.

'No, no, I want to dance,' she insisted. 'Listen to the music – it's sensational.'

'But I want to kiss you,' he murmured in her ear, smelling her hair and feeling her body close to his.

'Then kiss me here,' she said, offering her mouth to his.

He looked at her. Her eyes looked distant, and it finally occurred to him. 'Have you taken something, Emma?'

'Just a little half a pill, that's all. It's wonderful.'

Stanley decided he'd better lay off the booze for a while, she might need some looking after. 'Oh well,' he shrugged, 'I guess I'm the only one here who hasn't. And I might as well take advantage of you while you're bombed.'

They swayed to the music and he kissed her. And the kiss to Emma was delicious. It went on and on and on. His tongue gently explored her mouth and his lips moved on hers, sometimes engulfing her upper lip, sometimes her lower, then his whole mouth, open on hers, as their bodies seemed to meld into one. Everything was in unison with the music, she thought. It was a dream, a wonderful dream where every sensation was perfectly matched.

Both she and Stanley were oblivious to the fact that Michael was staring at them through the crowd, his euphoria fading into thin air as he watched them. *No*, his mind screamed to him, *this can't be happening*. He'd danced with Emma himself earlier and he'd been aware of her sensuality. He knew she'd popped a pill; he'd told Mandy to give her one. But her sensuality had been for him. Not Stanley. He made his way through the crowd.

'Mind if a brother cuts in, Stan?' he asked, his voice like ice.

'Oh. Sure.' Stanley stepped aside, feeling a little foolish, aware that they must have been making quite a spectacle of themselves. He looked about self-consciously but nobody was taking any notice, so he watched Michael and Emma whirl about the dance floor. The tempo of the music had quickened and Emma was laughing and enjoying the pace of the dance. Michael was forcing a smile but Stanley could tell he was displeased. Christ, the man was possessive, he thought. Poor Emma. It was sick.

'Want to party on?' Michael asked. 'I've laid in crates of champagne and we're all going back to my place.'

'Oh yes,' Emma laughed, 'I want to party on all night.'

At least twenty people ended up back at Michael's. He wasn't too happy to find Stanley amongst them. He deliberately hadn't extended him a personal invitation and he was irritated beyond measure when Emma refused the offer of a lift. 'No, it's okay thanks, Michael,' she said. 'I'll go with Stanley and Derek. You can drive some of the others and we'll meet you there.'

The music was loud and most of the gang seemed still to be on a high. But Michael needed a boost. Half a dozen people gathered around him as he put the glass board on the coffee table and started cutting the coke.

They passed the board from one to the other, ceremoniously snorting a line each, even Derek. Derek had decided to be in anything that was going that night. He'd worry about tomorrow

587

when tomorrow came, he told himself, Mandy was right, this was the night of a lifetime.

'Emma.' Michael called her over. He wanted to get her away from the crowd in the corner which included Stanley. 'Your turn,' he said. 'Come on,' he urged when she hesitated, 'this is our big night. Share in it.'

Why not, she thought, as she accepted the tightly rolled hundred dollar bill. She remembered the one and only time she'd snorted coke before. She'd been with Michael then too. They'd been working on *Halley's* and it had been a buzz. She snorted deeply and then fought the desire to sneeze. Yes, he was right, this was their big night, she must share in it.

Stanley watched from the sidelines. It was mad to snort coke on top of the pills they'd taken, he thought, and he was angry with Michael for leading Emma astray. There was nothing he could do, though, Emma was too far gone to listen to him. Besides, he himself was too drunk to tell anyone what to do. He avoided the champagne and had another beer.

It was Mandy's idea to take the party to the basement. 'The pool!' she shrieked, and started stripping off her clothes. 'Hey, everybody! The pool!'

In minutes, clothes were flying everywhere. Naked and semi-naked people were running down the stairs and throwing themselves into the pool with gay abandon. The music was turned up even louder, two crates of champagne were carted downstairs and the party continued.

Not a bad way to sober up, Stanley thought as he stripped down to his underpants and prepared to join the throng. In the middle of the pool, Mandy climbed aboard Derek's shoulders and together they called for a battle to the death. 'Fight! Fight!' Mandy yelled and Derek, between her thighs, was laughing so much he could hardly stay upright.

Stanley grabbed the half-naked Emma and heaved her onto his shoulders. 'We'll take you on,' he said, and Emma squealed with delight. Stanley wasn't sure whether he'd joined in the horseplay merely to feel Emma's thighs about his neck or whether he'd wanted to avoid the possibility of them ending up around any other man's neck, but he threw himself into the fray and soon he and Emma were the champions, beating every couple who took them on.

Michael was the only person not joining in the fun. Nobody noticed him standing fully clothed by one of the marble columns looking down at the frolics below. He studied Emma's breasts. He studied her buttocks which clearly showed through the wet lace panties which clung to her body. And he studied her thighs, locked either side of Stanley's face, and her ankles hooked behind his back for leverage.

Michael was sweating. Were they lovers? Had Stanley been possessing Emma all the while without Michael's knowledge? He thought of the gun in the dressing-table drawer upstairs. Maybe the gun wasn't meant for Karol Mankowski after all, he thought. Maybe it was meant for Stanley.

No, he told himself, that was madness, insanity. Calm down, calm down. Emma was uninhibited because of the drugs she'd taken – she wasn't used to drugs. Michael had been aware of the sexuality in her when he'd danced with her. She could be anybody's tonight. But not Stanley's, he thought. Not Stanley's. Not anyone else's either. He made a promise to himself. Mine. *Mine*.

He downed his champagne and poured himself another from the bottle on the railing. Then he turned his back on the gleeful squeals and shrieks and poolside frolics and crossed to the coffee table. Meticulously, he cut two more lines of coke and snorted them.

He sat back for a minute, waiting for the extra buzz. The music stopped but no one came upstairs to put on another CD – they were too busy splashing and giggling below.

Michael got up, went to the kitchen and took a bottle of Bollinger from the refrigerator. He put it in an ice bucket on a tray with two fresh glasses, and carried it up to his bedroom. He put it on the table by the window, then he set out another two lines of coke. She might want an extra lift by the time she came upstairs, he thought.

And, when he was sure that everything was in order, he turned the video on. High in the wall, behind the air vent, it started to quietly whirr.

He sat for several minutes planning his attack. Somebody downstairs put on another CD, the theme music from *Once Upon a Time in America*. One of his favourite CDs, one of his favourite movies. Haunting. 'Amapola.' The party was starting to quieten down a little. Good, he thought, she'd be getting mellow. Not sleepy. Oh no, still on a high. But playtime was over. Now she'd want the real thing. She'd want the feel of flesh upon flesh. She'd want the moment she'd been waiting for, the moment he'd been waiting for. Yes, they were meant to be one.

Michael could have laughed as he walked downstairs. There was no competition. Just Stan. Poor stuntie Stan. How had Stanley ever thought he'd get a look in? Michael was the only person in Emma's class. Emma was a creator, just like he was. And he was the creator of *Earth Man*. It was his invention. If they only knew to what degree he'd manipulated its success. Oh yes, Michael had the power. And Emma responded to power. Every woman responded to power.

There was no one in the living room. Whoever had changed the CD had returned to the pool. Good, they could all stay there while he and Emma went upstairs.

From the ground-floor landing, he looked down at the pool. Several people were still splashing about, but in a desultory fashion; others were sitting around, some half-naked, some wrapped in towelling robes, sipping champagne and talking. The party had mellowed. Emma was in a corner talking avidly to Derek who was raving back, neither of them really listening to each other.

Out of the corner of his eye Michael could see Stanley in the opposite corner trying to help one of the film crew follow 'Amapola' on the guitar. Michael loathed guitars and he loathed people who brought guitars to parties. But it was a welcome sight. He was sure that Emma loathed guitar players too. His eyes were on Emma as he slowly descended the stairs.

'Hello, Derek,' he said. 'Having a good time?'

Derek halted mid-conversation and swivelled eyes that were completely out of focus somewhere in Michael's direction. 'The best, the best, the best,' he said. The man was off the planet. Michael turned towards Emma.

But to his utter astonishment, before he could say anything, her mouth was on his and her body was pressing insistently against him.

'Michael,' she murmured and he could feel her tongue flicking across his teeth.

The room vanished as he held her to him. 'Let's go upstairs,' he whispered.

'Yes, yes,' she said.

Nobody seemed to notice them go, not that Michael would have cared if they had. Derek's glassy eyes were still focused on nothing and the splashing in the pool, the buzz of conversation and the strains of 'Amapola' continued, oblivious.

In the master bedroom, he closed the door and she snorted another line. 'Music,' she whispered, 'let's have music.'

He took a perfunctory snort himself, he certainly didn't need any more and, as he ripped his clothes off, he grabbed the first CD he could lay his hands on and put it in the player built into the bedhead. It was a remaster of an old Donna Summer recording.

He poured the Bollinger but they only downed half a glass before they attacked each other's bodies. She was as ready as he was.

Donna Summer was moaning 'Ooh, love to love

you baby, ooh love to love you baby, ooh love to love you baby . . . '

Then they were on the bed, naked, and he was driving himself into her. It was everything that Michael had hoped for, lived for. Her skin upon his skin. Their flesh mingling into one. This was no videoed fantasy that he would relive tomorrow. This was real. This was Emma. He was possessing his own Emma. And she was clinging to him, begging for more. She was his flesh and blood. And now she was his. Finally his.

He felt good. Strong. Powerful. And although her passion was exciting him, he knew he could go all night. His own pleasure was of no importance. He wanted to drive her into a frenzy. It didn't take long. Her answering thrusts quickened and she started to cry out. He drew back. Only fractionally. Just enough to tease. Enough to keep her on the knife edge of ecstasy. Any moment now, he told himself, any moment now . . . 'Ooh, love to love you baby, ooh, love to love you baby, ooh, love to . . . '

Suddenly she stopped crying out. He could feel she was on the threshold. The time had come. He would give her the greatest pleasure of her life. Yes, my darling, he thought. Yes. Now. He placed his right hand on her neck, positioning his fingers over her carotid arteries and he started to squeeze.

It was a game he'd played before. He would release the pressure at her moment of orgasm and the sudden rush of blood to her brain would intensify her pleasure. He squeezed, gently at first, then gradually applying more pressure.

She gasped in ecstacy, her eyes rolling back in

her head. She started to writhe but he refused to let go. Then she was bucking wildly and he was bucking with her, the two of them rivetted together. He loved her. He had loved her for years and now they were one. Forever one. He wanted to die at that moment. He wanted to die for the sheer love of her. And he wanted her to die with him. In ecstacy. Together. 'Ooh, love to love you baby, ooh, love to love you baby . . . '

He could feel her climax. There was no need for his own pleasure. His energy was spent, in any case. He lay gasping for air. He looked at her, and she looked back at him. But there was something wrong.

A glimmer of light found its way through Michael's fogged brain. She wasn't looking at him, she was staring at him. That was what was wrong, she was staring. And her mouth was open. And she was terrifyingly still.

'Oh God, no!' He smacked her face but still she stared back at him. 'For Christ's sake, no!' He felt for her pulse. 'Oh Jesus,' he panted, 'sweet Jesus! Emma! Emma!'

Help. He had to get help. 'Emma, Emma,' he whimpered as he pulled on his trousers.

'*Ooh, love to love you baby, ooh love to love you baby, ooh love to love you ... .*'

Stanley was in the living room. Still half-naked, he was squatting beside the stereo in his damp under-pants ferreting through the CDs when Michael appeared on the upper landing. 'Get real, Toddie,' he was calling downstairs, ' "Duelling Banjos" is a bit out of your league right now. What else?'

'Help me,' Michael panted, and he grabbed the railing for support.

As soon as Stanley saw Michael he knew that something was terribly wrong. But he'd known something was terribly wrong when the man had come downstairs to the pool half an hour ago. The glassy eyes, the tight smile, the air of supreme confidence – all the signs Michael displayed when he was drugged out of his brain – but there had been something else. Something driven, something insane. 'Hello, Derek. Having a good time?' Michael had asked, but his voice had a strange, intense edge to it. Stanley had known then. Of course no one else had noticed.

He'd watched as she kissed him and he'd watched as the two of them went off together, Stanley cursed himself. He should have stopped them.

'What is it? What have you done?' He was already racing up the stairs.

'I've killed her. She's dead,' Michael whimpered as Stanley pushed past him and into the bedroom. 'She's dead. I've killed her.'

Stanley stared at the body on the bed. 'Oh, Christ!' he said as he knelt beside her. He lifted her and thrust a pillow beneath her shoulders. Then he arched her head back and placed his mouth over hers. As he alternated between breathing into her and pumping her chest, he kept saying over and over, 'Breathe, Mandy, breathe. Can you hear me, Mandy? Breathe, Mandy, breathe. Can you hear me?'

As he said it, the fog in Michael's brain slowly

cleared. Of course! This wasn't Emma. It was Mandy. When he'd gone down to the pool to get Emma it had been Mandy who'd kissed him and thrust herself against him. It had been Mandy who'd come upstairs with him and Mandy to whom he'd made love. How could he have thought it was Emma?

But that meant that he hadn't killed Emma. On the instant of that realisation, Michael's panic disappeared and he felt suffused with a sensation of utter calm. *Stanley has killed Mandy*, he thought. He watched as the half-naked Stanley ground the heel of his palm into Mandy's chest. 'Breathe, Mandy, breathe.' *Stanley has killed Mandy.* That's certainly what it looked like – and that's what it would look like through the lens of the video camera. . .

Michael quickly pulled on his jacket. He positioned himself where the camera could see him. 'What have you done, Stanley? What have you done?' The camera microphone would pick that up.

'Breathe, Mandy, breathe.' Stanley didn't hear a word as he locked his mouth over hers. Even better, Michael thought. It looked as though he was mauling the girl, raping her even. It would be easy to edit the tape. And the soundtrack. It was what he was good at, wasn't it? Give him enough footage and he could create whatever fantasy he chose.

'Stan! Stop it! For God's sake, what are you doing?'

'Breathe, Mandy, breathe.'

Michael thought of the gun in the top drawer.

He'd be defending Mandy's honour, wouldn't he? Then he realised that the dressing table was out of camera range. Damn. No good. The gun would look too premeditated. The killing of Stanley needed to be impulsive, accidental. He could hear himself saying, 'I was simply trying to stop the man.'

Then he saw the bottle of Bollinger sitting on the dresser, clearly in view of the camera. Yes, that was it.

'Stop it, Stan, leave her alone!' Michael grabbed the bottle of champagne and smashed it with all his might across Stanley's skull. The bottle didn't break, but there was the sound of cracking bone and Stanley slumped forward on the bed.

Michael dropped the bottle and ran to the door but he didn't leave the room. He turned and looked at the bed. He was well out of camera range and the lens would be seeing what he was seeing. Stanley's body sprawled across Mandy's, her eyes continuing to stare blankly up at the ceiling.

He only waited a moment. Then he went downstairs. It was time to tell everyone to leave. After they'd gone, he'd ring the police.

CHAPTER SEVENTEEN

THE PICTURE IN THE top television monitor remained relentlessly still. Not a shred of movement. Just the bodies of Mandy and Stanley sprawled on the bed. Blood seeping from the wound in Stanley's head, spreading a deathly red stain across the white linen, Mandy's eyes still blindly riveted upon the ceiling.

The picture in the bottom monitor was more active. The basement camera covered the downstairs door which opened from the swimming pool to the steps leading to the street above. As an extra security precaution, Michael never used the basement entrance. Access to the pool was always via the stairs from the living room. Now people were hurriedly dressing, preparing to leave. Emma was asking Michael something but he was shaking his head as he rounded up his guests and directed them upstairs.

'He's getting them all to leave,' Karol said. 'What's the girl up to?'

Franklin didn't answer. He continued to stare at the row of monitors in the corner of the security room – the monitors which, for a full six weeks now, had been permanently linked to Michael's security system.

It was nearly seven o'clock in the morning. He'd come as soon as he'd received Karol's call: 'You need to see it, boss,' was all Karol had said.

Karol hadn't contacted Franklin until he'd realised that Michael had killed the girl. Jesus Christ, he'd thought they were just screwing.

Franklin had arrived in time to see Michael's attack on Stanley.

Together they'd watched as Michael prepared to go downstairs. Karol glanced at Franklin, awaiting instructions. Was he to call the police? Was he to go around and sort out the situation himself? But there were no instructions.

'We do nothing,' Franklin ordered, sensing the enquiry. 'We wait and see what he does next.' Karol stood beside him, eyes glued to the monitors.

What could they do? Franklin wondered vaguely. It was too late to save the girl. Or Stanley. Ultimately, it was too late to save Michael too, but maybe, just maybe, they could save the Ross family name.

Franklin watched Michael hurrying the guests into the living room. Presumably the boy had a plan, he thought. Was he going to ring the police once he was alone? Yes, he might just get away with it if he did that. Stanley had killed the girl. It could certainly look that way and, loathsome though he found it, Franklin would support the theory. But as soon as Michael was cleared of any involvement, Franklin would have him committed – for good. Quietly, privately, and with no fuss. Yes, he'd have to make sure of that.

'What's she doing?' Karol asked as he watched Emma beside the basement door. It was frustrating; he couldn't see her clearly behind the others.

But Franklin didn't hear him. Despite the plans forming in his mind, the old man felt numb as he watched the last of the guests, including Emma, leave the house by the front living room door. His grandson was an insane killer.

As soon as everyone had gone, Michael busied himself around the living room. Franklin and Karol found it difficult to see what he was doing – he kept walking out of camera range – but he appeared to be tidying up.

'He's clearing away the drugs,' Karol said.

'Good. That means he's going to call the police. If he plays it right, he should get away with it.'

Karol looked at Franklin. So that was the old man's plan – he was going to help cover for his grandson. Karol nodded. Personally he couldn't see why Franklin should waste his time caring about a madman like Michael Ross. The boy had always been a lost cause, in Karol's opinion. But Karol wasn't there for opinions. He knew that. He was there to do Franklin's bidding. And if Franklin Ross wanted to save his grandson, then that's what Karol would help him do.

For several moments, Michael disappeared from view altogether. Then he reappeared in the bedroom upstairs. He didn't even glance at the bodies on the bed as he cleared up the cocaine on the dressing table. He knelt beside the safe in the corner, carefully stacking away his drug supply.

'Come on, boy,' Franklin muttered. 'Hurry it up. Ring the police!'

'Boss. Look.' Karol pointed to the bottom monitor. The basement door which led to the steps and the street outside was slowly opening. 'The girl,' he said. 'She's come back.'

Emma quietly closed the door behind her. She looked about and then she walked towards the stairs.

'What the hell's she up to?' Franklin barked.

'So that's what she was doing,' Karol said, 'she was unlocking the door before she left.'

As Emma slowly started up the stairs, Franklin grabbed his cane. 'Get the car,' he ordered.

It had been cold outside on the steps and Emma's breath came out in short bursts of steam as she climbed the stairs. She wasn't sure why she'd come back, but she hadn't believed Michael when he'd said Stanley had gone home. Stanley wouldn't have left without telling her. And she hadn't believed Michael when he'd said a police contact of his had telephoned saying the place was going to be raided. Something had happened, she was sure. Something had happened that prompted Michael to get rid of them all.

At the top of the stairs, she looked about the living room. No one there. Michael must be upstairs, in the bedroom.

Her heart was racing and a terrible fear overcame her. It's the drugs, that's all, she told herself, still feeling decidedly strange – drug-induced paranoia, that's what it was. She was behaving like a fool, she told herself. No doubt she'd get upstairs and find that Michael had put himself to bed. But she couldn't help thinking that if there was a raid imminent, why wasn't he in the living room waiting for the police?

She looked up at the landing. The bedroom door was ajar. Quietly, she started to climb the stairs.

Michael closed the door to the safe, crossed to the table and picked up the telephone receiver. Then he remembered the video camera, still filming behind the air-conditioning vent. He turned off the switch inside the walk-in cupboard. As he closed the door, he heard a noise. There was someone on the landing.

He quickly crossed to the dresser, took out the gun and trained it on the bedroom door as it was slowly pushed open.

Emma stood there. She saw Michael immediately but she didn't really take in the gun. Her eyes focused on the bed.

'Oh God.' She stood frozen to the spot. 'Oh God, what's happened?'

'Emma.' Michael slipped the gun into his pocket. 'It's terrible. They're dead. I was just going to call the police.'

But Emma wasn't listening. She crossed and knelt beside the bed. 'Oh God! Michael, what have you done?'

'Stan killed her, Emma. I came in and he was attacking her, so I . . . '

'Call an ambulance,' she ordered.

'He was killing her, Emma ... I had to do something – '

'I said, call an ambulance. He's alive.' The fear had left Emma. Stanley was breathing. What should she do? She mustn't move him. No, she mustn't do that. She looked at Michael. 'For God's sake, call a bloody ambulance,' she snapped again.

But Michael just stood staring at her. 'He killed her, Emma,' he said. 'Stan killed Mandy.'

She rose and crossed to the telephone. But, before she could pick up the receiver, Michael's hand was on hers.

'No, don't do that.' She looked at him, looked into the eyes of a madman. 'Stan doesn't deserve to live, Emma,' Michael said slowly. 'He did a terrible thing. He killed Mandy.'

Emma fought to stem her returning fear. She had to take control, had to reason with him. But how did one reason with a madman?

'Yes, he did a terrible thing,' she said. 'But we still have to call an ambulance. And then we have to call the police, all right? The police will sort everything out and he'll be punished. Now let me use the phone.'

She picked up the receiver again but he ripped it out of her hand. She tried to grab it from him. 'For God's sake, Michael, he's dying!' she yelled.

'Let him,' Michael snarled, and he swept the telephone off the table and onto the floor.

As Emma made a dive for it, she felt something hard press against the back of her head.

'Don't do that,' he said, and she turned to see the barrel of the automatic pistol pointed at her temple. She could fight the fear no longer. Terror overwhelmed her and she froze, staring up at him.

'I don't want to hurt you, Emma,' he said, and very gently he helped her to her feet. 'I love you. You know that. Now come on, let's sit and talk.'

He led her to the foot of the bed and sat her down. She was terribly aware of the bodies of Mandy and Stanley directly behind her. She was also aware, as Michael sat beside her, that the gun was no longer pointing directly at her. He was holding it in his right hand and resting it on his knee as he put his left arm around her shoulders. The shred of reason she was fighting to maintain told her that, if she could lull him into a false sense of security, he might relax enough for her to make a dash for the door. If she dared.

'We don't need Stanley,' he said. 'Just like we didn't need Malcolm. Or Marcel. It's you and me, Emma. It's always been you and me. There's no room for anyone else, you know that, don't you?'

'Yes,' she whispered, sick with fear and realisation. 'Yes.'

He drew her to him, cradling her head against his chest. 'You know how much I love you, don't you, Emma?'

'Yes,' she whispered, staring in terror at the pistol resting on his knee. 'I know.'

He started to rock her gently back and forth. 'It was beautiful when we were together,' he murmured, 'when I thought it was you.' She didn't dare say anything. 'I didn't know it was Mandy. It was you and me, and we were so close.' He stroked her hair. 'So close, and I wanted us to die together. That's how beautiful it was, do you understand?'

604

'Yes,' she whispered. 'Yes, I understand.' She didn't resist as he raised her head.

'I love you,' he said. And he kissed her. His lips were soft and his hand caressed the back of her neck.

'Let's die together, Emma.' His mouth travelled down her neck and she watched as he raised the gun from his knee. Oh, dear God, he was going to kill her. 'I want you to be mine forever.' His right arm circled her and he pulled her to him in a close embrace, his breath warm against her neck. 'Love me, Emma, love me,' he whispered. And she felt the gun drop from his hand onto the bed behind her.

Now, she thought. Now! And, with all of her strength, she pushed him from her. But Michael was too quick. As she started for the door, he grabbed at her coat. She tried to wrestle out of it but he stood and pulled her to him. Once more she was in his embrace and once more he had the gun in his hand. She stopped struggling as she felt the barrel press against her ribcage.

'I didn't want it this way, Emma,' Michael said, as she felt the gun travel towards her heart. 'I wanted to love you before we died ... '

'Put the gun down, Michael.' It came from the doorway. Two silhouettes were framed in the early-morning light.

'Put the gun down,' the voice said again. Michael knew that voice.

Franklin and Karol stepped into the room.

Emma held her breath as she felt Michael tense beside her. The gun was against her left breast. Any moment, she thought, any moment now.

'You heard me, Michael. Put the gun down.' The voice demanded obedience. It always had, and Michael found himself automatically lowering the pistol.

'Grandpa,' he said.

'Put it on the bed and then we'll ring the police and sort out this whole mess.'

The gun remained in Michael's hand, but he'd forgotten it was there. It dangled loosely by his side and, despite the fact that his left arm still encircled her, Emma started to breathe a little more freely.

'Stan killed Mandy, Grandpa.'

'Well, we can certainly make it look that way.' Franklin gestured at the telephone. Karol picked it up from the floor and replaced it on the table. 'Now put the gun down,' Franklin repeated as he lifted the receiver.

Something in Emma snapped. In an instant, the fear left her to be replaced by cold, blind fury. One person was dead, another lay dying and all Franklin Ross could think about was safeguarding the character of his family. He was prepared to sacrifice Stanley Grahame to preserve the precious name of Ross. Even if Stanley were dead, it was a shocking proposal. What about Stanley's name? Stanley's family? What gave Franklin the divine right to assume that the Ross honour was superior to that of others?

'He's alive,' she said. It was an accusation.

Franklin was genuinely taken aback. It hadn't occurred to him that the man might be alive. He'd been so occupied with his scheme to save Michael that he hadn't given a thought to Stanley

606

Grahame. It certainly complicated things.

'Did you hear me, Franklin?' the girl snarled. For the first time he looked at her and he could see the scorn blazing in her eyes. 'Stanley's alive and I'm calling an ambulance.'

But the harshness of her tone jolted Michael out of his compliance and, as she reached out towards the telephone, she broke the command Franklin held over his grandson.

Emma was ordering Grandpa Franklin around, Michael thought. That couldn't be right. And she certainly couldn't leave him. They were together now. Soon to be together forever. He pulled her back beside him. His arm locked about her waist and the gun once more snapped into position against her heart.

Yes, that was better. He was the one who was in control here. Not Emma. And not Grandpa Franklin either. Not any more. Michael felt elation. A sense of freedom overwhelmed him. Freedom from Grandpa Franklin. At last.

'Put down the gun, Michael,' the voice once more commanded, 'and let Emma go.'

'No, Grandpa.' Michael smiled at Emma who stood, transfixed, the gun at her breast. 'Together forever,' he whispered. He would shoot her through the heart – he wouldn't destroy that beautiful face. 'Emma. Emma, my love.' His finger slowly started to ease back the trigger, but a movement he caught from the corner of his eye momentarily distracted him.

Grandpa Franklin had given a sharp nod, a signal. What did it mean? Michael turned to see.

In the instant that it happened, he was thirteen

years old again. He was staring through the wind-screen of a car and Karol Mankowski was standing there, his arm outstretched, the sights of his gun trained firmly on the person behind the wheel. In a second the blonde's head would shatter and her blood would splatter Michael in the back seat, and Karol would have saved his life.

'Grandpa!' he cried.

Michael's head didn't shatter. Karol shot him clean through the heart. It seemed kinder to Franklin to do it that way, he thought, as Michael fell dead to the floor.

Epilogue

FRANKLIN DIDN'T TRY to suppress the story. He didn't try to whitewash the events of that terrible night in order to preserve the Ross name. In fact, it was Franklin himself who handed the videotape over to the police.

'There's your evidence,' he said. 'The murder of the girl, the attack on the man, it's all there – even the performance he put on for the camera. He obviously intended to frame Stanley Grahame.'

Franklin was tired. He felt empty, defeated. He wanted to get the whole wretched business over so he could return to Australia. He would never come back to New York.

'The one incident not covered on that tape,' the old man continued, 'is the killing of my grandson and that was carried out upon my instruction. It was the only way to save the girl.'

'Emma Clare,' the lieutenant said, nodding to the young officer who was taking notes.

'That's right. Emma Clare. My granddaughter.'

* * *

As soon as the inquest was over, Franklin took Helen to Australia. They were married at Araluen.

Emma didn't attend the ceremony. She stayed in New York to be near Stanley. His skull had been severely fractured and he'd been in a coma for three days, so the doctors had feared permanent brain damage. For several months after he regained consciousness, he suffered bouts of memory loss but slowly, with Emma's help, he regained the threads of his past and, six months after leaving the hospital, he was ready to start work again. He accepted an offer on a big-budget Disney film due to start shooting around Christmas. 'Special effects only,' the doctors warned. 'No stunt work. Another skull injury and you won't be so lucky.'

'Oh well,' he shrugged philosophically, 'it's time, I guess. Nobody loves an aging stuntie.'

Emma refused his offer to come and work with him. She'd long since left the Ross Corporation and had started writing her novel. The novel she had promised herself she'd write since she was a young girl. She had the time to do it now. And more than ample funds to support herself while she wrote. Since the death of Michael Ross, *Halley's, Blue Water History and Earth Man* had become three of the greatest money-spinning movies of the decade. Even *The Breeders* had a resurgence at the box office when it was re-released. As co-producer Emma had points in all four films and it came as a surprise when she found herself a wealthy woman.

'What's the novel about?' Stanley asked.

'Oh, a family saga style thing,' Emma replied vaguely. She didn't tell him about the journals. The journals were her inspiration.

When the invitation to Franklin and Helen's wedding had arrived, it had arrived with a large parcel and an accompanying note from Franklin. 'This is your heritage, Emma,' the note had said. 'You're a Ross, whether you like it or not. Come to Araluen. Please.'

Inside the parcel were the journals of George Franklin Ross. Emma couldn't help herself; she was drawn to them like a magnet. The sense of history captured her completely. The sense of belonging. Her great-great-grandfather was speaking directly to her. Franklin was right. Like it or not, she was a Ross.

The urge to go to Araluen was strong. She wanted to see the old stone barn that George had built, she wanted to walk amongst the vines that Richard had planted . . . But she resisted the urge. She refused to be dictated to by Franklin Ross. Besides, she told herself, she couldn't leave New York until Stanley was well again.

But Stanley had been out of hospital for months and had accepted the Disney job when the telephone call came. There was no excuse for her not to go back.

'Penelope died early this morning.' Franklin's voice sounded strange down the line. Not as authoritative as she remembered. 'The funeral's on Tuesday. Will you come to Sydney?'

'Yes,' she said. 'I'll be there.'

'Will you stay long?' Stanley asked when he saw her off at the airport.

'I don't know,' she said. 'I'll stay for Christmas, then see what happens. I might even have the book finished by the new year.' Now that Emma had made the decision, she was glad she was leaving. She needed space. Space from New York and space from Stanley.

She knew she loved him. She knew she always would. But she didn't want an affair. Not yet. He was too much a part of her past. Too much a reminder of Michael. Memories of the three of them were inescapable when she was with Stanley. And Emma needed to forget Michael.

Stanley sensed her evasion. 'Do you want me to butt out, Emma, is that what you want? Just tell me to leave you alone and I will.'

'For a while, Stanley,' she answered. 'Just for a while.'

'Fine. How long's "a while"?'

She smiled and kissed him.

Penelope's funeral was a grand affair. She would have been pleased. All the right people were there, all the pomp and ceremony. Franklin had arranged it himself and he'd spared no expense. There was no more animosity left in him. It was the least he could do for her.

'Will you come to Araluen?' he asked Emma.

'Yes.' She'd known she would.

Franklin was a different man, she thought. Was it just because he'd aged rapidly over the last six months? Or was it Araluen? Probably a mixture of the two, she decided. But there was a sense of peace about him now. The desire to dominate had gone. She watched him as he sat with Helen on the front verandah overlooking the vineyards. It was early evening, Franklin was sipping a glass of his best hermitage, and they were chatting and very comfortable together.

New Year's Eve tomorrow, Emma thought. She'd nearly finished the book – another two weeks should do it. What then? she wondered. Back to New York? She missed Stanley. But she would probably miss Araluen more if she went back.

'I'm just going for a walk,' she said as she crossed the verandah.

'Dinner in an hour, dear,' Helen reminded her.

Emma loved Araluen. She loved it with a passion she'd never known was in her. She walked through the vineyard watching the patterns of light play on the vines and the colour of the earth change in the deepening dusk.

She'd joined the workers amongst the vines all through the hot December. She'd wanted to. She'd revelled in the smell of the soil and the feel of her hard-earned sweat. And now she was as brown and fit as any of the farmhands. She often saw Franklin watching her as she worked; his expression was unfathomable, but somehow touching.

There was no point agonising over a decision now, she told herself as she looked back at the homestead in the distance. She'd worry about whether to stay or go in two weeks when she'd finished the book.

Emma hurried back to the house. She mustn't be late for dinner. Unpunctuality annoyed Franklin.

As it turned out, Emma didn't have to wait two weeks to make her decision. Franklin made it for her the following night. New Year's Eve.

The three of them dined alone. The cook had the evening off and Helen prepared a beautiful meal. Chopin's 'Nocturne' was playing quietly in the background. Franklin was still dictatorial enough to insist that nothing but Chopin was played at Araluen and Helen couldn't be bothered rebelling. It wasn't worth it. Anyway, she liked Chopin.

They dined late and it was eleven o'clock before they left the table and took their coffees and liqueurs out onto the verandah. It was a hot summer night, but the verandah was positioned and designed to pick up the slightest breeze that wafted up from the valley. Old George had made sure of that, Franklin thought. For someone with no experience he'd been a clever builder. But then Grandfather George had always been ruled by common sense. He should have learned that from the old man, Franklin thought; it was something he hadn't applied too much to his own life. Franklin had always wanted power. Too much power.

He was feeling very mellow tonight. Perhaps it was the wine. He took another sip from the glass; a good red – one to be proud of. Franklin never drank liqueurs or spirits. He'd even given up his evening Laphroaig. These days he could only drink wine.

Perhaps it was the fact that it was New Year's Eve, he thought. Nineteen ninety-four. He was eighty-nine years old. It had been a long life. Not much more of it to go now.

He looked at the two women as they sipped their liqueurs. It had taken him all of these years to understand women, he thought. Well, that was wrong of course – he didn't understand them. Not one bit. But it had taken him all of these years to appreciate them. He wondered at the mess he'd made of his life. But it wasn't too late, was it? Not for the future generations.

'Half an hour to midnight, Emma,' he said. 'And then it will be the new year. A good time to make decisions.'

'What decisions?' she asked. He'd taken her by surprise. How had he known she'd been agonising over what to do?

But he hadn't. 'I have an offer to make you. And you must decide whether or not to accept. I think now is a good time.' He looked at Helen. It was obviously something that they'd discussed.

'I want you to take over,' he announced.

'Take over what?' Emma asked, confused. Was this going to get complicated? she wondered. She'd had a little too much to drink.

'Everything,' he said. 'Well, primarily Araluen,' he added, as an afterthought. 'Araluen is obviously where you belong, there's no decision to be made there.' He put his glass down and sat back in his comfortable wicker chair. 'I shall die soon and I want to leave it all to you. There has to be a Ross at the helm.' Emma stared at him blankly.

'It's not as daunting a prospect as it appears,' Franklin continued. 'The Ross Corporation runs itself, you'll have a wealth of experts at your beck and call. And of course Helen will be around to help you.' He glanced at Helen who nodded and smiled back at him. She and Franklin had discussed the matter fully. 'Of course, you would have to change your name to Ross, but that's a mere legality.'

'Oh. Is it?' Emma felt a dangerous surge of rebellion. The old man was reverting to type. The dictator was rising to the surface.

But Franklin refused to recognise the danger signs. 'Emma,' he said leaning forward in his chair. 'You are my blood. You are my sons and my grandsons and I'm asking you to accept what is rightfully yours. And to take responsibility for it.'

Emma couldn't resist. She laughed. The wine had certainly gone to her head. 'You mean you're asking a woman to take over the Ross empire?' she said.

'Yes, I am.'

Her smile faded. 'You really want your pound of flesh, don't you?'

He nodded.

Emma and Franklin stared at each other for a long time. Then she asked, 'Does that mean I get to change the music?'

Franklin considered for a moment. 'I think Helen has some Mozart there.'

* * *

616

Three months later Stanley arrived at Araluen. 'Okay, so you told me to butt out for a while,' he said. 'But it's a week short of five months. I figure a week short of five months constitutes "a while".'

She showed him around the property with pride, quoting George's journals as she took him on a guided tour through the old cellars and the original vineyard. 'Cuttings brought out from France, Stanley. Grenache and hermitage. Richard got them from Dr Penfold.'

'How's the book going?' he asked.

'I'm about to do a deal with Pan,' she grinned. 'They seem really excited about it. Hey, I can show you the Grange, Penfold's original home.'

Stanley was quickly realising that he would have to rethink his plans. Emma was not about to allow herself to be whisked off back to New York. Not now, possibly not ever. Sure, this was a pretty part of the world, he thought, but, hell, they were moviemakers. 'Don't you miss it, Emma?'

'What?'

'New York. The movies.'

'No.'

Yes, he'd definitely have to rethink his plans.

It happened a fortnight after Stanley's arrival. Franklin went for a walk. 'I'm going for a walk,' he said. 'Just down to the old stone barn, sit in the sun for a while.'

'Take your scarf, Franklin,' Helen said, handing it to him. It was a fine afternoon but there was an autumn chill in the air.

Franklin dutifully took the scarf. He'd decided

617

to tell them where he'd be. There was no point in causing unnecessary worry. If all went according to plan, they'd find him at dusk. He hoped he had the strength of will that Grandfather George had had.

'Can you really do it?' he could remember himself asking. These days it was easy to remember one's childhood.

'I think people can do whatever they set their minds to,' Grandfather George had answered. 'If they're strong and they have the will.'

He walked through the cellars feeling the coolness of the stones and breathing in the smell of wet hessian and he marvelled at the fact that some things never changed.

Then he walked around the side of the old stone barn. The side away from the homestead. Where he'd sat with Aunt Catherine as she'd sketched the old vineyard. Gently, he eased himself down on the ground and looked around at his world. It was a good world. And he was leaving it in good hands.

Franklin had discussed his imminent death with Helen. She was prepared. And Emma? Well, Emma was like Grandfather George, wasn't she? All the passion of the land and the common sense to run it. Pity he hadn't known her earlier – he might have learned something from her.

No, he wouldn't have, he told himself. He wouldn't have learned at all. He only ever learned from his mistakes – and then always too late to rectify them. Catherine. Millie. Penelope. He'd been wrong, hadn't he? Wrong every time. Not that it mattered now. Emma would make up for all that. And she had a good man by her side, which pleased him. That was right. A woman needed a man by her side.

He could hear Catherine laugh at the thought, but he didn't care. So he was old-fashioned – was there anything wrong with that? A man needed a woman too, he was prepared to admit that, and he thought fondly of Helen.

He looked out over the old vineyard as the autumn sun warmed his face. The timeless vines. They would outlive him. They would outlive Emma. And they would outlive Emma's children. They would always be there. It was a wonderful thought.

The light was changing now. Was dusk coming on? It was early if it was. 'Use your peripheral vision, Franklin,' he heard Catherine say, 'and you'll find ... that the earth is red and the mountains purple, and ... ' Then Never-Never Everard's voice took over and Franklin was at Mandinulla ... you'll see colours you've never seen before,' Never-Never was saying. 'They shimmer like magic. And then, beyond the shimmer, mirages. Sometimes a whole lake.'

Franklin could see it all. His world was a shimmering lake of colour. And beyond the shimmering lake was the timeless network of the vines. It was truly marvellous.

They found him just as he had anticipated they would. At dusk.

JUDY NUNN

Kal

They hugged each other and there were tears in Rico's eyes as he held his brother tightly to him. 'Find gold for me, Gio. Find gold for me at the bottom of the world.'

Kalgoorlie. They called it Kal. It grew out of the red dust of the desert over the world's richest vein of gold. People were drawn there from all over the world, to start afresh or to seek their fortunes.

People like Giovanni Gianni, fleeing his part in a family tragedy. Or Maudie Gaskill, one of the first women to arrive at the gold-fields, and now owner of the most popular pub in town. Or Caterina Panuzzi, banished to the other side of the world to protect her family's honour.

The burgeoning town could reward you or it could destroy you, but it would never let you go. You staked your claim in Kal – and Kal staked its claim in you.

In a story as sweeping as the land itself, bestselling author Judy Nunn brings Kal magically to life through the lives of two families, one Australian and one Italian. From the heady early days of the gold rush to the horrors of the First World War, to the shame and confrontation of the post-war riots, *Kal* tells the story of Australia itself and the people who forged a nation out of a harsh and unforgiving land.

BOOK ONE

THE MIGRANTS
1892

CHAPTER ONE

'*V*ide '*o mare quant'e bello,*
Spira tantu sentimento,
Comme tu a chi tiene mente,
Ca scetato 'o faie sunna.'

A light snowfall started to blanket the earth as the men's voices rang out across the mountainside. The men ignored the snow as they squatted around the open fire, clutching their mugs of red wine, their coat collars raised, their woollen caps pulled down over their ears.

'*Guarda, gua', chistu ciardino;*
Siente, sie' sti sciure arance . . .'

Giovanni's voice was raised above the others'. Although the youngest worker at the camp, he was the only one who could play the concertina and he always led the evening song. Besides, he had by far the finest voice. At least that's what Rico thought as he glanced fondly at his younger brother as they sang the haunting 'Torna a Surriento'. Several of the dozen or so men sang well, and all were of robust voice, but Giovanni, with his fine natural tenor, was a joy to the ear.

Half an hour later the men acknowledged defeat— the snowfall had all but extinguished the fire—and, with mugs freshly refilled, they retreated to their tents. But, from Giovanni and Rico's tent, the concertina played on.

''*Vide 'o mare quant'e bello . . .'*

Gradually, the men joined in and, from tent to tent, their voices once more rang out until the wine was finished and it was time to sleep.

THE FOLLOWING MORNING it was Rico who first saw the four figures trudging up the mountain track, their bulky wool-clad bodies black against the snow.

They looked tiny in the distance. Four dark dots. But then everything looked tiny in the Alps. Even the fir trees, thirty, forty feet high and shaggy with snow, were dwarfed by the landscape. And in the summer months, free of their white disguise, the massive grey boulders, some of which were as large as the village church, looked like pebbles on the side of the mountain.

But amongst the magnitude of nature's architecture it was the village itself that looked tiniest of all. Nestled in the valley far below and built of rock quarried from the very mountains which dwarfed it, the village looked defiant. Its church bell rang importantly on Sundays, its stone chimneypots puffed busy smoke into the Alpine air, and its people lived their lives ignoring nature's surrounding statement that human existence might not be of vast importance in the ultimate scheme of things. Against the backdrop of the mountain splendour, the village and its people were a testament to the wonderful audacity of man.

That it was Rico who first saw the girls was no accident—he'd been watching for Teresa since the dawn light first cut the icy air. While the men scraped clear the small stone fireplace and fetched dry wood from their tents to boil their mugs of thick, black coffee, Rico stood stamping his heavy work boots in the snow, his black eyes searching the track to the village for the first sign of the girls.

'She is coming,' he said to Giovanni as his brother handed him a tin mug of scalding coffee, so hot he could feel the warmth of the metal through his thick leather working gloves. 'See? There.' He pointed. 'She is coming.'

It wasn't long before the other men noticed the girls and gathered to whistle and heckle as they passed by.

There were always girls climbing the mountain at this time of the year, peasant girls from nearby villages and farms, crossing the Alps to work in the chalets during the heavy tourist season when extra chamber-maids and serving girls were required. The workers always whistled and heckled—but nothing more. They themselves were peasants, employed by the government to work in the stone quarries, or to chop the timber for railway sleepers, or to dig the railroad tunnels and service the tracks through and over the Alps. They came from similar farms and villages and they knew the girls to be good Italian virgins, just like their sisters. They would never dream of accosting them.

For the most part the girls enjoyed the flirtation. Some pretended they didn't and marched past with their noses in the air but, more often than not, they smiled saucily at the men and called out their own cheeky responses as they walked on.

This morning, though, was different. This morning the girls stopped.

'Teresa!' Rico ran to the tallest of the group. He took her in his arms, lifted her into the air and kissed her passionately. She returned his kiss with equal ardour and the heckling died away as the men watched in envy. The couple's lips finally parted and, arm in arm, they walked several paces away where, oblivious to their onlookers, they again fell into each other's embrace.

Giovanni was the first to initiate a conversation with one of the other girls. She had been standing closest to Teresa as the couple kissed and had stared with open-mouthed fascination at their passion.

Teresa and the other two girls wore heavy skirts hitched up at the waist with twine to prevent the hems from dragging in the snow. However, the raised hemlines revealed no tempting display of ankle, just heavy walking shoes and thick woven leggings. They wore bulky overcoats and large woollen shawls draped over their heads and shoulders.

The girl who attracted Giovanni's attention was different. She wore men's trousers, far too big for her, tied at the waist with a length of rope. Through the open front of her coat the swell of her breasts was visible beneath the coarse fabric of her shirt. A long woollen scarf was woven around her head and neck in the style that many men adopted when they worked in the bitter cold.

Giovanni walked over to her. 'You look like a boy.'

She glanced down at the trousers. 'They are my brother's,' she answered. 'I did not want my skirt to be ruined.'

Each of the girls was carrying a knapsack, on which was tied a pair of snowshoes. As several of the men drifted over, they put their bundles down and prepared to stop for a chat. Giovanni was determined to keep his girl to himself and as she eased her knapsack from her back, he took it from her.

'Let me help you,' he said, managing to edge her to one side. 'My name is Giovanni.' The girl gave him a friendly smile and her blue eyes danced, but she did not offer her own name in reply. Her skin was milky white and Giovanni noticed that a wayward auburn curl had escaped the confines of her scarf.

'Where have you come from?' he asked, fascinated. She was beautiful.

'My family has a farm near Ridanna.'

'Ah,' he nodded. 'So how do you know Teresa and the other girls? They come from Santa Lena.'

'I do not know them,' she answered. 'My father made enquiries. There were no girls from Ridanna climbing the mountain and he did not want me to walk on my own, so he took me to Santa Lena.' She gave him a cheeky smile. 'I do not know why Papa did not want me to walk alone—perhaps he worried about the railroad workers.' Again the blue eyes danced. Laughter bubbled beneath the surface of her beauty.

Giovanni knew she was joking but he was defensive nevertheless. 'Oh we mean no harm, we are no danger—'

'I know,' she laughed. The young man was so serious, she should not make fun of him. 'I know you are not.' She cast a glance in Teresa's direction. The lovers were still in a deep embrace. Rico had taken off his gloves and Teresa's shawl lay unheeded on the snow as he raked his fingers through her dishevelled hair. A handsome woman with a strong-boned face and wild black tresses, Teresa clung fiercely to Rico's body as his mouth left her lips and started to travel down her neck. She appeared transported, her mouth open, her eyes closed.

The girl watched, shocked but fascinated. They were so blatant they might as well have been naked, she thought. They were making love, fully clothed, out here on the snowy mountainside for all to see.

She was suddenly aware that Giovanni was watching her with as much interest as she was watching Teresa and she averted her eyes, embarrassed.

Giovanni himself was a little embarrassed by his brother's behaviour and felt he owed some explanation. 'Rico is my brother,' he said. 'We also come from Santa Lena. He and Teresa have known each other for a long time, they are bound to marry some day.'

The girl's momentary confusion was over and her

smile was warm. Genuine. 'They love each other very much. That is good.'

Then as quickly as Teresa had fallen into Rico's arms, she thrust him away from her. 'Enough, Rico, leave me alone,' she cried laughingly. 'It is a full day's walk to Steinach and we must get there before dark.' He tried to embrace her again but she pushed him away. 'I will see you in four months,' she said, picking up her knapsack. She started up the track, turning to wave every few steps, and the other girls followed.

'Goodbye,' the girl said to Giovanni.

'Goodbye.' He watched the four of them as they trudged on up the track but he was really only looking at the girl.

THE FIRST HOUR wasn't heavy going. The track wound gently around the base of the mountain and there was not much climbing. The girls chattered and breathed puffs of white steam as they walked. It was cold but there was little breeze and the sun's rays would soon warm the air. It was going to be a fine day.

The girls were excited, undaunted by the eight-hour trek to Steinach, the little Austrian village on the other side of the mountain where a sleigh would be waiting to take them to the ski resort.

Teresa and her two friends had worked in chalets for the past two seasons. As they compared notes and giggled at stories about the incompetence of tourist skiers, the girl studied Teresa. Tall, handsome, strong, she wore her woman's sexuality like a badge of honour. The image of the lovers and their unashamed passion was still fresh in the girl's mind.

Caterina had never seen people kiss like that. She had just turned eighteen and she had kissed several boys over the past two years, one of them a number of times. She had even parted her lips for Roberto and once his hand had brushed her breast as if by accident. Her heart had pumped wildly at the time but she had suffered terrible pangs of guilt until confession the following Sunday. After that, she avoided Roberto, but she could not keep at bay the memory of his moist lips and the tantalising touch of his hand on her breast.

And now there was the image of Teresa and Rico. Rico had been strong, virile. He had lifted Teresa from her feet when he had embraced her. Caterina wondered momentarily what it might be like to kiss Rico's brother, the serious young man, the one who'd said his name was Giovanni. He was certainly very handsome. But she breathed a sigh of frustration and forced the images from her mind. It was not only sinful, it was foolish to torment herself like this. Determined to concentrate instead on the exciting new world that lay ahead, she tuned into the girls' chatter.

They were agreeing that it was wise to be especially nice to the Americans—they invariably tipped. The Italians, Austrians, Swiss and Germans rarely did, the English only sparingly and the French never. No, definitely the Americans, they said, and Caterina thought they were very sophisticated.

They were not. Of course, the girls liked to think they were. Each year they came back over the mountain with fresh tales of what was happening in the outside world. 'An Italian opera called La Tosca is famous throughout Europe,' they would boast. Or 'There is a famine in Russia and hundreds are dying.' But they did not really understand what they were saying. The farms and villages nestled in the Alpine valleys were rarely affected by the dramas of their far distant neighbours.

Next the girls gave Caterina an English lesson. It was the most useful language by far, they told her. Americans did not speak anything else.

All four of them were panting by now as the walk

grew more strenuous, but still they talked. Caterina learned 'good morning', 'good afternoon', 'good evening' and 'thank you'. One of the girls had a favourite phrase, 'I do beg your pardon', which she had learned from a very nice English woman the previous season, and they all agreed it seemed a very complicated way of saying 'scusi'.

Gradually the track became steeper and the girls' conversation finally dwindled as they conserved their energy for the climb ahead.

As THE MEN gathered their tools and prepared for the day's digging, Giovanni nudged Rico and signalled him to wait until the two workers who shared their tent had gone.

The workers' camp was comprised of four tents, the larger one a communal mess and the other three sleeping accommodation for between four to six men. Supplied by the company and constructed of strong canvas with solid wood supports, the tents were designed to withstand the harsh winter. A new tunnel was being built through the Alps and the men were contracted to dig and remove debris after the blastings.

'You are a fool, Rico,' Giovanni said when they were alone. 'Being so open with Teresa. If her father finds out he will kill you.'

But Rico only laughed. 'You worry too much.'

He looked like their father, Salvatore, when he laughed, Giovanni thought. Strong and confident, his sturdy body constantly poised as if to charge, Rico seemed afraid of nothing and Giovanni often envied him.

'There is no one here at the camp who comes from Santa Lena,' Rico continued. 'There is no one who knows Teresa or her father, so who is going to tell him?'

'What about her friends?'

'Girls never tell, Gio. They band together and keep

their secrets to themselves. You think Teresa is the only girl in Santa Lena who is no longer a virgin?'

Giovanni felt irritated. It was always annoying when Rico patronised him. At twenty-two, his brother was only two years older than he was, so what right did he have to act as though he knew so much more of the world? 'You are so clever,' Giovanni said, 'but what happens if you get her with child, eh? What happens then?'

Rico shrugged dismissively. 'So what?' he scoffed. 'We love each other. We will marry one day. Who cares whether it is sooner or later?'

Picks and shovels over their shoulders, they joined the rest of the men for the ten-minute walk from the camp to the tunnel face.

Glancing sideways at Giovanni as they walked, Rico chastised himself. He should not have been so condescending; Giovanni was offended, he could tell. Gentle Gio, with his man's body and his boy's face. Framed in soft brown curls, it was the face of their mother before time and hardship had greyed her hair and weathered her skin. And he had her eyes too, the same intense hazel which turned brown in anger. They were brown now.

There were depths to Giovanni which Rico could not understand. Why complicate life? he thought. One should simply grab it, devour it. Giovanni thought too much, that was his problem. He was too serious, too earnest. It made him vulnerable. The only time he seemed able to give himself up to the simple joy of living was when he had his concertina in his hands and his voice was raised in song.

Rico felt protective of his younger brother. Overprotective, he chided himself. He must stop treating Giovanni like a child, he was a man now. Indeed, when they wrestled it was all Rico could do to best him. Besides, how could Giovanni possibly be a child when he was seducing the most desirable woman in Santa Lena?

'You are one to talk,' he jested, trying to tease him out of his ill-humour. 'I am to worry about Teresa and her father? What about the widow?' He had Giovanni's attention now and he ignored the fact that his brother's eyes still flashed a warning. 'I risk the wrath of a village blacksmith,' he continued, 'and you risk the vengeance of the De Cretico family.' He shook his head in mock admiration. 'And you call me the fool. Ah, Gio, you are a brave man.'

Giovanni knew his brother was teasing him and usually he allowed himself to be humoured, but not this time. He wished he had not told Rico about Sarina.

But Rico continued regardless. 'Come, do not look so serious. If it were not for the De Cretico brothers I would boast to my friends of your conquest. The widow is the most desirable woman in the village—you should be proud.'

Still Giovanni did not rise to the bait. But there was no longer annoyance in his eyes. He was troubled; Rico could sense it. 'What is it, Gio? Something worries you. Is it the De Cretico brothers?' He slowed his pace a little. 'Tell me, I can help.'

But Giovanni did not slow his pace and Rico was forced to keep up. 'If there is any danger of discovery then you should be worried.' His tone was no longer flippant. 'The De Creticos are far more of a threat than Teresa's father.'

Rico was right. Giovanni knew that only too well. The widow was no longer an adventure—she was danger-ous, and Giovanni would do anything to be free of her. But he did not want to admit his fear to his brother. With their father and two older brothers away on contract work for most of the year, it was Rico who was the head of the Gianni family. When any Gianni was threatened,

Rico became fiercely protective and that worried Giovanni. If, in defending him, his headstrong brother were to take on the widow and the De Cretico family, God only knew what might happen.

'I can look after myself,' he muttered.

'Oh yes, I know you are discreet, I know you meet in secret. But I tell you, Gio, you make sure you leave her alone when the De Creticos come to the village.'

Giovanni finally slowed his pace and looked squarely at his brother. 'I said I can look after myself.'

'Oh you can, can you?' Rico smiled to himself. He was indeed proud that his younger brother was the secret lover of the proud wealthy widow who lived in the big house on the hill. If it were not for Sarina De Cretico's brothers-in-law he would most certainly have boasted to his friends about it. He nudged Giovanni with his elbow and grinned. 'You say you worry about me and Teresa— what happens if you get the widow with child, eh?'

Giovanni smiled back. It was impossible to be cross with Rico for long, he was so irresistibly good-natured. 'No chance of that, she is too clever.'

Rico roared with laughter. He had guessed as much.

THE MEN WORKED a six-day week. Sunday was their day of rest when, to a man, scrubbed up and looking their best, they walked the seven kilometres into Santa Lena to church. Sometimes the young unmarried men went into the village on the Saturday night and ate at the local tavern overlooking the piazza. After they had dined they would gather around the rough-hewn wooden bar and sing along to the piano accordion or take a bottle of chianti into the back room and play cards beside the open fireplace. Then, in the early hours of the morning, they crossed the road to the boarding house where they slept in clean, fresh beds. The married men never went into the village on a Saturday night. The married men always slept at the camp. Contract work paid well and they saved every lire they could, taking their earnings back to their villages and farms to help tide their families through the hard times.

Rico and Giovanni Gianni were the envy of the rest of the workers. They could go home every Sunday, see their family, sleep in their own beds. No matter that they had to set off before dawn on the Monday to return to the work site, it was worth it, the others agreed.

Rico and Giovanni often returned to the village on Saturday night also, but it was not to see their family as the men assumed. In the dead of night Rico would meet Teresa in the stables where her father worked and Giovanni would walk up the hill to the big house and Sarina De Cretico. Before it was light they would return to the small cottage on the outskirts of the village and steal into the back room they had shared throughout their childhood; when the family awoke, no one would be any the wiser. It was accepted that they returned late from the work camp and did not wish to disturb the sleeping household.

The following morning they would chop wood for the kitchen fire or watch their mother and their sisters make polenta for the evening meal and then the whole family, dressed in their best, would walk together to the church, just as they had done for as long as Rico and Giovanni could remember.

There was no reason for Rico to go to the village this Saturday. Without the anticipation of Teresa and her warm, luscious body waiting for him in the stables, there was no real incentive to make the trip which was always tiring after a hard week's work. He would see his family in the morning. Tonight it would be more relaxing to sit around the campfire and drink wine and tell stories.

Giovanni wished he could stay the night at the camp too, but he did not dare. Although he had been living at the camp for over three months now, the widow still demanded he see her every fortnight. Even if she were to demand a weekly visit he would have to oblige, he dared not refuse.

Rico gave him a lascivious wink as he set off. 'Can't leave her alone and keep your poor forsaken brother company, eh?' Before Giovanni could answer, he raised his tin mug of wine in salute. 'Go on, I envy you. Mine will have shrivelled and dropped off by the time Teresa returns.' And Giovanni started down the mountain track alone.

His thoughts were grim as he hugged his thick woollen coat and scarf tightly about him and jogged to keep warm. It was not that the widow had ceased to excite him in bed. Far from it. Even now, as he thought of her body and her abandonment and the tricks she played, he could feel the stirring of desire. But she had trapped him. Like a rabbit in a snare, he was powerless to free himself. And each time he went to her, and their passion was spent, he loathed himself for his fear and weakness.

He jogged faster to distract himself but still he felt like a man going to the gallows.

The blackmail had started nearly four months ago, when Sarina had announced, quite casually, that Mario and Luigi De Cretico were coming to stay with her. Everyone in the village was fearful of the De Cretico brothers, although no one knew precisely why. The De Cretico family had long since moved from Santa Lena to their wealthy homes and businesses in Milano and Bologna. They were rarely seen and they had done no harm to anyone in the village. Indeed, they had contributed generously to the local church and needy families. Perhaps it was simply because the De Cretico family had once been the most powerful in the district and the brothers still owned the tavern and many other properties in the village, not to mention several outlying farms and a large vineyard to the south. Perhaps it was because of the rumours that their city businesses had *Famiglia* connections. Whatever it was, the brothers were treated warily and with the utmost respect.

'They arrive tomorrow,' Sarina had said. Giovanni had simply stared back at her. The De Creticos had not been seen in the village for nearly a year, not since the funeral of their younger brother Marcello.

Sarina had laughed at Giovanni's dumbfounded expression. 'Oh do not be so frightened, my little bull. They will be here for only two weeks.' She always called him her *piccolo toro* and he usually liked it, but that night Giovanni realised the enormity of what he had done. If the De Cretico brothers ever found out that he had been making love to their brother's widow, they would kill him.

Sarina had kissed him as he left. 'Two whole weeks without *mio piccolo toro*,' she had said, and she'd pouted attractively before she closed the door.

Giovanni had not gone back. For a whole month he had not gone back. And when he saw her at church on Sundays, in her widow's black, he avoided her.

Then, one day, she was waiting for him outside. Waiting in the shadow cast by the heavy open church door. She had glided up to him. 'Come to me tonight,' she whispered. He could barely see her face behind the dark veil and he had tried to ignore her. 'Your life is in danger if you do not come to me tonight,' she insisted, then she strolled over to her trap where her servant waited.

And so he had gone to her. Late that night, as he had done so many times before, he stole up to the servants' entrance at the rear of the big house. And, as usual, she was waiting for him, her finger to her lips. Not a word was spoken between them as they crept through the narrow whitewashed corridor with its low wooden doors on either side. Giovanni held his breath—behind those doors were the servants' quarters.

He had always worried that the married couple who had been employed by Marcello would report Sarina's infidelity to the De Cretico brothers. But she dismissed the notion. They were elderly, she said; they retired early and their quarters were far from her bedroom.

Not a word as the lovers crossed the interior courtyard and climbed the wide stone steps to the surrounding balconies. Not a word passed their lips until they were upstairs in her bedroom with its tiny open balcony overlooking the village.

In the safety of her bedroom, Giovanni whispered, 'What danger, what has happened—do they know?'

'Not now,' she had murmured, slowly opening her gown. She was naked beneath and she placed his hand on her breast. As she unfastened his belt she caressed him through the fabric of his trousers. 'Not now. Make love to me. *Mio piccolo toro*, make love to me.'

And then they were on the bed together and she was moaning and thrusting herself back at him. Then riding him on top. Then pulling him ever deeper and deeper into her, ankles around his neck. She was insatiable. Fingernails digging into his naked back until the pain was exquisite. Biting his neck. Whispering obscenities in his ear. Giovanni had been as transported by her abandonment as he always was. There was nothing but the two of them and the blackness of the night and the heat of their passion. Nothing else had mattered. Nothing. Still he had the presence of mind to pull away from her just before he ejaculated. She had taught him that.

She was ready for him as usual, the small hand-cloth beside the bed instantly to the fore. It never ceased to amaze him. But, as she had explained, there must be no sign of semen on the linen when the servant did the laundry. She could surreptitiously wash a small hand-cloth herself; if she were to wash bed linen it would naturally arouse suspicion. It nevertheless amazed him that at the height of her uncontrolled passion she could display such presence of mind.

They'd lain panting for several moments. Then Giovanni had turned to her. 'What has happened? You said my life was in danger.' But she appeared not to have heard him.

'Why have you not come to me, Giovanni?' she asked. 'It's been a whole month.'

'Your brothers-in-law . . .'

'Mario and Luigi left the village a fortnight ago. You know that, everyone does.'

'You said danger,' he had insisted. 'Why could my life be in danger? Do they suspect something?'

Sarina's pretty face had hardened. When she frowned she looked every bit of her thirty-three years. The difference was quite extraordinary. Animated and smiling, with her soft blonde hair and her dimpled cheeks, she could easily pass for a twenty-two-year-old.

'Answer me, Sarina. Do they suspect something?'

She sat up, not bothering to cover her nakedness. 'Not yet.'

'Then why did you say—'

'But they will if you stop coming to me.' He had looked at her, puzzled for a moment. 'If you stop coming to me I will tell them,' she had said simply and her eyes had been hard and ruthless. Unable to speak, Giovanni had stared back at her, his expression one of utter disbelief. 'I will send a message to Mario in Bologne. I will tell him that you raped me.'

GIOVANNI COULD SEE the village in the valley below. The black sky above it was clustered with smoke from the fires which would burn slowly throughout the night. It was late; only a few cottages displayed the lights of their candles or lamps. There was no light evident at the big house but he knew Sarina would be waiting for him, there in the dark.

His life had changed since that night. He had tried to reason with her. He had even tried to pretend that she was joking, although he knew she was not.

'But how can there be any joy in our meeting?' he had finally argued.

'It is not joy I want from you, Giovanni,' she said. 'If you value your life you will come to me.' Sarina did not want to sound hard and ruthless, she knew it was not attractive. She would much prefer to have beguiled him. To have sat on his strong young thighs, her legs linked around his waist, running her tongue along his perfect boy's lips and pretending surprise as she felt him become rigid beneath her. But that would not work, not this time. He was too frightened. Everyone was too frightened of the De Creticos. So she had to be hard. If she remained celibate until the brothers found her the husband they promised, she might never know a man again. 'And you will continue to come to me for as long as I wish,' she said.

From that night on Giovanni's entire existence had become one of self-loathing. He loathed the fact that Sarina continued to excite him. He loathed the fact that he served her like a stallion. He wished he could make himself impotent—then the widow would quickly be rid of him.

But as he crept around the outskirts of the village, passing his family's cottage in the dark, even as his pulse quickened with fear at the thought of discovery, Giovanni could feel the contemptible fire in his groin.

Khaki Town

Judy Nunn's no.1 bestseller was inspired by a true wartime
story that remained a well-kept secret for over seventy years.

It seems to have happened overnight, Val thought.
How extraordinary. We've become a khaki town.

It's March 1942. Singapore has fallen. Darwin has been
bombed. Australia is on the brink of being invaded by the
Imperial Japanese Forces. And Val Callahan, publican of
The Brown's Bar in Townsville, could not be happier as she
contemplates the fortune she's making from lonely, thirsty
soldiers.

Overnight the small Queensland city is transformed into the
transport hub for 70,000 American and Australian soldiers
destined for combat in the South Pacific. Barbed wire and
gun emplacements cover the beaches. Historic buildings are
commandeered. And the dance halls are in full swing with jazz,
jitterbug and jive.

The Australian troops begrudge the confident, well-fed
'Yanks' who have taken over their town and their women.
There's growing conflict, too, within the American ranks,
because black GIs are enjoying the absence of segregation.
And the white GIs don't like it.

As racial violence explodes through the ranks of the military,
a young United States Congressman, Lyndon Baines Johnson,
is sent to Townsville by his president to investigate. 'Keep a
goddamned lid on it, Lyndon,' he is told, 'lest it explode in
our faces . . .'

Other titles by Judy Nunn

Sanctuary

On a barren island off the coast of Western Australia, a rickety wooden dinghy runs aground. Aboard are nine people who have no idea where they are. Strangers before the violent storm that tore their vessel apart. While they remain undiscovered on the deserted island, they dare to dream of a new life . . . But forty kilometres away on the mainland lies the tiny fishing port of Shoalhaven. Here everyone knows everyone, and everyone has their place. In Shoalhaven things never change. Until now . . .

Spirits of the Ghan

It is 2001 and as the world charges into the new Millennium, a century-old dream is about to be realised in the Red Centre of Australia: the completion of the mighty Ghan railway, a long-lived vision to create the 'backbone of the continent', a line that will finally link Adelaide with the Top End.

But construction of the final leg between Alice Springs and Darwin will not be without its complications, for much of the desert it will cross is Aboriginal land . . .

Other titles by Judy Nunn

Tiger Men

Van Diemen's Land was an island of stark contrasts: a harsh penal colony, an English idyll for its gentry, and an island so rich in natural resources it was a profiteer's paradise . . . *Tiger Men* is a sweeping saga of three families who lived through Tasmania's golden era and the birth of Federation and then watched with pride as their sons marched off to fight for King and Country.

Elianne

A sweeping story of wealth, power, privilege and betrayal, set on a grand sugar cane plantation in Queensland. In 1881 'Big Jim' Durham ruthlessly creates for Elianne Desmarais, his young French wife, the finest of the great sugar mills of the Southern Queensland cane fields, and names it in her honour. The massive estate becomes a self-sufficient fortress and home to hundreds of workers, but 'Elianne' and the Durham Family have dark and distant secrets; secrets that surface in the wildest of times, the 1960s . . .

Other titles by Judy Nunn

Pacific

Australian actress Samantha Lindsay is thrilled when she scores her first Hollywood movie role, playing a character loosely based on World War II heroine Mamma Tack.

But on location in Vanuatu, uncanny parallels between history and fiction emerge and Sam begins a quest for the truth. Just who was the real Mamma Tack?

Territory

Territory is the story of the Top End and the people who dare to dwell there. Of Spitfire pilot Terence Galloway and his English bride, Henrietta, home from the war, only to be faced with the desperate defence of Darwin against the Imperial Japanese Air Force. From the blazing inferno that was Darwin on 19 February 1942 to the devastation of Cyclone Tracy, from the red desert to the tropical shore, *Territory* is a mile-a-minute read.

Other titles by Judy Nunn

Beneath the Southern Cross

In 1783, Thomas Kendall, a naïve nineteen-year-old sentenced to transportation for burglary, finds himself in Sydney Town and a new life in the wild and lawless land. *Beneath the Southern Cross* is as much a story of a city as it is a family chronicle. With her uncanny ability to bring history to life in Technicolor, Judy Nunn traces the fortunes of Kendall's descendants through good times and bad to the present day . . .

Heritage

In the 1940s refugees from more than seventy nations gathered in Australia to forge a new identity – and to help realise one man's dream: the mighty Snowy Mountains Hydro-Electric Scheme. From the ruins of Berlin to the birth of Israel, from the Italian Alps to the Australian high country, *Heritage* is a passionate tale of rebirth, struggle, sacrifice and redemption.

Other titles by Judy Nunn

Floodtide

Floodtide traces the fortunes of four men and four families over four memorable decades in the mighty 'Iron Ore State' of Western Australia. The prosperous 1950s when childhood is idyllic in the small city of Perth . . . The turbulent 60s when youth is caught up in the Vietnam War . . . The avaricious 70s when WA's mineral boom sees a new breed of entrepreneurs . . . The corrupt 80s, when greedy politicians and powerful businessmen bring the state to its knees . . .

Maralinga

Maralinga, 1956. A British airbase in the middle of nowhere, a top-secret atomic testing ground . . . *Maralinga* is the story of Lieutenant Daniel Gardiner, who accepts a posting to the wilds of South Australia on a promise of rapid promotion, and of adventurous young English journalist Elizabeth Hoffmann, who travels halfway around the world in search of the truth.

Other titles by Judy Nunn

The Glitter Game

Edwina Dawling is the golden girl of Australian television. The former pop singer is now the country's most popular actress, an international star thanks to the hit TV soap *The Glitter Game*. But behind the seductive glamour of television is a cutthroat world where careers are made or destroyed with a word in the right ear . . . or a night in the right bed.

The Glitter Game is a delicious exposé of the glitzy world of television, a scandalous behind-the-scenes look at what goes on when the cameras stop rolling.

Centre Stage

Alex Rainford has it all. He's sexy, charismatic and adored by fans the world over. But he is not all he seems. What spectre from the past is driving him? And who will fall under his spell? Madeleine Frances, beautiful stage and screen actress? Susannah Wright, the finest classical actress of her generation? Or Imogen McLaughlin, the promising young actress whose biggest career break could be her greatest downfall . . .

Centre Stage is a tantalising glimpse into the world of theatre and what goes on when the spotlight dims and the curtain falls.